NIGHTSCRIPT

VOLUME TWO

EDITED BY C.M. Muller

CHTHONIC MATTER | St. Paul, Minnesota

NIGHTSCRIPT: *Volume Two*

FIRST EDITION

Cover: "The Lonely Ones" (1899) by Edvard Munch

Additional proofreading by Chris Mashak

Nightscript is published annually, during grand October.

CHTHONIC MATTER | St. Paul, Minnesota
www.chthonicmatter.wordpress.com

CONTENTS

New Strange

First things first: Whether you are new to *Nightscript*, or a devoted returnee, thank you to the Nth degree for giving this little journal of "strange and darksome" tales a try. Volume One was a resounding success, exceeding all my expectations and earning a score of positive reviews. I can only hope that the edition you now hold continues to charm. Herein you will encounter stories by both established authors as well as two newcomers whose bylines I suspect you'll be seeing a lot more of in the years to come. I could go on and on, I suppose, expounding on the spectacular nature of the twenty-one tales which follow, analyzing each, telling you what makes them tick, but I'd much rather issue a gentle directive and return to my curtain of night.

To wit: *Turn the page, good reader. The carnival awaits.*

C.M. Muller

The Carnival Arrives in Darkness

Michael Griffin

1. Subject in search of a beginning

SUBJECT WAITS DISUSED, days beyond count, lonely endless nights in the unlit soundstage which was once, long ago, a textile factory in some Eastern European country. Subject can't remember the name of the country, or what the factory used to make. He barely recalls his arrival. It's been so long.

He wishes The Storyteller would stop waiting on his muse and do something. The very subject of inspiration bothers him. He grows impatient, sometimes frustrated, even angry. He allows himself to blame The Storyteller, at least until he remembers The Storyteller is waiting too, far away, in another country where the light is different, the skies are dry, and people speak a language that Subject barely remembers. The problem is, The Storyteller has a life of his own to live while he waits. Subject has nothing like that. Waiting is all he has, hoping for another opportunity. For The Storyteller to find the story, or for the story to find him.

Before this, Subject had something important to do. The Storyteller used Subject as a stand in for himself in many films. These took place in other locations, less exotic, more comfortable for Subject to remain throughout the gaps in between. Then The Storyteller purchased this place and brought Subject here to wait, with this promise: "This is where the next story will be."

Subject might like to pass the time with the Girl Who is Love, but she stays out of sight, content in solitude. They've been intimate before, though always in front of a camera, surrounded by crew. Subject dwells in his mind upon those instances, visualizes scenarios. Some of the pictures he replays in his mind really happened, some are imagination. In this sense, Subject invents a story of his own. When he thinks of the Girl Who is Love, Subject tries to approach the puzzle from all different angles, to imagine other possibilities for what it might mean.

His efforts always come back around to the same thing. It's pretty clear she only loves him in movies.

2. This place, the way it looks and sounds

THE CONCRETE FLOOR is gouged as if heavy metal constructs have collapsed and sharp broken pieces dragged across the vast rooms. The windows are smudged with dust and grease aged to waxiness, so the light within is always diffuse, cinematic. In the corners and stairwells accumulate curling flakes of paint which look picturesque and textural so this mess is allowed to remain, though technically it is a kind of decay and brokenness which certainly someone should repair. Some of the spaces are littered with shattered asbestos tiles fallen from the ceilings and ventilation ducts. In winter the light goes gray but the temperature does not become cold. In summer the spaces are illuminated blue in morning, gold in evening, but the factory never warms.

In the big room, columns stand in rows a few meters apart. So many columns, hundreds of them in white stone, points on a grid. This place was crafted many years ago by masters, trained artisans of a high culture. The adornments are elegant, almost like an other-worldly museum, yet the lights buzz like a vibrator and the water stinks of sulfur and the ceilings drip even when there's been no rain for weeks.

Outside is a world of breathtaking old world opulence gone utterly to seed. Derelicts lie dead in alleys, junkies tremble delirious in gutters, the fallen stepped over by hollow-brained smiling decadents wobbling on cancer-weakened bones, outfitted in suits and dresses handed down six generations.

Inside, every day is grainy black and white, more filmic than cinematic. Nothing movie-worthy is happening, at least not yet. Maybe it never will. Life looks exactly like film, though, flickering with profundity and heartache even when it's just life, waiting for meaning to arrive.

The way things sound here took Subject quite a while to perceive. The sonic atmosphere only rose to the level of his conscious awareness after he'd remained a long time alone. Suddenly it was there, or he realized it had always been. Underlying everything, even in the perfect absence of movement, is a soundtrack of persistent industrial noise. The mechanistic grind of the factory, though all the old iron machines have vacated and in their place only drop-cloth-covered modern tools of art remain. Clattering trains pass at distance, their enormous weight shaking loose a cloud which covers the city. A deep ambient substrate, a dark rumble of the ordinary sounds of life slowed and pitch-shifted, imbued with mystery and threat.

Was it always like this, or did Subject himself change it by coming here? Could he shift the world somehow, just by waiting and listening?

3. Problems arise, just like in a story

SUBJECT WAKES TO find the animals have gotten loose again and run wild throughout the factory. One by one they're running into concrete walls and dying. He catches some, restores them one at a time to their pens. If this is all this place offers to keep him occupied today, he doesn't like it. Subject keeps chasing until he's exhausted, so sweat-drenched and depleted finally he drops to the concrete floor amid the several bodies of the dead things, and drops effortless into the sleep from which the run-amok animals awakened him.

He wakes again later, shaken by a wild party full of music and danger and aggression in another part of the factory. Many arrivals, of course including The Storyteller. It looks like finally a story might be about to happen, but Subject has heard no hint, seen no script. Not even an outline or storyboards.

Everyone is celebrating, he learns, because The Storyteller has gotten married. This is something nobody expects. The stories are never about things like this. Sudden marriage, new wives appearing out of nowhere.

The Girl Who is Love emerges from her corner of the factory to join the party. It's always interesting, seeing The Storyteller alongside the Girl Who is Love. In stories where Subject stands for The Storyteller, the Girl Who is Love stands for some real girl The Storyteller must have fallen for in the real world, long ago. Nobody knows who. All of them presume that whoever the girl is, she must be similar to the Girl Who is Love, just like Subject is to The Storyteller.

The Storyteller's new wife is nothing like the Girl Who is Love.

4. Shedding demons and the cause of delay

THE ONLY ACTIVITY Subject has to occupy his waiting time is to mind the animals in their pens. He waters them, feeds them, trying never to look at them directly. The animals give him an anxious, unsettled feeling. It's unclear what they are exactly, maybe some halfway thing between cat and pig.

The Storyteller has banished his own demons one by one and placed the demons into the animals so they don't get loose and fly back into him. Each of the animals contains one demon in a living, squirming sort of prison. A few spare animals empty of demons are kept on hand in case another animal dies and something has to be done with his demon, or in the rare event of The Storyteller happening to show up unannounced on the verge of shedding yet another of these horrible squalling things. The Storyteller hasn't emptied himself of a demon in quite some time.

The animals remain important to The Storyteller as reminders, repositories of all his old problems. Sometimes he looks at them with a queasy sort of fondness, the way Subject might revisit old letters from neurotic college girlfriends. Subject doesn't understand why The Storyteller doesn't just send the demons away. Put them in the animals and get rid of them. Stow them in a place out of sight. Get rid of the reminder. Maybe all these demons around, maybe they're the reason the story ideas have stopped.

The Storyteller used to make stories all the time. Then after that, he told stories less often, but still worked on story-making more than he did anything else. Gradually he trailed off. Now every day The Storyteller gets closer to the glowing light of the absolute. With the passing of time, greater and greater meaning is carried in his every word. Now he hesitates before he speaks. Each utterance, so important.

Once he was good natured, full of quirky fun. Now he seems half monk, half alien. Sour and beatific, profane and profound, he radiates enlightenment gleaned from a million flickering tea lights left burning on a Himalayan monastery courtyard in a land and in a time very remote.

He's changing so much, leaving this world behind so fast, he might only have one story left. At most two, before he transcends this mortal plane and rises into clouds, soul hissing out of him like a balloon propelled by the force of escaping life-essence.

5. The Storyteller comes around to his Subject

SOMETIMES THE STORYTELLER comes to visit, starts pacing the rooms and talking to Subject about things as if he needs help figuring out some part of a story that has come to him. Because Subject stands in for him when the stories are filmed, The Storyteller seems to equate such discussions with the sort of brainstorming a creative artist might usually perform alone. Subject is glad to help. Anything to bring about the next thing.

At these times Subject often grows excited, certain the story's about to start. The Storyteller's life is so much like fantasy, he increasingly gives the impression he's coming up with some kind of strange surreal ecstasy, full of symbolism and the disconnection of dreams when really all he's doing is planning a party or a road trip.

Because his life has become like this, The Storyteller has less and less use for real stories. Everyone ends up painting pictures with this thick tarry paint all over their fingers. Everyone's topless in tuxedo pants painting faces on each other's chests then acting out the voices of what those faces might say. Everyone's making screaming rackets in the recording studio and deciding, Let's put out a record.

A wild scene breaks out. Threatened violence, unrequited love. A carnival of dwarves and limbless Asian acrobats held in an abandoned lot. Sudden eroticism bursts in the room around a drum fire spitting sparks like fireworks. The whole city whooshes with the escape of all the air at ground level, like consensus reality is about to be sucked up into the sky. A dream as big as the universe. Another big bang, another starting over. Then after all that, it turns out to be just another music video.

6. *Creation of a different end*

Subject is exhausted, so tired of waiting. Yes, there's accomplishment in standing for a great man in the telling of his stories. The Storyteller is certainly a great man. The stories, though, have apparently stopped. Where does that leave Subject? He's so depleted now, so demoralized. He forgets about the demons, the animals, forgets even to listen for footsteps beyond the door. For the first time he stops straining for any hint The Storyteller might be arriving to make things happen.

Something has to change. No more waiting, passively hoping for the universe to be clarified, explained by someone else. Time to remake things. Remake himself.

At the window, Subject gestures tenuously at smudged glass. Clear light streams through the mark left by his fingertip. He looks around, takes inventory of all he has at his disposal. Raw materials for art, for life.

It's so easy to modify surroundings, change details. The dilated mind perceives vast potential, an infinite array of possibilities, like rearranging zeroes and ones in the program of the world. He strips objects of their old names and bestows new ones. Knocks down walls, slathers paint. Everything changes, conceived at the speed of thought. It looks different in the new light, this old factory, changed from the way The Storyteller made it.

Not different enough. Not a new start.

Where walls stood before, he places doors, and makes doors where walls have always been. The floor shakes, the ceiling trembles. A great atmospheric rush, an interior cyclone, the inexorable whooshing escape of all air from the soundstage. In its place, when he dares inhale, he finds a new atmosphere. Smells of oil paint and turpentine, of whiskey and typewriter ribbons, these remind him of the past. Memory aches, like a severed limb regrowing. In the telling of Subject's unfolding story, he remembers himself. Life events unspool, recycling scenes of passion and regret. He relearns long-forgotten truths.

When the first part of his work is finished, when the place has been entirely remade, he blackens the windows with tar in rejection of the distracting light. The mystery deepens. Darkness is no longer a threat, but a soothing and encompassing warm bath. An inducement to dreams.

Now everything's quiet.

While Subject contemplates what to create next, The Girl Who is Love approaches, the only sound her footsteps echoing off new walls. She reaches out, uncertain. The way she looks at him, barely visible in the near-black room, he knows. Something is different. Can she have any idea how deeply she lives in his thoughts? Unsure what she intends, part of him wants to break away, to avoid risk.

Some clenched, desperately fearful part of himself slowly unwinds. Not everything has to be clear. Some matters can remain unknown, shrouded. This obscurity vibrates with a kind of poetic beauty.

He reaches out, touches her hand.

She speaks her real name. Subject speaks his own.

Should he open up his story, let her join? No, better to show her the way to destroy. Help her tear down all she knows and rebuild from scratch. Observe as she renders each new detail, molds and shapes a world entirely her own. Then so acquainted, only when each grasps a perfect counterpart to what the other holds, open up. Offer to intertwine.

These new rooms come alive with sound, movement. Ideas arrive unsought, barely visible at first. They flutter and spin, wild fish twisting in the air until too tired they fall, like chips of paint cracked loose, like asbestos tiles fallen from high ceilings. A rhythmic churn of industrial machines in motion drowns out the old subliminal hum. The laughter of new arrivals. A party, a multitude. A carnival underway.

Eyes open, alert in the familiar dark, aware of each other and the infinite potential of things, they wait only for the next act.

In the Dark, Quiet Places

Kristi DeMeester

My sister is the first to find the buried things. The things no one is supposed to find.

"Tessa," she says and offers up her dirt-stained fingers. "Come and look."

Cupped in her palm, a tiny jewel the color of blood glitters. Around it, a thin gold band encrusted with red clay hints at something that had once been beautiful. Like my sister. Before Henry found her. Before he put the baby inside of her and then took it away. He didn't even let us have a funeral.

"Might be worth something. Could probably sell it down at Lucky's Pawn. Pay the gas bill," I say, but her eyes are bright, more blue under this December sky than the green they are in April, and I know she won't sell it.

The dirt flakes off the band, and she sticks the entire ring in her mouth to suck off the grit before she spits it into her palm.

"Somebody may have lost it. Could pay a reward for a return. It'd be stupid not to try and get something for it, Lou."

"Don't call me that." She whips back to face me, and her face is pulled back so her teeth are exposed, and it's hard not to stare at the long, vertical scar that runs down her cheek and neck.

I whisper that I'm sorry, but she's already turned away. It's hard not to call her Lou. I've been calling her that since I was little, and then Henry came and stole it away, and she giggled every time she heard him say it.

Louisa, I wrap my tongue around her birth name, and the taste of something sour floods my mouth—hot and thick—and I resist the urge to spit.

When Henry came, he took more than her name from me. This mirror image of myself. Her face is my face. Her eyes, my eyes. Between the two identical sisters, he chose her, and he wrapped her in soft words and hard fists. If the son of a bitch wasn't already halfway to hell with worms crawling in and out of his eye sockets, I'd kill him myself.

Lou has slipped the ring onto her finger, and she's humming to herself. A song I remember from childhood. Something our mother would have sang while hanging the laundry or cutting potatoes. A song to distract yourself from the darkness snapping at your heels.

"Let's go. It's getting late," I say, and she pulls herself up. The hem of her dress is dirty, and there are two dark spots where her knees have pressed into the earth. She doesn't speak as she walks beside me, but her fingertips trace again and again over the ring she wears. The more I look at the ring, the more it looks like the ring our mother kept in the top drawer of her dresser and never took out. "It was my grandmother's. When she died, she told me to bury it somewhere out in the woods, deep under the roots of a tree if I could manage. Said that ring was full of the old magic; the kind she'd learned from her own father when she was a girl. The kind that she taught to me. Even after I did what she said, it always came back. Next day, I'd open up my drawer, and there it'd be. After awhile, I figured there was something inside of that ring that didn't want to be lost," she told us and left it at that. But there were nights when I would hear her in her room talking, and I would tiptoe to her room and press my ear to the door, but I never heard another voice responding to her.

Every now and then Lou and I would wake in the morning to find the house empty, our mother vanished into the woods behind the house. She tried to teach us how to listen to the earth, how to watch the moon, but I was never interested, and I assumed that Lou wasn't either. When my mother died, we buried her with that ring. The ring that I could swear is on my sister's finger right now.

The house is cold when we let ourselves in. The air pushes against me, and I tuck myself tighter into my coat. It's been weeks since we had heat. My tips barely cover the mortgage and electricity, and Lou hasn't worked since what happened to her.

Outside, full night has fallen, and shadows leak into the living room from the two large windows at the front of the house. I pull the curtains, and my mother's old words are in my ear. "Mind the dark now, Tessa. Like a mouth waiting to gobble down the soft bits it can find. Like men. When a man moves in the night, he's full of the dark. Make sure you mind that, too."

A shiver creeps down my spine as Lou walks ahead of me. She flips each light switch she passes, but the rooms feel dark despite the dull glow.

She's still humming, and the sound makes my head hurt. "Could you stop?" I ask her.

"Stop what?"

"Humming like that. It's annoying, and I'm getting a headache."

When she turns to face me, her scar is bright red. It looks raw and chafed as if she's been raking her fingernails back and forth over the thickened skin. "I'm not humming."

I open my mouth to respond to her, but she opens her mouth, too. A perfect, pale circle covering her teeth, and I go quiet. I head for the kitchen and try to ignore the sound of my sister's footsteps as she goes to her room and closes the door.

I make a sandwich but don't eat it. Lou's voice hangs stagnant in the air. Whispers I can't quite make out. A lilting, lullaby kind of voice. A voice that should sing children to sleep.

I throw the sandwich in the trash and put my plate in the sink. Fiestaware. The only china my mother passed on to us when she died. For twelve years, it had been just me and Lou, and then Henry came, and everything changed.

I fall asleep on the couch to the sound of my sister's voice, and I dream I am washing her hair. Warm water cascades over my wrists, and the shampoo smells of apple. There is blood in the water. There is blood under her fingernails. I take her fingers into my mouth, and I wish, again, that I had been the one to do it. That I had been the one to push the knife deep inside Henry's belly.

When I wake up, it's full dark, and the moon streams ghost light over the recliner and coffee table. Lou must have fallen asleep because the house has gone quiet. No more whisperings leaking into the air like smoke.

It's when I sit up, my back cracking, that I hear it again. My sister's voice. Softer now. More distant. Coming from beneath the ground.

I stand and gather my coat around me and shove my feet into my old black boots. The wind stings my cheeks when I open the door, and I stand on the top step. Waiting. Listening. Because I don't want to go out into the yard. I don't want to find out what it is she's doing.

"Lou," I say and wince, remembering the way Henry said her name. "Louisa?"

She doesn't answer me, but I can hear her more clearly now. Syllables play tricks in the air, dip low and then rise and reverse back on themselves, so the words sound like another language. Something harsh and lyrical at the same time.

I find her under the house. Tucked deep inside the crawlspace with her back bare and streaked with dirt. Muscles flex and shift around her ribcage, and I wonder when it was she got so thin? How I didn't notice her frame growing lighter, the sockets of her eyes deeper?

"What are you doing?" I shift from one foot to the other trying to keep myself warm, but the cold sleeps deep inside my bones.

"I buried it in the dark places. He told me to forget it. That it had never happened, but I found where he'd put it." She turns to me, extends her arms, and there's what I think is blood on her hands, but when I look closer, it's only the deep red of Georgia clay.

"Buried what?" I say and swallow the oil slick feeling in my throat. I don't think I want her to answer.

"The baby," she says and extends her right palm outward. A pill bug traces a path over her hand and up her arm, followed by two, then four more, and soon her arm disappears, the appendage nothing more than a part of the roiling dark.

I blink, and her arm is smooth and pale once more. Tucked inside of her palm are a handful of milk teeth. I think of the baby that Henry killed, but it wouldn't have had teeth yet. They shimmer like tiny pearls, and then she closes her fingers around them, and they're gone.

"Come inside," I say and reach for her, but she shrinks away from me. Pulls her knees up into her chin.

"Can't. You saw what I found."

"Somebody dropped a ring, and you found it. It doesn't mean anything, Lou," I say and hate the fear in my voice. Hate that I'm thinking of my mother in that pine box, the ring winking from the dark as we pressed our lips to her cold forehead. I clear my throat, but it doesn't keep my legs from shaking. I sink into the dirt.

"The ground took so many things from me. I fed it blood, fed it my past, and now it's giving back everything I've lost. Don't you see?"

"Come inside. It's cold, and you're tired. Come inside," I tell her. Her shoulders slump, and she shifts herself onto her hands and crawls towards me. Obedient. Compliant.

I scoot backward and we make our way out from beneath the house, and soon we are both on our backs in the grass staring up at a wide ribbon of black sky. Lou laces her fingers through mine, and our breath is full of ice and stains the air with puffs of white.

I let the cold carry me down and down and down, imagine all of the shadowed things that move underneath, how they must carry our secrets long after our bodies have finished feeding them. Their pincers and tiny mouths filled with the skin and marrow of the man my sister imagined she loved.

Lou sits up, and together with our hands still clasped, we make our way into the house. I don't question her when she crawls into my bed, curls her body tight against mine the way she did when we were girls and the nights were long and freezing.

I dream of the dirt, dream of bugs circling my bare flesh, tasting the salt and sweat of my skin. And then, I do not dream at all.

THE LIGHT COMING through the window is early morning gray, and the spot where my sister slept is empty. My nose is running, and my cheeks are chapped from the cold.

A dream. A weird dream, I tell myself, but there is red clay smeared on the pale blue sheet, and I trace the streaks, the grit flaking against my fingers as I follow the marks.

"Lou?" I call, but there's no answer, and so I swing my legs over the edge of the mattress. Beneath my feet, there's a small dusting of the red clay, and I dip the tip of my sock in it, trace my sister's name and my name in the dirt. Stupid. Like a little girl with a crush and a notebook.

Pictures line the hallway. Black and white imprints of a time when we were two girls with bare feet and wild, tangled hair. Lou waving from the very top of the pecan tree that fell two years back after a nasty storm. Me and Lou, our faces bloodied with the deep red insides of a ripe watermelon. Our mother holding each of us in her lap, her two girls caught tightly as she smiled clear and beautiful into the camera. Finally, a picture of my mother only, surrounded by long grass, her face and hands lifted to the sky. When we were young, Lou and I would ask her about it, ask her who took the picture and why she'd been standing in the middle of the grass like that and what was it she was looking at, but she would smile her secret smile and tell us sometimes there were things in this world that belonged only to yourself and those secrets were best left kept.

"Is it the old magic?" I asked her once, and she pulled me onto her lap and hugged me tight.

"Something like that, little one. I wish," she began, but I was squirming down and running out the door, and I didn't know what it was she had said. What it was that she had wished for me or my sister.

Lou isn't in the kitchen either, and I pull a glass from the cabinet, run the tap, and wait for the water to go clear. Outside the window, mist rolls across the ground, and a dark form bends to meet it, its arms filled with something I can't quite make out. But I know the way it moves, know the posture. The gait. As I know myself. Know the skin I've inhabited all these years.

The screen door slams behind me when I step onto the porch, and Lou glances up at me and then back down at the bundle she carries. Fabric. Something flimsy and airy. Something with lace. Something the pale color of a spring morning.

I think she'll turn away from me or she'll run, but she lets the fabric tumble from her hands.

"Do you remember, Tessa?"

Clutched in her hands are two dresses. Identical scooped collars and skirts that flowered when we would balance on the back of the tiny heeled shoes our mother bought us and spin and spin until we thought we would be sick.

"We were twelve," I say, and she points to a tear on one of the dresses. The lace comes off easily in her hand when she tugs at it, and I think I've forgotten how to breathe.

"This one was yours. Remember?"

"Where did you find that?" My heart is pumping rabbit fast in my chest, and something deep in my gut aches.

"I wanted to kill him. Wanted to turn him inside out for what he did to you, Tessa. But I was so small, and so were you. And then he ran away, packed up everything and left, and the police couldn't find him, and you stopped talking for such a long time. Every night Momma came in the room and held your hand while you slept so that you would feel safe, but it didn't keep you from waking up screaming. Remember?"

"Stop it," I say, and she shakes her head. Inside of the blurred motion, I can see the face of the little girl who followed Deacon Bishop into that empty Sunday School room, but it wasn't my sister who went. It's my face peeking out from behind the veil of dark hair. I scrub my fists against my eyes, and it's only Lou's face. Only Lou, her fingers full of thin fabric.

"Didn't you feel pretty when you wore it?" she says and offers the dress to me.

"Get the fuck away from me," I say and swat away the lace. It piles against the ground. A death shroud for all of the memories we've buried.

Lou tips her head back and laughs, her voice climbing higher and higher until she's screaming instead of laughing. The pill bugs are back, and they cover her hands like gloves.

"I felt pretty the first time, too. The first time Henry put his teeth against my throat and told me to cry because he liked the sound. Even then," Lou says and lifts her hands to her face. The insects creep along her skin, trace the outline of her scar—a singular line streaking up her face before disappearing into her hair.

"You could feel it every time he opened me up. Couldn't you? Sister. You choked and drowned on my tears, and you knew. Because I knew when Deacon Bishop took you into that little room. Felt it when he ripped you open, and oh God, Tessa," she says. Her eyes are wet. I want to go to her, to smooth her hair back from her face, but I cannot move. "Could you feel it when the baby died? Could you feel it when I killed Henry?"

My mouth is dry. I nod my head. When he took the knife from her, I knew. I could feel the pressure of his hands on her neck, could feel the anger pouring out of him, all darkness and red and heat, and I opened my mouth to scream, but my sister swallowed her sounds. Even when he drew the blade over her face, she stayed silent.

"Help me. Help me find all that we've lost. Let it help us."

"Let what help us?"

"Momma knew. She understood. About the things that move in the places where no one likes to look. She knew how darkness can leak into a person and stain them. She knew the places to hide, and she told me about them. You never wanted to listen, but I did. Before she died, I learned what I could."

My sister leans toward me and wraps fingers through my hair. She smells of mint, and I press into her, match my body to hers, the heat from our skin rising into the December air. When the pill bugs creep onto my arm, I flinch, try to pull away, but Lou holds me tight. So tight I think my bones will snap in two.

"It's okay. It's okay," she says, and her voice is our mother's voice. It is my voice. It's Henry's voice, and Deacon Bishop's voice, and the morning sky goes pitch dark, and all around us is nothing but dirt for burial.

When a police officer came looking for Henry, my sister served him coffee with hands that did not shake. He pretended to watch her mouth, but his eyes betrayed him. Instead, he watched that angry, wet slit in her face. Watched it pull and strain as she answered his questions; as she told him Henry had gotten drunk and they'd fought before he took off. No, she hadn't heard from him. No, she didn't know where he could have gone. Yes, she would be sure to call if she heard from him.

He asked me questions, too. Asked if my sister and I shared the house. Yes. Henry hadn't lived there but might as well have with how frequently he stayed the night. Asked if I'd been there when Henry came. No. I'd been at work. He nodded and pressed his lips together in a tight line.

Before the officer left, he looked again at her scar. Made no attempts to conceal it as he reached out to touch her shoulder. "If he does come back, I'd put him in the dirt. But that's me," he said and then was gone. No one ever came back to the house after that.

"I should have helped you bury him," I say, and the insects cover my lips.

"No," she says and pulls me forward. "Come and see."

The pill bugs are in my mouth now, they pattern over my tongue and teeth, and I choke as they flood down my throat, move under skin and muscle.

Stumbling, I follow my sister into the woods, her hands prodding and tugging me onward. "I can't see anything," I tell her, but she keeps moving.

When she lets go of my hand, I pitch forward, my knees scraping against rocks or wood. I can't tell which.

"Help me," she says and pushes my hand into the dirt. "Dig," she says, and then her voice drops away, and I reach out for her, but there is nothing but cool air.

"Lou?" I whisper, but she doesn't respond. I say her name again and again until I am shrieking into nothingness, but still my sister doesn't answer. I flail, arms and legs pumping uselessly against the cold earth, but still I cannot find my sister's body. Cannot find the heat in the space she occupied only moments before.

When the bugs crawl up and over my calves, my thighs, I claw at my skin, try to brush them away, but they keep coming, faster and faster.

"Don't we deserve something beautiful?" Lou's voice coming from beneath the ground, and I push my fingers into the earth and draw up handfuls, toss them to the side. Soon, my fingertips go raw from scratching at the dirt, but I ignore the burning and open up a hole in the earth beneath me.

I find Henry's body first. His face bloated and pale. Almost shimmering down there in the dark, and I uncover him bit by bit. The checkered shirt he wore, and Lou's blood on his hands. I spit on his face once I've worked him free from the dirt.

The bugs cover his hands, nibble at what's left of the blood.

It doesn't make sense that he still looks like this. Like he's only just been put to ground. I dip my fingers in the gash in his abdomen, and when I pull my hands away the blood is warm.

Something vast has opened its mouth. Something that has long slept beneath our careful steps. I can feel it move, can feel it shifting below me in the safe place it created.

The bugs circle against my cheek, their tiny legs scattering my tears, and I clench my hands against the dirt.

"What am I looking for, Lou? Tell me what I'm looking for."

"Something beautiful," she says again, and darker shadow appears to my right. It glistens, and then my sister's face appears, the insects parting so I can see her eyes, her teeth.

"Do you remember how they couldn't tell us apart? Sometimes even Momma got us confused. But Henry always knew the difference. There were nights I wanted him to find you instead. Wished that just once he would get mixed up, but he never did. And now..." She points to her scar, traces her fingers over the seam Henry left on her.

She takes my hands. My sister. My other. All of our broken little pieces buried. Waiting. "Help me," she says, and we go into the dark together, our fingers filled with cold earth.

The sound is small at first. Something to fit inside of your palm and hide away, but as we pull back the dirt, it grows louder, and Lou smiles. Not one, but two voices crying.

"Please, please," she whispers, and her words are something like a prayer. Something like begging, and together we find little fingers and little toes and little mouths opened wide, and we hold them close to our breasts. Our daughters.

We wipe the dirt from their hair, and we kiss the tops of their heads, and they curl into us. Safe. Protected. Cradled and far away from anything that might do them harm.

Far beneath us, a hungry mouth opens and sharp teeth turn crimson as it swallows down all of the sorrow and blood my sister has offered it.

Our daughters look up at us from faces that mirror the other; look up at us with eyes that have seen and understand everything the other has seen. A gift for two sisters who bled and dropped tears into the earth.

We tuck them tightly against our breasts, and together, we go up out of the dark.

Phantom Airfields

Christopher Slatsky

RANDALL STILL SAW Jacob's face in crowds.

He sat alone in his truck's cab, absorbing vestiges of warmth seeping from the vents. He found a purity in this ritual, parking near the airfield, basking in a sorrow so profound it surpassed suicidal thoughts, circling back to attain something spiritual. Life doesn't just pass from living to non-living; there were quiet moments in between, little snatches of sleep and dream and hope along the way. Such thoughts helped him get through each day.

A fist-sized hole had rusted through the floor on the passenger side. The snow beneath the truck was gray. Randall looked out his windshield at the expanse of white ground, still pristine, icy veneer yet to be damaged by any living thing. A tall fence stretched across the field, preventing the curious from trespassing onto the abandoned Sodder Airfield.

This geography drew him in, spoke in a language that refused to be ignored. Here the ground kept luring him back, seducing him to walk among the broken buildings. There were no longer any signs of the old runway—in spring, weeds grew over any trace of what this place had once been used for; in winter, snow obscured the remaining secrets. Randall breathed mist onto the windshield, ran a finger across it.

He watched a mangy dog dart from the trailer park on the other side of the street and into the woods. The animal held a filthy diaper clamped between its jaws. The sight of the stray's muzzle, slathered with excrement, made Randall think of metal implants in abductee's mouths, of devices surgically imposed to intimidate, to conduct bio-telemetric analyses.

The rest area was just a mile from here.

He'd stopped returning the detective's phone calls. Cooperating with the investigation meant accepting their interpretation of events. He was done sifting through photos of children's corpses. Done with everything.

He pressed his palms against his face, pads pushing against eyes, nostrils filled with the odor of gas station pink soap and grilled onions from the burger he'd eaten late last night. When he lowered his hands the dog was gone. He remembered the day it happened.

Remembered the panic and mounting grief. Running across the rest stop parking lot into the bathrooms, bellowing *little astronaut!*, his voice echoing between the empty stalls, the affectionate nickname perverse in his mouth.

Hands pressed against temples, running around the rest area picnic tables screaming *stop hiding dammit, stop hiding dammit!* Blaming Jacob for wandering away. Blaming Sarah for not watching their child closely enough. Blaming himself.

His wife's voice escalating, their son's name mangled by her screams.

Stop hiding dammit!

All he saw was their car in the parking space, no other vehicles, the open road beyond empty save for a glorious silver light that filled Randall's body with a trembling wonder at the majesty of a moment so potent it ruined him.

It seemed as if it had happened yesterday. He put his Styrofoam cup of coffee into the holder and stepped out of the truck.

A raven dipped its beak into a puddle of antifreeze fluid on the pockmarked blacktop that led to the trailer park. It shook its head. Feathers rippled like fur. Randall felt a pang of remorse. This creature meant no ill will, was only obeying its basic survival needs. But the poison would finish it off soon enough.

He slammed the door shut. The doomed bird flew away. The chill of the snow penetrated his boots. He sucked frosty air into a mouth sour with black coffee.

The trailer park was starting to wake up: chatter of right-wing AM radio talk shows, wheeze of an unidentified instrument played by clumsy hands. Probably a child's recorder, borrowed from school, presumably much to their parents' dismay. The sky was bright with a post-snowfall glow. Randall's ear lobes stung. White plumes of exhaust spiraled from worn mufflers as people began their daily commute.

He didn't need to worry about going to work; the final wave of layoffs at the mortgage company saw to that. His ineffectual boss had crumbled under pressure from corporate and now a dozen employees were desperately seeking new ways to supplement their income. Nothing but time these days.

He followed a familiar path towards Sodder Airfield. Scuffed his feet through gray slush, slid down an embankment beneath a closed bridge. Concrete pylons prevented vehicles from passing over from either lane. He walked along a shallow stream. Clumps of gravelly ice on the surface made disconcerting sounds, rasping like teeth scraping against aluminum foil.

He ducked through a gap in the 12-foot high fence. Corroded wires snapped. Bureau of Land Management property, but Randall had yet to come across any security monitoring the land.

He passed over nearly a mile of level landscape before arriving at the abandoned airfield. Sodder Airfield had once managed P-40 operational overflow during WWII, but all that was left was an ILS antennae, the upper half having long fallen to the ground to sink into the soil, winter-yellow weeds covering any remaining metal. The low generator buildings had crumbled into empty squares decades ago. There was one wooden shell Randall thought may have once been a guard station. On the other side of a knee-high fence, beneath a mound of snow, a row of battered 50-gallon drums sat, the bottom of most having rusted away.

He paused to stare at the spaceman spray-painted against a slab of concrete leaning like a dislodged piece of ancient dolmen. No matter how many times he saw the graffiti, it filled him with an indefinable dread.

He studied it for the hundredth time. It reminded him of the Solway Spaceman. The puzzle of that photograph, the menacing figure looming behind a child—did they mean to abduct her or merely observe? It all promised a life far more exciting than what was available here. Of better worlds where mysteries were benign and parents couldn't be destroyed in one brief moment.

The graffitied figure's helmet was a perfect circle, the artist utilizing cracks and pits in the concrete to add a decayed effect. The crooked jaw was sloppy, a spattered application that captured an otherworldly appearance. A hint of a human skull lurked behind the visor, teeth faintly visible.

Randall noticed a slight decline in the landscape, a subtle depression deepening further away. The ground had been flat every time he'd roamed previously, but now sloped into a shallow crater about the circumference of the water fountain in the center of town.

When had this occurred? Had the weight of the snow collapsed an underground bunker or storage area?

He pondered this new mystery for several hours before heading back to the truck.

"I DON'T THINK Chloe and I can stay in the house, Randall. I don't like coming home anymore." Sarah nestled their baby daughter securely under her arm, deftly twisted the cap tighter on a sippy cup. The diner was filling up fast. A movie must have just let out at the theater next door.

Randall saw Jacob's mannerisms in Sarah's gestures, in her black, tightly curled hair, the tapered shape of her hands. She was so much like Jacob in so many ways.

He reached across the Formica table for his daughter.

"You need to stop going there," Sarah said.

"Where?" Randall paused, hands frozen in position to take Chloe.

"Don't play dumb. You know what I mean. The airfield."

Randall lowered his empty hands, picked up a glass of soda, held it tightly, the cool surface firm under his grip. All he had to do was let go and the glass would shatter on the diner's chipped linoleum floor. Or squeeze it as hard as he could until it fractured into slivers. Create one pristine simple moment.

"Wide open space. Helps me think."

"Isn't that what your therapist is for?" Sarah shifted their daughter to the crook of her other arm. Chloe began to wriggle.

Randall slid his glass away. "I can hold her you know. You don't have to do everything."

Sarah looked up abruptly, surprised by his offer.

Chloe rejected the sippy cup. Her fussing became louder.

Sarah had kicked Randall out of their house four months ago. Days later, a terse text message confirmed she'd initiated divorce proceedings. Randall knew she needed time and distance. They'd never be the same again, but a respite might help. They'd done their best to remain cordial. Sarah had even agreed to meet him once a week, usually at their favorite greasy spoon, to spend time with his baby daughter.

Chloe was whining now. A piercing wail that all babies acquire to announce their distress, to force parents to drop what they're doing and come running because everything revolves around children. This is what's expected of them; nothing left to do but obey the commands of an infant, even if it meant your life was effectively over.

Randall took a sip from his soda. He could bite down and break the glass against his teeth, lacerate his gums, express his helplessness with howls and drooled blood foam, a stupid pointless tantrum of violence. Fantasizing about hurting himself was the only semblance of control he had these days.

Chloe was screaming. A shrill-voiced creature reminding Randall of his inability to protect his family. A terrible thought ran through his head—what if their daughter had devices implanted inside her, something that influenced her behavior? Something to control Chloe, and in turn her parents, manipulating them to react in ways they wouldn't normally react?

Keeping them from learning the truth about what happened to Jacob.

Randall tamped down an atavistic urge to break the glass over his child's skull. To shut her up so he could gather his thoughts, have a normal adult conversation with his soon-to-be ex-wife. A few moments of peace and tranquility. Stifle the acidic panic that filled his gut, spilled from pores like sharp vinegar.

One terrible moment. He loathed himself for even thinking of hurting his daughter.

Sarah bobbed Chloe in the air. Made cooing sounds to calm her down. A young couple at the booth next to them looked over, frowned in annoyance at this intrusion on their date night.

"Stop going to that airfield. There's nothing there. You disappear for days sometimes, and I can't get ahold of you. What if detective Curtis needs us to identify something?"

Randall heard a car alarm in the distance. He imagined himself bobbing in the air, through space so cold it snagged his skin like hooks. He could see the curve of the planet in the distance.

Sarah changed tack. "I can't go into Jacob's room anymore."

Her voice pulled Randall to attention. "Why's that?" His mouth felt dry despite the pool of sweet cola on his tongue.

"I thought I saw..." Sarah gave a weak smile, not trusting herself to explain what she may have encountered. Chloe made deep gulping sounds, gagging on her own phlegm and frustration.

"You saw Jacob?" Randall asked.

Sarah's eyes burned. She hesitated.

"What did you see?" Randall persisted.

"I don't know. It was, someone, someone in his room. I thought it was him at first. But that can't be." She lowered her head to look at the untouched mound of eggs benedict on her plate. Breakfast dinner had always been Jacob's favorite. She pushed a fork through the thin hollandaise sauce.

"A shadow, a car drove by and its headlights made it look like something silvery was moving in the bedroom. A silver light. Just a car."

She seemed to grow older in that moment. A filter of time applied over the lens of how Randall remembered his wife. He thought she'd grown more lovely as time progressed. The haunted were capable of depths of compassion most were not capable of expressing. Those who'd suffered tragedy were less likely to trivialize the tragic.

"Just a light Randall."

Sarah touched the dry, coarse knuckle of his right thumb. She looked at him with a trace of resolution. She'd always care, though they'd never share lives again, their tremendous loss a chasm that kept them apart. Her eyes were bright. Pupils wide.

Randall couldn't stop thinking about broken glass and Chloe's head dangling limply. He heard himself before he knew what he was going to ask.

"You saw an astronaut in Jacob's room, didn't you?"

Sarah began to cry.

RANDALL RETURNED TO Sodder Airfield the next morning. The sun had just risen, soft-edged shadows and clumps of snow melting away under its glare. It was too early for people to start waking up. He liked these calm moments when he could look to the sun and it wouldn't harm his eyes.

He began walking towards the airfield.

Sarah left a voice message saying she and Chloe would be out of town at her sister's place, so Randall couldn't see his daughter until next weekend. He knew this may or may not be true; she'd prevented him from visiting before. He didn't care anymore.

His Survivors of Child Abduction support meetings offered 60-minute increments of gray mouths opening and rarely closing, smacking teeth against tongues, against palates, forming words into sentences of self-help platitudes. They talked at great lengths about how Randall must never give up hope.

He couldn't argue the point. Hope helped snag a few hours of sleep before the sobbing woke him up. Hope meant that Jacob might actually be safe and sound, and the slim possibility this stubborn insistence wasn't a phantom in a distressed brain to ameliorate the shock of it all.

Little else had come of therapy save for a steady prescription of Paxil that made Randall feel as if his head was as empty as outer space.

He'd once confided to his therapist about his theory regarding Jacob's fate. But she'd countered with bizarre scenarios: a cabal of child abusers had tricked Randall with magician's props, deceived a grieving father's susceptible mind. She spoke of a conspiracy of kidnappers, of military technologies, sonic machines that scrambled minds, intravenously administered drugs to distort perceptions—all manner of trickery utilized to concoct artificial memories concerning stolen children. Pseudo-memories to protect him from accepting that his son had been led from a rest area bathroom to a stranger's vehicle.

Randall found her allegations far more outrageous than his own hypothesis. As time passed, however, nothing seemed real. The depths of grief assailing him at every turn held a false aspect. Mind controlling machines implanted by a conspiracy of pedophiles was just as incomprehensible as a child being whisked away by a stranger.

Tragedy was absurd in all its manifestations.

Jacob hadn't wandered over to the vending machine near the bathrooms, fascinated by the soda can lighting up every time he pressed the button while his parents argued over whose turn it was to change Chloe's diaper, oblivious to their son's whereabouts. This could not be how lives were crippled.

The sky was enormous this morning, so clear and pale he could still see last night's stars. The airfield's crater was a dark oval from this distance. As he drew closer, a chartreuse glow caught his eye. He moved towards the source.

The glow was emanating from something on top of the snow in the center of the crater. He slid down the shallow embankment. There were no footprints, the snow was undisturbed.

A translucent spaceman.

An action figure, articulated better than those he'd played with as a kid. Glow-in-the-dark plastic casing, magnetic ball and joint limbs. Jacob had been obsessed with astronauts and rocket ships—he'd been playing with something like this when they'd parked at the rest stop. Randall put the toy into his jacket pocket.

It had to be Jacob's. No parent should ever have to be submerged beneath the vast reach of hopelessness.

As Randall began the trek back to his truck he saw a silvery orb float behind one of the concrete structures. He explored the area but found nothing unusual. He looked up into the sky, then around the rubble to see if a Mylar balloon had been caught or deflated at ground level.

He didn't find anything.

RANDALL WANDERED THE house like a phantom the first few days after Jacob disappeared, not sure how to proceed with the day-to-day routines. Lifting a toothbrush to his mouth had become an effort. He'd quit shaving, neglected to brush his hair. Even today, eight-months on, he still felt like a ghost buffeted about by gentle gusts, pushed through darkness from room to room on currents his weak soul was unable to resist.

Tonight he crawled through the unlocked window of Sarah's house. The divorce proceedings forbade him from coming onto the property—this was no longer his home, but Chloe and Sarah were still at her sister's place and Randall couldn't resist. The lure to return to his old home was second only to the call of the airfield.

He stepped into Jacob's bedroom. Sarah had kept the room exactly as it was the day he was taken. Bed perfectly made, toys in their place. Even the dirty clothes hamper remained untouched.

He reverentially touched the dresser, the bed, bookshelves. Opened the closet. Rows of shirts, never to be worn ever again. He ran his fingers across the fabric, luxuriating in the memory of his son—the smells, the tactile warmth of the cloth. He was touching the garb of someone holy and they were going to step out of the closet any moment now, lay a hand on his brow, tell him everything was going to be alright.

There was a piety in forcing himself to experience this heartache again and again. Scrolling through baby photos on the computer. Hearing his son's laughter in videos of their trip to Yellowstone Park. Breakfast dinners. He was a pilgrim seeking penance, the thought of his son's absence a whip across his skin. He wanted to die.

If only they hadn't let him out of their sight. If only they hadn't dropped their guard to allow the monstrous to intrude.

Randall had a recurring dream shortly after Jacob's abduction. In the vision, an astronaut opened his bedroom door, peeked in with its bulbous shiny head moving ever so slightly as it watched him. It shut the door.

Then opened it again.

Closed.

Opened.

The helmet glistened like wet skin. Its smooth gray face reflected a cartoon frog nightlight near the bed, like star shine on the surface of a placid lake. The head jiggled as if it was going to fall off. The spaceman floated into the bedroom.

It was the size of a child.

The intruder tilted its head from side to side, surveying the room. The front of its helmet, where Randall assumed its eyes were located, turned to him.

The eyelid of its face slid open.

Randall wasn't sure if he remembered the dream accurately, or if he'd borrowed it from his son. His memories felt loaned, passed back and forth between those he loved, slightly distorted each time like a psychic game of telephone. He felt as if he were recalling an event that had occurred in some other time, on another path he'd neglected to follow.

He no longer remembered when or why he'd given his son the *little astronaut* nickname.

He allowed the memory of his dream to recede, like a tide pulling strange life back into its depths. He walked into the kitchen. Weeks after the tragedy, he'd been standing in front of the refrigerator, wondering whether to box away their son's art or leave it tacked to the door with magnets. He'd moved a magnet aside to expose Jacob's scrawled signature. The paper had fallen, slipped beneath the fridge.

That day came back all over again. He collapsed on the floor, shook with great heaving breaths, feeling as if he'd betrayed his boy once again. Destroyed a fragile piece of history.

The day of the incident, when Randall, Sarah, and a sleeping Chloe had returned home after hours at the police station, the couple just sat quietly on the living room couch and didn't speak until Sarah said she was going to check on Chloe then go to bed early. Randall drank in a failed attempt to forget everything. He woke in the morning to find a deep gouge out of his left thumb, a dish rag collecting most of the crusty blood. He didn't know how he'd hurt himself. Never found anything in the house broken.

He'd never retrieved Jacob's drawing from beneath the refrigerator. As far as he knew, it was still under there.

It seemed like yesterday. He wriggled his fingers into the gap beneath the fridge. There was nothing.

He found himself in the living room. He turned the TV on, the volume muted. An anthropomorphic train smiled, rolled its eyes crazily as it sped down a track. Jacob's favorite show.

The engine's face was human. The gray metal organic, as if it could sweat. If Randall placed his palm against the surface he'd feel warmth instead of cold steel, pulse of vital liquids pumping inside, hot exhalations from between the train's pouty, full lips.

This was deeply unsettling.

He turned the TV off, went back to Jacob's room. He placed the glow-in-the-dark astronaut toy on a shelf, then exited back through the window.

RANDALL LISTENED TO Sarah's voice message. Detective Curtis had found a new piece of evidence. Randall hadn't bothered to check his phone in days, much less return any calls, so she'd gone to the station to identify it by herself.

When he heard the abject devastation in Sarah's voice he knew that the pants found buried in the woods near the trailer park were the ones Jacob had been wearing that day. He knew they'd still be cuffed just the way Jacob liked them.

Randall didn't need to listen to the rest of the message.

The cab of his truck spun. He pressed his palms against his face, drooling hot saliva onto clammy skin. He thought of tracking devices sliced into muscle tissue, machines injected into blood, sewn beneath skin, sending electrochemical signals to the brain and nervous system. Underground bunkers filled with the soft bodies of children. Manipulations and a universe that maims and kills and abducts, all to some mysterious end.

This must be why the ghosts of Sodder Airfield called to him, the reason the past taunted Randall with its secrets. Like the Nazca lines, the Wurdi Youang in Australia, the Carnac stones. Sites visible from above.

A memory of Jacob years ago, sitting in his high chair, contentedly chewing on a mushy portion of toast.

A memory of Jacob in his perfectly cuffed pants.

A memory of Jacob.

Randall let the remaining voice messages play as he howled silently into his open hands.

HE PARKED IN front of the trailer park near Sodder Airfield. He sat in silence. The cab stank of stale coffee. The morning was clear and crisp. The snow deep, the sky bright. He held a box cutter in his hand.

He left the truck, walked towards the faded runway, to the familiar dilapidated buildings and chunks of concrete.

The box cutter's hard plastic handle was cold.

Randall planned to hurt himself, then curl up in the center of the crater and bleed out. Maybe that would force them to bring Jacob back down.

But the airfield had changed.

Antennae now sprouted from the earth like monstrous insect palp, the molted remains of something that had long departed this planet. Their tips flaunted blinking lights. Rows of these pencil-thin antennae ran through the center of the airfield. The metal was putty-colored, as if the alloy was decomposing. Their topmost points swayed in the wind hundreds of feet above, swinging back and forth with a strange metallic hum audible on the surface of the planet.

Randall approached the depression. A flash of silver caught his eye.

An astronaut stood in the center.

It turned towards him. The blue sky reflected off its featureless face.

Randall didn't know if it was a plastic helmet, or aged bone brittle from the abuse of months. Its cranium was cracked, stained a putrid yellow, as if a sickness was leaking from inside. The visor was thick as a cloudy cornea. A perfectly aligned row of gleaming teeth was visible within.

The astronaut scrambled out of the crater, shuffled towards Randall. Its skin flaked away like old crinkled aluminum foil. Silvery specks mingled with snow that had somehow already been polluted with a lead-colored substance.

The lights on top of the antennae grew brighter.

The spaceman stumbled, its short legs and the snow preventing it from moving any faster.

Randall waited patiently. He wasn't afraid.

The astronaut's helmet began to fall away, the thin cord connecting skull to neck fraying from too much jiggling. A broken toy that had been played with too much.

Its arms and legs moved in a familiar manner, the tilt of its shoulders all too recognizable. It was so very small. Just a child.

Randall dropped the box cutter in the snow, ran to the astronaut. Fell, regained his balance, ran until he embraced the small corpse.

He said *oh my my my little astronaut* because any other words were out of reach. He held his son against his chest, cradled his wobbly head to prevent it from dislodging. Wept until his lungs burned, the sensation dissipating into the vast cold emptiness of the morning. He wasn't sure what to do, didn't know what was expected of him as a father.

He couldn't open his son's visor and view the familiar face. To look past the time and decay, to see what he'd set out to find all those months ago would confirm every fear, every desperate certainty that there was no joy to be found in a world governed by entropy. Everything rots. The world dilapidates. Everyone will vanish into nothingness.

Children are taken away from bathroom rest stops.

Little astronauts never return home.

So he told Jacob made-up stories instead. Old ones heard many times, new tales he'd never had a chance to tell. He spoke of his boy's first steps, first words, favorite toys, told him about his little sister, how his mother missed her son so much. He recounted every maudlin parent cliché he could imagine. But Jacob never made a sound or even acknowledged he understood anything at all.

Randall continued until the tiny graceful presence of his boy lulled him into the first semblance of comfort in far too long. His face touched his son's helmeted face. His grip loosened.

He felt his son's head waver, then tumble over his shoulder onto the ground. The head gouged a shallow furrow in the snow as it rolled away towards the crater.

Randall wanted to call out, to halt its progress. Wanted his boy put back together, to be a whole child once more so they could be a family again. But his limbs ached, unwilling to move his sore body any more than was necessary to maintain a heartbeat. He stared at the dirty snow.

His life wasn't worth Sarah's life. Or Chloe's. Wasn't worth Jacob's life. Maybe things had worked out for the best. He loathed himself so intensely nothing could harm, humiliate, or affect him in any manner he hadn't already inflicted against himself.

His boy's body dissolved into silvery bone meal in his arms. The dust trickled from his lap to the ground, then dispersed on a sparkling breeze. Randall tasted sunlight.

He didn't deserve to see the dust speckle the air with resplendence. Didn't deserve to see his son's head fall into the crater, the air around the hole shimmer with a glorious fervor the color of nebulae, the diaphanous form of the reconfigured child astronaut ascend, picking up speed the higher he rose towards the exosphere.

Randall kept his gaze below, mesmerized by the patterns and pocks in the snow. He only deserved to stare at filthy ice.

Jacob waved at his father far beneath him, but Randall couldn't rescue his son from oblivion. Couldn't even own up to his responsibilities as a parent and reach out. Couldn't save his family. Couldn't save himself from eternity.

Jacob kept waving, but Randall remained motionless until he became nothing more than a speck on the surface of the planet.

Then the little astronaut faded into a pinpoint of silvery light.

Then they were both nothing at all.

En Plein Air

J.T. Glover

A GUST OF WIND boiled off the James without warning, flattening cattails and clumps of spikerush as it swirled around the inlet where I was painting, and of course it caught my canvas. The morning's work rushed away from me like a sailboat before a storm, taking my light easel with it. Just as I was sucking in breath to howl with frustration—it shuddered to a stop in midair. Two pale hands held it fast, reaching around from the back.

"Whoa," said a woman with frizzy brown hair as she looked around one side at me. "I expected a lot of things today, but not an easel attack."

"Damn, I'm—thanks. That wind came out of nowhere."

"Been there," she said, smiling.

The woman walked toward me and set the easel back in place. I was instantly delighted and wary when I saw her umbrella, pochade box, and other painting supplies. On closer inspection, I noted that her gear was highly customized and showed the kind of wear that came with long use.

"I'm Sharon," she said, sticking out one hand.

"Delia," I replied, appreciating her firm grip as we shook.

"The wind comes up suddenly here sometimes."

"Yeah? This is my first time. Usually I paint out in the country, Goochland or Louisa, out that way."

"Nice," she said, nodding. "I've been out there a few times, but I'm a city girl. I probably paint right here more than anyplace else. Something about the way the light falls, and this stretch of Cherokee Road doesn't get much traffic."

"Huh. Didn't mean to poach."

"No worries! I don't own it, and every so often people come by here anyway. I don't think it's actually all that scenic, but it's isolated enough that people sometimes assume it is. They don't hang around very long."

She nodded amicably and walked a little distance away, far enough to be out of my picture plane.

Courteous, and not falling all over herself to tell me about her work. How quaint.

The woman wasn't a complete exception among artists I met in Richmond, whether life drawing at VisArts or touring galleries on First Fridays, but an awful lot of them just seemed to want more followers on their Instagram. Sharon appeared to be most interested in painting, and that's what we both did, mostly in silence, for the next couple hours.

The wind didn't kick up that strongly again, but the clouds thickened partway through, going a slate gray that promised rain. I'd chosen this spot at random while driving along the river, thinking it was a nice blend of dry land and tidewater, and as the light faded, I was mildly surprised by how the shadows thickened, falling into a startling range of hues and values. Most people wouldn't have considered it beautiful, but it was the kind of challenge I liked as a painter.

By the time I packed it in, a thin drizzle had started to fall. I walked over to Sharon, halfway thinking about seeing if she wanted to grab lunch. She'd popped her umbrella, though, and even if it was there to diffuse sunlight, it didn't do a horrible job of keeping off the rain, and she was still at it. Her brushstrokes were fewer and more precise than mine, and large piles of paint remained on her palette, even after most of a day's work. Her picture was dark and muted, entirely unlike my cheerfully over-bright painting.

"Hey," I said, "thanks for saving the day earlier. Are you..."

"I think I'm still going to go a little longer."

"Okay. Well, don't get caught if it storms."

"Will do! Maybe see you again."

I said the same and walked off toward the embankment that led up to the road, slogging through brush and the band of trees, mostly elms and redbuds, that started where the ground angled up. When I had everything stowed in the Jeep, I looked back toward the river. She was still working, carefully and deliberately. From this distance her painting stood out like a wedge of night in the rain.

That week I stayed late at the office, trying to finish a new client's website, and painting had to take a back seat. By Thursday I'd overdosed on screen time, and I saw style sheets every time I closed my eyes. When I hung up my coat and dropped the keys in the bowl by my front door, I knew just where I was headed for the night.

My apartment was in a subdivided house in the Fan, an old brick building that sat on a corner of Grove Avenue. It was close enough to the bustle of Robinson Street that I could meet up with friends at Starbucks or a bar five minutes from my door, but my block sat in one of those oases of quiet you get sometimes in Richmond. I'd lived there since I got my first design job after VCU, and so far I hadn't wanted a house badly enough to move, or found anyone comfortable enough to bring home for good, so I stayed where I was. Shabbily ornate window frames and chipped bricks had been plenty elegant to see me into my thirties, and the tiny parlor that the landlord had apologetically offered as a living room served nicely as a studio.

Visitors occasionally commented on the odor of linseed oil, but I never noticed it anymore, so the smell in the studio that evening took me aback. It was a little bit oil, a little bit miscellaneous art junk, and something like...standing water, undisturbed for long enough to grow algae. My ancient tortoiseshell, Rollo, had died during the winter, and I hadn't been able to bring myself to replace him yet, but he wouldn't have stood for this. I smiled sadly, imagining him squeezing behind boxes and jumping from shelf to shelf, trying to find the source of the stink.

I circled the room until I stood in front of the canvas I'd started the previous weekend. Even under color-balanced lights, the thing wasn't right. I'd always been drawn to the Fauves, and Pop, and the garish proclamations of poster art, but somehow my painting no longer looked so vibrant to me.

What the actual fuck? You aren't supposed to paint like a web designer. You have a style, and that's it—right in front of you.

No matter what I told myself, though, something felt off about the picture before me. I loved landscape paintings, however uncool some of my college teachers had said they were, but subtle palettes weren't my thing. Never had been.

So why does this one feel weird to you? It's not like all the rest of your paintings went bad.

Looking around my studio was unexpectedly distracting. It was as if I were peering through a pane of dirty ice. The bright, high-chroma colors that I loved were a mess. The self-portrait I'd been lazily hacking away at for a few weeks looked dead as a monochrome underpainting, despite the wild impasto and glass granules I'd worked into it. Not bad, just...not for me, not right now. It was the strangest sensation, like looking at pictures from childhood, at a part of myself walled off by time.

"You need a change of pace," I said aloud. "And it's summer, so why not?"

That felt right, and the thought of sun and fresh air was a tonic after the long week. I wandered back toward the kitchen, thinking vaguely about making some stir fry. I paused at the bookcase in the hall, looking at spines and gravitating almost unconsciously to a book of Charles Burchfield's winter landscapes. I pulled it out, glad I'd held this pale, slender volume back from the thrift shop box the other day. My appetite vanished as I studied gray skies and empty houses. The pages weren't free of color, but it was a near thing. Soft rain started outside, and something coiled up inside my heart, sleepy and well satisfied.

THE WEATHER STAYED shitty for a while, but on a Sunday late in June I finally got my act together, hopping in the Jeep and tooling around town from Short Pump to Manchester and back again. Nothing felt quite right, though, and I quickly got tired of dodging church traffic while waiting for inspiration. Soon I was following that same cracked, potholed road along the James River, looking for the place I'd last painted. I found it soon enough, and although there weren't any cars parked nearby, I saw a familiar shape out in the dead field. I parked on the muddy shoulder and hoofed it down the embankment and through the trees.

"Hello again," I said. "No wind this time."

Sharon turned and gave me a little smile. "Maybe later. Doesn't look like rain today, but we're going to get a cold spell soon."

I made a noncommittal noise and started setting up within earshot. After I figured out my scene, I took a surreptitious look at Sharon's work so far: mostly brush and stagnant water. Not surprising, given what she'd said last time, and the fact that she could have passed for Wednesday Addams if she were twenty years younger. What she'd laid down so far struck me as—

Beautiful. All that brown ought to feel like just an imprimatura, but it's got polish. What does she have on her palette? Looks like umbers, sienna, ochres, white. Dang. Girl knows how to paint.

In the face of that, I was at a loss. I looked into my paint box, and that moment in the studio the other week echoed in my mind. These tubes before me were too bright. Couldn't do for painting unless I mixed them to mud, so that was what I did. Sap green blended with Venetian red, dioxazine purple with Hansa yellow, and before long I had a palette full of no-colors. With them in mind I looked around, eventually settling on a cluster of stumps where the water deepened, with a stand of trees off to one side.

As I worked into the painting, the world faded away like usual, but the color did as well. What remained were mostly darks and lights.

"Wow, that's toned down," Sharon said some time later, when she'd paused for a drink and come over to look.

I looked away from the canvas and blinked to refocus. She was smiling almost sardonically. It struck me that I didn't know her at all, not really, and yet we seemed to mesh perfectly in our desire for uninterrupted painting. It was a thin bond, perhaps, but camaraderie nonetheless.

"There's something about this spot, isn't there? Makes you feel like, well, lots of things don't matter."

"I guess," I said slowly. "I thought I just needed a change of pace. Back to basics."

"Hmm. Well, I like what you did with the trees there. Is this going to be that stump's root structure?"

I looked where she was pointing and saw that I'd somehow rendered it less fully than I'd thought. Looser than my usual brush-work, the tree faded into rough strokes that could have been many things—worms, braided hair. Seeing how the shadows came together, possibilities floated through my mind. Finally I felt lethargy creeping over me as I tried to imagine what it was supposed to be.

"I guess I'll know eventually," I said.

She laughed. "Everything becomes something eventually, even dust."

THE WEEKS PASSED, and my color sense kept changing. It was strange, given I painted to free myself from the strictures of design work, but when I gazed out at the world, increasingly I sought out shadows and dying plants. They were always there, of course, because that's the world.

One day I drove out to Louisa and wandered the back roads until I found a big field lying fallow for the summer. The remains of last year's crop made a web of fibrous browns and almost-blacks atop the soil. I found myself looking for hollows in trees and dark spots in the sky.

What's this about? I like Sharon's work and all, but...

I tried to put it out of my head. I squeezed out this color and that on my palette, wanting the purest hues, entirely unmixed, but before long I found myself taking a swipe of this or that and dulling what lay at the end of my brush. It wasn't like I was trying to paint landscapes full of nothing, but that's where I kept ending up. I felt frustrated by it, but there was a painful satisfaction in looking at my canvas and then back at the world, thinking about the canvases stacked in my studio, or hanging on buyers' walls. Today I felt like I'd painted a secret world that nobody else could see, one where no decay was possible, because everything had already happened.

Two kids walking a dog came into view, crossing the opposite corner of the field from where I'd set up. They were wearing vibrant-looking shorts and tank tops, and their golden retriever sported a red bandana around his neck, but clouds had occluded the sun and washed them out. I heard their high, sweet voices raised in argument, and the dog was dancing around them, and yet I felt removed from it all—cut off in a way that normally didn't happen when I was painting outside. It was the *opposite* of why you were supposed to paint outside. The clouds passed, but not before the kids vanished into the trees, joining the rest of the shadows and leaving behind only silence.

As the light was starting to fade, I looked at the canvas carefully, trying to decide whether I liked it or not. Eventually I took out my pocket knife and cut a slash through the heart of it. Usually that gave me a perverse kind of pride—knowing that I had judgment enough to recognize my failures—but this time I felt only tired, a failure for having brought nothing to life. I looked back at the field, wanting to see what had drawn me there in the first place, but night had taken it.

A LATE AUGUST heat wave turned my apartment the kind of unbearable that only happens in old brick buildings, where you actually *bake* if you stay inside. I drank endless iced coffees, ate cold bean salad for dinner, left for work early to get more air conditioning than my tiny window units put out. The Fan got even quieter as wealthy residents headed out to the beach. Painting was on hold along with everything else, aside from one disastrous attempt to "fix" an old painting I'd kept lying around.

One day I decided to take a sketchbook over to the VMFA, wondering why I hadn't done it sooner. A few blocks' walk later, I was entering the vast, cool lobby, passing the greeter and guard, and picking up one of their collapsible sketching stools at the coat check. There wasn't a traveling exhibition on at the moment, and apparently other people were equally forgetful about the pleasures of a cool museum, because that day I was alone in most of the galleries where I walked.

Eventually I settled down in early American, homing in on Hiram Powers' *Cleopatra*, a sculpture that I always stopped to see. The glowing white marble stood out against the deep red walls, and I felt some of my heat-daze lift as I gazed at her cool bosom and shoulders. Pencil flew over paper, and minutes turned into hours.

After a time I stopped and really looked at what I'd drawn.

The Egyptian queen's face had taken on the structure of Sharon's. My sometime painting companion *looked* out at me with dead eyes and half-rotting skin, and that felt…

Right. It feels right. *Jesus Christ. What is wrong with me?*

I thought of the spot down by the river, and how things got quiet there. When I stood there, the world seemed not to matter. Nothing mattered in that place. I looked back at Cleo, but she was pensive and silent. Her world had ended long ago, and even if her lips had moved, I could never have understood what she said, no more sense in her words than the whistling of the wind.

A WEEK PASSED. The heat dwindled into the false autumn that sometimes comes to Virginia early in September, cooling the ground before roaring back like a dragon in October. One day I got some time and walked out into an afternoon glowing with a peachy, golden light. There was only one place I wanted to go, of course. The ground under my feet was both soggy and full of sun-scorched grass, and everything was silent apart from the chuckle of the river.

Standing there, I felt color fade from the world. My heart pounded as I looked around, half-wondering if I'd see Sharon, but there was no sign of anyone. In fact, there was nothing in sight to indicate that there were still people. No planes, no empty bottles, nothing. The pounding of my heart eased, and I felt myself sinking into a half-torpor.

This patch of ground stagnates, endlessly. This is an honest-to-God damned place, but I'm not going to let a fucking field get the better of me, however many ghosts or demons or whatever there are here.

I looked upriver toward a spot where big rocks rose out of the water and made my choice. I started blocking in the bank on my canvas panel, even as I grumbled about the shade of blue that I'd toned the upper half months ago, back when nothing could be bright enough. Now the color blared out at me like an alarm, volume beyond tone or sense.

"Going to have to knock it back," I murmured, barely aware I'd spoken.

I got into a rhythm after a while so that at first I didn't notice when Sharon arrived and started setting up her own rig. I opened my mouth a couple times, trying to make the right words come out, to ask *something*—if she'd been painting here a long time before I first showed up, if she had been someone else once. Flash of tightness in my chest as I started to open my mouth, and so I turned back to painting.

The sun, when it started to set, burned a scarlet so clear that it could have come straight from a tube. My palette knife swept in blobs of ivory black and terre verte before I knew I was going to do it. Soon I was looking at a muddled, almost-warm color that might have glowed in cracks where the sun never shone and Hell was close at hand. Sharon came over and placed one hand beside the pile of paint. Her flesh had turned ashen as the day I'd sketched her in the museum, her veins blue-black in the sunset light. Next to *her* my paint shone with hectic radiance.

"See?" she said. "Color comes from contrast."

I looked up at her, watching how her cheeks changed as the sun touched the horizon, turning a vivid pink.

"But I don't always paint at this time of day," I said, "and I sure don't look at my paintings only at this time of day."

"I never look at mine again after I've finished them. They're dead things."

Her expression was wistful, and I wanted to know why she still came here to do this. Far downriver some people had gone out onto the rocks, and they were throwing something back and forth. Too distant to tell for sure, but they looked like high school kids, just on the verge of adulthood and at the end of sweetness.

"Paintings help me remember," I said slowly. "They tell me who I am, what I saw. When I look at them, especially the newest ones, I know that I'm still alive."

Sharon turned to face me, and her eyes were black like dusty basalt. She removed her hand from the palette and looked at her own setup, then back at me. The sun was bleeding the last of its light for the day, and her face had gone flat and entirely unreadable. She walked away then, toward the trees between us and the road, and soon she was gone. I didn't know what to do about her easel and paints, so they stayed when I left.

That was the last time that I saw her. As time has passed, my vision has weakened, and if the colors don't come clear like they used to, that's okay. My paintings are as bright as I can make them, with nothing to dull their riotous, vibrant cries of life. In my mind's eye, clear and cold I see her hand, and I feel the call of that place, where life drains out of the world. With each brushstroke I paint out the darkness, holding onto the light that lingers before sunset, staving off the grays and browns that creep in with the night.

The Inveterate Establishment of Daddano & Co.

Eric J. Guignard

WE HANDLED THE undertaking arrangements for them all: Bosses, capos, killers, tough guys—once you reached certain levels in a family, it was known you'd be cared for when the time came, like part of a benefits package. And we were strictly neutral territory, no affiliations. We didn't take sides, didn't ask questions, didn't exclaim how it was that some poor schlep had his kisser blown off, how we'd have to pack the skull with sawdust like a punching bag just to keep its shape, and cover it with a wig and more makeup than Carole Lombard so his mother could hang rosary beads over him one last time. We did good work and we earned respect. Every outfit came to us over the years: the North Siders, the South Siders, the Circus Cafe Gang, Egan's Rats, the Forty-Two Gang...I could go on.

Daddano & Co., that's our signage, been there near a century. My father was in the funeral business for forty years until his heart went kaput while sitting on the crapper one mornin'. His father started the business in 1872. Grandfather Daddano apprenticed for an Irish prick who made him dig graves from sun up 'til sun down. Nothing but gravedigging, fourteen hours a day, earnin' twenty-five cents a week.

"Hell with that," Grandfather said. He figured digging was the hardest part of the mortuary game, and he was doin' it already on his own. The easy part was rolling in bodies. So he set up shop on Halstead, and his first service was for the Irish prick, if you catch my drift.

"Simplest business in the world," Grandfather said. "Everyone dies. Ain't no shortage of that."

From day one, he never had to go seekin' clients, either, and that goes for all us Daddanos. People got a way of knowin' who to do business with, who they can trust, who can get the job done right, and in that way Grandfather's name got passed around.

But I'm runnin' my mouth the wrong way. You don't wanna hear about my family's history. You wanna hear about the Massacre.

It's all people want to hear about these days. Thing is, everyone else died that morning, so who's gonna buy the word of some old funeral man over what the coppers trumped up? Not even you, I bet...

I was only fifteen at the time, my father still alive, running Daddano. Al Capone and Bugs Moran were warring all over Chicago, which meant a boon in business for us. I dropped outta school to work full time with Father, and that pleased him a lot.

"Education is for the phonies," he'd say.

Anyway, I'd been helping him around the funeral home since I could toddle. As I grew, so too did my responsibilities, and while other kids in the neighborhood were playin' ball or lifting pockets, I was doing autopsies, embalming, going out to pick up stiffs in our stake bed delivery truck or maybe the old hearse if it was someone important. Sometimes he'd go with me, sometimes one of the other help went.

One of those help was a mortician named June whose hair was whiter than a snowstorm. June was maybe fifty, sixty years old though his hair had been colorless since birth, one of those pigmentation defects, I heard. June also carried a knife scar like a big crescent moon running under his right eye down to the corner of his mouth where a tooth was missing. My whole life, he'd been working for my father, but me and June barely ever said more words to each other than *mornin'* and *night*.

That day though we were together, taking the delivery truck to make a pick-up, and June outta nowhere says to me, "Johnny, you wanna know about death?"

I'd been helping my father so long I could tell you where the renal artery ran through the major calyces and whether a hematoma expansion was two hours or six past its onset. I'd seen a thousand dead faces wearing every ghoulish expression that would cause your nightmares to wake up crying. So I answered, "What's there to know? We're livin' now, and then we ain't. We got it better than most, then someday it's all over."

His voice lowered then, and he says quiet, "I mean real death, Johnny. Not just seeing the shell death leaves behind, but the act of dying. You never seen a man really die, have you?"

And that was true, though I never thought about it before. Every mutilation, every disease, every murdered dame and run-over kid and suicide and accident had come to me after the fact. It never struck me that the moment of transition was important. Just like waking up, I thought. One moment you're sleeping, then you're awake, and in the end, it goes the other way.

He nodded when I said nothin'.

"You're going to see it today," June whispered. I remember his breath stank like wild onions left in the ground two seasons too long, and when he paused between words, he chewed on the side of his tongue the way other men might roll a toothpick between their teeth. "You're gonna find out plenty, Johnny."

Those few words sent a chill so far down my back I could've pissed an icicle. My father liked June 'cause he worked hard and never said 'no,' but that cinched it why I'd kept my distance in the past. The old man was creepy as a sewer bug. And, Christ, the way he had to say my name in every sentence!

Though I had a thousand things I wanted to say, I kept 'em to myself. That was our business, remember? We didn't ask questions. June closed his eyes and went silent, as if the exhaustion of talking to me called for a nap. Which was fine, since I was driving and preferred my own company. In those days it didn't matter how old you were to operate a vehicle. If your feet could reach the pedals and you could see over the wheel, you could drive. And, friend, I started drivin' fast.

I probably looked like one of those little wind-up toys, my shoulders hunched and head craned over the wheel, arms jerking left and right as I veered around slow-poke traffic. There wasn't no rush otherwise, but I was gettin' edgy.

Then outta nowhere, June's eyes pop open, and he begins muttering some gibberish words I never heard in my life. I thought maybe he had Russian or Bulgarian family, and that's the language he was speaking, on account it sounded almost lyrical, the way monks might chant down in the bowels of a relic monastery.

I noticed too, while he mumbled, June kept looking behind us, his eyes darting from the rearview to the side mirror. I followed his gaze and thought I saw the flash of something darting in the street after us, flitting along the storefront walls where shadows were deepest, growing long when the street gutters ran into sewers, receding when the sunlight bounced off windows. Boarding houses and coffee shops blurred by as I sped, but that sense of something chasing after us kept pace just fine.

June's muttering changed back to words I was plenty familiar with, and I almost drove us into a light pole when he said, "Don't ever fuck with me, Johnny."

"What're you talkin' about? I thought me and you were on the level."

June eyeballed me strange. "Maybe we are, maybe not. I heard you all those nights, whisperin' I was a loony."

My heart could've hauled itself outta my mouth and swan-dived into my lap, and I wouldn't have been more surprised. "I've never said anything like that about you!"

"You've been warned, Johnny. Oh, yes, warned I ain't loony at all."

"Yeah, okay, I've been warned."

I thought to ask if he'd been drinking a Mickey Finn of formaldehyde, but the way June's pallid forehead popped beads of sweat in the cold air made me keep my tongue.

I ain't told you yet, but our pick-up that morning was to be in a mobster's mechanic's garage. See, we were going to a warehouse owned by Bugs Moran for his hatchetmen to use in chopping up hot cars, fencing stolen booze, turning stool pigeons to sausage, whatever... and here I was, more nervous by the old man sittin' next to me.

It was Father who'd taken the phone call last night, though when June heard about a pick-up at the garage, he offered to do the job with the haste I never seen a dog beg for porterhouse steak. Father said fine, but to take me along, I needed more field experience. June might have nodded his assent, 'cept you could tell he wasn't happy about it, way his lids slitted down the tiniest of bit.

Father didn't tell me squat about the pick-up, just gave me the address, and said to let June do the talkin', and for us to use the truck, so I knew it as another backstairs affair.

Reason we used a stake bed delivery truck instead of the hearse was that it blended in with the city, nothing memorable about it, just a rattletrap rusting at the edges of its doorframe, could have been a regular delivery of lumber or some hayseed cartin' his wares to market. Half the corpses we picked up, the men who hired us wanted to keep the matter quiet. Forget about the movies, nonsense like "sending a message to the enemy"; that only inspired guarantee of reprisal. It was better an unliked man simply vanish, and no one knows nothin' about it.

So here comes the brick face of S.M.C. Cartage Garage. I slowed as I drove past, to make the first right into an alley and circle around to its rear entrance, while that impression of being shadowed still lingered ominously, like something leaping through the air after us, one leg at a time, the way a child takes great strides over cracks in the sidewalk.

Halfway down the alley, June says, "Stop the truck," and I did.

He climbed out, clenching his fists. "I'm going in the front."

Once he left, I didn't feel that sense of being followed anymore, and only later did I consider it was waitin' for June.

At the time, I was nothing but relieved to be rid of both him and that spooky vibe of bein' watched. June walked toward the street past moldering tires and bags of trash, and I continued through the alley to park in the garage's dingy rear lot, backing up so the tailgate faced the rear steel door.

Since the door was closed, I stayed in the truck, checking things out through the side mirror.

My father usually did all the talking with customers, me and June and the other help doin' the legwork, but I got to know our clientele by face, by name, by rep, even if they didn't know me from Shinola. Like I said, sooner or later every outfit came to do business with Daddano & Co.

Which is how I recognized the man right away who opened the

garage back door: Al Weinshank, one of Moran's men. You see a mug like that, ya don't ever forget him. He was a gorilla, near six feet and a couple hundred pounds of muscle, with a towering pompadour of oiled hair that added another half-foot in height.

I got out to meet him.

He says, "Kid, you with Daddano?"

"Yes, sir."

"Truck ready?"

"Yes, sir."

"All right."

Then a fat guy dressed to the nines comes to the doorway, smokin' a snipe. Weinshank turns to him and they whisper to each other. The other guy nodded.

Past them, through the open door, I could see inside the long narrow garage there were four or five other men, only one of whom looked to be doing any actual mechanic's work, his head concealed under the hood of a dismantled coupe.

Weinshank and the fat man whispered something else, and I overheard a bit, "...comin' here to booshwash with Kachellek."

Kachellek.

Like I said before, we ran a tight operation at the Daddano business. We kept our mouths shut, did our part, and people knew to come to us for sensitive disposal matters.

But that don't mean business was always hunky-dory, either...

Some months back, Weinshank and a Moran lieutenant, Albert Kachellek, had cornered June in the stairwell outside our shop.

They pushed June around, slapped him, affirmed the usual threats for a debtor to pay up. Seemed June had run up some gambling dues with Kachellek, and the tardiness in payment turned issue.

I saw the fracas through a window and told my father, and he went out and ran them off. Not that I bore any love for June's well-being, but it was bad for business. And not that the men feared my father so much to scram, but they respected him enough to not worsen the scene.

Before they left, I overheard Weinshank sayin', "Don't make us open the side of your face again, Juney. And Al Kachellek's still got your last tooth."

Then they had a big laugh.

Is this what June was talkin' about, getting "fucked with"? Was he in over his head with debts? Were the threats gettin' to be too much? I wondered why in hell he'd want to come here, if he knew the garage held men who were leaning on him...I wondered too if the sick feeling rising in my guts meant every guess I made about that question ended in a bad way...

Someone from in the garage shouted, "Close the goddamned door, Frankie, whyn't you give the world an eyeful!"

"Aw, loosen your girdle," the fat man shot back, with a hint of foreign accent, before returning inside, slamming the door after him.

Weinshank came to the back of the truck, inspectin' within.

"All right," he says, "Your pops does good work."

Then he walked to the alley I'd come through, peering both ways to see if anybody'd been watching.

The garage door opened again, and a new guy comes out, half-readin' a newspaper. He was slim, balding, normal as any Joe accountant. The door closed automatically behind him. "Hey, your father said you need something?"

"My father? He ain't around. He's back at the shop on Halstead."

Accountant-Joe lowered his paper. "Old man you came here with, white hair, chews on his tongue real funny-like. Said you're his son?"

I made a face at him, confused, and maybe it's 'cause I didn't say anything back that the guy felt obliged to add, "I dunno. Old man said, 'My son is coming for us.' Took that to mean you were lookin' for something...What the hell's he got me runnin' around for?"

I shrugged, like what-the-fuck was I supposed to do about it? Though the next thought crossing my mind was a given, that because June told me *not* to think him loony, I immediately started judging he really had cracked a lid.

Weinshank comes back around the truck, as if readin' my mind, "Who you talkin' about, Adam? Loony Juney in there givin' you crap?"

It was then the first scream roared so suddenly from the garage that my heart almost burst outta my ribs. The other two men's eyes went big as dinner plates, and the one who looked like an accountant dropped his paper. He pulled back the lapel of his suit coat, and out came a revolver from his shoulder holster, though he didn't look in any hurry to go use it. That scream sounded...I don't know, *unholy*, pitched too high, too gurgling, and finally cut off too quick. The ensuing silence pretty much seemed as terrifying as the scream itself.

Weinshank shoved past us both as a second scream erupted. There was this barrage of submachine gun fire inside the garage, shouts, curses, the slapping sounds of revolver slugs hitting cement. Weinshank flung open the door and bolted inside.

The garage door hovered open just a second, before closing again on its own. And in that one glimpse, I saw the closest to Hell I'd ever care to know.

My impression of the scene was a raging whirlwind, one of those small dervishes that blow up off the lake sometimes, swirling leaves and shit into the air, only here it was blood and shell casings and a couple severed heads, all of it fuzzy, like how a blob of dust and grime clumps together. You ever look real close, there's no hard edges to dust, it just seems to fade in and out of existence at the edges.

Now imagine that fuzzy dust in the size and shape of a man, but every part of it always moving, as if an invisible wind blew over it from every direction at once.

Yeah...it was something like that.

The fat man who'd come out with Weinshank—Frankie—was squirming over the hood of the dismantled coupe, only it wasn't really Frankie anymore, but a severed gut spilling its insides and a pair of legs kicking up like a Rockettes routine.

Someone fired a Tommy submachine gun at the swirling dust man, and the roar was deafening, louder than a factory of dames at their Graybar sewing machines, just *rat-a-tat-a-tat*. The bullets ripped into it, passing through without doin' jack squat, like you're shooting at air. Someone else stumbled past, minus a head, his arms flailing around like all he'd done was lose balance.

I'll give credit to Weinshank, he must've seen the same things as me, and he didn't even blanch, just rushed right at the...*whatever it was*...his gorilla hands curled to battering ram fists, though I knew exactly the fate awaitin' him.

And I ain't even told you the worst of it. June—June was just standin' there with blood raining over his face, watching the whole thing and laughing and laughing, a horrible shriek you couldn't ever imagine coming from someone's voice. And that look of goddamned *glee* on him...it'll haunt me the rest of days.

Then the door closed shut.

I backed up real slow, and this panic took over. I turned alongside the tail of the truck, and all I wanted to do was hide, I couldn't even make it another ten feet to the cab to drive away, so I just dropped and crawled underneath between the tires.

Meanwhile the balding normal guy—*Adam*, Weinshank had called him—stood there, pointing his revolver in two hands at the door.

The shooting inside abruptly stopped, the screams, the cries, all those sickening sounds ended like a switch got thrown off.

I thought the machine gun fire had been loud, but that was nothin' compared to the *rat-a-tat-a-tat* of my pounding heart, and we're not even done yet. A voice calls out to me from the garage, and my nuts just scrambled up into my stomach.

"Oh, Johnny-boy, where are you? Johnny, come meet my son—"

The door slammed open. There stood June in all his loony glory, that snow white hair now soaked red and standing on edge, his eyes glaring near to poppin' out of his head, and him chewin' on the side of his tongue. Blood and gore splattered over his coat and his face, and his arms were outstretched like he thought I was right in front of him and he was gonna grab me up in an big happy embrace.

I don't think he even saw Adam. The gangster pulled the trigger of his revolver—*Pop! Pop!*—and June's eyes went bulging even more. His legs sorta gave way real slow, and he dropped to his knees in the doorway, two neat little smoking holes added to his chest. The life seemed to fade from him real quick as his mouth went slack and his head rolled down, and a bubble of blood popped at his lip right where the crescent moon scar connected...

Then *it* came out.

The whirlwind was silent as clouds, but if it had a voice, I knew it would've been howling. It twisted around June, straight at Adam who fired the pistol again, each shot carefully aimed into the center of the dust man. For all the good it did him, he might as well have been slappin' it with a wet noodle.

That swirling form of soot and grime sorta surrounded Adam, and then it expanded outward, and took Adam with it, expanding him I mean, so he came apart at the seams as if nothin' but a rag doll, his legs and arms and head all pulling off in different directions. Adam's gun fell to the ground inches from me, though I knew it didn't matter if it landed right in my hand and the trigger under my finger, cocked and loaded; it wasn't gonna do any good. I stayed where I was, frozen.

After that, the whirlwind kinda slowed, hovering there awhile, gazing down at Loony Juney's corpse, and it almost seemed like the wind holding it aloft began to soften, as if some despair got the better of it. I took a closer look than I would've wanted...the swirling dust was still in the form of a man, yet seein' it nearer, I realized it wasn't just any man, but a thousand men, ten thousand men, a horde of faces all sifting and overlapping each other, layer upon layer upon layer that you could see through, but fuzzy too, and mucky and wet and ethereal, and Christ, it's just so hard to explain, y'know?

It wasn't no ghost, not like that, but it wasn't no human either, and it didn't seem right for a demon or some boggieman...it was something else entirely, which even now I still only vaguely comprehend.

See, there was somethin' fluttering around in that whirlwind's figure, and I don't think anyone else would have recognized it, though bein' raised in a mortuary I knew right away the small string-wrapped slip of cardboard for what it was: A toe-tag.

And after all these years tryin' to settle it out, the best I can tell you is it's something there ain't a name for. It's the little scraps of death and residue that accumulate together the way motes of dust collect to form clumps under the hutch, or the way grit always seems to build in the same board cracks until it overflows to spill across the floor. Give it chance, and that buildup keeps going, those dust clumps grow in no time at all.

You ever neglect sweeping beneath a couch or bed for awhile and then amaze at the mass of gunk that's festering down there?

Think of that gunk in your home, how it happens to us all—dust bunnies you might call it. Now think of that gunk in *my* home, Daddano & Co., decades upon decades of death filling our halls, and the worst kind of it, the remains of mob men and pushers, wife beaters, assassins, pimps, whores, thieves and all their ilk and leaders. Flakes of their skin, drops of their blood, strands of their hair, remnants of their hatred, their viciousness, their corruption, all slipping under a loose floorboard and *growing together*.

Looking back, I think it's June all along, hardworkin' employee that he was, stayin' late and closing up the doors after me and Father and the others gone to bed. June found that mass...or maybe it found him. A gust from the fan, a dropped nickel rolling past the crack...a scent of something moldering, or maybe June lookin' for that lost toe-tag, whatever it was, he found the creature, made cause with it, and tried to control it like a pet dog. Loony Juney who'd probably been beaten down all of life had found his chance to rise up, as fleeting as that chance was.

Anyway, my story about the massacre that day ain't even finished yet. 'Cause I was still cowerin' under the truck while watchin' the dust man continue to swirl over June's body. It hung in the air a few minutes, kinda circling June, touching him, waiting for I don't know what. Then real carefully, like trying on a new suit, the thing sank down into June and filled the old man back up with itself.

There was a twitch of limbs, a fluttering of eye lids, and June pulls himself up, as if he'd been faking death all along. Only those two bullet holes over his heart don't lie.

He opened his mouth, and a little puff of dust billowed out, and he only says one word, "*Johnny...*"

It was June's voice too, but aloof, like our work here was done, and we needed to get back to the shop, bein' on the clock and all...only it wasn't June's voice either, 'cause it was dry and wispy as bones rubbing against each other. June began to walk toward the truck, so as he got closer, my perspective of him changed by scale, my line of sight falling from his air-holed chest to his waist, then his legs, and finally just a pair of scuffed black loafers a foot from the fender.

I was tryin' not to cry or piss myself, when I heard sirens in the distance, gettin' near fast. June's feet turned away, hesitated, and he—*it*—walked off down the alley.

Afterward, the police didn't have any clues, never mind what I told 'em. There were seven dead men torn to pieces, and I mean literally, a hand here, an ear there, a pile of guts draped over someone else's legs.

So they framed it all on Al Capone. It was convenient since him and Moran had been warring, and the coppers wanted him bad. Capone was a thorn in everyone's ass back then, he was so popular with the public that judges wouldn't sentence him 'cause fear of backlash. Capone gave people jobs, donated to schools, set up soup kitchens for the poor, all out of his own pocket, for God's sake. Chicago loved him, all except the cops who knew where he was getting all that money from in the first place.

Yeah, that garage massacre pretty much put Capone outta business, ironically blamed for something he wasn't responsible for in the least.

He was never convicted of it or anything, but the media crucified him, and people began riding him for the crook he was. The federal government took notice too, and they're the ones who ultimately got him, trumping up tax offenses.

I'll tell you somethin' else too, that I don't hardly tell anyone. To this day I see fellas lookin' like June once in awhile, out of the corner of my eye, never aged, just blending in with the crowd but for that snow white hair and crescent moon scar, and I don't like to think where they're going, what they're doing...

So there's my story, friend. Take a look at the pictures that day in the Cartage Garage, why don't ya? The real pictures, I mean, if you can find them, not those staged phonies, the ones where Hollywood actors were brought in and laid on the ground with a daub of blood at the corners of their mouths. Anyone with a nickel's worth of sense can make those out as shams; the story that each mobster was riddled with at least fifteen bullets apiece on Valentine's Day don't even match the images, let alone how they *really* ended up lookin'. Anyway, it is what it is, I guess, and folks say history is only what we agree it to be.

And I don't know any more than that. I'm just an old mortuary man.

White Elephants

Malcolm Devlin

Jimmy watched as Penny the Pocket Lady walked through the village fair. She was an unfamiliar figure: bright and varied of color, moving with confidence through the drab and familiar local crowd.

"A pound in my palm, a prize in every pocket." Her voice was sing-song and accentless. As she walked, her skirts and apron—buoyed up by acres of angel-white petticoats—sashayed before her like the sails of a tall ship pitching in a squall.

She was, Jimmy decided, the most beautiful person he had ever seen in his life. Being only nine, he wasn't sure if this revelation had any weight, but it didn't matter. He was completely entranced and little wonder: she had a flurry of blonde curls and round pink cheeks that shone like polished apples in the mid-afternoon sunlight. She smiled too, all the time, at everyone, and surely that was a sign of beauty? Or maybe that was inner beauty. Something important, he was certain.

Her apron was a patchwork of pockets, a matrix of brightly colored pouches that gaped open invitingly, each heavy with the weight of something precious stowed inside. The kids from the village followed her with a guileless fascination they would ordinarily reserve for the new and the unexpected. Obedient to her sing-song command, they paid in coins that she'd spirit away, and agonize over which of her pockets to choose until, eventually, they stepped forward and reached deep inside to find what they had won.

"Must have got the idea from that book," Jimmy's father said. "What was it? That treasure hunt one. The hare? Remember the hare?"

Jimmy's mother was looking across the green where stalls had been set up on trestle tables.

"Moira's on the White Elephant," she said. "Jimmy, aren't your friends around?"

She didn't wait for a response to her first comment, nor an answer to her second before she was off, pitting the dips and furrows of the village green against her bright red patent leather shoes.

The White Elephant stall sold everything and anything, and behind it, there was Mrs. Moira Mercer from down-the-way. Her arms were crossed and she wore the look of someone who had been saving all her conversation and analysis for the right outlet. She watched Jimmy's mother approach expectantly.

Jimmy and his father stood together on the edge of the green. His father was a thin man with a thinner mustache and he was wearing a grey tweed suit that seemed more appropriate for the church than for the fair.

"Well, sport," Jimmy's father said, patting his son on the top of his head, an automatic gesture calibrated for a boy who had once been shorter. His eyes flickered around the gathered crowd. "Was there something you wanted to see?"

Jimmy shrugged. The fair was mostly the same as it was every year. The same layout of the stalls, the same games that sounded like orders: *Throw The Hoop*, *Climb The Rope*, *Kill The Rat*. There used to be a small Ferris wheel that arrived on the back of a truck, its hanging carriages sheltered with brightly colored awnings. But that hadn't been back since it stalled two years earlier, stranding Mrs. Tunney in the car at the top for three hours until the fire brigade had arrived to rescue her like a cat stuck in a tree.

The White Elephant stall was Jimmy's favorite. Two years earlier he'd found a tattered board game missing most of its pieces and all of the rules. He'd salvaged what was there to make his own game that he was pretty sure would have been exciting if only he could have found someone willing to play it with him. He didn't dare approach the stall while his mother was there because she'd think he was following her and she hated it when he did that.

"Isn't that Kim over there?" his father said. "Don't you want to go play?"

Jimmy felt his father's hand on the nape of his neck. A gentle push, a less gentle intent.

He glanced back to see his father's smile being slowly eclipsed as he surveyed the assembled tents for something specific.

"Can I have my pocket money?" Jimmy said.

His father's expression crinkled in annoyance, but he didn't look down.

"You'd better ask your mother," he said. "Now then, run along now."

And it was *his* turn to be off, stalking across the grass to the private-looking tent beside the old cricket pavilion, the one with the sharp smell of spilled beer coming from it, the one with the men standing outside, smoking and looking morose.

Kim lived two doors down on Miller's Lane. She was older than Jimmy by nearly a whole year, and while Jimmy didn't have a sister, Kim would sometimes pretend she filled the role, often to the extent that made Jimmy think he probably didn't want a sister after all.

"Have you been to the Pocket Lady yet?" Kim said when Jimmy got near.

Jimmy shook his head.

"I think she's sexist," Kim said. "She gave me this and I think she only gave it to me because I'm a girl."

She held out a small pink tube that glittered ever so slightly.

"Glue?" Jimmy said.

"Lip gloss." Kim shook her head in disgust. "Ben got a torch. Just a small one, but a proper, working torch. It's very unfair. Next time I see my Aunty Pat, I'll tell her."

Idly, she scratched the back of her hand and Jimmy noticed how it looked a little red, a little shiny.

"Have you cut yourself?" he said.

Kim shook her head.

"I must have walked past some stinging nettles or something," she said. "It's only itchy. It doesn't really hurt."

She always had been brave. She could climb trees and jump over the brook behind the churchyard while Jimmy was content to just watch and admire. He didn't even want to imagine the look his mother would give him if he hurt himself.

"But you should really have a go," Kim said. "There might be good things in there, you just have to know which pocket to pick."

Jimmy looked at his feet.

"I don't have any money," he said.

Kim looked sympathetic, it was a new expression of hers and it looked like she'd been practicing in a mirror.

"Well obviously, I would lend you something," she said. "But I can't because I'm saving up."

"What are you saving for?" Jimmy frowned, it sounded like a very grown up thing to do.

"An automatic label machine," Kim said. "You can type in little messages and it prints them out on black sticky tape."

"What do you want one of those for?" Jimmy said.

"So I can label things, of course," Kim said. "And leave messages. And letters. And ransom notes no-one would be able to trace."

Jimmy sighed. It did sound like something worth saving up for. He wished he earned enough pocket money to be able to save up for something worthwhile. As it was, he only really got anything when he badgered his parents, and even then he got so little, so rarely, that he spent it as soon as he could for fear it would just get tidied away when he wasn't looking.

Kim scratched her hand again.

"Well you'll have to hurry," she said. "You don't want to be the last and she doesn't have all day. She might run out of things in her pockets. Did you hear what Stan got?"

"No," said Jimmy.

"He got one of those little tools for getting stones out of horses hooves." Kim hooked her finger to demonstrate.

Stan didn't have a horse, but tools were always useful. Then again, it might not have been true at all. Kim sometimes said any old thing just because she knew Jimmy would believe her.

Once, she'd told him how the night sky was dark because it was actually full of spiders.

"Really, it's sunny all the time," she'd said, "but when it's night, all the spiders crawl across the sky and block out the light. Billions and billions of them, all crawling over each other. All those legs and eyes and teeth. You can sometimes see the sun glinting through the gaps in them and people think those are stars. That's why stars flicker and shine. Because the spiders which surround them are moving all the time."

Jimmy hadn't slept for a month after that. Even now he insisted on a night-light and made sure the curtains were properly closed before he went to bed each night so he couldn't see even an inch of the dark outside.

"Well, you should get some pocket money," Kim said again. She looked a bit distracted, like a fly was buzzing around her. "You should talk to the Pocket Lady. She'd like that." She scowled at something Jimmy couldn't see and waved her hands ineffectually. Then without another word, she turned her back on him and walked away into the crowd.

JIMMY DIDN'T WANT to go near the Pocket Lady until he had the means to have a turn himself. He didn't want to risk being sent away, disappointed as she flashed that smile at him.

So he watched from a distance as little Susie who lived above the Post Office turned in a coin and contemplated the choice before her, absently tugging at her pig-tails, her brow furrowed.

He watched as she reached a decision and her hand hovered over one of the blue pockets on the top row. Then he saw how she plunged her arm in deep, her face creased with concentration before she withdrew her prize.

He saw her look of exaltation as she held up the pack of playing cards she'd won in her red and shining hand. And as he turned away from the scene, he buried his own hands deep in his own pockets but felt only the seams of their empty linings, sharp along the backs of his knuckles.

JIMMY TRIED HIS mother first. She was still at the White Elephant stall, talking to Mrs. Moira Mercer from down-the-way. He tried to be stealthy. He started at the far end of the crowded table and, feigning an interest in the things the stall was selling (old wooden nutcrackers, yellow ivory chopsticks, pots with missing handles, handles with missing pots), he crept closer.

They were talking about the allotments, where they had neighboring plots of land and how, across the path, Mr. Cromwell had planted something new.

"It's beautiful," Mrs. Mercer said, "but it's invasive. I don't like the way it seeds."

"I'll have words with the committee," Jimmy's mother said. "Perhaps they can make him see sense."

She and Mrs. Mercer had their backs to Jimmy and their voices were curiously muffled in that adult way, engaged in subjects that children tune out of by default. Jimmy edged a little nearer, his hands tracing the wares before him (old hardback books with faded color covers, horse irons, dominoes, napkin rings with old family crests on them) but even as he got closer their conversation struck him as guarded and opaque.

His mother was a tall woman, taller than his father, and she seemed tall in more than just her height. Even when she was standing next to Jimmy, she sometimes seemed such a long way away, and she often spoke to people with her head tipped back as though, by doing so, she could make herself appear grander still.

Now they were talking about Mr. Cromwell's new bride, who was much younger than the wife who had died.

"She's beautiful," Mrs. Mercer said, "but she's intrusive. I don't trust her motives."

"I'll have words with their landlord," Jimmy's mother said. "Perhaps he can make her understand."

Jimmy continued pretending to be fascinated by the bric-a-brac, (a pocket calculator with the "6" button missing, a box of assorted chess pieces, a candlestick holder, a compass, a fire shovel), until he was close enough to reach out a hand and gently tug the fold of his mother's skirt as though it was a bell pull.

A broad hand descended from his mother's lofty heights and gently batted him away.

"Jimmy, dear," she said, looking down at him, "you know I don't like it when you follow me around like a lost little dog."

"I just wondered if I could have some pocket money," Jimmy said. "Please," he added, being careful not to stretch the word out to two plaintive syllables because he knew from experience it would only make things worse.

His mother sighed.

"You should ask your daddy," she said. "It's his turn to give you pocket money, he is an accountant, after all. I'm talking to my friend, and you're being very rude indeed."

Moira glanced down at Jimmy and gave him a brief this-is-how-it-is sort of smile.

"Daddy said to ask you," Jimmy said. "There's a lady with pockets and everyone else is doing it. Stan got a tool for getting horses out of hooves."

"Well bully for Stan," Jimmy's mother said. "Go and find your daddy and tell him that mummy said it was his turn to give you pocket money. Go on now, run along. Off you go."

And she turned back to Moira and they were talking again like he hadn't been there at all.

THE TENT INTO which Jimmy's father had disappeared was on the far side of the green, just next to the old cricket pavilion. Jimmy tried to look through the tent's doorway, but a large red-faced man in a green wax jacket blocked his way and muttered something disparaging about his age. Jimmy retreated, craning his neck to peer inside, but he saw only a black fabric screen that blocked his view.

Around the back, there was a stack of barrels and wooden pallets and behind them, Jimmy found a split in the tent where the canvas hadn't been tied down properly. Confirming he was alone, he resolved to be brave in a manner that might impress Kim when he next saw her.

The canvas was heavy and blackened around the edges, but the split was just about big enough for him to crawl through on hands and knees.

Inside, it was darker than he'd anticipated, heavy black masking drapes hung around the interior walls forming a private arena in which a small congregation of men were sitting on assorted wooden chairs.

Most of the men had their backs to him, but from his hiding place in the folds of the heavy curtains, Jimmy recognized a few faces from the village. Mr. Halter from the school was there, and so was Mr. Newson from the garage. No one was talking, the men just sat patiently ignoring each other as though they were waiting for their turn in a barber's shop. Mr. Halter was staring into the middle-distance and Mr. Newson was playing a game of patience, his cards stacked into columns on the grass before him.

None of the men were paying much attention to the raised stage area at the back of the tent, which was curious, because Penny the Pocket Lady was standing on it.

Or so Jimmy thought until he looked closer. The dress was certainly hers. It was big and layered, its wide, expansive skirts patchworked with many, many colorful pockets, each heavy and ripe and so beautiful he almost wanted to break from his hiding place and explore them all. But it was only the dress and nothing else. Penny the Pocket Lady didn't seem to be inside it anymore, and instead, her empty garments stood unsupported, like a headless, handless mannequin.

As he watched, it started to sag and deflate ever-so-slightly. At first, Jimmy assumed it was because dresses weren't supposed to stand so straight on their own, but then he noticed a hand grasping its shoulder, squashing the fabric down and misshaping it, so the personless costume lurched to a stoop, listing to its side like it was reaching down for something it had dropped. Another hand joined the first, flattening the dress further as they pawed at its ribbons and folds, and then a figure emerged from behind the billowing cloth, a thin man in a grey tweed suit.

"Daddy," Jimmy said. Quiet enough that no one heard him, loud enough to convince himself that what he was seeing might be real.

The other men in the tent didn't seem to be paying much attention to what was happening. Sitting on a barstool, closest to the stage, sat a younger man whom Jimmy recognized as Mrs. Givens' eldest boy, who was spending the summer working on the farm. The lad looked up from his paper to glance briefly at the stage and check his watch before he returned to the sports section. His expression was serious, but also incurious.

On the stage, there was something altogether changed about Jimmy's father. His face was bright and red and glistening like he'd been too-long in the sun, and there was a hunger in his eyes that Jimmy didn't like at all. He watched as his father worked feverishly with a vigor that was quite uncharacteristic of the man he knew. With flailing arms, he smoothed and flattened the dress so it lay across the stage in a broad circle like a lily pad. Then he was on all fours, crawling across the ruched fabric, burying his face in the mass of pockets. He moaned in a peculiar happy-sad way and his body racked with angular convulsions. When he came up again for air, cords of saliva snapped at the corners of his mouth and his eyes looked wild and bloodshot.

Mr. Newson sighed. He scooped up his cards; he shuffled them and dealt himself another game.

Jimmy's father crawled his way to the centre of the dress where the bodice had flattened into a ruffled O. He wrestled free of his jacket, sending it sailing offstage. He was still struggling with his shirt when he reached the inky hole where the Pocket Lady herself had once emerged, but it was empty now and without hesitation, Jimmy's father started to crawl inside.

Headfirst he went, greedy and eager. With an unpleasant urgency, he dragged his way deep into the dress and it was as if there was a tunnel underneath the stage, because even as his feet disappeared, flapping into the gaping neck-hole, the garment itself remained resolutely flat across the wooden boards.

Jimmy didn't move. It was only when the empty costume started to stir that he began to back away, hiding himself deeper into folds of the curtains. As the garment grew on the stage, as if something was inflating it from the inside, billowing outward, then snapping upright, Jimmy had retreated so far, his back was tight against the white canvas of the tent's exterior.

He stayed long enough to witness a curl of blond hair corkscrew out of the top of the bodice, and he saw how Mrs. Givens' boy folded his newspaper and got to his feet; he left the paper on his stool, and he opened his wallet. Taking out a single coin, he stepped forward towards the stage.

JIMMY DIDN'T GO back to the fair. The fair didn't seem safe. Everything that had happened was all the fair's fault.

Normally when he hid, Jimmy didn't expect anyone would look for him, so he never really made much of an effort to hide properly. Once when his father had come home from work, he hid behind the post box down the street, waiting for someone to step out the front door and wander where he was. A dozen people must have passed him by, but he still wasn't sure if anyone had seen him. Certainly no-one came to look for him from home, and he concluded that *this* was the secret to hiding successfully. You just need to be the sort of person who people don't look for, and then you can hide where you like.

With this in mind, he made a nest for himself behind the wheelie bins around the back of the pavilion. He curled up into a little ball and screwed his eyes tightly shut as though by doing so, he could make the world go away for a spell. But his own personal darkness was spotted with flashes of light and he didn't want to imagine there were spiders inside of him as well, so he opened his eyes again and waited for something decisive to steer him.

It felt as though he waited for a long time before he finally decided to emerge, but he couldn't really be certain. No-one passed his hiding place and eventually, the music and chattering voices of the fair had dispersed. There had been some raised voices: someone shouting something about Mr. Cromwell's allotment of all things, but they too had subsided quickly and now there was no sound at all. No people, no cars, no wind, there didn't even seem to be any birdsong. The only thing he could hear was the heavy *tukka-tukka-tukka* of his own heartbeat that seemed so loud amidst the silence that trying to remain hidden felt futile.

The stalls were all still set up on the green, but the fair appeared to have wound down completely, a flurry of drink stirrers and plastic cups from the refreshment stand cluttered the path, paper napkins danced in the breeze.

To Jimmy's surprise, everyone was still there, but they were lying in the grass silently, flat on their backs and staring up at the sky. Each lay alone, neatly arranged like fallen dominoes and no one was talking because everyone seemed to be asleep. Jimmy picked his way around them gingerly. He knew them all, his grey crowd of locals. There was Kim and Stan and Ben and little Susie who lived above the Post Office. There was Mr. Halter, Mr. Newson, Mrs. Givens' boy. They all looked so tranquil, and each lay with their swollen hands, red and shiny and bright like ripe rosehips, resting gently on their chests, fingers stretched and distended like roots, rising and falling as they slept.

His mother was still standing. She was still talking to Mrs. Moira Mercer from down-the-way and when Jimmy tugged at her skirts she looked down at him with a stern expression.

"Jimmy, dear," she said. "Did daddy give you your pocket money to spend?"

Jimmy shook his head, he was close to tears, he wasn't sure if he could say anything without making a fool of himself and embarrassing his mother in front of her friend.

His mother pursed her lips.

"Well there's nothing I can do, now, is there?" she said. She gently lifted the hem of her skirt so Jimmy could see how there was a bole of knotted bark where her lovely red patent leather shoes should have been. She sighed deeply and then reached into her bag. Beside her, Moira glanced down at Jimmy and gave him a brief this-is-how-it-is sort of smile.

"Well, if I must be the grown up," his mother said. She fished out a pound coin and passed it down to him, then she glanced across the green to where Penny the Pocket Lady was standing alone amongst the sleeping villagers.

"You'll have to hurry," his mother said. "It looks like you're the last and she doesn't have all day."

And with that she turned away again, and she and Moira talked and talked and talked in voices that were as intelligible to Jimmy as the sound of the wind in the trees.

THE COIN FELT too light in Jimmy's hand. He wondered if it was even real, like one of those chocolate pennies his grandmother used to give him at Christmas. For a moment, he imagined if he were to clench it in his hand it might break and melt in the same way.

He glanced up at Penny the Pocket Lady who was waiting for him on the green and he wondered if he might use the coin to go somewhere else instead. Somewhere on a bus maybe, or on a train. But she was as beautiful as a flower in bloom, and the dress was as colorful as a rose garden, anywhere else would seem black and white and empty in comparison.

Penny looked down at him as he approached her, and she smiled her lovely, lovely smile. Up close, she smelt like freshly cooked currant buns and custard and tea.

"A pound in my palm, a prize in every pocket," she said.

Jimmy smiled at her.

"I'm tired," he said and her smile widened, her sympathy genuine and unaffected. Her hand found his and her long, elegant fingers gently unwound his fist, claiming the coin buried inside like it was a seed hidden in a gnarled burr.

Jimmy looked down at the pockets in her apron. They gaped at him hungrily. They were bright and inviting, their throats glistening with something slick as tree sap. Jimmy chose the green pocket, the one in the very middle. He reached into it, unafraid.

It was so deep, so dark, so full of life.

Reasons I Hate My Big Sister

Gwendolyn Kiste

#17: *She always embarrasses me.* Especially when we're in public. I wish she would act normal for a minute, but I might as well ask the sky to rain free lipstick because let's face it: she'll never change.

WE'RE SHOPPING AT the mall when the first flap of flesh sloughs off Elise's arm.

"How strange," she says as if her body comes undone every day, and it's all a minor inconvenience.

Next to us, a woman picking over a bin of discount makeup nearly faints at the sight of the skin as it ripples and falls from my sister's arm. One customer shrieks and another and another after that, the screams going right down the line like keys on a piano scale.

The shop empties, all except me and Elise and the staff behind the counter.

I sigh. Today was the first time Mom and Dad let Elise borrow the car and take me with her, and it'll probably be the last time too.

Because I don't know what else to do, I squint at the remnants of my sister's flesh, curled like lace ribbons at our feet. The mountain of tissue looks oddly beautiful. Everything about Elise looks beautiful. Even the way she lifts her arm curiously to the light and inspects her new wound has an elegance to it.

I move in closer to see what she sees. From her wrist to her elbow, all the skin has peeled away. There's no blood. Beneath the places where skin should be, there's something tough and iridescent—a casing of armor over her bones.

Outside the store windows, a few spectators gape and point and whisper about Elise and me. Red-faced, I back against a wall of tacky bangles and wish I was someone else.

#29: *She's the center of attention.* I'm invisible anytime she's around. She was born first, so I guess she's had more practice at getting people to notice her, but it would be nice if someone would pay attention to me for once.

THE DOCTOR SHINES a light in Elise's eyes while my parents and I gather next to her hospital bed. Dad left work early, which isn't a good sign since he always says he "doesn't believe in taking half-days" as though they're as mystical as elves or something.

"I got to ride with Elise in the ambulance," I say to him and Mom when they arrive at the emergency room, but neither of them care. All they're worried about is the diagnosis.

"We need to keep her here to ensure she's not contagious." The doctor makes notes about my sister. Lots of notes. He types in an electronic file for almost ten minutes. My parents don't notice how he smirks to himself, but Elise and I see that goofy expression on his face, and we know what he's thinking. Elise is an anomaly, and white coats live for anomalies. She means publications, case studies about a brand-new ailment, trial and error experiments no one's ever done because no one knew a girl could swap skin for scales. If what's on her arms are scales. I hope not. Scales are for reptiles, and my sister's not a lizard. At least I don't think so.

I fidget. "Will I be quarantined too?"

"Your younger daughter is not yet showing symptoms," the doctor says to my parents, and though he's answering my question, he speaks as if I'm not in the room. "But keep her out of school for now. We're recommending everyone who came in contact with Elise stay at home until a normal incubation period has passed."

"What's normal?" I wonder aloud and already know no one will answer me.

"Maybe we're all supposed to shed our skin," Elise says, running her fingers over the new flesh. "And everyone else has forgotten how."

En route to the hospital, she shrugged out of the skin on her other arm too. Now she reclines in bed, two sleeves the color of moonstone peeking out beneath the sheets.

"Were there any early symptoms?" the doctor asks.

"There was an itch," Elise says. "Mom told me to leave it alone, and it would heal. Guess she was wrong."

Our mother stomps one foot, her eyes squinted and fists bunched up like a child who skipped a nap. "Did you leave it alone like I said? Or did you keep picking it? You probably did this to yourself."

Elise laughs. "I gave myself scales? That's some trick."

My sister's words lilt in the air like raindrops against a tin roof. I love to hear her voice. Some nights, at bedtime, she croons me to sleep. I tell her I'm fourteen and too old for childhood things, but she keeps on singing. And I let her.

But tonight there will be no lullabies. As they drape a clear plastic shell around Elise's bed and usher my parents and me down the hallway, I fear there will never be lullabies again.

#48: *I'm no one because of her.* I have no name, no identity of my own. I'm just "Elise's little sister." Without her, I don't exist.

TWENTY-ONE DAYS—that's the incubation period the doctors choose for a disease they know nothing about. I curl like an inchworm in bed, my arms around my ears so I can't hear my parents arguing. Across the room, Elise's mattress feels emptier than anything in the world should.

As long as she's in her cocoon at the hospital, we can't see her. No visiting hours, not even a phone call. She's far away from me now. That voice of hers might as well be in another galaxy.

Three weeks pass, and I slink into homeroom, chemistry and algebra textbooks withering in my arms. The solemn gazes tell me everyone already knows about my sister. Her picture hasn't been on television or in the local papers, but after the scene at the mall, it shouldn't surprise me they heard. But it does surprise me. Because even though Elise is still in the hospital and my parents can barely look at each other without crying or screaming, I want so badly for everything to be normal.

At lunch, a boy I don't recognize sidles up next to me. "So what does she look like?"

I nudge a mound of coleslaw with my spork. "I don't know," I say. "We haven't seen her since the doctors put her in quarantine."

A second boy materializes on my other side, and sandwiched between them, I feel trapped.

"But what did she look like that last time?" This boy is also someone I've never met, but he's speaking to me like we're friends. Maybe he thinks I'm desperate for him—with his football shoulders and wide grin—to notice me. Maybe I am. But not like this.

"Well?" the boys say in unison.

I don't answer. I leave my tray on the table and walk away. They're too slack-jawed to follow.

In the girls restroom, I hide in a corner stall and sob. The tears are silent. These last three weeks, I've learned to cry without making a sound.

After school, my parents pick me up, and it's not until we're halfway to the hospital they tell me about Elise's operation scheduled that evening.

"It's risky," they say without inflection, "and the doctors aren't sure she'll make it until morning. But it's the only way."

"The only way for what?" I ask.

"For her to have a normal life."

Outside, the buildings bleed past like melted oil paintings, and I wonder if it's already too late.

#86: *She gets all the breaks.* If I had only half of her good luck, I sure wouldn't waste it like she does.

WE DON'T SPEAK in the hospital waiting room. My father does the New York Times crossword puzzle, and my mother watches a trashy talk show with a bunch of women gathered in a circle tittering like hens on the way to the slaughter.

I sit alone, waving my feet back and forth in the chair and staring at my scuffed black Oxfords. The shoes are hand-me-down from Elise. My whole life is borrowed from her.

Fourteen hours later, after my feet no longer wag and the newspaper's retired to the trash and the television plays only midnight infomercials, a solemn doctor with lines around his mouth shuffles through the double doors and tells us the operation was a success.

A full-body skin graft, they call it. Unprecedented, because even in bad burn cases, the victim has more skin left than Elise. Since the last time we saw her, the flesh on her legs has gone too.

"Can we see her?" I ask, and the doctor nods.

Bright-eyed, Elise sits up in bed and examines her new shoulders and elbows and knees. Her body's a patchwork quilt of dead people's skin.

"It doesn't seem right to wear them around like this," she says, marveling at the stitches. Between the borders of the skin grafts, there's blood seeping out, blood that must not belong to my sister, because my sister's skin doesn't bleed anymore.

I scrunch up my nose as pus dribbles down her white hospital gown. "I liked your old arms better."

"Me too," she says with a grin, and I realize she means the scales.

I glare at her. "Not *those* arms."

After a week of recovery, the doctors let us take Elise home.

"I'm glad it's over," our mother says.

But the new skin doesn't last. It falls off in clumps, and her hair goes with it. I find tufts of pink flesh and blond tresses in the sink, in the trash, in our closet.

"Are you picking at it again?" Our parents hover over Elise, their faces soaked in sweat. "If you are, we'll have you padlocked in bed until it heals."

"Won't make any difference." She stares out the window past the trees behind our house. "Who I really am will come through one way or the other."

"You can't reason with her," our mother tells her Rotary friends over a pot of tea in the parlor. "She won't listen. She's never listened."

All the ladies nod their heads as though they understand, but they aren't here for scones or sympathy. They're here for a glimpse of my sister.

And Elise obliges, reclined in the nearby window seat, her scales showing through her lace shirt with an almost defiant glee.

"Why don't you commit her to full-time care?" a blue-haired woman whispers.

"No one will take her," my mother says, eyeing Elise who pretends not to hear. "We've checked. They refuse to house such an unusual patient."

At this, Elise smiles and digs one finger under her flesh until it bubbles up and plops to the floor like pancake batter.

I get a broom and sweep up the mess.

By the end of the month, the graft is gone along with the skin everywhere else—her torso, her neck, even her face.

There's not a stitch of flesh left on Elise's body.

#99: *Anytime she does something wrong, I end up sharing her punishment.* Is that fair? Of course not, but if your family can't trust the oldest, they'll never trust the youngest.

OUR PARENTS KEEP us home. No more school. No more trips to the mall. We even get our groceries delivered—money in the mailbox, brown bags left on the porch—so no one can see what my sister has become.

Elise doesn't care. She reclines in the grass, arrayed in a skimpy two-piece bikini she bought for our annual Myrtle Beach vacation. Thanks to her, we'll never see the beach again. Our consolation prize is a fenced-in backyard where the local kids poke holes in the wooden posts so they can watch my sister. Watch and wonder.

"Can you see her?" we hear them say.

Blinking in the sun, I don't belong out here where the others stare. But then I don't belong anywhere. In the yard next to my freakshow sister is good enough.

It's bright and hot and sticky, especially for early April. I squeeze a sunscreen bottle, and the white goo spurts into my hand. I offer Elise a smear, but she shoos me away. Her new skin's got its own protection, thick as a layer of mortar, so she doesn't have to worry about sunburns anymore.

"Do you think I'll grow horns?" she asks, her eyes closed and toes pointed toward the willow trees that loom over the fence like towering skeletons, frail arms extended to the heavens. "Or maybe wings? I've always wanted to fly."

"Don't talk like that," I say. "Anyhow, the doctors think your body might be done. How you are now is how you'll stay."

"How about a tail? A tail could be fun. I could swing it at my enemies when I get angry."

"Stop!" I plug my ears and hum an old folksong Elise taught me. I hum it out-of-tune, as loud as I can, but it's not enough. I can still hear the melody of her giggling.

Her eyes are open now, and she and that skin edge closer to me.

"Leave me alone," I say, though I know she won't listen.

"What would you want?" Her tongue traces the outline of her mouth, the soft pink flesh juxtaposed against the scales. "If your body could be anything, what would you want it to be?"

"I would be me," I say. "Like I am now."

She snuffs. "How boring."

Elise stretches out her body, long and taut, and sighs languidly like the heat and the grass and the caustic smell of me rubbing SPF on my shoulders are all too much. Her swimsuit—pastel blue and white polka dots with little ruffles around the edges—is supposed to make her look like a 1950s pinup girl, and maybe in another life, she would have been the reincarnation of Bettie Page or Betty Grable or another gorgeous Betty, but not now. Now the bikini clashes with her iridescent skin. I want to tell her so, want to tell her how ridiculous she looks lounging and stretching and parading around like an alley cat in heat, but my lips can't form the words, not while I'm staring at the way she shimmers in the sun.

Is she beautiful? She can't be. Mom and Dad whisper to each other, sometimes when Elise and I can hear, about how strange and ugly she's become.

But I think they're wrong. I think she's lovely.

She runs her tongue across her teeth, and the front two topple out of her mouth and into the grass.

"That's new," she says and digs through the dirt to retrieve the pieces of herself. "And not as good as wings."

The boys at the fence scream out her name and chortle and cheer for more. From their front-row seat, they enjoy seeing Elise come apart like a ragdoll drawn and quartered.

"Out of here!" I storm at them, my arms flailing madly and fists ready to beat their faces to pulp.

They see my expression and retreat, but not before one of them yells "Monster!" and the others laugh in refrain.

Nestled in the grass, the teeth cradled in her palm, Elise's bottom lip quivers, and for a moment, I'm sure she'll cry.

But she's doesn't. She just shrugs.

"That's evolution for you," she says and closes her eyes to nap.

#101: *She's crazy.* She cares about all the wrong things, and no matter what I tell her, she won't listen.

One by one, Elise picks out her teeth and collects them in a jar on her nightstand.

"Do you think if I leave them under my pillow, the tooth fairy will bring me something nice?"

"Stop that," I say and bury my face under a mound of pillows and sheets.

Her new teeth soon emerge, and new fingernails too. Thick and sharp. Everything on my sister has edges now.

Our parents no longer speak to her. They barely speak to me either. All their conversations are on the phone, whispers to doctors and family members, plans they make to take care of this "problem."

Elise ignores them. She creeps around the house on legs that seem longer and arms that can reach higher.

"How can you be okay with this?" I ask her.

"What would you have me do? Sob? Beg? Hide in shame?"

Her voice is foreign and guttural. I don't know if it's her new teeth, glinting beneath the bedroom light, that make her sound different, or if it's something else, something inside her morphing and contorting out of sight.

"This is who I'm supposed to be," Elise says, reclining in bed. "What's wrong with that?"

She slumbers, but I cannot. There are no more lullabies to guide me to sleep. When the quiet becomes too heavy to bear, I tear off my sheets and tiptoe to her mattress. She murmurs something soft and distant but doesn't awaken.

Beneath her faded linens, I pull Elise close. Still dozing, she rests a hand on my arm. Her fingernails like daggers trace my skin, and I'm sure her claws—and that's what they are, claws—will shred me, but the blood doesn't come. Elise knows how to use her new body. I wonder how, with no one to teach her, she already understands so much.

Dreaming secret dreams, she turns away from me, her shadow tucked to the wall like a fetus in utero, and I lie there alone and study the grooves in the ceiling.

Even though she's right next to me, I suddenly miss my sister.

#103: *She's always too far ahead.* No matter how fast I run, I can't keep up. She'll beat me in any race, because I didn't know we were racing in the first place.

ELISE DOESN'T WALK upright anymore. In biology class, I never paid much attention to the definitions of biped and quadruped, but I know the difference now. The difference is sitting at the dining room table and taking her meals like a person, or curling in the corner like a dog and lapping her nourishment from a pretty silver bowl.

"If she can't use a chair, what else can we do?" our mother asks incredulously. "Let her lie on the table and eat?"

I grip my silverware until my knuckles go white. "You don't trust her, do you?"

"That's not true," our father says, straightening his posture like a politician at a podium. "I trust *Elise*. But whatever's inside her, it's taken over. That thing is not your sister."

I wish Elise could tell our parents they're wrong, that she's still the same person she's always been.

But she says nothing at all. Her voice has left her. That's the hardest part. Not the scales or the claws or the teeth or all the glares and gossip she's brought upon our family, but her voice—the voice that used to sing me lullabies at night, the one that promised me that if there were monsters in the world, she would slay them for me.

But now I've met a monster, and Elise can't help me.

The next morning, the doctor makes a house call. He doesn't do it for Elise. His charity is for the other patients.

"Everyone's scared of her," I overhear him saying to our mother. "They don't want to use the exam room after her."

I assume he's here with a litany of pills and potions, a last-ditch effort to revive my sister, but he hands my parents just one orange bottle.

"Put the tablets in her food," he says.

Our mother reads the label. "How many?"

"All of them."

That night at supper, I push food around my plate, but my parents don't notice. They only care that Elise refuses to eat.

They fill her silver bowl with discolored meat and shove it at her face, but Elise bares her teeth, and they recoil as she darts to the bedroom.

I shove my meal across the table. "What did the doctor say today?"

"That your sister is dying," they say plainly. "There's nothing else they can do."

But that's a lie my parents want everyone to believe so they can justify what they're about to do.

I crawl under Elise's bed and find her hiding there. "You know what they're planning, don't you?"

She stares into me, and I know she understands. We sit together in silence and form a plan.

After our parents have their nightly argument, our mother sobbing and father screaming and cursing God, the government, and everyone else alive, they lock their bedroom door and go to sleep. They always lock their bedroom now. They don't trust my sister not to use those claws and teeth for what they're good for.

With a careful hand, I open our window, and Elise and I head for the trees.

In the darkness, I stumble, but she moves with the grace of a dancer. It's the first time I've seen her full form, gliding out in the open.

Everyone else is wrong. She *is* beautiful.

We reach the willows, and I kneel next to her.

"It's time," I say.

But she doesn't move. Her shape spirals around my legs as if to protect me.

"You don't need to worry," I say, my hand trembling against her cheek. "I'll be fine. You go. Find somewhere they won't follow you."

Elise hesitates, those dark eyes fixed on me, and I want to wrap my arms around her neck and never let her go. But I know I can't.

Slowly, I uncoil myself from her and step back.

"Goodbye," I say.

Her new legs don't fail her. She's faster than I expected, maybe faster than she expected too. She moves like the wind, in sync with the trees and the earth and the air. Elise is part of this place now. She belongs here—away from the suffocating cacophony of those who will never understand.

At the tree line, she turns back, and for an instant, I see a fragment of Elise in those eyes, a fragment of a seventeen-year-old still giggling and singing and just being a girl.

A flash in the moonlight, and she's gone, vanished into the forest like a delicate fog at sea.

I stand and shiver in the night and wish I too could belong somewhere.

I wish I could belong with her.

105: *I hate my sister.* I hate her because she was here, and I hate her because she's gone. I hate her I hate her I hate her. Only I don't hate her. And that makes missing her so much worse.

I'M BACK IN school, finishing what's left of the eighth grade, when a hunter claims he got Elise. You can almost hear the audible sigh of relief in town. Since she escaped, everybody's been waiting to hear she was caught, and though no one will say it to me, even my parents hope she's found dead, not alive. It would finish what they started.

The newscaster shows a picture of the dead animal on television. The thing is small and brown and probably a deer with mange. Whatever it is, it looks nothing like Elise, and I want to tell them so, want to tell them they're wrong. But if they believe me, they'll keep combing the woods for her.

She's safer if I lie.

I wear one of her dresses to a quickie memorial in her honor. It's just me and my parents and a local camera crew that plasters the spectacle on the six o' clock news.

"I'm glad it's over," my mother says as we shuffle to the car and drive home as a family. Or what's left of a family.

On the last day of school, the teachers take us to the public pool.

"Helps you start fresh for the summer," they say.

The rest of the kids jump in headfirst, splashing and screaming and celebrating the end of another year, but I don't follow them. On the gray cement at the shallow end, I tremble and don a white cover-up over my polka dot swimsuit.

"You coming in, baby?" a boy calls to me from the water. He looks like the same one from the cafeteria who asked me about Elise, but then all the boys look identical, so I can't tell for sure.

"Yeah, come on, *baby*," another says, and they all start mimicking that word in a childish singsong.

Baby. Like I'm their baby. Like I belong to them.

That's when I feel it, deep beneath my muscles. An itch. I don't have to hold my arm to the light to know what it means. From somewhere faraway, Elise tells me what to do.

I shrug off my cover-up, and the white cotton flutters to the cement along with a trimming of my skin. The first boy sees it. Then the second. And suddenly, none of them are catcalling me anymore. From the chlorine, they're staring, the same wide-eyed stares at the mall that first day with Elise.

But this time isn't like before. My cheeks don't flush, and I don't back away and wish I was someone else. Instead, I smile. I close my eyes and smile.

And I wait to hear their screams.

NEARNESS

Ralph Robert Moore

CORIANDER IS SITTING cross-legged in the grass, bare knees poking out from the hem of her dress, looking down at the long green blades.

Something big pulses out from behind her back, hanging in the air.

Furiously beating its wings, hovering blur of color right in front of Coriander's face. Her eyes widening as it carefully lets its diminishing effort lower itself towards the grass, its little ridged feet opening, clutching already for the blades before it reaches them.

It snares a blade in one foot, then stretches out its other foot with rapid, spasmodic dips for another blade. Once it has a blade clutched in each foot, it flaps less and less, its tiny head pointed downwards to gauge how much its weight is causing the blades to sink, the blur above its bent head gradually widening out, slowing, into peach-veined, red-gold wings. The blades it's gripped curl unhurriedly down to where their tips snag against, then thread into, the green beneath them.

The blue embossed edges of its wings flap a last time, striking adjacent grass, and then its weight is accepted, the natural springiness of the blades it's clutching lifting up, a fraction, the butterfly.

Square wings fold up neatly above it, exposing the glossy blackness beneath.

The little dark head twitches around, antennae lagging a moment behind each jerk. It points its gaze briefly at the huge, fuzzy bulk of Coriander, then tilts its head sideways to an angle a human could never manage. Stretches its neck out towards a nearby grass blade. Tiny turtle's jaws vibrate against the side of the sprig, and when it retracts its head to where it is no longer eclipsing the blade, there's a ripple-edged half-moon missing.

Holds its head absolutely motionless, not even swallowing, and then, unexpectedly, its small ebony head twitches in a sneeze.

Coriander tosses a piece of popcorn at the butterfly. The popcorn misses, but the butterfly lifts off anyway, flaps away.

Past where the butterfly fluttered down atop the grass, two pairs of bare feet slipped from their sandals face each other, leather thongs deflating amid the faraway cries of children.

Coriander rolls her chubby neck back, looking up.

Nana is sitting sideways on the green bench, touching her smile with a long fingernail, talking to the younger woman who had been going by on the walk, but then stopped when Nana said something about her hair. Who, after talking to Nana for a while with her long arms curved gracefully to her hips like a vase, walked over and perched sideways on Nana's bench, facing her.

"I was right, then," Nana says.

The younger woman laughs, raising her eyebrows. Big eyes look off, brimming with something, then she glances sideways at Nana and smiles. "Is it that obvious?"

"Nana, she wants to walk."

"Go ahead baby, but don't go anywhere I can't see you."

Coriander shuffles away from the bench, putting one foot in front of the other, patting the air before her with both hands with each step, the bag of popcorn swinging back and forth, lifting her arms to balance herself, banging the side of her head with the bag, blinking.

She falls sideways onto her behind. Cranes her head around to look back at the two women, who are laughing and touching each other's forearms, and decides not to cry.

She lowers her face, lips working, looking around her person to be sure, after her landing, that her dress is down and both shoes are still on. With a few cross-sounding grunts she manages to get the long plastic bag of popcorn straightened out across her lap. Colorful balloons with unheld strings are printed up and down its length. She pushes her short hand deep into the throat of the bag, head turned the other way, scrabbling with her virtually nailless fingers to get past the popcorn to the slices of bread at the bottom.

She drags one out, spilling popcorn over her legs, and, eyes squeezed shut, tosses it with great gusto into the air.

It lands beside her.

Three pigeons flap down immediately a few feet away from the bread slice. Coriander slaps her nose with both palms, excited. She begins swaying back and forth on her behind, watching the three birds pick their way sideways through the grass. None of the three pigeons face her directly at any point, though they do occasionally give her a nervous glimpse of their profiles.

Somehow, by moving further away, bending their heads up under their wings, they've managed to get a little closer. One looks big and normal, but the second one's wings don't fold fully behind it, like they're dislocated, and the third has two ratty-looking white feathers stuck to the bottom of one of its salmon feet.

"Your name is Pecker and your name is Sunday and your name is Groceries."

They percolate their heads at the sound of her voice. The tiny flat eyes of the one with the mismatched wings start to catch more light, like it's worried.

Soon all three are moving closer to Coriander, and Coriander is very excited, looking at the bread slice like it too may start moving.

But then Coriander sees that they're not pointing their profiles at her anymore, but at something behind her. She twists clumsily around on her waist, wet mouth hanging open.

A few yards behind her, the grass blade tips are whipping quietly back and forth on either side of a swath of grass getting pulled down, disappearing.

The three pigeons jump up into the air, two of them crashing into each other like helicopters.

Coriander fumbles some popcorn into the air to bring the pigeons back down, but by now they're halfway over the treetops.

A coppery hull from the popcorn is stuck under one of her translucent fingernails. She slowly points that finger out towards where the grass was moving.

She blinks.

The blades, though, are now still.

Is something, beneath them, hiding?

Her eyes stare down, and then, happily, much closer than she thought it could be, the grass stirs right in front of her knees.

She leans forward, peering into the criss-cross of blades, and spots something large, flat sliding towards her.

Leans forward too far, losing her balance, small hands not strong enough to brace her fall, face dipping into the blades, chin nudging against something rough.

She pulls her face up out of the grass, lips open in a laugh.

Sits upright again, grabbing her wispy blonde hair, giving it a two-sided tug, still laughing.

What was hidden in the blades rears itself up until it's only partially concealed by the grass. It's big and flat and dark.

"Pretty bird. Where are your feathers and your wings and your head?"

The large, squarish bird slides a little closer. A long, boneless leg without a foot curves out towards Coriander.

She aims a handful of popcorn at the leg, the three pieces bouncing away from each other as they land.

Another leg emerges from underneath the other side of the bird's front, curling into a moist spiral on the grass. A third leg oozes out a little bit halfway down the left side of the bird, but then does nothing else.

"Wanna bread?" Coriander spins a slice at the bird. It lands on its flat, rough back. A fourth leg, with a gum wrapper stuck to one of its stiff segments, snicks itself up from underneath and lays across the bread slice.

"Coriander?"

"She wants to stay!"

But Coriander dutifully gets up on her feet. She wobbles a bit at that height, one shoe accidentally stepping on the bird's back.

The front of the bird makes little wet clicking noises. A long yellow-red beak, three colorless bristles sprouted on it, stickily pushes out. Down the length of the bird on either side a buzzing starts, and wide, dark wings flick out, then draw in to where they're close to the body.

"Coriander!"

Coriander stops at the walk and carefully turns around to wave goodbye to the large bird still lying concealed in the grass.

"Cory, look at me baby, this is Sarah, she's going to come over to our house tonight for dinner, isn't that nice? Did you fall?" Nana wipes at Coriander's chin with her thumb. Coriander stands still, concentrating on keeping her balance.

Nana looks at the pad of her thumb, then at Coriander's chin. She pulls a lipstick-stained tissue out of the waistband of her shorts, spits on it, and starts rubbing it, despite Coriander's facial protestations, against her chin.

Coriander looks at the other woman while her chin is being wiped. Sarah smiles down at her, her short black hair making her teeth look whiter and bigger.

"I guess your mom takes pretty good care of you."

"She's not my mom."

Nana tosses the wad of tissue onto the grass.

CORIANDER GOES DOWN the stairs backwards, on her knees. When she reaches the bottom, she turns around and toddles through the hall.

She stops at the wide, square doorway between the hall and the living room.

Nana and that Sarah are on the sofa. The coffee table in front of them holds two melting drinks on magazines.

Nana is in her bikini. Sarah is in a long dress, but the hem is above her knees.

Nana has Sarah's bare feet up on her shoulders, digging her fingers into the curling soles.

Sarah is lying on her back on cushions propped against the side of the sofa, hands twitching like she wants to stop what Nana is doing.

"It doesn't tickle so much when you press in so hard."

"People don't realize how sensitive feet can be."

"That feels really good. Right there."

"Right here? Right here below your toes?"

"Yeah."

Nana works in silence for a moment, biceps flexing. "People should have their feet massaged more often."

"Oh. I like that, between the toes, like that." Sarah shifts her legs, resting her feet more comfortably on Nana's shoulders. "This is so relaxing." She brings her hands up to her ears, letting her eyes droop. Takes a deep breath. "No one ever took such care with me before. I don't deserve it." Sarah's mouth starts trembling. She sniffs moistly, starts crying, her face red.

"Baby, what are you doing here?"

"She doesn't have anything left to do."

Nana swings Sarah's twisting feet away from her neck, onto the coffee table.

"Go outside and play, sweetheart."

"What's Nana doing?"

"Aunt Sarah has a lot of pain, and Nana's trying to help her."

"Hi, Coriander."

CORIANDER SITS ON the flagstone terrace behind the house with her legs out in front of her, shoes pointing up, hands braced behind her to stay in a sitting position. A black ant pokes around on the slab her right fingers are spread across, but she doesn't see it.

She rolls her head back, snarling one side of her lips down and making a clucking sound with her tongue, looking up at the sky. She stares directly at the sun, squinting almost immediately, sliding her stare around the rim, eyes watering, head hurting.

Fluttering rush in front of her. She rolls her head forward, looking for a moment like a woman.

Two pigeons hobbling around on the flagstones, pecking at wood chips.

Coriander shows them her pebble encrusted palms.

"No food. Sorry."

They fan back a few sidesteps at the sound of her voice.

"Your name is Nana, and your name is Corider."

Out of the ragged line of trees at the rear of the property a large bird flaps with ungainly determination towards the terrace. It has trouble lowering itself, sticking things out to try to right itself as it touches down. Once it's on the patio, it tucks its wings in close to its body immediately, making it look like an immense, flat beetle. It starts sliding forward towards Coriander.

The two pigeons cringe backwards up into the air, turning their wings around and flying away, feathers puffed out.

"You found out where I live!"

The bird advances low on the ground until it's within petting distance. Coriander strokes its rough, brittle back, crooning every third or fourth note of a lullaby.

She tilts her head to one side, feeling the coarseness of the bird's back against her fingers.

"I don't have any food for you."

The bird crawls forward until it's at the taut hem of the skirt stretched across her chubby legs. Coriander reaches forward to pet further down its back, smiling with her mouth open.

It tilts the front of its body up, climbing onto the hammock formed by her skirt.

This close, half in her lap, she can see its flat, wide back isn't just one dark color. There are speckles of emerald and sapphire along one side, and a jigsaw splotch of pale topaz on the other side, at the rear. She raises a vertical finger, and meticulously outlines the splotch, feeling the slight welt of its border.

"Coriander!"

"She's out here."

"Ugh, what's that?"

"It's her bird."

Nana takes a puff on her cigarette, walks over, then backs up a step in her bare feet.

"That doesn't look like a bird, baby. It looks like a huge horseshoe crab or something." She folds her arms, lifting one pink heel off the terrace. "Don't let it crawl on you like that."

Sarah reaches down and hauls Coriander by her armpits out from under the bird. The front of the bird lowers very slowly onto the flagstones.

Nana, looking at the plucked loops of thread on the front of Coriander's dress. She turns to Sarah. "Baby, you shouldn't handle something like that. It might have some kind of skin disease."

"Cancer."

Nana reaches out and down, slaps Coriander across the face.

Coriander's face snaps back to where it was before, now half white and half red. She lowers her eyes. After a moment, she bursts into tears.

"Jackie."

"Fuck, I don't know why I did that. Honey, get up off the ground. Nana's sorry." She undoes the bun in her hair, shaking her head to let the long hair fall out of its descending swirl.

"We're going to the store, want to come? We have to buy lemons. You can ride up front with Sarah and me."

CORIANDER SITS ON a bar stool at the counter dividing the kitchen from the breakfast nook, swinging her head to follow the two women bustling back and forth.

Nana lowers a Flintstones glass filled with ice and Coca-Cola onto the counter in front of Coriander.

When the toast pops up, Sarah's shoulders jump.

"Easy, kid."

Sarah bows her head, cheeks blushing. "I hope this is a good idea."

Nana puts a painted fingernail on the rim of Coriander's drink, lowers the glass curve away from her sucking lips. "How does Aunt Sarah look, baby?"

Coriander sighs, rubbing her elbow on the granite. She gives a quick glance at Sarah, who's standing with her arms out from her sides, smiling kindly. She's wearing a short, sleeveless dress with a buttoned-up collar.

"Very pretty, I guess."

Nana thrusts her shoulders back, breathing in to deepen the cleavage of her low cut top. "How about Nana? Am I beautiful?"

"She thinks you're very beautiful, Nana."

Sarah puts a white plate down in front of Coriander, removing from the plate two of the three toast slices. Spreads mayonnaise on the remaining one. With her index finger she brushes the wispy blonde hair out of Coriander's bored-looking eyes. Coriander shakes her face until the hair falls back, then turns her head away, studying the calendar on the wall.

"Coriander, Nana tells me you've never had one of these before." Her voice is soft. "I hope you like it. When you're a big girl and a boy takes you to a restaurant for lunch, this might be what you'll eat. So this way you can try one now to see if you like it."

Coriander keeps watching the calendar. Out of the corners of her eyes she can see Sarah carefully unfold a lettuce leaf out across the toast slice, the edges of it making little curly lines in the mayonnaise.

When Sarah lifts her fingers away, the leaf relaxes, rising up slightly.

"You don't talk a whole lot, do you Coriander?"

Coriander deliberates a moment, still looking off, then shakes her head.

"I didn't talk much either when I was a little girl." She lays two rolled slices of turkey on top of the lettuce, which lowers it again. The rounded blade of her knife swirls more mayonnaise over the pale meat. "A lot of times, I just liked watching people, learning about them. You too?"

Coriander stays quiet for a moment, then clears her throat. "Sometimes." She makes her face look more stubborn.

Sarah goes to stroke Coriander's hair, but hesitates. Instead, she picks up the bacon. "Sometimes I think you've got five feet of problems on a four foot shelf, sweetheart." She arranges the bacon on top of the mayonnaise turkey in neat, crinkly rows. She picks up the last piece of bacon and stands it upright on the others, making it bend in half and address Coriander. "Hi, Coriander."

Coriander slips her head down onto her little bicep, looking exasperated, but her eyes are a little less red. "Bacon can't talk."

Sarah holds the second piece of toast, covering one side of it with mayonnaise, then places it slathered side down on top of the sandwich, glancing quietly to see if she still has Coriander's attention. "I'll bet you think this sandwich is through now, don't you?"

Coriander gets a sophisticated look on her face. "Maybe you're gonna cut it in half."

Sarah smiles, then picks up the knife. She tilts it into the mayonnaise jar again. Coriander watches despite herself.

Sarah spreads a layer of mayonnaise across the top of the sandwich.

Coriander sits bolt upright. "That's silly!"

"No it isn't."

Coriander rears back on the stool, sternly watching as Sarah drapes a few glossy slices of ham across the mayonnaise-topped sandwich. Her eyes switch warily from Sarah's face back to the sandwich, where three rounds of sliced tomatoes have been added. She shifts uneasily atop her stool.

"You made a big mess and you have to clean it up."

Sarah says nothing. She works in profile, putting more mayonnaise on top of the tomato slices. Coriander juts her lower lip out, then flexes it up over her upper lip, kissing it against the cleft below her nose, eyes narrowing uncertainly.

Sarah places the third toast slice on top. She turns full-faced towards Coriander, winking.

"Now that's a sandwich, isn't it?

Coriander grabs both hands around her Flintstones glass and slants it to her mouth, breathing through her nose, looking sideways at Sarah, then at the sandwich. An ice cube bangs against her teeth, making her blink.

Sarah pushes four toothpicks down through the stack. Each toothpick has a different colored plastic strip curlicued at its blunt end. Red, blue, yellow, green.

To cut the high sandwich she uses a knife with a very, very long serrated blade. Instead of cutting it in half she cuts it in four, corner to corner, each quarter held together by one of the toothpicks.

In turn she picks up each fat, multi-layered triangle, holding it firmly in her fingers while she pokes the sharp end of the toothpick out through the bottom slice of toast, then places each of the four parcels on their sides on the plate.

With a moment's hesitation, raising her head, sad-eyed, reaches out and strokes the little girl's hair. Coriander lifts her eyebrows, smiles shyly.

Nana stands at the other end of the counter, resting her elbow in her left hand, smoking a cigarette. "There you go, baby. Now you have a club sandwich. One more step towards becoming a woman. Thanks, Sarah."

"Can I share it with my bird?"

"No. I told you I don't want you playing with that thing. It smells, and it's making you smell from handling it so much."

"I don't smell."

"You sure do. I told you that two weeks ago, and you keep deliberately disobeying me each and every day."

"Would you like some milk to go with your sandwich, Coriander?"

Sarah's head twitches. Nana hurriedly stubs out her cigarette.

The doorbell ding-dongs again.

BY THE TIME CORIANDER has carefully toddled down the dark hall, trailing one pudgy hand along the white wall to keep her balance on the carpet, the men's voices are booming in the foyer.

"Who's this?"

Nana turns her head away from the two big men in their suits, lowering her eyes at Coriander, whose hand whirls in the air as it leaves the wall. Nana's hair is stretched up away from her face. She looks very pretty and small. Sarah is standing behind Nana, bringing her hand up to her close-cropped hair to pat it, smiling nervously.

"Baby, go back and finish your sandwich."

One of the big men strides over, standing in front of Coriander, blocking her. He squats down to Coriander's eye level. His big, pale blue stare rolls around, inspecting Coriander up close. He smells sweet and harsh and salty. Coriander turns her face away, making a fat fist.

"You didn't tell me you had a kid. Jeez, look how small her face is." He puts his hairy hand up in front of her. Coriander makes a lemon-eating expression, looking sideways at the short white lines across his wrist. "Her face isn't any bigger than my palm!"

The other man comes over from behind the first one, half-squatting at his back. "She's a little young for you, Jilly."

"It's not my kid. She's my granddaughter. It's a long story."

"We don't have time for long stories, Jackie. The ice is melting."

"Baby, Mrs. Roediger will be coming along any minute." Nana clicks her little purse open and peers inside. "Finish your sandwich and watch TV until she gets here, OK?"

"We could wait a minute."

"Sarah's an old Nervous Nellie because this is her first date in a long time."

Sarah, trying not to look irritated, glances at Coriander and shrugs.

Coriander raises her shoulders up, lowers them back down.

CORIANDER LIES IN bed on her back. The room is dark, but her eyes are still open. Her legs, under the covers, only go a third of the way down the length of the mattress.

Rapid scratching at the window.

She purses her lips, struggling to throw the covers off her chest. Her ten toes switch back and forth until the tiny balls swing down against the rug beside her bed. She falls over once on her way to the window, her shoulder speeding a duck up and down on its wheels across the wooden floor.

Climbing on her hands and knees up the cardboard packing boxes containing all that's left of her mother, to the window. Once she gets the latch unhooked, her bird's bulk pushes the French window open wide enough for it to ooze through, feathers and tubular sloughs of scaly skin floating in the air.

The bird crawls onto Coriander, pushing her down onto her back on the top cardboard box.

And is just as quickly knocked off her pajamas. She watches, amazed, as a book slides down the wall on its spine, pages vibrating like a pair of horse's lips. Raises her head to look for her bird. Lying at a tilt in a shadowy corner far away.

Mrs. Roediger stands in the doorway, light behind her. She picks up another heavy book and sends it shuffling through the air at the bird.

"You're hurting him!"

"Are you out of your mind?" Mrs. Roediger bangs her foot down on the floor at the bird, terrified look on her face. "How did it get in here? Did it bite you?"

Coriander swings a bare foot over the edge of the box she's on, crying. "You're jealous!"

With a spread of wings far wider than would ever be expected from a creature its size, the bird scrabbles up the boxes to the open window and wriggles through backwards, the long, luxurious wings twitching through after it like antennae.

A SOLITARY PIGEON pecks around the border of the flagstone patio. After every few dips of its head, it nonchalantly points its profile at the bag of bread in Coriander's lap.

"Shoo away."

The untended grass at the edge of the patio starts waving in one spot.

Coriander hoists her bag high for her bird to see.

The pigeon, startled by Coriander's sudden movement, fans its wings.

Darkness moves to the edge of the patio, rising out of the green grass, uncoiling five legs across the nearest slab.

The pigeon swivels its head around on its humped shoulders until it has its profile to the uncoiled legs. Its feathers puff, making it look bigger, then it keels over sideways on the slab, one leg sticking up.

Coriander's bird starts to glide happily across the terrace.

The bird stops. Starts to vibrate, a whistling whimper coming out of it.

"Get the hell out of here!"

Coriander's small mouth drops open. She turns around in her sitting position to look over her shoulder. Nana is standing behind her with a carton of milk in her hand.

The bird pulls back a little from the slab it was crossing, slides forward on it again, retracts again.

"Get the hell out of here." Nana hoists the carton higher for the bird to see.

It vibrates, slamming the underside of its front down repeatedly on the flagstone in frustration.

The carton hits the side of her bird, spraying white across its back and the grass.

It lifts straight up off the terrace, into the air, hovering.

Coriander waves desperately at it, beckoning it to her, curling her little fingers in towards her shaking chest.

It moves across the air to the nearest tree.

As it disappears into the high foliage, dozens of birds flap out and away.

Coriander tries not to cry, because if she cries her tears will blind her, and she won't be able to see where her bird goes.

It flaps to the next tree, darkness wriggling into the green, but the birds in that treetop also wing away in all directions.

A tear slides down.

It tries tree after tree, each top emptying as soon as it arrives, on and on, until the trees receding in the twilight are as small as puffballs, and the birds turning their backs, specks.

"If it comes back I'm going to kill it."

"She hates you!"

"You don't understand." Nana absently rubs her thumb over the pads of her fingers, feeling the milk on them, glances down at the front of her silk blouse, which is soaked with milk.

"Look at your hands."

Coriander balls them into fists and sticks them up her dress, out of view.

"Don't do that." Nana bends over, pulls Coriander's hands out, twists them around. "Look at your palms."

Coriander's big eyes stay on Nana's face. She scrunches up one side of her lips. "Nana, Nana, looks like a banana."

Nana crouches down on her haunches and slaps Coriander on the knee. "Smell them, baby."

Coriander brings her yellowy-orange palms up to her face. Sniffs them.

She rolls her head back haughtily, mouth open, switching her chin left and right, upper teeth motionless.

Her nose wrinkles.

She wipes the side of a nostril with a yellowy-orange index finger, then leans over, throws up sugar and spice and little wriggling globs of phlegm.

CORIANDER CRAWLS LIKE a little baby through the interior dimness past the chair legs and table legs to the archway.

Past it, in the well-lit kitchen, Nana and Sarah are talking to each other.

Coriander raises her eyebrows and holds her breath, settling on her stomach, face propped in her pudgy hands. Nana and Sarah's high heels look huge and their heads look tiny from this angle.

"You have to go."

Sarah puts the long knife down on the counter beside the mounds of diced vegetables. "I do, don't I? It's starting all over again. That's what I keep thinking, it's starting all over again."

Nana tilts her head to one side, trying to smile. She pulls a few tissues out of the wall dispenser and holds them out to Sarah.

Sarah looks at the fluffed-out dispenser. "Did you have a conversation like this with June? Maybe even right here where we're standing now?" Sarah stops crying long enough to laugh. "You know, I think my whole life has been shaped by conversations I've had in kitchens."

"June didn't have your strength. She got so tired of getting her insides burned, but she wouldn't cry. You have to. What else can you do?"

Sarah makes a goofy face, eyes still red. "Tell me and we'll both know." She lowers her eyes, embarrassed.

Nana glides over to her, putting her long nails on the top button of Sarah's blouse.

"You don't have to."

Nana trails a nail down the bridge of Sarah's freckled nose. "I want to, hon."

She undoes the buttons one by one down to the belt of Sarah's skirt, then pulls the front tails out so the two sides of the blouse fall open.

Sarah looks away, wobbly smile on her face, holding her arms at her sides.

Nana raises a hand to the upper swell of her left breast. "Right here?"

Sarah peeks down with the look of someone watching a needle go in. "That's it. It's so frightening when you first feel it with your fingers."

"It could be innocent."

Sarah dips her head, cleft between her black eyebrows, looking at Nana's face. "I don't trust my own body anymore."

Coriander's bored, propped-up face glances at a shadow, above the sink, against the window. She gulps, craning her head forward to look more closely, chin lifting out of her palms.

Three black eyes protrude against the glass, swaying slightly in the evening breeze.

Bites her lip with her two longest teeth, looking up past the eyes tapping against the pane to the stout latch clasping the upper and lower window frames together.

Sarah buttons the front of her blouse, watching her fingers push hard curves through soft slits. "I should probably go."

"Of course you should. I'm the one who told you to."

Sarah does the top button, drawing her collar together. "I mean go from here. From you."

"Stay. Please stay." Nana reaches her hand out, but doesn't touch Sarah's forearm.

"Here she is."

"Hi, baby, how long have you been standing there?"

Coriander looks down at her bare feet, then up at the two tense women again. "She just stood here now."

"Hi, Coriander. Did you enjoy your nap?"

Coriander nods solemnly. She raises and lowers her shoulders at Sarah. "She thinks she did."

Coriander waves her arms as Nana sails her backwards through the air to sit on the counter, legs dangling, beside the colorful mounds of diced vegetables. Puts a hand down on the counter to steady herself, turns around to look at the dark window above the sink. There are curly white lines scratched into the glass from the outside.

"I have to get going, Jackie."

"Cory, we don't want Aunt Sarah to go, do we?"

Coriander scoots her rear end closer to the edge of the counter. Now she can see, past her twitching knees, the far away tiles of the floor below. She puts a hand on the top of the dishwasher door just below the countertop. It starts yawning open, steam rising out.

"Careful, Coriander." Sarah puts her hands on Coriander's waist and lifts her up to her.

"My, you're heavy."

Coriander puts her arms around Sarah's neck. "Don't go, Aunt Sarah. My bird will eat you."

Sarah slides her forearm under Coriander's rear end so she can pull her face back enough to look into the little girl's eyes. "That thing went away, Coriander. It won't be coming back." She strokes the little girl's hair. Looks across to Nana.

"SARAH CAN'T COME over, sweetheart." Nana rubs the back of her own neck. Her lips look flatter than they usually do. "I'm going to see her later, and I'll tell her you asked about her."

"Could I come too?"

"It's not a good idea. It'll just give you nightmares."

Coriander leans forward over her legs, begins picking at the carpet pile.

Nana looks away from the frantic little fingers digging into the nylon loops.

"Do you still have bad dreams about that thing that used to come over here?"

Still in her bent over position, Coriander shakes her head.

"That's good. Now you know it was bad, right?"

Coriander keeps pulling at the pile. "She didn't when she first met it, cause it was so close all the time she kinda got used to it, but then when she saw it go away, and like how all the other birds that were her friends were afraid of it, plus how it made her hands and everything look…"

"I think you were afraid of it all the time, baby. I could see it in your eyes, even when you were petting it."

Coriander's bent head nods. "She was scared of it but she didn't want to be scared of it, cause then it would know, but it really scared her every time when she'd have to put her fingers on it for the first time when it would come back. Sometimes when it wasn't there she'd forget how scary it felt to touch it. But then it kept coming back, and then she'd want it to be near because she wasn't touching it for the first time, she was touching it for the second or third time, and that was a little less scary."

She reaches for the two big knobs, head still down, and turns both at the same time, not wanting to talk anymore.

A lopsided, silvery circle warbles over the intersections.

Nana watches, red-eyed, as the knobs twist circle after circle over the first one, rotating around and around and around amateurishly, darkening and expanding across the neat, modest rectangles.

Nana picks up the Etch-a-Sketch from Coriander, whose fingers still twirl a moment in mid-air, and turns it upside down, giving it a few firm shakes. "Nana has to get ready. Just draw straight lines, baby, OK? This thing isn't designed for circles."

She stands up, knees cracking, and puts the toy back down in front of the child. "Nana's going to tighten her drink a little, and by then your babysitter should be here."

"Will my babysitter make me a sandwich?"

Nana walks away, high heels dangling from one hand. "I'll ask him to, baby. We'll see."

Coriander makes a face, then returns to her Etch-a-Sketch. The intersections are gone, but most of her circle is still darkening the upper left corner.

NANA WARILY SPIES on the well-lit kitchen, one liver-spotted hand on either side of the doorway, looking from there at the microwave, the island bar, the refrigerator, the cabinets and ceiling, the floor, the counters, the window over the sink. The green readout on the black-faced microwave pulses from 6:49 to 7:00.

She enters cautiously, advancing step by step into the alert illumination, head cocked, trying to figure out the source of the little tone noises in the air.

At the far end of the living room, behind the curved back of an easy chair, Coriander is sitting on a shadowy patch of the carpet. She raises her head with a defensive look of explanation ready on her face.

"Baby, what are you doing?"

Coriander's thin fingers, so small it's hard to believe they each contain three joints, type another dozen times against the raised squares on the telephone's base.

"I'm calling my mom. She wants to talk to me." She makes a stern Shhh! face and clumsily lifts the receiver up under her scraggly blonde hair, against her reddened ear, eyes blank.

Nana takes the receiver away from her and hangs up on nothing.

"You can't call your mother. I don't want to keep going over this, baby."

Coriander raises her grasping fingers up towards the phone, which is lifted away to its rightful place, a covered stretcher rolled down a corridor to a restricted area.

"Maybe I'll call Sarah."

"You can't call Sarah either. She's with your mom now. You have to go to bed, baby." Nana's fingers push a gray lock off her forehead. It immediately flops back down. "You're so tired. Thank God you don't know how tired you really are."

THE COVERS ARE up to Coriander's chin.

The ionization in the room changes. The bare wire hangers in the closet tinkle against each other. A small pair of pink pants draped on the bureau relaxes, slides over the bureau's edge onto the floor. The pattern of wrinkles it pools into shifts shadows, subtle as an oyster in a shell after a squirt of lemon.

Coriander points a finger out from under the covers. "Stop it!"

A sepia-toned sketch of mushrooms and lieder-hosen children revolves upwards on its surprised nail, now hanging upside down on the wall.

The window scratches at the room.

"I don't let you in!"

The scratching responds, louder and more intelligent-sounding, until the bottom half of the window jerks up an inch. The latch at the sill pops off in an arc, bouncing down her mother's boxes. Multi-jointed claws, ten of them, curl through the open sill onto the bottom of the window, pressing against the frame so forcefully each claw flattens out.

"Not fair."

The bottom half of the window slams up, lightning bolts across its panes as the shards fall forward.

Cold air rushes in against the wallpaper.

Her bird pokes its wide front over the sill, letting its legs explore ahead of it, all the way down the staircase of boxes to the floor. Talons grasping the room's carpet, it reels its body bump by bump down the boxes.

Coriander raises her little head, distressed, pulling her feet up under the blanket, keeping both worried eyes on the footboard of the bed.

The top of the bedspread twitches against the bottom of her chin as her bird latches onto the hem resting on the floor.

The bedspread twitches some more, meaning it must be climbing up.

"You scare me."

Leg segments slanting every which way, her bird hoists itself bat-like over the edge of her bed.

She draws her stubby legs up even higher, knees against her shoulders.

It plucks its way up the length of the spread with the elaborate leg movements of a large insect.

Hesitates below where her body starts under the covers, pointing its flat front at her. Because its legs are extended further than she's ever seen it do before, it's able to raise its abdomen six feet above the bedspread.

Tilts its front end down at her, mewing.

Coriander pulls the covers up to the bottoms of her nostrils. "You were a bad bird because you scared all the other birds away, plus you made my palms all different colors."

It mews, creaking on the scaffolding of its many legs.

"You scare me."

The abdomen, suspended six feet in the air, twists moistly this way and that.

Coriander lets one little hand appear above the top edge of the bedspread. "I know you don't have any friends. 'Cept me." She looks at the piled boxes, then at the front of her bird. "I do feel sorry for you 'cause all the time you go into a tree the other birds fly out."

Her bird advances, lowering itself. A talon scratches Coriander's cheek, drawing blood.

"Hey, not so rough." Avoids looking at it, eyes terrified.

As it does every evening, the bird yanks down her blanket, hoists itself up the length of her ladders and snakes pajamas, crawling wide and flat towards her face. Coriander pushes its shoulders up with a great deal of effort, raising its body though not disengaging its talons, so that she can see the mass of brain tumor corals underneath, and all the little whipping legs. As the bird settles on her face, she puts her short arms around its body in a frightened embrace, a little girl forced to once again get used to it.

It scrabbles behind Coriander's head on the pillow, nudging her neck forward to settle behind.

Coriander reaches out a hand, trying to be like Sarah, petting the fur sprouting around a segment.

"But you're always my friend, whether I want you to be or not."

Her bird settles comfortably on her nape, clicking irregularly to itself, legs retracting, tilting Coriander's head even further forward, roosting atop the blonde down of her nape, the delicate little hairs a mother loves, which are already discoloring.

This Lonely Hecatomb

Christopher Ropes

AMANDA WAS TIRED. Tired of the funeral and tired of her dad being dead. Tired of his friends and her own friends trying to comfort her and tell her what a great man he'd been. Yeah, he had been great, but none of them knew why. His greatness came in the quiet moments at home, where he'd teach her that the meaning of being a strong black woman in the world was choosing her own path and pursuing it. Her former friend, dear, militant Cynthia, notably absent from the funeral despite knowing Amanda and her dad since the women had been little girls, didn't see it that way. "You're too fucking smart to study white man's Western history, Mandy," she'd said. "You need to focus on studying our history, our future, the realities we face in this screwed-up country." The argument had lasted two hours and resulted in Amanda studying European history, just as she'd planned, Cynthia going on to specialize in African-American studies with a minor in Poli-Sci, and the two not speaking again.

Amanda's dad told her to follow her own genius. She cared about history, not from the dominant white male perspective, but similar to how Howard Zinn, or maybe even Michel Foucault, had studied it. The history of the little people who'd made things happen. The history of the people ground down by the system, but making it go on with their blood and bones and hard work and sometimes their carcasses. He said, "You'll study everything from Ancient Egypt and Greece and Rome, to the world wars, and you'll see, you'll connect the dots, between our slavery here, and the Holocaust, between the Roman gladiators and the southern plantation 'bucks.' You'll see, hon, that the world is a big ole mess of unconnected dots just waiting for someone with your brain to put it all together. And you'll change the world in your own way, not the way some gal tells you you've got to. That's not freedom, darling. That's not."

But this damned wake and funeral and the post-funeral gathering, it was all too much. She'd had her hand shaken, her entire body smothered in usually unwanted embraces, all meant to comfort her, just like the empty words about how her dad had been the best man the speaker ever knew. She remembered one night when she'd been crying in bed, she must've been seven or eight, and he came upstairs with her teddy bear she'd lost outside earlier. He'd spent an hour and a half searching the dark yard and woods surrounding the house with a barely functional flashlight, just to bring her that teddy bear. That counted for more with her than any number of donations to civil rights-minded politicians, or speeches given to the plumbers' union, or benches at parks and plaques at zoos that bore his name because some rich liberal had decided to donate in the wake of his accident.

Across the living room, near the hors-d'oeuvres table, she saw her good friend Jackie and her ex-boyfriend Dante. Dante had been the rarest of combinations in high school: a sensitive and even artistic jock. They probably would still have been together if Dante hadn't moved from New Jersey on a football scholarship to the University of Michigan. Her dad had always loved Dante. She started to tear up a little and then forced them back. Dad wouldn't have wanted her bawling a flooded river at the reception.

Jackie broke away from Dante with a small smile and nudged her way through the crowd to Amanda's side. "Hey, sweetie, how're you holding up?" she asked, touching Amanda lightly on the forearm. Her hair smelled like wildflowers and her black, modest dress with a delicate, silvery floral design on the left breast was the most tasteful article of clothing in the room. Jackie was always the stylish one. Amanda looked down at her own dress, a slightly shabby dark gray thing she'd found among her mom's old belongings. She sighed. Her mom...also gone, going on a decade now.

"I'm getting by, Jackie. But...it's not easy. I'm about ready to call up Cynthia, call her the 'c' word for not showing up today, kick all these people out of my house, and turn Mobb Deep up to 10 on dad's stereo. And throw out that nasty fruit salad." They both laughed at that, looked over to the table where Dante was quietly warning someone away from that very food item.

"That's seriously fucked up, Cynthia not showing up. Didn't your dad help her pay her first semester's tuition when there was that screw up with financial aid?"

Amanda nodded silently. He'd done that and set her up with a single occupancy dorm and a sky high food allowance, too. He'd felt bad for her that her parents were both dead. And now that Amanda was in the same boat, she wasn't going to let down her tough bitch armor for a moment to comfort her onetime best friend.

"Screw her, Mandy. You're not losing anything by her not being here or not being your friend anymore. You're not losing anything but dead weight."

Mandy shook her head, like it was agony to move. "No, Jacks. I am losing something. I'm losing the ability to trust the goodness in my good memories." She glanced over in Dante's direction, and back at Jackie. Jackie took the hint, "Yeah, girl, go see him. He still cares a lot."

The two friends hugged tight and then parted, Amanda finding the image of an escape pod jettisoning from a spacecraft floating into her head. Eyes back on Dante, and not in La La Land, she squeezed between people and away from their attempts to "console" her, to get to her ex. "Damn," he said, looking her up and down. "Just...damn."

Amanda laughed. "Bullshit, Dante. This dress is probably twenty-five years old now, and the seams are starting to fray. Either you don't have functioning eyes, or you're looking at Jackie." But he looked striking, she noticed. Dark blue suit with a dark red tie, perfectly tailored to his athletic frame, a Rolex on his wrist, shoes shining like twinkling starlight and, of course, salon styled hair and a recent manicure. "You're looking all right, though, I can tell you that."

Now it was Dante's turn to laugh. He'd always kept himself immaculate. "Society expects a woman to look perfect, so I'm going to put the same demands on myself, until that ends," he used to say. Some people thought it was a line, like they thought a lot of stuff that popped out of his mouth was simply designed to sound good, but Amanda knew it wasn't. Dante was the most genuine person she'd ever known other than her dad. "I couldn't come to your old man's funeral looking like a bum."

"You've never looked like a bum!"

"Pffffft. Anyway, how's grad school treating you? When's your master's thesis due?"

Amanda paused, reluctant to talk about the impending thesis that she hadn't found the time to devote to at all. It was supposed to be about the use of sacrifice in antiquity, particularly in Greco-Roman culture, as a method of propitiating the gods, but also controlling the populace. Citizens of the empire were less likely to act in ways displeasing to the gods, that is, the heads of state, if they knew that the gods themselves had been invoked to secure the success of some undertaking. The larger and more ceremonial the sacrifice, the more control over the citizenry it afforded.

"It's not really coming along at all. It's just...this..." she waved her hand around the room, taking it all in. Dante nodded. "I gotcha. Just doesn't seem fair..." he said, and then trailed off into respectful silence. They stood like that, side-by-side, not uttering a word, until ten minutes later, when Amanda had to go use the bathroom.

"I'll be back, Dante. I promise." He nodded and there was so much sorrow in it, she wanted to hold him. She couldn't permit herself that, and left for upstairs. On the way, she nodded at Jackie, who gave her a strange look that seemed to fall somewhere between "I'll miss you" and "Bon voyage!" *They think they're never going to see me again*, she thought, wondering why, and then wondering why she felt the same internal sense of departure. Permanent departure. Maybe I should go somewhere. *Maybe that's what I need. To be...away. Elsewhere.*

She had to endure three more hugs and an "I'm so sorry, he was a wonderful, wonderful man" as she edged her way up the stairs before getting to the bathroom, which was just emptying out. Squeezing through the half-open, half-closed door was an elderly, Mediterranean-looking man she didn't recognize. He smiled at her, and gave her an "I know a secret you don't" look, before traipsing, quite merrily, down the stairs. She went in and stood completely still, her eyes on the floor, utterly unsure of what to do, feeling paralyzed.

On the white tile floor, she saw a pattern of sticks and roots arranged into the number "99." All the branches could have been brought in from the woods behind the house. Maybe that man going down the stairs had done it? Surely, someone else seeing that would have said something to her, about an odd arrangement of tree limbs on the bathroom floor. Right? It only made sense that someone would bring that up.

Seeing her face in the mirror, Amanda was shocked by how unsurprised she looked. *Was I expecting something like this? Is this what it's all been leading to?* She looked out the bathroom window, to the backyard and the woods beyond. She saw the man from the bathroom walking towards the woods. He stopped, turned, and thumbed his aquiline nose at her, and went back to strolling towards the forest. She knew it then, she was going to follow him, and those woods from her childhood were summoning her.

MEMORIES DRIFTED UP on the shores of her mind and she wound her way deeper into the woods, the house and its guests vanishing behind an explosive outrage of New Jersey autumn leaves. The crisp air tingled in her nostrils and smelled somehow both clean and bloody. She passed the oak tree that used to have a tire swing on it. Carved into it was the number "99." She merely nodded.

Her dad had put up the tire swing, of course. Her beautiful father, President of the local UA Plumbers' Union. The man who taught her to never be afraid of being herself. The man who took on the duty of raising a teenaged daughter by himself, while still juggling his many union responsibilities and being a dedicated civil rights activist and political force. Sometimes, it was his influence that decided who the local Democrats would have running for town offices. Occasionally, he had stretched further, his greatest triumph being a powerhouse campaign fundraiser in support of the first ever African-American elected to Congress in their district. And he made a tire swing. And that's the part of him that made her heart sing and scream defiance into the void of his absence.

A car accident. But some of the wounds didn't make sense. He had cuts and abrasions that weren't consistent with the accident. Had someone hurt him before he'd gotten in the car? Was he actually a murder victim? The investigation was still open, but seemed to be going nowhere. Amanda didn't think they'd ever figure it out. The detective in charge had told her not to get her hopes up and, if there was one thing she was good at, aside from finding the details in history that got overlooked by the average Western historian, it was not getting her hopes up.

Be serious, she thought. *I've got no hopes right now to get up.*

There was a bluff that she'd fallen down at the age of five. She'd skinned her legs up pretty badly, but the worst part was that her foot got stuck, stuck in a hole down there, must've been on a root, but did roots tug at your ankle when you tried to free it? Did they tighten their holds? She'd just been a kid; that was all obviously in her imagination. Obviously.

The tree at the top of the bluff had been the tree her dad later said he'd found her teddy bear beneath. Did she lose it when she fell down the bluff? Was that part of the same memory? She didn't know.

There was a carving on the tree. The letters XCIX. *99*, blazed in her head, and she swallowed the sharpened rock she imagined was in her throat. And, below that, more carving in the shape of two figures. One, indistinct, standing behind the other. The one in the foreground, a detailed portrait of a person, empty eye-sockets staring from the bark at her, the expression on its face more one of resignation than fear. And the indistinct figure was massive, and appeared to be holding aloft some kind of clawed hand or a blade. She touched the carving and her fingers came away red and wet. Once, that would have sickened her. Now, she merely shook her head and sighed with bitterness.

Up ahead, there was a clearing. Her father had always warned her against going there. The one time she'd disobeyed, all she found were empty liquor bottles, ragged shreds of porno magazines, and what she later learned were joint roaches. She hadn't gone back there, because it had still given her a very bad feeling, far worse than knowing there were delinquent teenagers using it as a party spot. When she'd asked him why she shouldn't go there, his only response had been, "It's old. Too old."

Entering the clearing was like having a stone rolled onto her chest. She had trouble breathing, the weight pushed her breath from her lungs, and her heart felt compressed. There was no evidence of teenagers partying anymore. Instead, she saw laid out on the ground, in eleven rows of nine, what looked like serrated and warped bear claws, each tipped with a spray of blood. Ninety-nine claws. She looked at the last one and knew everything she needed to know about what had happened to her father.

There was something rustling in the woods behind her. Something loud and large. Making no attempt to be silent, and not in a rush to get to her. It knew she wasn't running anywhere. Amanda thought back to her studies for her thesis on the hecatomb. One-hundred creatures sacrificed to one of the gods, often Apollo, Athena, or Hera. She looked up and saw the Sun staring down at her. It seemed to be smiling, a dark and secret smile. Maybe that's why the heat seemed to be rising, like a hand slinking underneath her clothes and leaving a trail of damp sweat behind anywhere it slid on her skin.

With a tiny whimper, Amanda raised her eyes back to the path she'd traveled from the house. The way was blocked by what appeared to be the entire crowd from the reception, including the man with the aquiline nose, standing in-between Jackie and Dante. Dante had his arms across his chest and was rocking from foot-to-foot. He did not meet her gaze. Jackie was smiling gently, and threw a small wave.

The rustling became louder, insistent. The sunshine continued to pour down on her and the man with the Mediterranean complexion and the nose of a Caesar shouted, "One-hundred! One-hundred! One-hundred!" The rest of the group picked up the cry. Then, he stepped aside and a familiar face appeared. Cynthia. Licking her lips and staring at her one-time best friend. For the first time since he'd died, Amanda wept for her dad.

Cynthia sucked in a deep breath. She raised her hands in the air and Amanda was immediately filled with a sense of *presence* behind her. A sense of *expectation*. The stone-faced young woman cried out for the assembled friends, acquaintances, and strangers, "Kneel before our high priest! Hail the high priest!" Her call was echoed as everyone gathered fell to their knees.

There was a sensation almost like static and white noise tickling the skin of Amanda's back. A blast of warm air that felt almost slimy, like the roots of a tree deep in mud, encircled her neck. The rustling had stopped directly behind her. She heard a swooshing sound, like a scythe being swung back in preparation to strike. In that briefest moment of her brief life, she was back in the tire swing. She was holding her rescued teddy bear. She was hugging her dad before he left for work the morning he'd died, something she'd not done because she was too busy primping in the bathroom when he left. The moment passed and she was alone in her skin and in her fate.

She wondered about ninety-eight other people, and decided that it was too late for that to matter much. They'd all had their own burdens, their own lives, their own endings. She wondered if her own burdens, life, ending, mattered. And she saw the entirety of her dad's burdens and life and ending washed away in a blaze of murderous light. He'd died in the early afternoon, coming back early from work, to surprise her on her last birthday, her 23rd. He'd never made it. She knew why the investigators weren't telling her what they'd found and why his funeral had to be closed-casket.

The Sun caressed her cheek, kissed the top of her head, and in an act of solar mercy, burned out her eyes.

100.

APARTMENT B

Steve Rasnic Tem

TOM CHOSE TO bring very little from his old life into the new apartment. A few clothes, a few random artifacts, but most of his clothes and furniture were new. "I hope you won't take that the wrong way," he told his adult son. He knew that might sound as if he didn't care about his son's feelings, which wasn't true, but he didn't have all the language he needed to explain himself. The reasons were complicated and hard to understand, even for him. But if he were to greatly simplify he would say that he needed to avoid pain. He didn't want to feel haunted anymore.

Of course he still kept photos of his son and his dead wife, and he hung some of them in his new bedroom in a place of importance—on the wall just above a sock drawer in his new chest of drawers, so that he might look at them as he dressed each morning. But they had no real relevance in his new life. His son lived hundreds of miles away, and his wife—he no longer had his wife. Over the three years since her death that had become somewhat easier to say. He was in this new life and in this new life he was unmarried. The only sane thing to do was to accept that. You shouldn't live in the past—people always said that, didn't they? Living in the past was something everyone did, but everyone seemed to agree it wasn't healthy.

He had never lived in an apartment before. He had gone from his parents' house into a small house with his new bride and from there into increasingly larger houses until their son had left home and their interests had stopped expanding. His wife had liked to sew and play with clay. He'd liked to read, and tinker. Now no one did any of those things. Whatever life was left to him was unusually free of distraction. Someone else might have used the word "empty," but Tom refused to.

His new second floor apartment had two bedrooms—one he would sleep in, and one he would put things into until he could think of a better place for them. The living and dining rooms were combined, and relatively small. The kitchen was an island of sorts in the middle, small enough to discourage a long stay, which was fine with him. He had never really understood cooking, and intended to eat pre-prepared meals and salads from the local deli, or perhaps some soup or stew from a can.

Off the dining room there was a small sliding door and a balcony beyond—something he had never had before. He ventured out onto this narrow platform his first evening in the new apartment, and saw that his son had placed a lawn chair from the old yard as furnishings —something he hadn't asked for but could see the sense in. He sat there for almost an hour and looked out and down on the large back lawn of the complex. He was glad he didn't have to mow anymore, or plant, or worry about how people felt about the outside of his house, and what they therefore might assume about what went on inside his house. What they might assume about him.

Other people were out on similar balconies and one or two of them waved. He did nothing to encourage them, and they stopped. Here and there were traces of a lit cigarette or an illuminated phone screen. Tom let the darkness swallow him, and when he went back inside doubted anyone noticed.

The first few nights sleeping in his new home felt like overnights at some lower-priced motel. This was a good thing—he felt it relieved him of any responsibility for the experience. By week's end, however, he was feeling critical of the bed and the color of the walls, and wondering why people cared so little anymore about standards and good service.

He did dream, but not about his dead wife or his distant son. He dreamed of trips never taken, cities never visited and yet oddly familiar, meetings with strangers who were so like friends from his past he felt like he had known them forever. They were inviting him on a journey, it seemed. They didn't promise he would like it, but they made it clear he had no choice.

He had taken early retirement and so there was no particular plan to his days. He usually woke up when the sun came up, but his new bedroom window was shaded unpredictably so sometimes hours would pass while he debated whether it was a new day or not. He tried a simple clock to fix the problem, but he finally had to get rid of it. He didn't like the way it sometimes sped up, sometimes slowed down, and sometimes didn't appear to change at all. He decided he didn't really need it—his body and his circumstances would somehow tell him what to do.

He didn't leave the apartment the first several weeks. He didn't even open the front door. There was no real necessity—he had plenty of food and other supplies—but he recognized the strangeness of it. He'd never been in the least socially adept, but he'd also never imagined himself a hermit before.

But he had been unable to shake off a peculiar sense of instability since moving into the apartment—an oddness of proportion or geometry. As if he were slightly too tall or his legs slightly too long to move around the space comfortably. And it seemed as if his lungs could never quite take in enough air. He didn't want to go outside until he had solved the puzzle of his environment—he didn't feel safe. He thought he might fall at any moment, and he knew what sometimes happened to elderly men who fell. Was he actually elderly? If he had the thought then perhaps he was.

So the first time someone knocked on his door Tom felt slightly frightened, especially since the knocks seemed to have some urgency behind them. He wondered, briefly, if the building were on fire. But wouldn't the smoke detectors have gone off? There were smoke detectors, weren't there? He knew there had to be, but he'd never noticed them.

The woman at the door appeared young, with her dark black hair. But she had the skin of someone older. He'd never been good with ages, and that lack of skill seemed to become more evident every year. Why did he even care about her age? He felt embarrassed, and he hadn't even said a word. She brushed past him and sat down on the couch.

He hesitated, not sure whether he should close the door or not, but fearful that someone else might force their way in, he shut and locked it.

The woman sat on the edge of the couch fiddling with the hem of her skirt and squeezing her knees together. "A family used to live here, the Blakes? Did you know them? Well, of course you didn't. That was years ago. They were a very nice family."

Tom couldn't imagine why she was here. But even if she were crazy she must have a reason. "I didn't know them." What else was there to say?

"No, I said that—there was no reason you should know them. They were a very nice family—that's all I meant to say, really. Is it just you here, by yourself? No family?"

"I have a son, but he's an adult now—he lives in another city." No need to tell her which city. No need to tell her he was a widower. He still wore the ring, and he saw her looking at it. But he'd put on weight since he first married and now the ring was too small to get off—he hadn't taken it off in years. He wasn't trying to be mysterious, or to convey a false impression, but taking his hand somewhere, getting the ring sawn off—that was a major step, wasn't it? He didn't even understand all the implications of such a deliberate decision. And wouldn't that be a bit of a betrayal, to deliberately damage the ring that way? He should put a Band-Aid over it until he could decide what to do.

"A lot of unattached people live here. I'm unattached. You'll fit right in."

Tom doubted it. When was the last time he'd fitted anywhere? He couldn't remember. "I haven't met anyone yet. I'm just getting—acclimated."

"Well then, I'm your first." She smiled, but it was a weak smile, as if she were somehow ill and simply trying to be brave. "But I'm not going to tell you my name. I'm going to let you guess it."

He avoided the couch and sat down in the burgundy armchair opposite her. Was she flirting? Tom couldn't remember what flirting was like. "That's alright," he replied, although he wasn't at all sure.

She smiled broadly, but said nothing. She seemed to be waiting.

Was he supposed to ask for clues? Finally she said, "So what do you do?"

He did nothing. He'd been spending all his time in his new life trying to figure out how to do more than nothing. "Retired," he said. "I ran an office. I had a staff. They did all the work, I guess. I kept them busy. Sometimes it was a challenge. People will just sit there, you know, if you don't give them something to do. I guess they call that purpose. People feel they require a purpose or they won't do anything."

What was this nonsense he was saying? His "staff" was two co-workers in the research department. They all did the same work—he was simply the contact person. Most of the time they had no idea why they were researching the subjects they were researching.

"It sounds important."

He nodded. He said, "Yes." This could not be farther from the truth. He apparently wanted to impress her, but he had no idea why. Had he been this way before he was married? He couldn't remember.

"It's good to take charge of things," she said. "Too many people just let things happen to them—do you agree?"

"Taking responsibility," he said. "That's what you're talking about."

"Exactly." She crossed her legs and adjusted the top of her dress.

"Will you excuse me?" He got up and went into the bedroom and shut the door. He pushed the knob in and twisted to lock it. He sat down on the edge of the bed with the lights out.

Without a clock he couldn't tell how much time had passed, but it seemed like a long time before he heard footsteps coming down the hall. The steps stopped in front of the bedroom—he could see two shadows in the narrow strip of light just beneath the door. Her shoes, he supposed. The doorknob turned back and forth and there was a rattle as she tried to open the door.

After a few minutes the shadows vanished and he could hear the footsteps in the hall and then in the living room, and then the front door opening. He held his breath. Then the sense of the room itself exhaling as the front door closed.

After a few minutes he crawled further up on the bed in the darkness and put his head down on the pillow. The lights were still on out there, but he decided that was acceptable.

Sometime in the middle of the night he grew cold and crawled under the covers, but he didn't open his eyes. He dreamed of walking in darkness, and every now and then a faceless voice would say hello, but he was always too afraid to answer back.

The next morning Tom got up and cleaned the apartment. Theoretically there wasn't a lot to clean. Since he'd moved into the new apartment he'd meticulously picked up after himself. His meals were pre-prepared and promptly disposed of. No stray ingredients or evidence of preparations to erase. And since he hadn't gone outside there had been no dirt or other debris to track in. His guest from the night before might have brought in something on her shoes, but if so it wasn't obviously detectable.

But Tom understood that dust was always a concern. Particles drifted through the windows, filtered down from the ceilings and even from the apartments on the third floor, an unknown amount traveling upwards from deep within the fibers of the carpeting, and there was always a certain percentage of dead skin cells—his and those of previous occupants—although the exact percentage appeared to be a figure of considerable debate.

The world renewed you, or replaced you—depending on your degree of optimism—at its own rate. He did not know how to feel about any of it. He scrubbed the floors and cleaned the surfaces as best he could—tried to rid himself of contamination. But he was haunted by the approximations of memory, by the unsupported promises of the imagination. His imagination suggested he might have everything, and yet he knew nothing was there, no matter how much that nothing clamored for his attention.

The next morning she let herself back inside, although Tom was positive he hadn't given her a key. He'd been sitting outside on his balcony again, following the comings and goings of strangers, and wondering if there might come a time he'd consider introducing himself. Even this tiny glimpse of an outside world was discomfiting. There were couples out walking their dogs, there were all those children playacting an actual life, there were all the legions of the dead, and the tantalizations of their laughter, the transient evidence of their happiness that dissipated in his scattered spells of reason.

She smiled at him as he entered his own living room. Her skin was as pale and as unblemished as the promise of sleep. She sat on the couch with some awkwardness, as if waiting for his next move.

"I'm sorry," he said. "I don't know what this is, but I'm not ready for it."

"I assumed you were lonely. I assumed you wanted some company."

"But I don't know how to do this," he said. "Is there someone I can call to come get you?"

"Could I just use your restroom? I know where it is—I found it while I was searching for you last night."

He nodded, said, "Please take your time."

She paused just inside the bathroom. "You know, the Blakes were much nicer neighbors." Then she slipped inside and shut the door.

Tom went into his bedroom, grabbed a pillowcase, and slipped the photos of his wife and son inside. He'd made a terrible mistake. He went back into the living room and looked around. Nothing here was his. He didn't recognize any of it. He opened his apartment door and left, carrying the pillowcase with the pictures close to his chest. He didn't bother to close the door behind him.

Once Tom reached the lawn of the apartment complex he turned around and gazed at it. It didn't look much like the brochure he'd received in the mail nearly a year ago, the one that had made him decide on this purchase sight unseen. It resembled a stack of concrete slabs, with stress cracks showing in the corners. The bushes around the garden level units appeared yellow and sickly. Not that it mattered a great deal, he supposed—apartments, houses were all pretty much the same—they were boxes for people to put their things in, and then to climb in afterwards and shut themselves off from the wind and the rain and the ones that might do you harm if they ever got in. At least the old house had had his history, however painful that history had eventually become.

He started down the sidewalk with no particular plan. He had some cash in his wallet and a credit card. He could always access his bank account if he discovered something he wanted to spend it on.

A variety of restaurants and other businesses lay on the other side of four lanes of highway. Their signage was incredibly bright and colorful. He passed a number of people on the sidewalk and their clothing was incredibly bright and colorful as well. Desperately so, he thought. Desperate reds and desperate blues. Desperate greens. Their eyes looked tired and pale, as if worn out trying to make sense of all the bright colors. Even the younger ones looked weary. Even their newer outfits appeared poorly cared for.

He hadn't paid adequate attention and brushed against a large man in a soft gray suit. The man stank of stress and a poor diet. Tom felt immediately embarrassed by his knee-jerk judgment when the man stopped and said, "Are you all right? Can I help?"

Tom had no idea why the man thought he might need assistance. Was it really that obvious? There was a looseness about the man's skin, as if it were a poor fit. "Thank you, I'm fine," Tom said.

The man went on his way, moving awkwardly as if in pain. It seemed to Tom that everyone he had seen today appeared ill.

A couple crossed over the highway to his side of the street holding hands. The way they clung together—Tom wondered what they feared, what they imagined might happen to either of them. They were really too young to know all the things that might happen. When they reached the sidewalk they gave each other a sloppy embrace, lips slipping off lips and then inhaling skin, makeup, whatever aftershave the man used. They appeared drunk, inebriated, but also intoxicated on themselves, and on the fact that they had each other. He wanted to give them some money, but when he approached them they ran away, laughing. Whether at him, or at the fun they'd found in each other, he couldn't say.

He didn't know how far he was from his old house. He'd stopped driving years ago, and since then had developed a poor sense of direction and distance. Not that it mattered in any practical sense. He'd sold the house and disposed of all its contents. That act was done and could not be undone. It was a terrible mistake, he realized now, but it had seemed like a good idea at the time. He had wanted to both escape pain and force himself into a new and useful life, or if not useful at least reasonable. The problem with such a strategy is that if you find you cannot complete the course you've laid out, if you come half way down the path and you discover it is the wrong path but you have given away all your resources, what do you do?

You die, Tom supposed. Such people died, or they wandered around in some kind of untouchable limbo.

It must have been close to lunchtime because there seemed to be a great number of people out on the sidewalk now and in the crosswalks. Tom couldn't have said for sure but this seemed like a reasonable guess. Singly and walking in groups, sometimes, many with name tags clipped to their pockets or hanging from lanyards. Some of them walked while eating—a sandwich or a protein bar in one hand, sometimes with a drink in the other, sucking through a straw or sipping or gobbling liquid down a long-necked bottle.

Some of them made pained noises when they ate or drank. Some of them gasped for air. Tom saw more of that loose skin he had seen before, loose and too pale and sometimes with dark shadows over where the blood vessels ran, where the blood pooled or where there was an old weakness or injury. Some had scabs or scratches. Some walked with the awkwardness characteristic of pain or injuries new or old. Some looked longingly for companionship and some of them actively avoided it.

Tom had nothing to say to any of these people. Tom had no idea how to make them feel better or provide even a moment's relief. He supposed he was like many of them but to identify too much, to accept that his experience was all too common, was to take away some of the validity of his pain. He should never have left his old house. He shouldn't even be here.

Without being aware of it he had entered one of those great stone and concrete plazas that stretched between buildings. Here was this seemingly endless plain of paved world anchored by monuments to technology and commerce. Populated by hundreds of people, perhaps thousands, milling about as if purposeless but of course many of these figures had their purposes timed down to the last minute.

Many were getting too close. He couldn't be sure if they had him exactly in mind or if simple space restriction were forcing them all together.

"No," he said plainly, and one or two nearby stopped in their tracks. "No," he said again, as a young man in a hurry ran right into him.

Tom went to his knees as more gathered around him. He held the pillowcase with the photographs inside up to his face. Several people were approaching. One of the women resembled his neighbor from upstairs.

He was very hungry. He hadn't eaten all day. And they kept coming closer to him, wanting him to rejoin the human race. But he wasn't having any of it. He wanted to do something, something else. He took out the photographs of his dead wife and his faraway son and began eating them.

UNDERSTAIRS

Jason A. Wyckoff

A FAMILY WITH several children previously occupied the house Gracie bought, leaving her to suffer the encumbrance of carpeted stairs. Gracie, being a single woman of taste, hated carpeted stairs. Nevertheless, she put up with the situation for nearly six years because the cost of buying a home—despite putting "no money down" against the principal—depleted her "cushion" (which the expenses of being a sociable single woman of taste in a new city prevented her from quickly replenishing). By the time she had the means to invest in remodeling, her wish list for improvements had grown considerably. And while several projects were by then absolute necessities (such as replacing all the rattling, ill-fitting windows which, in addition to contributing to mammoth winter heating bills, allowed in drafts of such a peculiarly disquieting nature that the simulated sound of breathing on the landing outside of her bedroom door kept Gracie awake more than one night through), the removal of the carpeting and the refurbishing of the stairs was the top item on her list.

Online reviews of local small business owners led her to engage

"Millett and Sons" contractors. The fifty-something man with broad forehead and crooked nose who managed her remodeling explained he was actually the surviving "Son," having retained the name when he inherited the business from his senior.

"And, since my daughters weren't inclined to follow in my footsteps, I got this little guy to help me out," he said by way of introducing Filipe as he put his arm around the much shorter man's shoulders.

Filipe took up his cue for the obviously-rehearsed but goofily endearing bit, beaming as he looked up at Millett and said, "Thanks, Pop!"—the only two words in English Gracie remembered him uttering during the entire renovation.

Millett, conversely, never squandered any chance to speak with his client. He seemed to relish each opportunity to explain the details of her house and the minutiae of their work on it. Gracie thought kindly enough of the older man that she didn't (often) wonder if his genial attention was tendered equally to customers who weren't pretty single women in their thirties.

And so Gracie thought it must have required a Herculean effort on Millett's part to restrain himself until after the steps were stripped, sanded, and stained before he mentioned the keyhole beneath the lip of the fifth stair.

"It looks like there's a secret storage compartment under the step," he explained. "It might have been used to store valuables or just children's toys. Probably there's nothing in there now, but who knows? Have you found any old keys in the house you couldn't find a use for?"

"No," Gracie replied. Though he seemed to try to hide it, Millett's obvious disappointment prompted her to ask, "Couldn't you force it open?"

Millett shook his head determinedly. "There might be a mechanism attached."

"What mechanism?"

For once, Millett declined to elaborate. Instead, he seemed to shrug off whatever importance he had ascribed to it and smiled. "Well, it adds a touch of character, anyway."

Gracie regarded the simple, brass clasp. "Don't you think a skeleton key would fit?"

"Eh." He waved off the suggestion. "Just wait. I'm sure the key will turn up."

Millett's prediction held true, though its fulfillment perplexed Gracie. Had she dusted more assiduously above the doorframe to the kitchen in an effort to clean the construction dust? It seemed more than possible—it was the only rational explanation. But Gracie was still surprised when she knocked the iron key with a greenish patina of rust to the floor.

Well, it's here now, she thought, which she found a particularly unsettling way to phrase her acceptance of its existence.

She was not shocked to discover the key fit and turned easily.

She couldn't say why she paused before pulling the panel down. Was she savoring the suspense? She wondered if she would be happy to discover something inside or relieved nothing was there. Perhaps she waited to stave off disappointment. She laughed at her foible and pulled the panel open.

"Oh!" she exclaimed. As the panel fell forward, it partially lifted the stair in front of it. Gracie felt a wobble in the wood and heard a loose piece knock softly against one of the longer boards. She envisioned a support strut freed from its locking notch swinging freely. The hypothesis seemed proved when she gently lowered both panel and stair step down into the vacant dark. She couldn't yet see anything in the space beyond. An idea occurred to her. She removed and pocketed the key, allowing her to fold the panel and step flat against the next panel down. She yelped again when the next panel angled forward—and lifted the next step down in front of it, which then folded flat. She repeated the process twice more to collapse the bottom four steps of her staircase into an accordion fold which flipped backwards at the bottom to fit snugly into an alcove in the floor. When she set them flat, she heard a click and saw a wooden button pop out from flush with the rail along the wall. She guessed what it might do and pressed the button to confirm her suspicion. She heard the twang of a spring extending and the soft shunk of a counterweight sliding inside the wall as the stairs unfolded and snapped back into place. Only the top panel did not close completely. She smiled with delight at the ingenuity of the simple design as she pulled the panel forward and proceeded once more to fold the stairs back down into the floor.

Even with the strange door completely open, Gracie couldn't see far into the hidden compartment. It seemed to go much farther back than she had expected, possibly the full length of the stairway. She went to her kitchen and retrieved a silver flashlight from her "assorted" drawer. She kneeled down and turned it on. Though it was a small flashlight, it emitted a bright, blue-tinted beam...which still couldn't dispel the gloom beneath the stairs. Gracie ducked beneath the opening and crawled forward on her elbows.

When she was halfway into the opening, she became terribly disoriented. She felt pulled upwards, so much so that she was forced to put her hands over her head to keep from hitting the underside of the stair. As her weight was forward and she was unbalanced on her knees, she knew she should have fallen on her chin, but somehow she remained upright. She then concentrated on the second distressing aspect of her disorientation. She had the feeling she had twisted at the middle, even though she knew she had not turned her torso. She looked down the length of her body and saw the feeling was wrong, and everything was in alignment as it should be. But the knowledge made her feel worse, because what she saw was at odds with what she felt—and what she felt seemed so extreme she thought her back should be broken and ankles facing front. Gracie was scared. She tried to lean back in hopes of extricating herself from the compartment, but her sense of the working of her musculature was so discombobulated she instead torqued forward and pulled on the stairs above her, turning to face upwards—which was immediately, unmistakably *down* as soon as her body had passed through the portal.

She slipped forward and smacked her wrist on another step. Her other hand shot out to keep her from falling further and she dropped the flashlight. It tumbled down a few steps before rolling out of sight, dropping through a gap where the vertical slat should have been. She looked back (and up—as though up the stairs, which should have been down, according to the bearings her mind clung to) but could not see into her house. The only light behind her was a dim slit at what must have been the top of the staircase—a staircase she now recognized by feel as being altogether different from hers. She considered that the underside of the stairs might not feel the same, but she was sure the cut was more coarse, the planks thicker, and the wood different. She curled her fingers around the front edge and felt neither rounded lip nor vertical board. She was quite sure she was sprawled on cellar stairs in a different house.

She tried to get her feet under her by easing her hips around the side. Her breath caught in her throat when her leg slipped forward and her buttocks slid hard down a step. She listened but heard no reaction from above. She wasn't sure if it was essential to be silent or not, but she couldn't very well explain her presence there, and with no knowledge of the house's occupants, she had no way to gauge their reaction to her invasion. She squirmed into a seated position and at last felt some sense of physical stability. Her thoughts were not nearly so steady.

She decided she needed to find her flashlight. She rationalized that if she'd come in—whatever way she had come in—then she could go back out again. As she sat, her eyes adjusted a little. It was late in the day but not yet dark. She realized there was some small amount of sun illuminating the room, though the light was terribly dim. She could just make out the outlines of narrow windows beneath the floor joists—windows made opaque with black paint.

She stepped gingerly down the last few steps to the floor. She could barely see, but she had at least some sense of open space at the foot of the stairs. She turned around beside them, keeping one hand on the staircase, and knelt down to reach underneath. The floor was cool cement, indicating an unfinished basement. Gracie felt a moment of delighted relief when, after only a few seconds, she located her flashlight; a moment repeated when it flared to life.

The basement opened to the right of the stairs and continued back behind them. Gracie swept the cone of light over a workbench running the length of the wall in front of her. Well-worn tools for carpentry and for landscaping cluttered the surface of the rough bench and hung from hooks in a dirty white pegboard behind it. A long table sitting parallel to the workbench was covered with large sheets of curling paper. Gracie stepped closer to see what was on them. Sifting through, she saw on each sheet a hand-drawn rendering of some sort of contraption accompanied by smaller detailed insets of construction phases and operating instructions. Only a few scrawled, nearly illegible words were paired with each machine, and at first glance Gracie thought she could never derive the mechanics involved from the drawings. But she soon understood how uncomplicated they were—though clever, too, in their simple utility and balance; she might have called the designs "elegant" if such a word hadn't seemed at odds with such boxy and artless forms. She identified a short cabinet whose door opened upward to become a table, supported by a shelf which swung out to reveal another narrow shelf behind it. Another drawing showed a bar stool with interlocking legs which collapsed flat when a latch was released and the seat turned clockwise. There were many others, including some whose purpose was unclear, but none whose operation was complex enough to require arrows on the dashed lines to indicate the direction of motion.

On the other side of the table were stacks and piles of building supplies, as well as several partial contraptions (whether in-progress or abandoned, Gracie couldn't say). She thought there could be no reason to further explore the basement and was about to begin considering what means of egress she might use when something on the back wall caught her eye. She navigated through the wood and metal skeletons on the floor to get closer.

As she suspected, a map had been tacked up. What interested her more was the wealth of notes pinned to it and the tracks of yarn tied between them. The collage was so dense the parchment underneath could not be identified as a map of the city until she stood before it. The strings came together in a mass in the northeast quadrant. The location meant nothing to her, but Gracie guessed she stood at its center. Many of the notes pinned to the map looked as though they had been there for years. Most read "open" or "closed," though some which read "open" were given the addendum "locked"(Gracie wondered at the distinction), while others had a large "X" or some other scribble bleeding into the fading paper.

A sudden dread came over Gracie. A chill caressed her skin. She moved the light, following a red thread, tracing its course to a terminal pin stuck in the map right where her house would be.

A crisp red square emblazoned with black ink noted, "Open—locked—lost key."

Gracie gasped and staggered backwards. Her heel hit a board and she stumbled into one of the unfinished forms. It began to topple. Gracie's arm shot out as she squat and she managed to grab a two-by-four crossbar right before the entire thing crashed to the floor. As her breath whistled through her teeth, Gracie gently lowered the board to the cement.

She listened. She listened for a full minute, but heard no sound in the house. As she waited, understanding came to her: She had come through a corridor between the houses. Somehow. It was impossible; she knew that. But the impossibility didn't matter. What mattered was both the reality of the passage, and, perhaps more alarmingly, it's condition of *being known.*

"OK," she whispered, trying to calm herself with the sound of her own voice. "Yes. It's there. I'm here. So—how do I get *back*?"

She flashed the beam back at the stairs to confirm what she already knew: the steps were supported only on the sides; there were no vertical slats. It seemed unlikely—even allowing for the unfounded expectation that the gate of the return portal should match form with hers—that she could return through her exit.

"Well, I can take a damn taxi if I can just get *out*."

Again, she listened. Again, she heard no sound of movement overhead.

"Windows first, though," she breathed optimistically.

And then she noticed the other door, in the back corner behind the stairs. She bit her lip. Was it possible there were steps leading up to a storm cellar door on the other side?

She crossed to the brown metal door. The handle turned smoothly.

She had hoped to spy a sliver of light promising escape, but she saw there was no exit besides the door through which she'd entered. And though what she saw inside made her want to turn and run right back out again, she found she could not. Mystery beckoned.

The focus of the room was the altar on the broad table set against the far wall. In its basic form, it was not so different from an in-home shrine a devout Catholic or Buddhist might erect for themselves: It was low at the sides and rose to the middle; ornamental scrolling adorned the frame surrounding the central figure; partially melted candles played sentinel in staggered lines on the dark-stained wood. The figure to which the altar appeared to be consecrated was not one likely to be encountered in a suburban American home, however. If in fact, as Gracie thought, the two-faced idol truly did represent Janus. She had never before seen the Greek god represented as smooth-chinned and blank-eyed, and carved from obsidian.

Her attention drifted to another table, much like the one in the main room, likewise covered over with large drawings on curling paper. But while these drawings also depicted simple machines, their functions were inscrutable, and the annotations were far removed from the pithy scrawls on the other drawings. These notes included complex mathematical formulas. And though Gracie remembered little of higher function algebra, she guessed many of the figures incorporated in the formulas had never been used in classical physics or any other accepted science. Even tracing the curves of some of the symbols filled her with alien dread, as though instinct recognized the forbidden and the arcane.

Gracie awoke to her situation. She shook herself from the grip of curiosity with the epiphany that the answers which might explain the riddles before her were ones she likely would not want to know. She turned to leave. She nearly tripped as she kicked a large clot of dirt. She shined her light down on the floor. The four low, oblong mounds implied only one possibility.

Gracie whimpered and trembled. She grasped her flashlight with both hands. She knew she had no chance of keeping it steady, but she was terrified she might drop it and be plunged once more into darkness. She went back out into the main room and looked at the windows. Despite the nearly-opaque black paint, with her eyes better adjusted to the gloom, she now easily identified the bars on the other side.

She looked up the staircase. It seemed impossibly long, and she found herself wishing she need never climb it—and wishing she was already at the top. She crept up the steps. With each creak of a bowing plank, she paused to listen. Nothing. Creep. Creak. Silence. Creep. Creak. Silence.

At last she was at the top. And again she wished twofold, that the door was unlocked and that it wasn't. It was. She cracked the door and put her eye to the tiniest gap. The house was dim, dark enough to merit electrical light, but none was turned on. The hinges ticked with each inch of aperture.

She stepped out into a hall. The house was like any other clean, middle class, century-old two-story. Gracie saw the front door, at the end of the hall, at the foot of a flight of stairs. Her pounding heart urged her to dash for it, but she tip-toed instead, her head on a swivel, listening for any sound. Past the stairs the hall opened into a living room. Gracie craned her neck to scan the shadowed corners. Mere steps from the door, she paused. On the mantle over the fireplace sat a family photo. She cursed herself, but did not resist the pull. She crept behind a sofa and crossed a corded rug.

She had known before she picked it up. But the photo indicated an existence so discordantly unexceptional she couldn't help shaking her head in disbelief even as she gazed at the broad forehead and crooked nose of pater Millett standing behind his wife and daughters. As she went to set the portrait back down, she noticed the familiar-looking key which it hid.

Headlights swept across the room. Gracie yelped and ducked. A car pulled into the drive. She went back to the hall but realized she could no longer leave through the front. As she turned, she wondered if the back yard was fenced. And then she saw the tiny hole beneath the lip of the fifth stair.

She fumbled the key out of her pocket, catching it but dropping her flashlight. She heard something crack and the light went out. She picked it up with one hand as she miraculously fitted the key on her first attempt with the other. But the key wouldn't turn. She heard a car door slam. She scrambled across the living room, knocked the happy family out of the way, and snatched up the hidden key. Another car door slammed. She heard voices coming up the drive as she hurried back to the stairs. An unspoken prayer was answered as the key turned in the lock. She collapsed the stairs. She dove into the dark. She realized she didn't know how they closed from inside—the button was outside. She heard laughter just outside the front door. Her fingers scratched at the planks. It seemed the wrong way to do it, but she forced them up into place. And she heard the turn of the latch in the front door just as she fitted the last slat.

She didn't feel upside down as she had expected. Nor was she in total blackness. She turned and saw the familiar landing of her own refurbished house. She crawled out on skinned knees, and, in a single motion, leapt to her feet, turned and pressed the button to snap the stairs back into place. She lunged and smacked the final panel flat.

She sat in her living room in the dark for hours, listening to the quiet of her own house, trying to convince herself it was *her* quiet, inviolate. She deliberated: what had she truly seen? Perhaps nothing. No, of course, not nothing—she had followed an impossible portal to an occult workroom where bodies might be buried in the floor. Where there *might* be bodies buried in the floor. There had been nothing else to suggest malevolency—*if* the figure in the shrine was Janus. But even then: What God has not had evil done in his name? Gracie even chastised herself at one point for not being braver and investigating more thoroughly the strange papers in the dark back room. And she wondered why, of all the possible connections indicated by Millett's map, she had returned home—was it simply because it was where she wanted to go? Eventually she realized she was exhausted. She told herself the uneventful passage of hours proved even if he had known someone had been in his house, Millett—whatever his intentions—must not have known who it was. Her flashlight was still in her hand, so she tried to turn it on, but the bulb wouldn't light. After she'd found a switch on the wall, she saw the lens was broken and a shard was missing.

Her bedroom beckoned, but she was almost afraid to walk up her own stairs, as though they might open and swallow her. She upbraided herself for the hesitation, stomped up defiantly, marched straight through, slammed the door behind her, and didn't bother to change before she collapsed onto her mattress.

But tired as she was, Gracie could not fall asleep. She continued listening. Her fingers were cutting into her palms as though missing something to hold. She remembered the key and retrieved it once more from her pocket. She clutched it tightly and seemed to derive some relief from holding it, considering it, identifying it.

The strange key.

The key to the lock in the stairs.

The key to the lock she'd forgotten to lock.

At the first creak, she told herself old houses settle. At the second, she told herself even refurbished old houses settle.

But, because the tight seal on her new windows shut out all the old drafts, she could not account for the sound of breathing outside her bedroom door.

Her phone lay on her bedside table. Any requested aid would never arrive in time, but she grabbed it anyway as she sprang from her bed. Then she dashed to the door—not to lock it, but to go through. For, contrary to convention, but in consideration of just such a need, Gracie had affected a renovation of her own when she'd moved the hinges to the *outside* of her door so it would swing open, and if necessary, knock any hostile situated there down the stairs into a (hopefully) broken heap, leaving Gracie to rush down the hall to her studio at the front of the house, with its window access to the porch roof and the (hopefully) cushy lawn below. And if no one was there, then—well, she always reasoned it was better to be embarrassed than endangered.

She wasn't embarrassed. She shouldered the door open and smacked into a resisting body which, as planned, was pushed back. But she could never have expected the abrupt pivot in gravity that accompanied her emergence from her bedroom. The figure outside her door fell, but it did not tumble down the stairs—it tumbled down the angled ceiling before crashing flat against the front door.

Only the instinct to squeeze kept Gracie from falling on top of him. She dropped her phone, heard it clatter far below. Though she couldn't keep hold of the doorknob, she did so long enough for her legs to swing beneath her and to angle her descent towards the railing. She banged against it, grabbed, lost her grip, grabbed again and held half-way down the balustrade.

She looked down and saw a man limply squirming, trying to claw his way back from senselessness. With only the bleed from the porch-light illuminating his face, it was still possible to identify Millett, though some trick of the shadow produced a strange after-image as he turned his head from side to side, a second, smooth face of obsidian offset from the features of flesh; it disappeared when Gracie tried to see it, but flickered into view after she blinked and it pulled from the corner of her eye when she glanced away.

As she expected, the passage beneath the stairs was open.

Gracie briefly considered trying to climb up the railing. She could then crawl along the wall to her "escape hatch" window—with the hope that whatever phenomenon upsetting the pull of gravity was confined to her house. But she was angry. Her sense of ownership reared; the truce between home and world had been invalidated by intrusion, and she felt obligated to fight back, to make right her sense of security, and for Gracie, that meant eliminating the threat—of not just the man, but of the mechanism, as well.

She clambered down the balustrade, careful to keep her weight distributed amongst protesting spindles. When her shoulders were parallel to the top of the opening, she "opened" her body towards the wall and ducked under the step. She groped in the dark and propped her forearm across the first panel between steps, praying it would hold when she shifted to it. She contorted to slide her other hand under the stairs and folded her fingers around the next plateau. She let her first leg dangle into open space. Then the second. And just as she began to pull herself up, she felt two hands grip and pull on her toes.

She shrieked and kicked, got one leg free, tried to heft herself up, but couldn't. She kicked at the fingers clutching her foot and felt them drop away. She got her other forearm flat on the next panel above and crawled upwards—until she tumbled backwards down the cellar stairs in Millet's house. Her wrists and knees took the brunt of the impact on the concrete floor. Her arms and legs throbbed and wouldn't obey her orders. But she pushed through the pain and forced her feet under her, and though new stings shot through her as she pulled herself upright, she stood.

The stairs were empty; the door above was closed. Fortunately, a light was on over the workbench along the wall, or else Gracie knew she would be trapped in darkness.

She stumbled through the clutter, kicking carefully, worried she might not have the strength to stand once more. She paused at the thread-webbed map. She clutched two handfuls of layered skeins and pulled. She felt great satisfaction throwing the torn map and rumpled, multicolored mass to the floor, but she knew the act was only preliminary to victory. She had no particular reason to believe her course would affect the change she hoped for, but she pursued it with desperate certainty. She opened the brown metal door and entered.

There was little light to see by, but enough to recall the basic layout. She ignored the four mounds and the arcana-strewn table. She crossed to the altar. She grabbed the black, two-faced totem by the base. She was surprised by how cold it felt, but unsurprised at how heavy it was. As she brought it up over her head, she uttered a two-word prayer that the thing wasn't shatterproof. She lunged forward as she brought the totem down with all her strength against the wall. She could barely see the separation, but the telling sound heralded success—a sound followed almost immediately by a scream.

Gracie whirled around. The man's scream had come from the basement. Knowing she had no other means of escape, Gracie brandished the stunted rock base in front of her and went back into the main room.

She heard a horrid wheezing, and then saw a hand slapping the floor near the foot of the stairs. Thinking it might be her one chance to strike a blow before Millett recovered, she rushed towards him, ready to slam the base against his head.

Instead, she dropped the rock on the floor and gasped. There would be no need to pummel her adversary. Millett had already stopped moving, stopped breathing. The loss of blood from where his legs were cleanly shorn just above the knees had killed him; blood now dripping from stair to stair to pool around Millett's torso.

She'd closed the door on him.

"Honey, are you OK?"

The woman's voice came from the other side of the door at the top of the cellar stairs.

For a moment, Gracie didn't know what to do. There was no other exit. She'd dropped her phone when she flew out of her bedroom.

But Mrs. Millett didn't know that.

"I've already called the cops," she bluffed. "They're on their way!"

Gracie almost hoped to hear confusion or alarm, to have the door swing open and see the widow Millett there, wide-eyed with horror at the sight of her mauled husband. That somehow, she didn't know what had been happening in her house. That maybe she wasn't some other thing masquerading as one of the four victims in the other room. Though Gracie might never know the answer exactly, she knew something was wrong when no challenge was forthcoming. Instead, after a few moments, she heard low voices murmuring excitedly and a rush of motion. She traced the squawking of floorboards overhead, wondering if the daughters were being gathered as reinforcements or for exodus. Then the front door opened and shut. Gracie heard the car engine roar to life followed by a squeal of tires. She exhaled.

She looked at the base of the totem on the floor. She wondered what had caused gravity to go mad at the instant she'd opened her bedroom door. Perhaps she was right about Janus—and perhaps an old god from a faded pantheon had interceded, that the barest memory of a ghost of a god had flared with anger at his despoiled legacy and the abuse of his totem's power, tasking Gracie with its destruction (that clear inspiration of the rightness of action) even if it meant extinguishing the last of his deific might in the world. To Gracie, the specifics didn't matter. There was her world to think of, and her house to attend to. And good or bad, she'd prefer to allow in only the invited. She wiped down the black rock as she tried to remember if her fingerprints might appear anywhere else in the house. Discarding the stumps Millett left behind would be a more involved and gruesome task. Gracie hoped any permanent stains would be confined to the secret room beneath the stairs, a space she planned to lock away and never revisit.

As Summer's Mask Slips

Gordon White

As she drove to her father's house—now hers, she supposed—Sarah knew that she still remembered those woods too well to have a chance of really losing herself in them. Still, she wanted to wander the trails and desire paths once again and to shed her burden bit by bit like breadcrumbs in her wake. To let the forest carry it away, even if she might never find her way back to the empty home.

When she was younger, she'd spent her summers out here with her father, given free rein of the wild tract between his house and the lake below. But as she returned now, a decade later and on the cusp of autumn, it was almost a different world. She had always been back in the city with her mother by the time the seasons changed, so the unfamiliar smolder of the fall's colors around her as she drove further and further into the country made it seem as if she had caught the world in the middle of putting on, or taking off, a disguise.

In fact, she'd only been out to his house one time during a season other than summer. She'd come up during the winter for Christmas the year before she left for college. She recalled pressing her face against the living room's picture window, staring at the skeletal branches groping with their stripped fingers towards the hangnail of a moon. Just the sight had made her shiver in a way the snow on the ground never could have.

"The emptiness is beautiful, isn't it?" her father had said, but Sarah didn't think so.

For her, the summer woods were the real woods. The green and full of life woods, warm and wild. That vibrant, verdant thing was the true version and honest face.

The still and hollow woods, with the early nightfall and the knuckles of the forest gripping at the bone-sliver moon, that wasn't beautiful. It was something only an old man should find beauty in. Someone nearing the end of his life, consoling himself with frozen memories for the long dark sleep of winter.

Not something for her father to say. Not yet.

The next fall Sarah went to college, then found a job, and as the seasons rolled on she visited her father less often. Then he called to say that he'd gotten sick, or rather he'd been sick for a while but was only just diagnosed. He went to the hospital, he got thin and strange, and then he died. The changes all came so quickly that it seemed to Sarah as if that spindle-man that he'd withered into had been her real father, her winter father, hidden away and biding its time. As if the man she'd loved was a seed husk that had been ginned away into something raw and wicked.

Those thoughts of the end, Sarah worried, would be the ones to take hold and define him in her memories. She knew that it was best not to dwell in morbidity, though, and instead she should plant a garden of bright summer thoughts of her father and their time together. So, after the paperwork was done, she decided to return to his house with the aim of filling herself to bursting as she emptied it out. In this way, Sarah planned to gather and tend to those small sprigs of happiness, so that they might one day grow into a consolation.

But her resolve remained intact only as long as the drive from the city to the dirt road cut-off. The strength fell from her soles, through the car's floorboard, and crunched like gravel beneath the tires as she ground her way past distant neighbors, further and further towards her father's isolated cabin.

Why live in such a remote area? The question echoed across the fields as she pulled into the driveway beside his truck. It had been an adventure when she was young, but it wasn't too long before she was old enough to worry about him not just for being so far from everyone else, but for wanting to be. Even before they knew he was sick, she would get vivid impressions, like waking dreams, of him lying in the woods or sprawled face down in his kitchen with no one to help to him. No one to find him.

She had tried to laugh away these fantasies, calling them ridiculous. She didn't know yet how right she was. How absurd it was to think that her father would have been fortunate enough to meet some quick and silent end.

Sarah unlocked the front door with the key she'd gotten from his belongings at the hospital. There used to be a spare beneath the planter, but when she checked it out of habit, it was empty. Inside the house, however, her father's things were everywhere. A pair of old boots lay by the door, a coat on the rack. A paperback book was propped half-open on the arm of his chair, basking in the late afternoon sun. Everything was suspended mid-moment, as if he had just stepped out and would be returning any minute. As if she might suddenly hear the back door open, instead of just the chimes shivering in a breeze.

In the living room, photographs frozen behind drugstore picture frames bore silent witness as she took inventory. There was Sarah the high school senior. As a little girl on a trip to England. At her college graduation, in the last photo of her mother and her father near each other, but not together.

The banality of the milestones her father had collected filled Sarah's pockets, rooting her to the floor. As she looked from picture to picture, she realized that she was trying to pinpoint the moment when she could have seen death pushing through her father's features. When she could have seen his sick and barren self getting ready to emerge.

Even if she found it now, though, what good would it do? She couldn't go back in time to tell him, Look, there is this *thing* inside you. Even if she could, would it have hastened his sick self's emergence and dragged that winter out over years instead of months? Would finding it now smudge every photo of him from that point forward with the taint of her failure?

She had come to get away from these thoughts, but had not come far enough yet. Feeling the need for air, she exited onto the back porch and gazed out past the small yard at the wall of trees that encircled it. Although the leaves were baking away into browns and oranges, although it was not the forest of her young summers, it called to her just the same. It had the same rough shape and features, only just changed a little, she hoped. Time must have left her that much, certainly.

Walking out through the ankle-high and unkempt blades, a distant memory returned of how her father used to mow the lawn of the little house that they all lived in together when she was just a child. Sarah could see him standing in that fenced-in yard, drenched in sweat and the smell of cut grass. Even back then and back there, surrounded by other houses, the air prickled with the scent of the wild onions that encroached from the suburbs' small feral patches.

She remembered how the onions' roots grew all twisted together, spreading out to connect to one another at seemingly random points, but coalescing into a wild and angled whole.

Her father used to say that there were many paths to the water, she just had to pick one.

This, she thought as she entered the woods, is how I will confront the loss. By coming at it horizontally.

ALTHOUGH THE WOODS were altered by the years of her absence and the unfamiliar changes of fall, there was enough for Sarah to recognize her woods within it. She remembered the main path and the long walks that she and her father would take. Sometimes, on pleasant days, they would take out the old canoe he kept hidden a little up from the shoreline.

"Why don't we chain it up?" she'd asked him once as they paddled across the flat and muddy water.

"Who'd want to take this old thing?" he said. "I'm surprised it even floats." Then he shifted his weight quickly, rocking the boat just enough for Sarah to grab the sides and laugh.

"Besides," he said, "nobody comes down here but you and me."

"What about them?" She pointed across water to the small landing on the far shore. Sometimes a handful of men sat in folding chairs and held fishing poles, but never seemed to be doing much else. One time, one of them waved.

"Them?" Her father laughed. "They're too far away to do anything."

Even then, she'd realized that the outdoors had been such a part of his life that he'd wanted to make it a part of hers. He never said why, and with the loss still fresh she didn't want to push too hard against the still-forming scar, but maybe it was something from his own childhood. Maybe it was a place to retreat when the flat empty spaces beyond the trees became too much to bear.

But whatever woods her father had seen, they weren't hers. Her forest was only an echo of his. It was a place of memories. A place of lessons.

It was learning how to tie a knot or how to play real hide and seek, as he called it. It was learning how to find a trail. It was her father asking what kind of birds are they that sing these songs? What does it mean when they all go quiet?

What does it mean when the insects go quiet, too?

When nothing makes a sound?

It came back to her quickly in the now-silent forest, how the steady buzz of woods will break for an intruder.

Behind her, somewhere between the carpet of fallen leaves and those still clinging to the branches, a stick snapped and its report shot through the still world. Sarah froze, counting the seconds as if it had been a flash of lightning and she was waiting for the thunder.

But there was nothing more.

Only one crack without another could mean that it was just a falling branch or other singular event.

Or, her father reminded her, something that doesn't want to be found.

Sarah knew what animals sounded like and that they would only pause for a second before moving on, their unencumbered minds failing to comprehend threats that didn't immediately materialize. But even then, the insects and the birds should start right up again. Life should flow on around minor disruptions like the wind through the skirts of the branches.

It shouldn't be this still and this quiet. Not for this long.

Sarah began to walk again, trying to remember how to do it quietly. Slow steps, maybe, rolling heel to toe. Maybe toe to heel. Behind her, the lengthening shadows of the sentinel trees barely breathed in the faint wind. There was no movement yet, but she felt the weight of eyes on her, the gravity of observation.

The awkwardness of her steps struck her as abundantly absurd. As absurd as this unfounded sense of dread. As absurd as the possibility of being followed through the empty woods.

But not as absurd, she knew, as having this feeling and not doing something about it.

Further down the path, closer to the lake but away from the house, she remembered that the trail wrapped around a rock outcropping. The sharp angle would cut off the line of sight behind her and allow her a small distance, just enough to catch her breath. Beneath her quickening steps, twigs broke and the echoes behind her made a double set of steps for an imaginary ghost of a pursuer, pushing her to move faster still.

She was embarrassed for herself, acting like a child. But she didn't slow down.

Around her, the woods seemed darker than the afternoon sun should have allowed. The thick legs of trees stood in her way and the ground threw up root walls and bramble bolls that funneled her onwards. This should be the right path, she thought, but then why did it never seem to end? Would the next twist bring her around the safety of the outcropping, or was it hiding something else?

As she began to run, she thought how foolish she must look. Wouldn't that be just what people would expect from her father's daughter, running from shadows and barking at the walls like he had in his final days?

That was, of course, if there was nothing behind her.

Sarah flew down the path, down around the bend, and came to the hook in the trail that she'd been anticipating. Around it she ran, pressing her feet deep into the ground to make her mark, then further, further, then she leapt off the trail. The small leap carried her to a table of partially exposed stones that would hide her tracks until she could make it to a deeper leaf cover. Two giant strides then, and she was clear.

As Sarah made her way up the incline of the ground, she crouched behind the sparse cover of the brush as deftly as her youthful memories could pull her aging body. She remembered to distribute her weight on elbows and palms, knees and toes. Her palms sank into the cool, dark soil, and she remembered in her bones how to hide before she fully realized in her mind that she was doing so. And when she did realize it, when she was pressed into the ground and shadows beneath the dying overgrowth and watching over the trail from above, it struck her how ridiculous all this was.

But only if there was nothing there, of course.

Except for the percussion of her heart and the rasps of her breath, the world was silent. Everything else was silent.

Everything except the sound of breaking twigs, snapping like fingers, coming down the trail.

Down below, moving slowly with knees and elbows held high in a marionette's exaggerated gait, the man crept around the rock. A bushy black beard like a squirrel's nest bobbed with each tiptoed step. He wore a green field jacket and stained jeans, but his boots, even from the distance, were shiny and new.

Whether from the dim light or her own failing eyes, Sarah could not see his face clearly, but she knew she did not know him. Unbidden, the thought that came to her was of an uncomfortable photo of her father as a young man standing next to his own father—a silver-haired and wild-eyed presence that Sarah never knew. The character below was too thin and too strange to be either of them, really, but he had the same uncanny look of being out of place and out of time.

Sarah dug her fingers into the dirt as if she could pull herself down into it and away from him. The way the man swayed like a hollow tree in an unseen breeze made her nauseous. As his loose steps carried him past her hiding place, she could tell by the way he rolled his head from side to side that he was scanning the trail.

Against her better judgment, she shut her eyes. The methodical creak of the forest underfoot continued as he meandered past. She let herself exhale slowly in the self-inflicted darkness.

The sounds stopped. The forest was a tomb again.

She opened her eyes.

A few strides beyond where she had left the path, the bearded man had stopped. Oh please, she thought, oh please, keep going. She willed him onward, as if her prayers could convince unseen hands to pluck at him, cuffs and collar, and carry him out of her life.

But he did not move on. Instead, he bent at the waist, almost in half. Close enough to sniff the ground, Sarah thought, and to see where her footfalls ended. The lolling of his head became more agitated as he surveyed the ground, and the thinness of her defenses beneath the brush struck her in the stomach. The entire forest was thinner, weaker, than she had thought even a moment ago.

No, she thought, no, no, no.

Like a birdsong in the silence, her thoughts seemed to pierce the still world around her and the man stopped. As he drew himself back to his full and unsteady height, Sarah recognized the look of someone who felt the pressure of hidden eyes.

He turned head first, his body following. He looked back the way he had come. Then to the downhill slope off the trail, towards the lake and away from Sarah. Then, rolling like a searchlight, he turned towards the uphill slope, towards Sarah and her father's house beyond.

Calm, she thought, just be calm. Maybe he was a neighbor, or a hunter, or a fisher or even a meter man. Maybe he thought she was an intruder or that she was lost. Maybe he was here to help. What other reason could there be?

She should stand up then. She should call to him.

But she didn't. Instead, she watched as he raised his long, pale fingers to his face. She watched as he slowly peeled away his beard and crumpled it beneath deft, insectile movements before pressing the now abandoned disguised into a jacket pocket. Through the dimming light-dappled shade, Sarah could see the smile that split his naked face.

The man lowered onto all fours in the middle of the trail. It wasn't necessarily animalistic, but an exaggerated style of crawling that her father had once tried to teach her. One for cover and for quickness, for stalking and passing undetected.

Then he moved, scurrying into the undergrowth on Sarah's side of the trail and disappearing into the thin vegetation. The leaves whispered in his wake, spreading like the ripples from the canoe's prow as it cut the water. But that momentary susurration faded, and then the breeze began to blow.

Below her on the hill, she heard the fallen leaves shiver. But if it was the man, bent over and scuttling on all fours, or the reawakened wind worrying the ground, she did not know. The birds and the bugs were still catatonic, but the rest of the world seemed positively cacophonous as every creak and crinkle in the dead and dried woods around her seemed to cry at once.

Behind her, further up the slope, was her father's house. The house with doors and windows and locks. She knew the general direction was back towards the setting sun, but there was no direct path from here. She would have to stumble towards it, groping back for its safety.

Down the slope was the lake. More than one path to the water, as her father had said, and all of it was downhill. That way was a sure thing, the slopes all leading into a single depression and, from there, to her father's canoe on the embankment's high edge. But beyond that was the flat and empty water. Maybe there were fishermen, though, in their own boats or even on the distant landing, but she didn't know. There could be anything out there.

Small stones dug into her hands and legs. She became very aware of the fragility of the shell of the bush surrounding her. She had to make a choice, but which way to go? The house, of course, was clearly the safest and most familiar destination.

She would rise and turn and slowly, very slowly, begin to make her way back. If she could just get high enough, get close enough, she could find her way back and lock herself in.

But then the leaves rustled behind her on the hill, maybe fifteen, twenty feet away. They whispered to her of something circling around, cutting her off.

It was humming a song.

So Sarah ran. She burst through the flimsy concealment and sprinted down the slope, surrendering to gravity as it pulled her away from the noise between her and the house. She may have screamed, but she couldn't tell.

The velocity of terror guided her acceleration around trees and over stones. She stumbled as branches clawed at her clothes, her face, her hair. Everything in that forest seemed to drop its final pretense at summer and grasp with raw splinter fingers to hold her back, to never let her leave.

But she refused.

As she ran, her feet caught on the bones of bedrock that pierced the earth's soft old skin. The granite teeth of the ravine bit at her, the years having pulled back the soil to reveal the colossal skull of the world that had always been hiding beneath. She burst through clots of dry kindling and tore past an uprooted tree that squirmed with ten thousand legs in the gathering shadows. Down, she ran, towards the end of the forest and the rim of the lake below.

She could not hear anything above her own thrashing, but she knew that the man was still behind her. She knew, in her deepest heart, that he was dancing down the hill like a spider, the rest of his disguises falling off of him like the autumn leaves.

Oh please, Sarah thought or even said, please let it still be there.

Let the canoe be there and let it not be chained. Of all the things that time has made strange and taken from me, please let it have left me just this one.

And there it was, unclaimed by the years, perching on the lip of the embankment as if it were waiting to set off for the horizon's empty edge. Without breaking stride, Sarah gripped the bow, wrenching it down the slope and across the short and rocky bank. It groaned and gasped, but neither the nails of the undergrowth nor the teeth-sharp stones could hold her back as she flung it and herself out into the lake's cold and black expanse.

Her pants soaked through to her calves, her knees. Sarah shivered as she hoisted herself into the canoe, rocking wildly, then grabbed the paddle and smashed it against the dull water, beating her way further out into the empty spread.

She knew it wasn't very deep, as far as lakes go, but it looped around bends and inlets that spread like crooked fingers along the shore. On the farthest side, the fishermen's landing pushed out into the stagnant mirror of water, away from the woods and the pursuer, but away from the house, as well. Far away from the doors and the walls and any safety she could have found barricading herself in her father's old homestead.

But just then, and for just a moment, the serenity of the lake took Sarah like a drug. For just a moment she forgot the frenzy of the last few minutes. She forgot the havoc of the last few months, of all the death all around.

"How could anything ever be wrong out here," her father had asked her once. Years ago, under the clear blue sky and unblemished sun, with the strong summer forest cradling them in its palm, she couldn't disagree.

But now, with the wilting trees gripping the black lake under the bruising sky and the sun setting behind the house in the distance, she didn't know how it could ever be otherwise. She stared at the golds and reds of the forest and it seemed as if that whole shore behind her was burning with the dying foliage, giving off the smoke of the night. She could never go back; she knew that now.

She turned to look at the distant landing, but there was not a light or a soul to be seen. Of course it was empty. No one ever comes down here but you and me, her father had said. It was too late in the season, and surely too late in the day, and there was nothing on that far side but an empty shore and uncertain terrain. Many paths leading from the water, she imagined, but she didn't know where to.

So Sarah laughed. Laughed at the darkening plateau of the pond. Laughed at the absurdity and at herself and at the absolute isolation reflected back at her on every side.

And as she laughed, as she looked back to the silent immolation of the autumn leaves and the sunset consuming her father's house and the woods behind her, the man emerged onto the shore. Like the memory of a picture, his details were smeared beneath the gloaming's thumb.

She watched as he stooped to pick up fist-sized rocks from the water line. She watched him stuff them into the pockets of his field jacket.

Even now, as the darkness won the sky, she saw his glistening smile as his shiny boots broke the water's mirror surface. He smiled as he went in past his knees, past his stomach, past his chin. His head disappeared without any bubbles, leaving only a gentle ring of ripples that spread like the whisper of the leaves before it vanished.

The water was still again, its murky shadows concealing fish and driftwood and a grinning man and who could ever know what else. Sarah was alone here, in the wide spread of nothing, with only that thin membrane between her and that hidden depth and everything within it.

Sarah dug her paddle's blade into the waters and pushed forward, towards the far and darkening shore.

And Elm Do Hate

Nina Shepardson

1.

WYCH-ELM OR WITCH-ELM, n: A species of deciduous tree, scientific name *Ulmus glabra*, found throughout much of Europe and western Asia. Also known as witch-hazel.

2.

"ABNER? ABNER, WHERE are you?" Abigail turned in a circle, leaves crunching under her feet. "Abner, I give up! You win!" Her lower lip trembled, and she clenched her hands into fists. "I don't want to play this game anymore! Just tell me where you are!"

A cry came from where the sun was setting, so faint she almost mistook it for the wind. "Abby..."

Abigail sprinted toward the sound, weaving around tree trunks and ignoring the underbrush that tore at her dress. The wails grew stronger. "I'm here! I'm in the tree!"

Abigail pushed through the low-hanging branches of a pine and emerged in a clearing. A tall wych-elm stood in the center. Drooping boughs festooned with bright green leaves formed a cave around the wrinkled gray trunk. The branches were shaking, and Abner's shouts were clearly coming from somewhere within. "Abby! Abby, I'm in here! I'm stuck!"

Abigail slipped under one of the branches, its leaves brushing her face and hair like their governess's hands. It was dim under the tree, as if the sun had already set. She peered upward, but Abner was nowhere to be seen.

Then the tree trunk shuddered and bulged as if something was pounding against it from inside. Edging closer, she spied a patch of blue: Abner's checked trousers showing through a hole in the trunk.

Abigail jumped and grabbed a low-hanging branch. Swinging her legs up, she pulled herself into the tree and scrambled in toward the trunk. It was thick but hollowed out, and Abner crouched in the well in its center. His hair was mussed, his waistcoat was torn, and sweat streaked his face. "Take my hand; I'll pull you out!"

Abner reached up, his slim fingers locking around her pudgy ones. Abigail wrapped her legs around the tree branch in what their governess would have considered a most unladylike way, and yanked. At first, nothing happened, but then Abner began to slide upward. The tree trunk felt like it was molding itself around him, and Abigail could have sworn there was a popping sound when he finally came free. His hand slipped from Abigail's grasp, and he tumbled off her branch to the ground. "Abner!"

Abner stood up, wincing as he put weight on his left foot. "All's well, Abby, I've only twisted my ankle a mite." Then his eyes widened. "Abby, get down! Get down now!"

Abby put her hands on the branch and swung her legs down, hanging from the branch for a moment before dropping to the earth. "What—"

"Please, Abby! We must get home!"

"I'm not arguing with you, but—" Seeing how frightened Abner was, Abby stopped. She let him wrap an arm around her shoulders and helped him limp out from under the confines of the wych-elm's branches.

3.

All the birds in the forest they bitterly weep
Saying, "Where shall we shelter or where shall we sleep?"
For the Oak and the Ash, they are all cutten down
And the walls of bonny Portmore are all down to the ground.

—from "Bonny Portmore," a traditional Irish folk song

4.

COLONEL JACOB BRADFORD strolled through the forest, whistling a cheerful tune. His homecoming celebration had been delightful, but the soft breeze, the twittering of birds in the high branches, and the sunlight peeking through those branches to illuminate the forest floor were even more appealing. The unspoiled countryside where he had spent much of his boyhood had come to symbolize everything he loved, everything he had fought to protect.

He entered a clearing and saw a great wych-elm standing before him. Green leaves spilled down from a lofty crown like fountains, shifting in the breeze to reveal a trunk so big he wouldn't have been able to put his arms around it. Colonel Bradford ducked beneath the branches and sat down on the mossy ground, leaning back against the trunk with a grateful sigh.

The bark wasn't as rough as he'd expected; on the contrary, it felt soft, as if he were sinking into a down mattress. He closed his eyes, breathing deep of the rich smell of loam and leaves.

Colonel Bradford was disconcerted to detect another scent underlying the wholesome one. It was earthy, but not the smell of soil. Mud. It was mud, though the ground beneath him was dry. Mud, and the kind of rain that doesn't wash things clean but instead turns the world into a dreary, soggy mess. And rising up through the mud like bubbles, another stench, sharp and coppery. All at once, the softness of the trunk at his back wasn't the welcome comfort of a down mattress, but the sticky give of a trench wall soaked by never-ending rain.

He lurched to his feet, and something with the consistency of pudding pulled away from his back. He stumbled out from under the branches and into the open space of the clearing. Turning to look back over his shoulder, he no longer thought that the bowed branches resembled graceful fountains. Now they looked like green slime bubbling over the lip of a cauldron.

It's shell shock. Shell shock, nothing more. Beating a hasty retreat out of the clearing, Colonel Bradford almost believed that.

5.

A SPECIES THAT evolved on the open savannah will naturally be uncomfortable in an impenetrable forest, where predators and odder things may lurk within a few steps of the unwary traveler. We can see this discomfort reflected in traditional folklore: the witch who captures Hansel and Gretel lives in a forest, as do Baba Yaga and the Erlking. A number of modern stories intended to horrify center around trees or forests as well, such as Algernon Blackwood's "The Man Whom the Trees Loved" and H.P. Lovecraft's "The Tree on the Hill."

6.

HARRY LUMBERED THROUGH the thick underbrush, leaving the sound of heavy machinery and the smell of asphalt behind. Other members of the crew actually used their coffee break to drink coffee, but Harry had something better than that.

Nettles and saplings gave way to a clearing that exuded an air of seclusion despite being only a three minute walk from the new road. The single tree in the center of the clearing was magnificent, and Harry felt a fleeting gladness that their plans didn't call for them to chop this one down. With a grunt, he sat down against the trunk and pulled out his stash and rolling paper from an inside pocket of his coat. This was almost as comfortable as sitting in his recliner at home. The only things missing were the can of beer and the football game on the telly.

The foreman was annoyed when Harry didn't come back from his coffee break on time. As the hours passed and he failed to emerge from the woods, annoyance turned into concern. A few men who could be spared were sent in to look for him. The half-smoked joint they found beneath a stately wych-elm told them that Harry had stopped for a few minutes in this clearing, but they never did figure out where he'd gone after that.

7.

IN 1943, FOUR children found a human skeleton hidden inside the hollow trunk of a wych-elm in the Hagley Woods of Worcestershire. The skeleton was that of a human female who had died of asphyxiation in 1941. Although a definitive identification was never made, many believed the victim to be a prostitute known as Bella. After this speculation was voiced on a BBC Radio 4 broadcast, graffiti demanding to know "Who put Bella in the Wych Elm?" began appearing in the local area.

8.

UNLIKE THE OTHER trees of the forest, the wych-elm in the clearing didn't play host to nesting birds. No squirrels scampered through its branches, and no moles or foxes sheltered beneath its boughs. Even other trees left a perimeter around it, hence the clearing.

When the elm bark beetles arrived in the British Isles in the 1960s, most of the other elms in the region succumbed. Their serrated leaves turned yellow and brown, dried up and fell from the branches. But the wych-elm in the clearing was unaffected. Its leaves remained vibrant, and while its branches slumped, it was not from weakness.

A few arborists cataloguing the remaining elms in the area made note of the wych-elm. It was listed several times because each purple ribbon the arborists tied around its trunk to mark it as uninfected fell to the ground and was quickly subsumed into the loam. No one was present to watch the ribbons fall, but if they had been, they would have seen the trunk expand and contract like the chest of a breathing man, stretching until the ribbon snapped.

What they did notice was a spongy texture to the trunk, but this didn't make it into any of the written records, since the clear absence of withered leaves and beetle feeding galleries showed that the softness wasn't indicative of Dutch elm disease.

9.

ELM TREES HAVE a reputation for shedding branches even in the absence of wind. On some occasions, these unexpected falling branches have injured—or even killed—bystanders. As a result, several ominous folk aphorisms have developed regarding this genus of tree. "Oak do brood, and elm do hate," says one, while another warns, "Elm hateth man, and waiteth."

10.

Clara gasped as they entered the clearing. The tree in its center was huge, a broad gray trunk with striated bark crowned by a jungle's worth of leaves.

"Pretty impressive, isn't it?" Michael asked.

"This must be the oldest wych-elm in the whole county!" She poked at her tablet with a stylus. "You should definitely take measures to preserve this."

She stepped toward the gently waving branches. Michael suppressed the urge to call her back, or to reach out and grab her arm. He had passed the wych-elm many times on his walks through the woods, and had sometimes considered stopping to eat lunch in its shade. But going close to it had always made the hairs on the back of his neck stand on end, and he'd hurried away, glancing back over his shoulder as if he wanted to be sure that the tree wasn't following him.

Clara was barely visible through the leaves now. "I don't see any signs of disease or damage at all," she called back to him. Her voice was muffled by the greenery. "The bark is perfectly—"

Her voice cut off, and Michael was overwhelmed by the sense of an expected disaster coming to pass, like seeing two cars on a collision course and knowing they were going too fast for either of them to stop in time. "Clara! Clara, are you okay?"

Clara stumbled out from under the elm's canopy, her hair disheveled and her stylus dropping from her fingers. "I'm fine," she said, pushing strands of hair back into place. "I just got a little—the heat, you know."

In fact, it was a mild day, and the trees blocked enough of the sunlight that it wouldn't have been too unpleasant even at midsummer. But Michael nodded acceptance of her explanation. He could see Clara's stylus lying in the grass just at the edge of where the overhanging leaves slopped down to the ground. He certainly wasn't going to go get it, and he suspected that if he pointed it out to Clara, she would find some reason not to approach as well.

"Anyway," she said in an aggressively businesslike tone, "it's a very old, healthy tree, and whatever you end up doing with the land, you should make sure it's protected."

No, Michael thought, *I should make sure it's chopped into pieces, and have the pieces burned. Do it out on the open moor, and make sure no one breathes in the smoke.* He and Clara left the clearing, and as always, he looked back as they did. He couldn't be sure, but he thought that maybe some of the leaves had curled around the stylus and were drawing it up.

A Silence of Starlings

Kurt Fawver

EVERY MORNING FOR the past four years I've been woken by the whistles and trills of the starlings in the gnarled oak tree outside my window. They don't sing so much as converse and it's a conversation that's always given me hope somehow. It's a lot like my kids, so long ago. Behind closed doors, they'd sit in their rooms and talk to their friends on the phone and sing along to music and laugh at television shows. They were constantly making the noise of lives well lived. And I was always a bystander, a watcher through the window. I had no idea what they were really doing, what they were really thinking. But I could hear their energy through the walls, the doors. I could hear their dreams and desires bubbling over, their excited plans and personal celebrations, muffled and murmured though they might have been to my ears. And that gave me hope. There was passion and promise hidden within their rooms and even if they didn't share it with me I knew it wasn't too far away. The starlings out in the twisted old oak whose branches tap against my window pane give me that same feeling. I wake up to their chirrups and think, "Today is a day when things might get better, when things might change. There's energy in the air."

But the starlings didn't sing today.

I drifted awake and there was silence, so much silence I thought maybe I was dead. No birds. No wind. Not even a fragile tick from the alarm clock on my nightstand. Dead. I was sure. But then I heard the creak of a wheelchair down the hallway and the metronome beep of Harry Bernson's heart monitor next door and knew—no, that's not right, I *assumed*—I was still alive because surely eternity wouldn't include a house of infirmities like this one.

I rolled over and checked the clock. It had stopped on 5:55. I thought I wound it the night before, but maybe not. At my age, the mind contains more dark ravines than bright mountaintops. I fumbled for my wristwatch—a present from my Suzanne before she passed and, thankfully, digital—and the heat of panic began to spread up my spine when I saw the time. 10:41. The starlings weren't my only concern. I needed my pills.

The staff usually wakes us for breakfast and our morning medication around 6:30. We call those early morning rounds what they really are: the body count. Obviously, though, no one had been by my room to knock and make sure I was still breathing today. Maybe, I thought, they were running late or maybe they'd forgotten me. But that never happens. If it's one thing this place has going for it, it's efficiency. In and out, quick and clean—that's how everyone on the staff here works. I think it's mostly because the more time they spend with us, the more they have to look at us and the more they look at us, the more they're forced to realize that we're all just sacks of meat in various stages of spoliation. Not a pleasant thought for the younger set.

Having already overslept by hours, I decided to track down a nurse or an orderly for my pills and then shuffle down to the cafeteria to grab some food. A nice bowl of oatmeal with banana slices. Cup of coffee. Nothing fancy. I had to save room because today was different. Today wouldn't be a day like most other days, with me sitting by a window, wondering whether anyone would notice if I just walked outside and never came back. It wouldn't be like most other days, with me playing four-hour checkers games with poor Jenny Sturm, who has Alzheimer's. It wouldn't be like most other days, with me staring at the phone, willing it to ring, just once, and for someone to say hello and tell me they wondered how my day was. Nope. Today was different because I had a birthday party to attend and I was damned if I wasn't going to gobble up some cake and have a good time.

I checked the note I'd written to myself when my oldest son, Zachory, had called last week: "Camilla's 10th B-Day Party—Saturday, April 18—Zachory or Annie will pick me up by 2." This was only the second time I'd seen Cammy since Christmas. Such a good girl. Crazy smart. Funny. A lot like her grandma. I guess that's why they got along so well. I guess that's why I love them both so much. I don't see her often, though. I don't see much of anyone often. My daughter Janice and her partner Zora live two thousand miles away. My youngest, Nick, hasn't called me in nine months. And Zachory and his wife Annie are always so busy with their jobs; much too busy to visit. But sometimes they drop off Cammy for an afternoon and when Cammy's here, we have a blast. We race wheelchairs. We paint pictures together—a lion landing on the moon in a space suit was our last masterpiece. At Christmas, we had a milk and cookies-eating contest that neither Zachory nor Annie nor any of my nurses knew about. Sure, we both felt a little sick afterward, but if an old man can't indulge his granddaughter, well, then there's probably no point in growing old.

I pocketed the note and braced for shooting pains in my knees and hips as I swung myself out of bed. The arthritis was acting up, bad. I pawed at my cane—another present from my ever-adored and ever-missed Suzy—but my fingers could barely curl around its raven-headed handle.

While I was trying my best to loosen up my rusty hinges and pull myself off the bed, Patricia Cortez shuffled into my doorway. Her eyes were large and wild; they darted around my room, searching for something or someone.

"They're not here, either?" she asked me, almost pleading.

I stood with effort, so many joints popping I sounded like a New Year's Eve party just before midnight, champagne corks flying. "Who?" I asked.

Patricia kneaded her hands in a ritual of anxiety. "Katisha. Alexis. Franklin. Any of them. The nurses. Where are they? Have they been to see you today?"

"No." I shook my head. "I overslept. No one came for the body count today. Maybe we've all already died."

Patricia's jaw went slack and I could see a tsunami of tears cresting behind her frightened puppy dog eyes. It's been one of the curses of my life to never be able to say the right thing to anyone. Suzy forgave the awkwardness, the social fumbling. Maybe even loved me for it. She understood that I didn't want to be weird and distant, but I didn't know any other way, even with my own children.

"A joke," I said, forcing out a sputtering laugh. "Just a joke. Sorry. We're clearly still alive. At least as much as we were yesterday. Pinch yourself if you don't believe me."

She did, and seemed satisfied enough with the painful results. "Well, we still need our medications," she said. "Charmaine told me she went downstairs to the nurses' station an hour ago, but no one was in it. Some of the staff's cars are in the parking lot, but whoever drove them isn't here, anywhere. I think we're going to have to break in to the nurses' station. That's what Charmaine thought, too."

I considered Charmaine breaking down the door to the nurses' station. Eighty-one year old, four foot ten, ninety pound, hot tempered and always opinionated Charmaine Jackson, landing a flying kick to the door.

I grinned at the possibility. "Charmaine would be the one to do it."

Patricia took a step into my room, then paused, her mouth pursed as though she wanted to say something more. She glanced at my open window.

"Does it seem like the sunlight isn't quite right? Or is that me?"

I turned to look. I saw sunlight. Maybe it was a little dimmer than usual, a few shades more grey than white, but I didn't think it was all that notable.

"Probably just overcast," I said. I hobbled over for a better view. Outside, the leaves of the ancient oak where the starlings usually perched didn't stir. Nothing stirred. Not a bee or a butterfly or a bird or even a car on the street beyond the lawn. I moved into the light's direct rays, and, for no reason I could understand, I was overcome with a bout of shivers. Where the light fell upon me, it felt like a sheet of ice passing a hair's breadth above my skin. It had to be in my head, though. The power of suggestion and all.

I pulled the curtain shut and snatched up the television remote control from my nightstand.

Patricia wagged a finger at the window. "See? You see? It's not right. And the TV's not working, either. You might as well not even bother with that."

I turned on the television and was greeted by a big blue box that read "No Signal." A tiny knot formed in my throat. We definitely needed to find the nurses and the rest of the staff. We needed to hear from somebody that everything outside was okay, that we weren't adrift here, forgotten.

"See?" Patricia asked. "No TV at all. And don't bother 9-1-1. You get a weird clicking noise. The internet won't load anything either. I tried on the computer in the lounge. It just says 'No connections found.' Anyway, I'm going to keep checking rooms for the nurses. Someone must have seen them."

As Patricia turned to leave, I asked her, "Do the phones work at all? Can we call other numbers? Besides 9-1-1?"

She meandered out of my room and into the hallway beyond without responding. She probably didn't hear me. Very few of us can hear any sound quieter than a scream.

I hobbled to the room's phone and picked up the receiver. The usual dial tone hummed from some distant place where nothing ever changes and everyone is safe. I reached into the pocket of my pajama pants and drew out a folded slip of paper with the phone numbers for my children written on it. Whatever pair of pants I'm wearing, that piece of paper goes in a pocket. I guess you can call me a ridiculous old man, but just having those numbers nearby makes me feel a little better, like maybe my kids aren't so far away, like maybe just having that small connection means I didn't fail as a father. Sometimes I call and talk to the answering machines or the voice mail or whatever answers in place of my children. I don't say much. I never know what to say. I guess that's why they don't call back very often.

I tugged on my reading glasses, unfolded the paper, and dialed Zachory's cell phone. It kicked over to a prerecorded message. I hung up, the knot in my throat tightening.

I dialed Annie's cell phone. It kicked over to a prerecorded message. I hung up again and swallowed hard.

I thought: *Today is Cammy's 10th birthday. My note says so. I can't miss that birthday. She'll get a kick out of what I bought her: an easel and a set of paints that glow in the dark.*

I dialed Zachory and Annie's home line. It kicked over to their answering machine.

"Hi, Zachory," I rasped. "It's your dad. I hope everything's going okay there. We're having some technical problems here. Wondering if you are, too. I hope our plans for today haven't changed. Please call me if you can."

I hung up and immediately cursed my reticence. I should've said "I love you." I never forgot with Suzy. I was never anxious about saying it to her. Same with Cammy. It just comes easy with the kid. But with Zachory and Janice and Nick, I'm too worried about messing something up. I don't know what that something is, exactly, but it scares me and makes my other worries feel insignificant, even foolish.

I refolded the phone paper and stuck it back into my pocket. Maybe I could try Janice or Nick later, but I had to find my pills before I did anything else. Just holding the phone and creasing that old sheet of paper curled my fingers into claws and set wildfires in each of my knuckles. If I didn't pop a Rheumatrex and some Aleve soon, I'd be lucky to be up and about by the afternoon.

Creaking and cracking as though I were made of warped wooden boards and rusty nails, I shuffled to the elevator and took it to the ground floor where, it so happened, almost every mobile resident of our community had congregated. As I stepped out into the activities room I received some nods and a few furtive smiles, but the buzz of conversation in the room was tense, anxious. At the far side of the room, opposite the elevator, a small crowd had gathered outside the door to the empty nurses' station. They watched as Charmaine Jackson and "Iron" Eddie Person, who was once a star college linebacker, rammed the door with one of the heavy metal carts that the staff used to bring meals to bedridden residents. It took five good strikes with that battering ram, but the door broke from its moorings and hit the floor with a thunderclap. Everyone rushed the station, scrambling for their medication, their shots, their towlines to another tomorrow.

And that's when we heard it. As everyone, me included, tried to shove inside the station and snatch up pills, the phone rang. The home only has one main line. All our rooms have extension numbers. So for the nurses' phone to ring meant that someone was calling the home itself, and not one of us in particular. It could mean news. It could mean explanations.

Charmaine ducked beneath an outstretched arm and answered. "Hello?"

We all froze.

Charmaine scowled. "Who?" A pause. Then, again. "Who?"

She held out the receiver and yelled, "Liza! Liza Collingham! They're asking for you. I think."

Liza was one of the newer residents. A series of strokes had brought her here. She still couldn't really move her right arm or walk without support, and yet she flashed past me like a sprinter half her age.

No one else dared breathe.

Liza took the phone, said "Hello," then went silent. Everyone in the nurses' station stared expectantly. Charmaine whispered, "Tell them about the staff."

But Liza said nothing. She nodded twice and replaced the phone in its cradle. She looked up and smiled in a way I'd only seen in Renaissance paintings of mysterious, all-knowing women.

The room exploded in questions and accusations.

"Why didn't you say anything to them?"

"Who was it?"

"Did they say what was going on?"

"You could've told them we needed help."

"You should've said something."

I didn't join in. I was more interested in that weird smile.

Finally, under the din, Liza said something.

Everyone quieted and she spoke a second time, her words soft and sheer, as if her tongue had unraveled them from a spool of silk.

"They're coming for me."

Charmaine grabbed onto Liza's good arm. "Who? Who was that? I could barely hear 'em. A lot of strange noises in the background."

Liza patted Charmaine's hands and said, "They told me that my two daughters are coming for me."

More questions swirled: "Who told you that?" "Did they tell you why we don't have any television?" "Was it one of the nurses?" "Can I come with you?"

Liza turned to us, beacons of triumph glowing in her eyes. "They told me," she said. "The people on the phone. They told me. Maybe they'll call for you, too."

And the phone rang again.

OVER THE NEXT two hours, the phone rang sixteen more times. I don't know if seventeen is a magic number or has some kind of metaphysical significance, but that's how many calls came in, and every one promised a ride and a rescue. None of them were for me, of course, but that was expected. My family already had plans to pick me up and I couldn't hope for more than their promises. Even so, I loitered in the lounge with the rest of the mobile members of our community and secretly wished that my name might be shouted following one of the rings. That wish faded fast when I began to see how strange my neighbors who did receive calls acted after they'd talked to the people on the phone.

Except for Liza, who sneaked away to her room, every one of the recipients clammed up and sidled over to the grimy bay windows in the lounge, where they stood together in the cold light from outside and hummed low, monotone notes to themselves—not songs, mind you, but bare tones. To me, the humming sounded like that noise you hear when you stand under high voltage power lines. Martika Jessup, a woman from the first floor who sometimes played piano for us when her Parkinson's allowed her fingers to slow their frantic dance, said that those hummed notes made her uneasy because they weren't really notes at all but the frequencies between notes. Whatever our neighbors were doing, she said, had no basis in music. I didn't entirely understand what she meant but the humming made my skin crawl, too.

One of my casual acquaintances in the home, Paul Blackmon, a man I played chess with a couple times every month, was a call recipient. As he stood by the windows humming his anti-music, I hobbled up next to him, tapped his shoulder, and asked him what he was doing. He stopped humming and, without turning to me, said "Waiting for it to turn."

"Waiting for what to turn?" I asked, but he had resumed his humming and paid me no further attention.

During the spate of calls, only the seventeen people who received them and Charmaine, who insisted on manning the phone and screening all incoming messages "in case it was the authorities," heard the voices of salvation on the other end of the line. After my peculiar interaction with Paul, I asked Charmaine if there had been anything odd about the voices. She told me that they sounded "damn peculiar," but in a way that was hard to describe.

"Like when you set a record's speed just a notch too high," she said. "But also sort of like an answering machine that's not really talking to you so much as talking at you. Sends a chill right through me, though I can't rightly say why."

By the time the last of the calls had come in and the phone had settled into prolonged silence, it was after noon. The internet was still unresponsive, 9-1-1 was still down, and the staff still hadn't arrived. Our bedridden compatriots, many of whom lay in their soft coffins feebly moaning for aid, needed to be cared for. Although the rest of us were hungry and on edge, we tried to oblige as best we could. We wrangled pills and injectables and set off to help our siblings in enfeeblement traverse the terrain between mattress and toilet. As I stood with my hand on the paper-thin shoulder of a man whose name I didn't even know and tried to coax him to choke down a barrelful of capsules and tablets, most of which he spit up onto his chest, I could only think that whoever had called old age the "Golden Years" must have died young.

I fled to my room as soon as our goodwill mission had ended, my hands smelling of urine from inexpertly emptying catheter bags and my joints already beginning to protest against their extended use. I scrubbed my arms in my room's sink then tried the television again, but the only news it carried was that there was still no signal.

I slumped on my bed and stared out the window. Thoughts of dialing Zachory and Annie and leaving another message fluttered at my temples.

I glanced at Cammy's present, silver wrapped and patiently seated on the chair in the corner of the room. The girl was going to be famous one day, was going to do important things. She was too sharp and too creative not to. I remembered her second grade Christmas program. She wrote a fifteen-minute play about being kind to homeless people for it. The plot included ghosts and a talking dog and the president of the United States who, if I recall, was an astrophysicist named Lilac. The rest of the kids in her class performed and she and her teacher directed. I think that was the day I knew she was going to be someone who changed the world. I wish Suzy was still around to see her. I wish Suzy was still around for a million reasons. This is what it is to be an old man: every thought becomes a wormhole to the past.

A voice from behind shook me from the embrace of nostalgia.

"Have you been watching outside? It's scarier than the people downstairs."

Patricia Cortez again, on the threshold of my room. I wondered if she was patrolling our hallway, seeking any ears that might be receptive to her worries.

"What are you talking about?"

Patricia bumbled into the room and motioned at the window but refused to come any closer to it.

"You don't see? You don't notice?"

I looked. I saw the chill, grey-toned bowl of the heavens. I saw the imposing oak, devoid of avian or insect amongst its branches. I saw the lawn outside, a wild scrubland rarely mowed or groomed. And I saw the road that ran parallel to the home, chock full of potholes and in desperate need of line repainting.

"No." I shrugged. "What am I supposed to see?"

Patricia shuffled closer. "The cars," she whispered. "There aren't any. There haven't been any all day. I've been keeping track."

She was right. I waited and watched, but the road outside the home remained barren. Normally, vehicles of all manner pass by, as our wrinkled enclave lies just two miles from a large shopping plaza that includes a supermarket, a big-box store, and a Chinese buffet restaurant. Apparently no one was out shopping or gorging themselves today, though.

I stared at the road, curious where the cars had gone, a pin of unease stuck in my throat, and the road stared back, taunting me with the knowledge that it stretched to far off places well beyond the horizon, places I'd surely never see again.

I turned to ask Patricia whether she'd seen any airplanes or helicopters in the sky, but she'd disappeared from my room just as suddenly as she always appeared. Sometimes I thought that she must be a ghost that only I could see. In many ways the same could be said for all of us here at the home.

As the afternoon crept by, I loaded up on another round of pills and tottered my way back downstairs. I had to be ready if—no, no, when—Zachory and Annie showed up.

The call recipients were still in the rec room where I'd left them, waiting for their rides by the windows, humming their monotone hymn. I couldn't believe that some of them hadn't collapsed from exhaustion. Maybe the calls had imbued them with superpowers. Maybe a mystical energy generated by their hum had somehow shaved a few years of wear from their bodies. Or maybe the mere idea of jailbreaking the home, even if only for a few hours, had gifted them something that the sterile beige walls of the home seemed to constantly leach from us: a purpose to go on living.

Charmaine, still seated in the nurses' station and hovering over the phone, motioned for me to join her. I'd never seen her frown. When she lost half her toes to diabetes last year, she laughed about it and said she was never good at dancing anyway. When doctors told her that she was too old to receive a bypass operation for her clogged and failing heart, she shrugged and flipped them her middle finger. But today, in the dim light of the nurses' station where few people could see, the weight of worry dragged down the corners of her mouth.

"I've been thinking," she said as I walked in, "you're an intelligent man, a learned man. A former teacher, right?"

I nodded. I had been a teacher. I wasn't so sure about the rest of it.

"So what do you make of them?" She pointed to the hummers at the far end of the rec room.

I studied the backs of their heads, the unflinching postures. "They're very...focused," I said.

Charmaine chuckled but her frown somehow remained. "Yeah, a little too focused. Have you ever seen anyone their age stand in place that long? Their feet must be swollen up like cantaloupes. But that's not what I mean. I mean they're all a little off. Up here." Charmaine tapped her forehead.

I ran down the list of the people by the window and their infirmities. Blackmon, stroke. Greer, stroke. Cutter, Alzheimer's. Chandra, stroke. Reyes, Alzheimer's. Samuels, Alzheimer's. As I mumbled their conditions to myself, I realized I was repeating only two primary debilitations.

Charmaine could see the comprehension dawning in my eyes. "So why them?" she asked. "Why just people with brain injuries? Why do they get to go and not the rest of us?"

I had no idea. Maybe in the answer to that question lay the answer to all questions great and small. Einstein famously said that God doesn't play dice with the universe, and I believe it. God plays much more byzantine games, games that we don't know the rules for, games that we can't possibly understand though they're constantly played out around us, with our lives as their tokens and currency.

"We don't even know where they're going," I said. "Or if they're going anywhere. Maybe no one's actually coming for them." A length of anxiety knotted itself in the center of my chest as I listened to my own words. My hand reached for the phone number sheet folded up in my pocket. I slid it back and forth between my index finger and thumb. Perhaps if I rubbed hard enough, I could summon Zachory like a genie from a lamp. I had only one wish, after all.

Charmaine shook her head and shuddered. "I'm telling you, those phone calls. The voices on the other end..." She broke off mid-thought, suddenly distracted by the people at the window who, without warning or apparent reason, had changed pitch. Their hum was now higher, much higher. It was the skirl of a tea kettle's whistle but indescribably hollow, as though the sound that issued from their throats was an echo from much deeper within themselves or much farther outside our shrinking corner of the world.

Everyone in the rec room who could hear well enough to notice the change dropped what they'd been doing and looked past the hummers to the window itself—for what, none of us was sure.

The room suddenly grew dark, the four tall standing lamps in the corners of the room—lamps that remained on both day and night—becoming soft beacons in a hard-tossed, caliginous sea. Beyond the window settled an impenetrable murk. To call it black would've been wrong. Black implies a color, a substance, a tangible idea. What lay outside was none of those things. Gazing into it reminded me of lonesome nights filled with dreamless sleep and the longing for dead friends and lovers.

Liza Collingham broke from the group by the window and edged toward the reinforced glass double doors to the main entrance.

A pale red glow flashed out from within the murk. It could have been a car's taillights, but it could have just as easily been lightning or UFOs or the bloodstained eyes of a marauding demon.

"They came for me!" Liza called out. "Just like they said!" Before any of us realized what had happened, she pushed open the doors—from which swept a blast of frigid, soul-shattering wind—and walked through, immediately disappearing into the darkness without a sound or a stirring.

Most of the residents who had gathered in the rec room, myself included, were too stunned to say or do anything meaningful. We gaped at the entranceway, now an exit to anywhere. Icy cyclones continued to spin out from the darkness, the windows in the room rapidly frosting over and frostbite snapping at our noses, our fingers, the lobes of our ears.

"Close the goddamned doors!" someone shouted, but no one moved.

I tried to force myself forward, but my body wouldn't respond. Everywhere the currents from the doorway brushed against me, I felt the infinite heaviness of regret. I thought of the darkness in the hallway outside my children's bedrooms when they were younger. I thought of the muffled conversations they held at night, conversations I could never be a part of, conversations I desperately wanted to join. I thought of all the hugs I could've given, but didn't. Paralyzed in every way, I thought of distances even greater than that between the rim of the universe and the center of the human soul.

Unexpectedly and without notice, the people by the window dropped their hum back into its initial register and, outside, the murk disappeared—whether as a precursor or as a response it was impossible to say. Rather than dissipate like a fog or gradually fade into day as nights must do, this darkness simply winked away, its chill uniformity replaced by an abandoned afternoon.

The doors to the home drifted shut with an anticlimactic swoosh.

My thoughts returned to the present, where I found I could move again. In a daze, I shambled to the doors and peeked through. Several other equally curious residents joined me by the entrance. I feared, but half-expected, that Liza Collingham's lifeless body would be sprawled on the other side, frozen stiff or worse. But no. Liza was nowhere to be seen, dead or alive. For that matter, much of the world was nowhere to be seen.

The titanic oak trees and lilac bushes that normally graced the front yard, the gold and blue "Serenity Acres" sign posted by the home's driveway, the cinderblock dentist's office across the street, the fancy new gas station and convenience store next to the dentist's place, even the very tarmac road that ran past the home: all had vanished. There was no concrete foundation left at the dentist's office or the gas station, no gaping holes in the ground where the shrubbery and trees had once been rooted, no indication that anything had gone missing anywhere. Yet I wasn't crazy. Those things had been part of the view from the home since I arrived. It was a view that I knew too well, given that most days there's little else to do here other than stare onto a world we can barely recall without a frayed edge of sadness, a world we helped build and shape but that's perfectly content to continue on without us.

"Where's the gas station?" someone beside me asked.

No one responded because there was no adequate response to give.

After a few minutes of quiet disbelief, we all drifted back into the rec room where I checked the time. If the clocks could be trusted, it was a quarter past one.

My joints were already complaining again, so I took up residence in a cushy, hopelessly stained recliner and waited, keeping the front entrance in my direct line of sight. I no longer believed that I'd taste Cammy's birthday cake later in the afternoon, but I wanted to believe. I wanted a reason, any reason, to believe. So I watched the entrance, just in case.

Ten minutes passed. Twenty minutes passed. I kept watching the entrance, hoping Zachory's car would materialize on the other side, hoping Annie would stroll up to the doors. But neither happened.

By the nurses' station, an argument broke out between Charmaine and a wheelchair-bound man whose name I couldn't remember. He was trying to persuade people to push him outside while Charmaine was trying to prevent anyone from passing through the exit. The man said he wanted to go out to "smell the air today" because, as he put it, "you can tell a lot about the kind of day it is by the way it hits the nose." Charmaine had only to respond, "Liza Collingham went out there, now where is she?" to discourage any would-be volunteers.

As Charmaine and the wheelchair-bound man continued to bicker, the people by the window again raised the pitch of their hum. The argument immediately stopped. A few hearts probably stopped, too.

Just as it had before, the change in pitch coincided with the sudden appearance of the murk, which again slathered everything beyond the home in a thick tar of nothingness and leaked shadows into the rec room. Again a pale, red glow flashed out of the darkness and again one of the call recipients—a hunchbacked man named Vetterly—shuffled to the front doors.

Someone in the back of the room shouted "Don't go out!"

Someone else shouted "It's not your ride!"

And still another person began repeating the word "No" at increasing volumes.

Vetterly placed his hands on the door handles and was ready to yank them open when, from behind him, flew Charmaine Jackson. She grabbed both of Vetterly's shoulders and whipped him around to face her. He struggled against her grip and cried out, "Let me go! They won't wait for me! They won't wait!" but Charmaine refused to release him.

"Help me," she said to whomever could hear. "Help me hold him."

No one stepped forward to lend aid, as everyone's interest was intractably drawn to the lonesome gloom that seemed to wend its way into our souls. I felt it dragging me back to the past, to the frozen storehouse of memory. It became difficult to differentiate my lifetime already lived from the immediacy of the now. The past was so cold, so cold. It crystallized every passing moment and caused some people, places, and events from yesteryear to shatter in my mind's eye, to irrevocably fragment into a million tiny pieces that gently drifted over the surface of my thoughts like an early morning dusting of snow.

"Help me," Charmaine called again as Vetterly twisted and turned and tried to throw elbow jabs to her stomach. But I couldn't help. I was so lost in nostalgia that I was barely even in the room with her.

Charmaine and Vetterly struggled more, but Charmaine was clearly winning. She dragged Vetterly away from the door a few feet, then away a few more feet, and still a few more. As the two fought, the hummers returned to their original pitch and the murk again vanished. Vetterly toppled backward into Charmaine and both went sprawling, landing flat on their backs in the middle of the room with an unpleasant crunch and a curse from Charmaine.

With the murk gone, I regained my sense of time and place and rushed to the prone figures on the floor, where a circle was forming. Charmaine had broken out into a sweat. Her eyes were wide and her teeth clenched.

"Fool just fainted on me," she breathed. "Felt him give out right on top of me. I think I broke my hip. Damned rickety body. Damn fool Vetterly."

While a few people went off in search of a gurney for Charmaine, I bent down and put a hand on Vetterly's chest. I felt neither rise nor fall. I took his pulse. Nothing beat inside him.

I straightened with a series of cracks and said, to no one in particular, "He's not passed out. He's dead."

Everyone milling about the room shook their heads. A volley of questions and hasty conjectures bounced between us. "How?" "Just fell down dead." "What happened to him?" "We didn't let him go outside." "What do we do with him?" "Nothing to be done." Eventually, someone wheeled in a gurney and we managed to lift Charmaine onto it. Someone else dropped a blanket over Vetterly's body.

The people by the window paid no attention to any of the proceedings. They seemed to not notice one of their number was gone, lying lifeless only a few feet away. They seemed not to care.

After I helped find some pain medication for Charmaine, I returned to my post in the cushy chair opposite the exit and checked the time. It was closing in on two o'clock. I sat and I waited and I stared through the glass doors to freedom. As I kept watch, I noticed that the trees and grass in the front lawn, the macadam parking lot where staff and visitors parked, and the parking lots to the businesses across the road had all disappeared. I feared what another round of vanishing meant. I feared that I would never hear the starlings sing again.

Two o'clock came and went. Three o'clock came and went. Four o'clock passed by, showing me its middle finger. Still no one showed. At least, not for me. The darkness, though, the darkness came to visit again and again and again, and every time was the same—the people by the window raised their pitch, a glow flashed from the gloom, and one of the call recipients fled from the home, into the engulfing darkness and its subzero concentrate of yesteryears. Considering what happened with Vetterly, we let them leave without issue.

As the murk ebbed and flowed, it eroded more and more of the world beyond our door. By the time only three people remained at the window, even the sky and the ground had disappeared, lost to the erasure of the darkness, forever washed out and faded to an undifferentiated grey plain that recognized no horizon.

At eight thirty in the evening, the last of the call recipients wandered from the home, alone and as joyful as all the others who'd stepped outside. I can't lie. I wanted to venture outside, too. I wanted to go wherever the red light might take me. But I remained seated in my chair. I worried that I wasn't wanted by the light or the darkness. I worried that something terrible might happen to me on the other side of the exit doors if I wasn't wanted. I worried that, without Suzy, the only right and proper place for me was in this house of the dying.

I reached into my pocket and grabbed my children's phone numbers. I traced the ones and the twos with my thumb. Surely they would've called if they had the time. Surely whatever had happened today must have forced them away from the phone.

I thought about Cammy's present, up in my room, unopened forever, and a tear rolled down my cheek.

The starlings didn't sing today, that much is true, but, really, I suppose today's been like every other day after all.

AYCAYIA

Rowley Amato

ONCE, A YOUNG man named Hector Fuentes crouched on a jetty, taking water samples from the Gowanus Canal, when he looked down and saw a woman's face glaring up at him.

For a moment, he was too surprised to react. The face swished away like a pale ghost. A shock of adrenaline coursed through his body and the flask that he was preparing to dip into the canal dropped from his hands. It splashed into water stained the color of strong, black tea.

He glanced around the canal: a pigeon cooed on a patch of barbed wire. Insects droned and buzzed. Trucks and cars rumbled down the bridges that crisscrossed the water like stitches in an open wound.

Hector shook his head and breathed deep. The face he saw was just a trick of the sunlight, a rainbow in a slick of gasoline. A striper wandered in from the harbor, maybe.

He lay on his belly and peered into the toxic water, thinking of a story his abuelo once told him. Below him, dark eddies rose and churned.

HECTOR HAD SPENT most of his summer trudging along the Gowanus Canal in a kind of sun-sick fugue. He worked as an intern for a small nonprofit called the Friends of the Canal, collecting and cataloguing daily water samples at different points along the banks in preparation for the Superfund cleanup. The work was, he thought, rather excessive; the grant would end in September and the cleanup was coming soon after, so his time spent logging samples felt perfunctory, like homework in the last week of school before break.

Every morning, he drifted in and out of consciousness on the long train rides from his mother's apartment in Alphabet City, all the way out to Union Street. At the office, he checked in with his supervisor, a glum older man with a ruddy nose and wet eyes named Kowalski, who plugged numbers into spreadsheets in a cubicle at the farthest end of the office, dutifully filling out Hector's academic credit forms with little comment beyond the occasional, "Thanks for all your hard work." From the office, he would walk a few short blocks to the water.

The canal was just a New York oddity for many, but over the course of the summer, Hector came to appreciate its mysteries. It seemed to live a secret life of its own, in its little corner of Brooklyn.

He was mesmerized by its unnatural changes in color: one day it was a dark gray that swallowed up the sunlight. The next it was a bright, St. Patty's green, the result of whirling galaxies of algae that bloomed in the stagnant heat. After heavy rain, the storm drains vomited raw sewage into the canal and turned the water brown and fecal, the bulkheads threatening to breach and flood the streets.

He sometimes awoke, choking, in the middle of the night, the smells pervading his dreams. A noxious blend of sea and city: a base of sweet brackishness—the salt of the harbor—mingled with centuries of industrial and human waste, the sour, metallic overtones of VOCs, PCBs, PAHs, and other arcane acronyms. The stench grew stronger as he approached the water, and on hot days the air itself seemed to thrum with poison.

There was a malicious quality to the canal that disturbed Hector. His hands jittered as he walked its banks, waiting for a seagull's caw to break the fetid silence. He jumped when shadows passed over him, when splintery boards sagged under his footsteps. It had a strange effect on sound, and noises were sometimes audible from blocks away as they echoed and ricocheted down the twisting bends and tributaries. He often heard loud clicks, like the gnashing mandibles of an enormous insect.

In the late afternoon, whenever he was finished hopping from jetty to jetty, he would rush back to the office and drop off the day's samples in a basement with a bored assistant, relieved to be free from the canal's lurking predation. His coworkers invited him out for drinks at some Third Avenue dive every now and then, but they too stank of the canal, in their way.

HECTOR IMAGINED THE face again and again as summer dragged on, and soon it became a constant, niggling source of worry in his life.

Every now and then, he would catch a glimpse of something from the corner of his eye—a flash of white streaking through the water; a hand slicing the surface. But whenever he took a second look, he only saw trails of muck or shadows flitting under the surface. He would stare at lights dancing on the water for what felt like hours at a time, as if hypnotized.

Always, he sensed that he was being watched, and he would find himself spinning around when he heard those awful clicks, or when that dreamlike feeling of paranoia became too much to bear. He once caught a bedraggled cat eying him in the shade of an ailanthus tree, but never the invisible thing that stalked him. He regarded this presence as he did the gang of rats that always rummaged through the trash-cans outside his window late at night, or the patch of evil black mold that crept steadily across the bathroom ceiling.

He thought of his abuelo, and he wondered if he was losing his mind. If the Aycayia was real.

WHEN HE WAS young, Hector spent a summer playing dominos with his abuelo, Rafi. He was a slight child, preferring the company of books and videos and D&D monster manuals to that of his peers, who tossed baseballs in the park and threw slapdash fishing lines into the East River. The summer after sixth grade, several weeks into vacation, his mother (who worked long shifts in the Montefiore emergency room and returned home broken and exhausted) issued an ultimatum.

"Mira," she said. "You can either go play with your friends or with abuelito. You're not staying cooped up in the apartment all day."

Hector chose his grandfather.

At first, their time together was awkward and fumbling. Hector was quiet and nervous, the kind of boy who felt a flush of self-conscious embarrassment when he heard groups of people laughing on the street. Rafael Fuentes was loud and boisterous, a real old-fashioned Boricua who had a bushy gray mustache and wore a rumpled linen suit year round. He drew the attention of the entire neighborhood when he walked down Avenue C, and everyone seemed to know his name: the old Jewish and Italian holdouts, the twitching junkies, the defiant warrior poets, even the NYU kids, who treated the neighborhood like some rugged frontier outpost.

Rafi conducted himself in public and private with a certain grand showmanship, an ostentation that made Hector uncomfortable. He reminded Hector of a character in an old spy movie—the jovial, dark-skinned sidekick, armed with a pair of sweat stains and a toothy grin.

Every morning, Rafi would pound on Hector's bedroom door and the two would walk downstairs, carrying a white plastic table and some folding chairs that Rafi found squirreled away in the basement. They would meet the other men on 10th Street and play all day.

At around lunchtime, Rafi would slip Hector a few bucks to buy a pepperoni slice and a mango icee, plus (and here, he would always lower his voice to a whisper) a forty of Budweiser from the bodega down the block. Rafi always let him keep the change, winking as he cracked open the heavy bottle.

"Es nuestro secreto, hijo."

Hector became a strong dominos player in the summer between sixth and seventh grade. He quickly learned to slam the tiles down on the table and talk shit in the Nuyorican machine gun patter as well as any of the old-timers in the neighborhood. Many dropped by to chat, but the core group was always Rafi, Willy Vázquez, and José Silva. They seemed to live in a perpetual cloud of smoke, and Hector would return home reeking of cigarillos, with a headful of tall tales embellished with each telling.

These stories were relayed with a sort of repressed misery that Hector was too young to understand. Only later did he realize that they were mourning for their youths, for their island.

The men would often map out faded scars that traversed their bodies. A pink worm wriggling down Willy's ribcage was the result of a street fight in the Ponce slums (or was it from the knife of a crazed ex-lover?).

An accident with a pedal-powered thresher (or, sometimes, a shark off the coast of Vieques) had left José with a dappled, deformed knee-cap. A reddish half-moon on Rafi's neck was, he claimed, a parting gift from the Aycayia.

The story went like this: when Rafi was a young man, he left home and found work on a small coffee plantation up in the mountains. By day, he walked between the rows of shrubs, shaking the red berries free from their branches. Little green snakes and lizards fell with them, and he would nudge them away as he stooped to pick up the valuable fruit. The work was hard and grueling, and he would return to the huts late at night soaked with sweat, his arms covered in blisters, his back aching.

It was like this for months, every day in the hot sun and every night in the buzzing, mosquito-infested shacks. He kept most of his wages hidden in a tobacco tin buried in the loamy earth beneath his cot, sending a dollar or two home to his mother in the city at the end of every month.

On Christmas Eve, the overseer—a blanquito who strutted around camp with a rifle slung over his shoulders like John Wayne—surprised the hands with a few bottles of rum and a fat, squealing pig. That night, the workers celebrated with booze and mounds of spicy meat roasted in leaves hacked from the forest with dull machetes. Someone produced a battered, out-of-tune guitar, and during the celebration, Rafi danced and drank strong coquito for the first time, spinning and whirling around the bonfire.

When most of the other hands had gone to bed, long after the electric lights in the big house had darkened, Rafi staggered into the forest to relieve himself. A million pairs of eyes watched him as he trudged deeper and deeper into the woods, but he felt no fear. Owls hooted and the eerie, playful calls of coquís rang out all around him. Bats flapped overhead and other unseen things rustled in the undergrowth.

He walked for a while, content to just follow the moonlight that spilled through the rustling canopy. Soon, he came to a break in the trees and the rocky banks of a small brook that twisted down through the hills.

He dipped his hands into the water and sipped deep from his concave palms. The cool water dribbled down his chin. The moon hung high over the stream, its light casting everything in silvery blue. The forest was deafening, but he could hear a small, distant spluttering, a little plane flying low over the mountains in the west.

In the stream, a hand emerged from a shimmering moonbeam, pulling itself up. The hand grew into an arm, into a woman's torso and a bare breast. The woman had skin the color of dark rum and long hair that hung down her back in little black curls. Her body glistened with droplets of water, and her eyes were bright headlights shining out, illuminating troops of frogs and lizards and turtles lined up along the shore. She rose until her waist floated just below the surface. Rafi could see little silver scales running up and down her thighs.

As he told the story, Hector furrowed his brow. The other men listened in hushed reverence.

"She was the Aycayia," Rafi told him, sensing his confusion. "La diosa."

"Oh. A naiad," Hector offered, recalling his monster manuals.

"Hmm?"

"A water nymph…an aquatic fairy, I guess."

Rafi shrugged.

The woman beckoned to him.

Ven aquí, she murmured.

She spread her arms wide and Rafi moved towards her, splashing into the stream. The water rose up to his chest and he felt his feet slipping on the smooth rocks on the bottom.

Ven.

He scrambled deeper and soon he was right beside her. He reached out and touched her dusky skin, and she wrapped her slender fingers around his hands.

¿Por qué robas mi agua? she whispered in his ear.

Rafi nodded. "Lo siento, doña."

She smiled, pointing a long figure at his chest.

"I don't know why I did it," he shrugged, taking a drag from his cigarillo. "She was very beautiful. Quizás era una obligación. No sé."

Rafi bared his throat to the woman in the stream and she ran a finger along his arm. He could not pull himself away from her eyes, the brilliance of which blinded him, and left him seeing a crimson afterimage silhouetted against the stars.

He touched his neck and felt warm blood seeping over his fingers. The woman began to lick and suck at his neck. The experience was discomfiting, but, Rafi found, not all that unpleasant. He grabbed at her body, kissing at her and finding her smooth, amphibian lips. His blood dripped down into the cool, clear water.

She moved back to his throat. As she performed her work, he looked up at the night sky scattered with an impossible chaos of stars, and listened to the forest shriek.

SOON AFTER HECTOR'S summer with his grandfather, the neighborhood seemed to reach a breaking point. The trailblazing NYU kids were soon joined by yuppies in suits and shining black shoes. The Irish dive became a Duane Reade. The pizza place became an affected coffee shop. The plastic furniture on 10th Street was replaced with stained wood tables, where the new residents ate sixteen-dollar burgers and drank eight-dollar craft beers with silly, ironic names.

People moved away. Many of the junkies migrated, but some stayed behind, hidden in doorways and cellars, squatting in the few abandoned tenements left in the neighborhood. More police cruisers skulked up and down Avenue C. The older folks—Hector's mother, Rafi—watched these changes with a sense of unease, a weird mix of relief and wariness of things to come.

When Rafi got sick, his lungs black and rotten with emphysema, Hector visited him at the nursing home on Eldridge Street after school. He would sneak Rafi plastic water bottles sloshing with rum, given to him by the man at the bodega counter, who smiled sadly and waved away any offer of money. They played dominos with NY1 blaring in the background, and they never once spoke of the Aycayia again.

He thought often of his abuelo, that summer at the Gowanus Canal.

One day, Hector was walking up the ramp of a jetty on 8th Street. He hoisted his box of glassware up to his chest, when he heard a small splash behind him. He wheeled around, careful not to drop the box.

At the edge was the lost flask that had fallen into the canal so many weeks before. It wobbled in the sunlight, tossing discotheque colors in irregular little circles.

He felt like he was watching himself in a dream, terrified and enchanted by the canal's secrets, by its strange, kaleidoscopic power. Slowly, he put down the box and inched toward the flask. He wanted to stop himself, to pull away and keep from seeing what hid beneath the buckling jetty. He could only move closer and closer, until the edge loomed before him. He stooped to pick up the flask. He leaned out over the canal, some part of him knowing just what he would find.

The boards creaked and the insects sang and a thing with the face of a woman floated in the shallows below.

She stretched out just beneath the surface. Her black hair rippled around her head like seeping crude oil. Her skin was opalescent and seemed to sparkle in the sun—the mottled shade of oyster shells and gasoline. Her small breasts rose and fell with the rhythm of her respiration, as if she breathed air.

Her eyes seemed carved into her face, like black voids. They stared up at Hector, curious.

She pointed to the flask, which Hector clutched to his chest. He let out a dry, choked yelp. He fell to his knees and felt a battery of splinters stab him.

Yours. Her lips were motionless but he still heard her voice hiss in his ear.

He kept his eyes fixed, careful not to let them stray below her bare, jutting collarbone, down to her breasts. He mustered up the courage to ask her the question that had been nibbling away at the back of his mind all summer.

"Are you the Aycayia?"

She cocked her head.

"A mermaid? A nymph?"

The expression on her face was blank.

"What are you then?"

I am one who guides the water.

Her black eyes bored deep into Hector, who sat, paralyzed, on the jetty. It seemed like she was sizing him up, measuring him like a coiled snake.

You steal the water. I have watched you.

She wrinkled her nose. The creature rose from the canal, revealing herself below the waist. Hector gasped.

Her lower body was a single, fanned tail, covered in dense plates and spines. Slender, jointed legs flared from her sides and scrabbled at the air. She clawed her way towards him, hoisting herself up out of the water, her movement a grotesque, writhing puppet show.

She was not as Hector had always imagined her, as Rafi had described her.

She sat on the jetty and adjusted her position so that her armored tail dangled out over the water. She reached out a slimy hand. Her fingers were monstrously long and webbed, like the vestigial digits of a bat's wing. She grazed Hector's trembling chest, down to his belly.

You don't understand, she said. *I have watched this water for so many of your lifetimes.*

THERE ARE MEMORIES in the canal.

A girl walking along the edge, a boy beside her. Legs swinging out in the night. Fabric billowing. Warm overcoats.

There are words and ignored warnings; paths lit by the brightness of the moon, breath steaming.

She speaks of the canal and her love for the belching ships that chug and chug down the canal and out to the harbor and then on to strange ports, strange places nobody has ever heard of, where strange people look strange and speak in strange sounds, worshiping strange gods. The boy reaches and brushes blushing cheeks and she bristles but does not pull away.

Then, she turns, drawn by the glow of the big city, way out there on the horizon, towers shrouded in fog.

Then, she slips.

She flaps and he yells, leaping forward, scratching her wrist with dirty fingernails, grabbing at wind with calloused fingers. She falls and she sees his face, eyes wide against the moon.

There is darkness, then.

She awakes frigid. The bright moon faded, flickering. Oily tendrils wrap around her, tickling her legs, caressing her breasts, weighing her down, deep in the muck and the sludge. She can't breathe or scream and blackness devours her, down there in the muck, in the sludge.

Above her: shouts, dim flashes.

The girl is alive, down there in the muck and the sludge. Clothes and skin fall away until there is nothing but nerves and burbling muscle wrapped around a skeleton. Patches of chitin erupt across her flesh like some medieval rash. Legs fuse into a whipping tail. Legs burst from her sides. Fingers grow long and teeth grow sharp, and her soft, green eyes glitter black.

Her new body jitters and pulses with life. She crawls to and fro, over centuries of wood and stone and metal, over slimy bones of all manner of beast and man, over history layered in the sediment. She feels the canal flowing and leeching.

Memories creep along in the muck and the sludge. They slink towards her like a cat. They speak without words and she understands.

There were others before. When the waters ran sweet and clear and men and women waded through the shallows with sweeping nets. When the waters ran red with blood. When the waters ran brown with filth.

Even now, there are others—a lumbering turtle in the bay to the east; a monstrous eel, curled in the mud of the harbor. Sleek but dull fish in the tributaries to the north, patrolling their trickling little streams like sentinels.

There will be others after her.

But for now, she belongs to them. And everything in the canal belongs to her.

"EVERYTHING IS POLLUTED," the words escaped Hector's mouth in a hoarse whisper. "They're trying to clean the canal—I mean, the water. That's what the Superfund is."

She glanced toward the harbor, which lay fat and heavy in the distance.

And what is clean?

She turned back to him and gazed deep into his eyes. Slowly, her mouth curled into a smile, wider and wider until it stretched across her face like a gash.

Hector's stomach lurched.

Her massive jaws snapped open and she cackled, revealing rows of razor teeth that looped down her throat like a spiral staircase. Her laughter echoed out across the canal, shrill and metallic. Bony fingers clutched at ribs. He threw his hands over his ears, falling backwards.

She scuttled across the dock, faster than Hector would have ever expected, still shrieking with laughter. Hector inched back, cowering under her shadow.

You have no idea what you are doing, she roared. *You are nothing. You are less than nothing.*

She reached out spindly arachnid fingers and stroked his face. His cheeks were hot and red, and as she touched him, he was overcome with her aroma. The creature reeked of fish markets on Mott Street and sweating piles of garbage on Houston. She reeked of the rat traps in the basement and the rusty sewer main that had once burst in Tompkins Square Park.

It was every awful smell that had ever emanated from his city, from his Gowanus Canal—the shit and the chemicals and the brackish corruption; the unmistakable stench of death.

He tried to push her away, to clamber out from under her heavy carapace, but her spiny legs held him down with the expertise of a shrike. She wrapped her hands around his throat and squeezed. He clawed at her with feral desperation. Teeth hung inches from his face, and her tongue shot out and brushed against his cheek.

These waters are mine, she whispered. *You and your masters will never take it.*

Pain exploded as her jointed legs pierced his flesh, spreading him out across the wood like a frog under dissection. Her bare breasts pressed against his chest and he felt, to his disgust, a peculiar stirring. He tried to scream but her grip on his throat was too tight.

The story came back to him in flashes: his abuelo in the stream, under the stars. The woman standing before him, kissing his neck.

"My...my blood," he croaked. "Mi sangre."

Her fingers relaxed for a moment.

He tried to nod. "Please."

The creature loosened her embrace. She pulled him to a sitting position. His arms and legs were pinned, and he felt a sickening pop as his shoulders jerked upwards. She caressed his hair, squeezing and kneading the contours of his skull.

Shhhhhhhh...Shhhhhhhh...

Her breath tickled. He thought he was going to throw up.

She yanked back his head. His eye caught a patch of rusting scaffolding, an advertisement for a long forgotten neighborhood business. An odd landmark for the area, but one he saw every day during his rounds up and down the canal. It served as a milestone for him, a point by which he could judge how far along the canal he had traveled.

The creature's face pressed against his own. She licked him once more, drawing salty tears and sweat from his cheeks.

She pushed his head back and latched onto his neck, her mouth sharp and sucking like that of a lamprey. The pain was excruciating, but he could not scream, could not will the sound out. She moaned softly as she suckled at his throat.

Shhhhhhhh...Shhhhhhhh...

He thought of Rafi, of his mother and aunts. He thought of mermaids and his abuelo's Puerto Rico and the Aycayia. He thought of dominos and the DEP and the Gowanus Canal and his Loisaida, drifting rudderless.

His eyes glazed over, staring up at the bright, blue sky, while high above an airplane whined.

THE WHITE KISSES

Charles Wilkinson

NORVIN SOLD EVERYTHING and went down south. His new apartment was fully furnished and every item in it, including the plates, cups, bowls, and cutlery, even the toaster, had been designed by Korcorvian himself. Before leaving Norvin burnt his clothes in the back garden and bought new ones, close in appearance to those worn by the architect and designer in the one surviving photograph of him. For many years, Norvin had studied Korcorvian's work and thoughts; now was the time to live like him, without excess and superfluity of emotion.

He drew back the living-room curtains and looked out: no sign of the albino sitting on the bench that faced the sea. Then it happened for the third time that week. There wasn't a pattern, aside from its occurring only when he was in the apartment. Could he think of a simple way to describe it? It was as if a presence had "signed into" the space around him. Not like being possessed by a spirit or an alien entity; nearer perhaps to knowing one was stored on a computer. The metaphor of "signing in" was, he decided, the most appropriate. Whatever was interested in him had something akin to electronic access, which could be used at will. Yet the analogy was also apt since it was not like being viewed remotely; he felt as close as he would be at breakfast to another guest who'd signed into the same hotel.

He knew he would find nothing but checked every room. All was as he'd left it before going down to take his morning walk on the beach. Outside, the sky had been flat and white, apart from a wash of pale blue high in the heavens. In the middle distance, orderly small waves dissolved on the shingle.

There were no pictures on the walls of his apartment, which was painted magnolia. The white covers on the chairs and the beige bed-spreads, the steel and chrome in the kitchen, the pale ceramic tiles in the bathroom were all consistent with Korcorvian's aversion to bright colors. Norvin kept a few possessions out of sight in the pine ward-robes and chest of drawers. It was a privilege to be living in the last surviving building designed by Korcorvian. The least Norvin could do was to try to live as Korcorvian had done, eschewing the decorative and the clutter of conspicuous design.

Whatever it was that had been with him in the flat had gone. Signed out. He went into the tiny kitchen. There was no change in the light, only a suggestion that something had closed; he was no longer open to observation, his emotions legible. Norvin considered making toast and a cup of coffee, but instead poured a glass of cold water from the jug in the fridge. Since coming to the apartment, his appetite had been poor. He took his glass back to the living-room and gazed out the window at the bleached sky, the sea with its thin metallic waves and the sheen of the shingle beach. In the foreground, on the other side of the road from the apartment block, there was a lime tree and a bench. The albino was still sitting on it, at exactly the spot where the shade would have fallen had the day been sunny.

SUPERVISED BY AN overweight woman with dyed orange hair, the concierge put out the last of the metal chairs. The communal space on the ground floor of the apartment block was one Korcorvian had intended should be used for lectures. Most of the time it was empty. Light through the tall windows stamped white rectangles on a floor of polished hardwood. The area was used for the infrequent meetings of the Korcorvian Foundation. As a resident of the block and a member of the Korcorvian Society, Norvin was entitled to attend. He took a seat at the back. The concierge, an abnormally tall and thin man, worked speedily; just for a second, it was as if he enjoyed the benefit of an extra arm. The front rows began to fill up. Norvin recognized a few of his fellow tenants. After a whispered consultation, the concierge retreated with swift long strides in the direction of his office. A hush descended. Three men came through the front door; two of them made their way to the front, but the third peeled off and sat down next to Norvin, even though all the other seats in the back row were empty.

"Don't mind if I sit here, do you?"

Norvin turned to examine the newcomer, whose face hovered next to him. One of the man's eyes was a pale blue; the other discolored: the broken black egg of the pupil had leaked into the iris.

"The seat was vacant," said Norvin, looking away.

The man leaned even closer. "I'm a man that likes to have company. That's not a problem for you, is it?"

Norvin smelled an antiseptic mouthwash that failed to disguise the underlying odor of dental decay. At the front, a man who introduced himself as the treasurer began a detailed account of the Korcorvian Foundation finances. Norvin stared straight ahead, with what he hoped was an expression of rapt concentration.

"Member, are you? Of the Foundation," continued his neighbor.

Norvin gave a barely perceptible shake of the head.

"That's good. Neither am I. I just live here. Like you."

The treasurer was talking about an expense that might or might not prove to be tax deductible. Norvin craned forward, as though eager to hear the denouement of this fiscal adventure.

"No, we're both residents. That's what we," muttered the man. "Tenants of the Korcorvian Foundation. Tenants together. And what could be better than that? Eh, Mr. Norvin."

Norvin swung round."How do you know my name?" he said, just managing to keep his voice down. The man had a pale slithery face, the color of a bar of toiletry stuck to a basin in a fly-blown hotel; his mousy hair was unwashed.

"You don't mind me calling you 'Mr. Norvin'? I mean that's not a difficulty for you, is it?"

"I merely want you to explain how..."

"I see he's not here."

"Who?"

"The albino, of course. You must have run into him."

"As a matter of fact, I have. Who is he?"

There was muted applause for the finance officer and then the woman with red hair asked a question about the lift.

"Don't you worry, Mr. Norvin. He's not my type," replied the man, standing up. "Well, I must slip away now. But we'll meet again. And oh, by the way, when you've the time to listen to it, I've got a message from your wife."

TO NORVIN'S LEFT the night sky was uniformly black, indistinguishable from the hidden sea. Although there was a faint hiss of water on the shingle, he could see little further than the bollards on the promenade. Even the beach huts below had vanished. In front of him, a row of cast iron street lamps leaked yellow light. On the other side was the coast road; beyond that a cliff top with a terrace of houses, which tonight had a papier-mâché fragility. Slightly further up, there were modern hotels and blocks of flats. The Korcorvian apartments occupied the highest point and stood out against a navy-blue sky, the horizon flushed with inland light. More substantial than the surrounding buildings, the apartment block had a glow of nautical impermanence, as if about to lose its moorings and drift away down the wide river of the night sky.

Korcorvian had often drawn on marine design, even for projects far from the coast. Norvin was reminded that the lost abbey the architect had built for a silent order had combined traditional cloisters with the suggestion of a ship at the moment of leaving harbor on a spiritual voyage.

As he was about to turn back, Norvin saw something, perhaps fifty yards ahead, almost at the end of the promenade. At first, it resembled the head of a white owl with drooping wings; it remained stationary, as if painted onto a backdrop.

"No harm in getting out," said a voice from behind him.

Norvin spun round. A pair of stilt-legs and a gleam of long leather shoes. Then the concierge stepped into the light noiselessly as a spider.

"No, it's a change." Norvin agreed. He didn't know the concierge's name. It seemed rude to ask after having been in residence for months.

"Taking the night air?"

"Yes, indeed. What do you think that is?" said Norvin. But as soon he turned to point in the direction of the white shape it was no longer there.

"What? The bandstand?"

"No, I'm sorry; it's gone."

With the yellow light behind him, the concierge's expression was hard to judge.

"They said you were talking to him. You were seen."

"I'm sorry," said Norvin. "I'm afraid I don't know who you're referring to."

"Mogson, of course."

"I don't know anyone of that name."

"The man you were talking to during the meeting. Mogson."

"Oh him, it was only a very brief and one-sided conversation. He told me that he is a resident."

"He's in the basement apartment. Him and his electronics."

"Electronics? What is he?"

"That's what we'd all like to know. Why has he got all those machines in the basement? What does he want them for?"

"I've no idea. To be honest, I can't say I warmed to him."

"He arrived the day after you. Not the type we normally have in the apartments. Information is what he wants…and has. That much we are well aware of."

"Maybe. But I don't think that all of his information can be entirely accurate."

Norvin thought of the computers, the flat-screen television and the walk-in freezer he'd owned in the north. From time to time, he liked to remind himself he'd sold everything. Even the white goods. He was by himself, making a new identity in silence.

ALMOST MID-DAY. The sky had the washed out looked of denim worn for decades, so nearly white it was only memory that detected more than a hint of darker blue. With the tide out, the shingle too was paler. Colors were drying in the fabric of the world. Norvin walked towards the edge of the sea. The waves were small today, more like very thin wires. A faint grey-white blotch headed for the horizon. Most probably a ferry. At the strandline were clots of seaweed and a few sticks, some arranged enigmatically, on the verge of becoming pictograms left by a strange sea god.

He put his hand in the inside pocket of his jacket and drew out some newspaper cuttings, which he kept in a small transparent folder.

The article with a black and white photograph of Korcorvian was, as always, at the top. The architect was standing by a pillar, no doubt long demolished. Experts were divided as to whether it had once been part of a hospice or a priory. Korcorvian was very thin with a wasted face and round, steel-framed spectacles. He wore a white linen suit and a shirt with the top button done up and no tie. The photograph was badly over-exposed, so the skin was paper-white, the unruly hair a blizzard of snow. In his right hand, he held a broad-brimmed straw hat. This was the only surviving picture of Korcorvian, who had never sat for a portraitist and was famously camera shy. The books written about him concentrated on his work and ideas, for very little was known about the man—not even his age or nationality. It was claimed he had not been born with the name Korcorvian. There were theories he was a Finn or from one of the Baltic States, but nothing had ever been corroborated. He lived entirely alone, seeing only those with whom he was professionally obliged to come into contact and a few acolytes. Norvin became interested in Korcorvian when he read a monograph in which the architect was quoted as saying his buildings were designed as "spaces in which it was easier to forget." Religious life, he implied, was not about finding God but simply a way of not remembering the world. Dying was a chance to move closer to being liberated from memories, free from impurity.

Norvin put the folder back in his pocket. Although the sea was no rougher than before, he felt uneasy. The waves were thinner, somehow less watery, as though they were in the process of being transmuted into metal that could be used in a circuit board. He tried to remember whether water was a good conductor of electricity. The ferry, which he thought was going away from the shore, was now larger and therefore closer. The word "radiophonic" came into his mind. The sea and its clients were building connections and sending messages. It would be safer, Norvin decided, if he were to head back towards the shingle. He looked towards the Korcorvian apartments. Was it unreasonable to suspect the waves were being affected by the activity in the basement?

Just before Norvin reached the sea wall, he noticed the albino lying back in a deck chair outside a beach hut. As he was wearing tinted glasses, it was impossible to tell if he was asleep. He was dressed in a white jacket with a black shirt and trousers. Although it was beginning to turn cold, his relaxed posture was that of a sunbather. The other deck chairs were empty. Apart from the man and himself there was nobody on the beach. Norvin stepped a little nearer, but not close enough to establish whether the albino was breathing. For a reason he found hard to explain, Norvin could not bring himself to move further forward. There was something perfectly composed about the scene: the arrangement of man, deckchair, beach, and the backcloth of the sea wall. The muted colors and the angle at which the subject was positioned suggested the imminence of a photo-shoot. Norvin did not wish to put himself in the picture.

THE NEXT DAY Norvin found the furniture in his apartment covered by what he at first thought was a very fine white powder. But when he ran a finger over his bedside table, it felt like frost. His room was chilly, yet the windows were shut and the central heating was on, even though the radiators were lukewarm. Perhaps it had been unnaturally cold during the night. No doubt the frost, if that was what it was, would vanish as soon as the apartment warmed up.

He dressed quickly and went into the kitchen. That the windows were iced over implied he had been correct about the drop in the overnight temperature. He took a mug out of the cupboard and ran the palm of his hand over the kitchen table, leaving a dark arc. The cold tingle made him turn round to look for a cloth. Then without warning, the sensation in his hand intensified to something close to an electric shock. He went over to the sink and ran hot water over his palm until the pain slowly abated. Whatever it was had signed in again. He was sure it was close. The skin on his wounded hand felt thicker and heavier, as if an invisible glove had been rolled over it. The tingle turned to a faint vibration that was spreading though his body. Something had begun to search: was running a check on every bone, tissue, and blood cell. If necessary, it would destroy, restore, or reconfigure. It was essential to get out of the flat now. This second. Before the scan was complete. He grabbed his overnight case.

He was half way down the staircase before it stopped. After taking a deep breath, he flexed his fingers. Quite normal. It must have withdrawn for the moment. Logged off. One thing was certain: he would not return to the apartment, apart from one brief visit to collect essential possessions. He would find the concierge and explain he had to move out temporarily. Something amiss with the central heating. That would be an excellent excuse. Perhaps they would find him another flat in the building.

There was no one in the lecture hall or the lobby. All the chairs had been put away and the place appeared larger and emptier than before. Sunlight distributed shadows evenly over the wooden flooring. The door of the concierge's office was ajar. As Norvin walked over, he counted his echoing footsteps. It was important to remain in charge of his thoughts. The door opened before he could knock.

"Yes," said the concierge.

"Sorry to disturb you, but I was wondering if it would be possible for me to move to another apartment in the..."

"Hold on. Let's get the first point straight before you start rambling on. You said you were sorry to disturb me."

"Yes."

"Well, are you?"

The room behind the concierge appeared smaller than Norvin had expected. Although most of his view was blocked, he could make out part of the far wall, on which was a wooden keyboard.

"In a way, certainly. You might have been having a cup of tea or..."

"Fair enough. I can accept that. Now what do you want?"

"I'm hoping to move into another apartment in the building. There's something wrong with the central heating in mine. This is hard to explain, but I'd be more comfortable elsewhere."

"There aren't any vacant. The only thing you can do is swap with your mate."

"What mate?"

"Him in the basement, of course. Mogson."

"That wouldn't be ideal. We're not friends. And anyway why should he move just for me."

"He'd have to."

"Why?"

"Who's paying his rent?"

"I don't know."

"You are. Two apartments requested. One to be in the basement. Both paid for by Mr. Norvin."

The concierge glanced back into his office, as if he were checking that something was still in-progress. Or perhaps there was a very quiet animal in there.

"I don't see how that could possibly be true. I'd never even heard of this Mogson when I took my apartment."

"Paperwork," said the concierge, turning back to him. "That's what you need. Check it. Then check it again."

"I'm going to book into a hotel for a night and try to sort this out. I'll be back tomorrow to collect the rest of my possessions. In the meantime, please ask the other residents if they'd be prepared to swap with me."

"There's no harm in a change," the concierge said. "I take one myself from time to time. As you've seen."

"I'll be in tomorrow. I'll let you know how things stand then."

"That Mogson. He's not liked. You'd be all right here if it weren't for him."

NORVIN HAD TO be careful with money. As a member of the Korcorvian Association, he'd been paying a reduced rent for his apartment, and living cheaply, or so he thought. But failing to have his bank statements forwarded from the north had been a terrible mistake. Not only had he covered three months of Mogson's rent, he'd even given the man a weekly allowance. Of course, contacting the police was out the question, but at least he'd stopped the direct debits. Unfortunately Mogson's apartment was paid for up to the thirty-first.

Norvin looked around his new room: no accessories, not even a television: just an iron bedstead covered by an ancient eiderdown, a side table, one wooden chair and a hand basin. His overnight case was open on top of the bed. He tried to congratulate himself on having the foresight to pack the essentials: a sponge bag, pajamas, and a change of clothing. But that still left him with the problem of the diaries and the Korcorvian papers. Having them sent over would be inadvisable. The papers were valuable, but the diaries were more than that: they were evidence. There was no option but to collect them from the apartment himself.

No phone or radio on the side table; only one dirty glass mug of the type used at school dinners. The temperature was barely above that in his apartment. He would go out and walk around the town. For the first time, it occurred to him that he'd not bothered to explore the centre. He'd restricted himself to the apartment building, the beach, the promenade, and cheap restaurants nearby.

The town was full of small shops selling postcards and souvenirs. Now it was the end of the season many of the restaurants only opened in the evenings. In the narrow streets, a handful of puzzled holiday makers were starting to appreciate their cheap bookings came with a guarantee of indifferent grey skies. Resolutely dressed for summer, they gazed upwards, eager to discover unheralded delights on the higher storeys.

Norvin was about to return to the hotel when he turned down a side street and chanced upon the Korcorvian Café. Four o'clock. From the pavement the place appeared empty, but as he opened the door a bell rang and a pale thin woman emerged from the back. He ordered a coffee. The walls were covered with photographs of the architect's lost buildings: some as they had been before demolition or dereliction had won the day; others now little more than a single desolate arch or slabs of green, graffiti-covered concrete. Three grey stumps were all that remained of a seminary; a chapel once shaped like an ark, which had graced a crematorium, was level with the gravestones. There were plans for a railway station that had never been constructed. A much larger reproduction of the only surviving picture of Korcorvian hung over the fireplace. The chiaroscuro caused by overexposure had been accentuated: the architect's skin and hair almost as white as the photographer's flash.

The waitress put his coffee down on a table. Norvin turned round. For the first time he noticed an alcove not visible from the street. Mogson was seated right at the back, instantly recognizable though half of his face was in shadow. He was looking straight at Norvin.

"I thought you'd turn up here if I waited long enough, that's what I told myself. He'll be along. Don't you worry," said Mogson.

Norvin sat down and spooned sugar into his coffee.

"Don't you want to join me here in cosy corner?"

Stirring—and the rattle of a tea spoon.

"Ah well, time for Mohammed to come to the mountain." Mogson rose stiffly and walked over to Norvin. "I wouldn't mind another coffee. Though I have cash flow problems at the moment. But then you'd know about that." He made himself comfortable and picked up a brown sugar lump, which he crunched in his rotten teeth. "Have you seen our friend?"

"What friend?"

"Mr. White Man, Mr. Albino?"

"Yes, since you mention it."

"So have I. I've seen him all over the place. Moves about, doesn't he?"

"I suppose so."

"Ah yes, he moves—a lot. But have you ever seen him moving? That's what I'd like to know."

"What makes you think I'm anything like as interested in him as you evidently are?"

"Because…and you listen to this," Mogson hissed, leaning forward and pressing both of his arms down hard on the table, "I've been reading you! Right down to the last dot. Some people—they're cryptic, see. But not you. I know you—and you're a piece of filth!"

Mogson was half way across the table now, anger shining in his good eye, the swirl of blind mysteries alive in the other.

"That's rich, coming from you," said Norvin.

After seizing the sugar bowl in both hands, Mogson leant back in his chair and looked up at the photograph of Korcorvian. "Do you reckon they're related?" he asked, suddenly relaxed and matter of fact.

"Korcorvian and the albino?"

"Of course. Your hero and Mr. White Man, Mr. Albino, Mr. Motionless?"

"Korcorvian was celibate."

"And so now everyone's Mr. Pure too. Is that it?"

"None of this has the slightest thing to do with you."

"Is that right?" said Mogson, scooping up the remaining sugar lumps out of the bowl and putting them in his pocket. "There are those who know better, that's what I say. And it's about time," he added, smiling, "you heard your wife's message, isn't it?"

ON THE STEPS up to the Korcorvian Apartments, Norvin saw the woman with dyed orange hair coming in the opposite direction. Her eyes alighted on him for a second. He was too far away to detect her expression, but she averted her gaze well before they passed each other. Evidently she was one of the people who blamed him for Mogson's presence in the basement.

He was in the lobby when he remembered he'd left the key to his flat in the hotel. He could visual it, with its orange tag, lying on the top of the side table next to his bed, exactly where it had been since he had booked in. Nevertheless, he checked all of his pockets, just in case he had absent-mindedly picked it up: nothing, apart from the hotel keys. Their weight had deceived him into thinking he had what he needed. He was about to turn back when he realized the concierge would have a spare; the keyboard was in the office. The silence and emptiness of the lobby was so complete it was hard to imagine the woman with the orange hair must just have walked through it.

From where Norvin was standing, the office appeared to be shut. He heard himself walking, footstep by echoing footstep, and knocked on the door. No reply. He turned the handle and to his surprise the door swung open easily. Inside, the quality of the light was different, as if it had been falling on stone for centuries. There was a very faint scent of flowers. Norvin was reminded of a side-chapel. In the centre of the room was an armchair upholstered in a material the shade of grey smoke. Although it was positioned to face away from Norvin, he could see the back of a man's head, the hair albino-white and two pale hands at ease on the armrests. The keyboard was still on the far wall. To reach it, he would have to go round the chair and its occupant. But who would he find if he did so? Absurdly he thought he would see no more than what was there now: two hands and a head of hair, on the verge of disappearance.

He stepped back and closed the door. Was there no alternative to returning to the hotel? Of course he could always wait for the concierge, but how long would that be? Perhaps he should check the apartment now he was here. It would be ridiculous to trek all the way back only to discover the door was open all the time. And, come to think of it, how could he be sure he had locked it? He couldn't recall doing so as he'd fled.

The building was quieter than he could ever remember it. Everyone must be out at work, except possibly Mogson in the basement. He ran up the stairs. As he had expected, the door to his apartment was open. Everything in the living-room was normal. He touched a radiator; it was slightly warm. Possibly someone had come in to fix the central heating. All that remained was to collect his diaries.

The second he stepped into his bedroom a fierce light and the cold enveloped him. Everything, even his bed, was shrouded in snow. He walked over to the cabinet in which he kept the diaries and tugged the frozen handle. The drawer was locked fast. A simple solution: he would go to the kitchen and boil the kettle. As he turned round, he felt the first kiss burn on the back of his neck. It was no longer possible to tell where the door had been. The wall he'd walked through was ice-rink smooth. Now he started to slide, the carpet tiles turning to cubes in a gigantic ice tray.

The sky in the window reached unpigmented perfection and was disconnected, leaving a glow of artificial light. Something was pressing down on him, white-kissing his lips. One shock after another. He gave a little electrical dance, his last loose-limbed movements. What was her message? *Tell him I'll kiss him goodnight.* She would have been numb when she died. He tumbled and stared up at the ceiling: a good place to watch the frost accrue. Then later, after the light went out, she would join him, and they'd lie there together, knowing how carcasses hang in the dark.

Down by the River

H.V. Chao

By this, and this only, we have existed
Which is not to be found in our obituaries
Or in memories draped by the beneficent spider

— T.S. Eliot

THEY STARTED OUT at eleven—late for him, early for her. The sun in that run-up to summer was lordly, lolling at the zenith. Noon sprawled over hours.

At the trailhead, she turned to look back at him, shading her eyes.

"I'm sorry." She knew how he felt about apologies, but it just came out. "I know you wanted to get an earlier start."

At twenty-four, she still had the knack of sleeping in; there was something spoiled, even lewd about it. Awake and alone he had watched her, sunk in wrecked sheets as if on the sea floor, her dark hair the storm that had drowned her. In this and other things he envied her abandon. It was cool in the room, but when he stepped into the courtyard, he'd felt the heat of the coming day.

He bent now, in the shade of a pine, to shoulder the daypack. The air was cool against his shins but thick already between his shirt and back. "Well, we're here now."

It was something she might have said—but more brightly, meaning it.

He straightened, walking past her into the tunnel of woods. She caught his elbow. "Look!"

High and to the right a hummingbird fluttered, with its iridescent breast and a beak like a line of pencil lead, pointing this way and that. They stood watching for a moment.

"Do they ever stop?"

He looked puzzled.

"You know...*going*?"

He shook his head. "I've never seen one alight." Such a life flitted now through his imagination—one unbroken nervous hover, perishing heroically from sheer exhaustion.

"They must."

For a while the only sound was their footfalls. The trail was of beaten dirt that did not rise when scuffed, and clay that held each pebble embedded.

"See these?" He patted a tree marked by a patch of white like the rear of a fleeing deer. "If you get lost, keep going till you see another one."

"And if I don't?"

"Then turn around."

They came to a low stone bridge. The railing was crooked and rust-red, but smooth to the touch. Below lay a sheer creek over a dark bed, its burble barely audible. From the shallows rose a few thin beeches.

"It's okay, you know," he said then. "I was up anyway. You know me."

It was not so much waking as ceasing to sleep, or having it taken from him. His eyes were dry and his hands and feet cold. The aimless hours stretched before him, a cell. That morning, he had wandered barefoot over chill stone floors. The *chambre d'hôte* where they were staying was less of a B&B than a vacation rental—more rooms than they knew what to do with. On counter, table, couch, and rug lay their things, strewn for convenience. These scant belongings seemed greedy to domesticate the emptiness. But they had brought too little. The house seemed not so much inhabited as full of things left behind. In the stillness and gray light, he felt like a man perched on a suitcase in a train station, someone else's photograph of loneliness.

"It's true, old people need less sleep."

He snorted.

It's a start, she thought.

The woods had come alive around them, or they were just deeper in: ticking insects, bird chatter, scamper amplified by the rustle of dry brush. To the right, uphill, opened frequent clearings of dust and butterflies, low scrub laid bare to the blinding sun.

"Is it really just lizards?" It was hard to credit such racket to something so small.

"I'm pretty sure."

After a moment she said, "Tell me again why you hate apologies so much?"

He could be brusque, even dismissive about them. "I used to apologize a lot when I was young. I guess I just don't see the point anymore. It's all water under the bridge."

"But clearly it's not."

He clung to some core of the unforgiven, like a man who discards the fruit and gnaws the stone. "I just mean, they don't fix anything."

"They're not about fixing. They're about moving on."

"Yes, but they sort of force the point, don't they? Moving on is all you can do; eventually everyone gets around to it. I just don't like… being rushed."

"You'd rather stew?" She smiled. Small surprise, really. He hung on to so much else.

"Let's be clear: if the choice is between being happy with less, or completely unhappy, it's not really a choice. No sane person would choose unhappiness. And apologies remind me of that—how powerless I am to choose, or to change things."

"Is that how you feel about getting old?"

He stopped and turned. And smiled crookedly, despite himself. "Very good."

"And death?"

The question took him by surprise. The thing he professed never to worry about—had he spent his whole life fleeing it? Had his whole life been one of denial? Well yes, life was by definition death's very opposite, a refusal.

"What *about* death?" There, he had said the word. Younger, he had worried his unconcern over death made him a shallow person. He worried less now, he would have said, though she would not. "I've always detested simple things."

"Like the truth?"

"Rarely simple." Hated, too, the obvious, the irrefutable; there always had to be more to it. Take love, for example—the constant flux of desire and regret, selflessness and privacy—he loved in constant uncertainty. Or was it just that when you pared everything back, got down to the hard, obdurate kernel, he wanted there to be something to soften the blow?

She put her hand on his shoulder, raising one foot to her knee. "Can we stop? I think there's a rock in my shoe."

It was meant to be a hike of five hours or so; the kilometers made it hard for them, Americans, to tell. They were headed, following the river Méouge, for a hilltop village; there were several in the area: Antonaves, Upaix, Le Poët..."Which one again?"

"The one with the historic sundial." He folded the map—more of a brochure, really—and tapped the photo of a fresco on the back: a faded goddess beside radiating, Roman-numbered lines. They were to arrive just in time for a cool drink on a café terrace. The bounded European wilderness: civilized comforts were always in reach. Even lost without vista in a thicket, you were never far from a town that had been settled for ages. "We'll watch the old men play pétanque."

It cheered her, the thought of cobblestones, a stray cat, the steady trickle of water into a stone basin from a lion's mouth. She felt a rush of affection for these irrigating guardians and their fierce, cartoonish scowls. "How far are we?"

He watched her fiddling with her boot. "Well, back at that boulder where we turned left—how long ago was that? I think that was about a fifth of the way in, so..." After a certain point—probably a third—fractions ceased making sense to him as estimates. He could imagine having yet to go the stretch he'd come, or half again; imagining it four times over defeated him. Besides, it gave way to imprecisions, introduced too many variables. Half the journey ahead, and you were likely to cover it in the same time it had taken so far; but who knew how much your pace could vary from fifth to fifth?

"Say...a third?" He wanted to be encouraging.

She had laced up her boot. "Let's go."

It was hot now even in the shade. Gnats danced about their heads. They were like lunatics, plagued by the unseen. At one point he walked into a spiderweb and stopped, flummoxed by silk.

"What is it?"

He had blundered into one earlier that morning, strung across the courtyard. Had it been there yesterday, when they'd walked through, stopping to marvel at the peonies? Unconscionable, how quickly they surfaced, these signs of neglect and decay, emerging from closet and corner to bind the vibrant and the thriving. The bathroom that morning was cold as the grave. From the skylight fell a baleful shaft of gray. Alert after the courtyard, he'd found another spider just under the toilet seat, its web spanning the bowl, and in the tub, the tiny gnarled carcass of a third, like a hand clutching after fled life.

"I guess not many people pass this way."

"No—didn't you know about webs?" She liked telling him things, with a prickle of vanity; she could help it no more than her apologies. Perhaps it was because he told her so much, or discounted so much that she told him. "They put them up every night and take them down every morning."

So it was everyday, and not accrued disrepair. He felt some meaning had been lost. He said, "Or forget to."

Slowly they had risen through the layers of vegetation, and emerged now on a ledge above the gorge. The other side was clearly visible, barer still at the same elevation, scrub in sparse clumps studding the scree slope or clinging to the limestone tiers.

"Reminds me of...chest hair." She was flushed—from effort, not reticence. "This one ex."

He took her by the shoulders, turned her around. "Look."

His nose was close now to a few damp strands pasted flat against her nape, which smelled of soap and sweat. Touching thumb to forefinger before her face, he framed the scene. Back the way they had come, clouds saddled rounded hills with shadows, a dappling at odds with the greenery overlying gray escarp. Three hot air balloons dawdled in the blue above.

"Oh right," she said. "I always forget."

"To look behind?"

"I guess I figure I'll catch it on the way back."

"We're not coming back this way."

"Next time, then."

The next times, the somedays of which her life was so full, simply because so much of it still lay before her. No: life was fickle and difficult. Full of friends you never saw, that restaurant—*unforgettable! What was it called again? I can't believe it's been so long! We have to go back!* Long after the rare call from an old friend was over, promises hung ghostly in the air.

"Do you always think there'll be a next time?"

"Do you never?"

"I used to be like that."

It was one of the more condescending things he said. The funny thing was he didn't mean to condescend.

"No, not all the time," she agreed.

The terrain was constantly shifting, up and down, never a harsh grade but a broken wave. It was not hard going but she was just breathless enough. She tried humming, but the rhythm of her footfalls on the rutted dirt was uneven and jostled the melody, like a vase from a table on a train.

"So you've really never...broken up with anyone before?" He took the water bottle from his pack and handed it to her.

She took a sip and passed it back. "I've never had to: does that sound pathetic?"

"You mean they've always left you?"

"No, it just sort of happens...falls apart, I guess. Unravels."

"You both walk away from the wreckage."

She rolled her eyes. "Oh, there's never any wreckage, just...less, one day."

She was bashful about hurt and surprised by pettiness, resentment. She always wanted to be on the folksong side of a breakup: serene and moving on, beyond bitterness if not regret, beyond her years, looking back with an aerial wisdom compounded of tears and clear sight, having let go and forgiven. A safe place from which to contemplate the beauty of what had been.

It was a nice idea. The end of love, for him, was always bound up in anger and blame. The time and generosity, at worst wasted, at best simply spent.

"Not the things you did *with* someone," he tried to explain, "but the things you did *for* them."

"Those are the only things you can't regret," she said.

It was her eyes that made him wonder. Pale, brilliant, like light in ice, a lens for any meaning. Aloof from her face, they were its most riveting feature—ageless, unlike her lined hands, which were the oldest part of her.

They picked their way along the ledge, one hand on the beige, crumbling flank from which it had been cut. Sometimes a yellow flowering of furze relieved the arid drab.

"It's part of why I picked you. Of the two of us, you seemed likelier to hold on." Lest it make him feel weak, she added, "I feel safe with you."

He snorted. "Funny. It's usually women who go in thinking it'll last forever."

They climbed in silence, breathless, sweating. The exposure was brutal. The limestone mesmerized, a history of force in the undulant lines, like wood grain on a larger, coarser scale. Then the forest received them again, their sunstruck eyes failing in the new gloom.

He said, "I think we're past the peak."

"Oh, so soon?"

"It's good to have it done with." He heard the flirt in her voice a minute late.

"Women take longer, you know." She plopped down on a rock. In a grove off the trail, a massive trunk lay in the ferns, fallen to splinters.

Still sitting, she bent forward, reaching for her ankles. She had taken her hair down, and now it slid bit by bit from her nape, like a curtain with a weighted hem. Her boots were dusty.

With the back of his hand he smeared sweat from his brow, then stood watching her, thumbs tucked under the straps of his pack. "If we were crossing the desert, we'd be sleeping off the burning hours and marching later when it was cool."

She sat up, slowly, luxuriantly. Her smile was dazzling. "Why don't we do it in the woods?"

Time passed differently for the two of them. Take this trip, for him: each day felt long enough while light lasted, but by evening seemed abruptly fled, like a favorite song that comes on the radio and ends before the traffic light has changed. In the silence broken only by raindrops he would realize he had not really been listening, and now it was too late. There was dwelling in the moment, and dwelling *on* it—dwelling *on*, she pointed out, always happened after.

"You're always so...happy, afterwards." What he meant was self-sustaining, contained. Unto herself. Dreamy and harboring secrets, as if she took whatever he gave and held it suspended inside, a honeyed lozenge under her tongue.

They were not yet past that early fascination with each other's bodies: groping, ingenuous, instinctive. That movie moment, always from overhead, when two people chastely draped in sheets fall away from each other sweating, pleasantly surprised...She rolled over, slowly, onto her back. "Aren't you?"

The trip to France had been his idea—a gamble, but not really. Once on the ground it seemed hers in its fullness; it seemed to spring from her. She gave it life. "Are you glad we came?"

Solemnly she nodded, a rustle of leaves against her hair.

"But you always say yes," he sighed.

It was her kind of company, uncomplicated, easy on him. Not that she was obedient, merely obliging. She went along freely with things, with the smile of someone nodding to a song—private, enticing. Her complaisance was compelling, replete with its own reasons. As if in agreeing, she were the one leading him along.

"Hey, I started it," she said.

The world was coming back to him now: patches of damp, nettle, needle, thatch. Nature was never as comfortable as it looked. The soil beneath them was probably teeming, swarming. On the shattered trunk beside them, a millipede performed its sluggish, gleaming roil.

There was afterglow, and afterhollow. After sex, he always felt chastened, reduced, settled without being clarified. How to explain that comedown, the littlest oblivion, a pinprick of loss in a sea of satiety? Or a drop of color spreading in water soon to recall it only as hue. A familiar heat like trapped wings blossomed in his upper back, faltering toward the extremities: a sign of exertion. "*Ah, la petite mort...*"

"What's that?"

"I've told you before."

"Oh, right." She raised an arm straight up at nothing in particular, sighting along it at the empty sky. "What about it?"

He was up on one elbow, combing leaf debris from her hair. "Do you think you sleep better than I do because you're so young?"

The important thing was she was younger, or that was the least important, once he got over it, and in these early days, he had to get over it again and again, alternately guilty and amazed. He had felt compelled to beg from total strangers, the world at large, understanding if not forgiveness for the difference in their ages. She had taken it in stride. These things happen, she said equably. They were to be enjoyed, or refused, but not worried over. It was just part of them now, who they were together. How had he managed to live so long, fretting so much about what people thought?

"I mean, I'm old enough—"

"Don't say it!" She crossed her arms over her head to ward it off.

"—to be your father."

"My who?"

They both laughed.

"But seriously," he said.

She was up on her elbows now too. "Well, if you're so worried, there's always the campsite rule."

"...only you can prevent forest fires?"

Who, me? she mouthed, eyes moon-huge. "No, doofus. Leave it better than you found it."

He studied her: her startling eyes, her smooth body, her strange hands, years older than the rest of her. The vaunted honesty of nudity—if only. Bare flesh was the best liar; it had the most innocent face.

"I think I can manage that," he said at last. "How about the other way around?

He could be such a baby, sometimes. "Not everything different between us is because I'm younger."

"Not everything," he said, "but a lot."

HE WAS A photographer—not people, no, he'd said when they first met. Landscapes. A show of his, in a small gallery. What he sought, through the lens, was beauty. He had been to stark places, difficult places, in search of it, and some contingent illumination of the soul.

"I like to think...if you're lucky enough to encounter it, you shouldn't get to walk away unchanged." It was a line if she'd ever heard one, except that he went on. "But you do, of course. That's the worst part."

He was at peace now with weather—atmospheric oddities, shimmering aurora—changing only the “nothing” that poetry is supposed to. What was it, exactly, he had expected? Something he’d never admitted to himself. “But you keep at it.”

The stem of the wineglass was cool between her fingertips. “Why?”

His face had flickered with amusement, or abashedness. “Well—you still have the pictures.” Later that night, he had asked to take hers.

On her belly in his bed, she shrugged. “I thought you didn’t take pictures of people.”

“You’re the first girl I’ve dated who didn’t mind having her picture taken.”

“Were they all that ugly?”

“That’s mean...I was thinking it had more to do with smartphones.”

She had two rules, she told him the next morning. I won’t be mistaken for someone else. I won’t go anywhere, do anything you’ve gone or done before. I want everything to be new. Life’s too short for anything but first times.

He had his own theory about relationships. In the first few heady days, you saw everything, and after that, less and less. You knew, right from the beginning, what would one day drive you apart, but somehow you managed to forget. All he’d said was, “Well, don’t you move fast.”

“Hold up a sec,” she heard him call out now. Since lunch, he had been lagging behind. It had been one thing or another, a sip of water, a stop to catch his breath, a thorn through his sock pricking his ankle.

The trail cleaved mostly to cover, stands of hornbeam and holm oak. Short and small-leaved, they were a poor filter for sun, so that shade, too, was violently spangled. It was giving him a faint headache. He kicked up what he thought was a pebble, but its flight seemed too graceful, unrelated to his dragging boot. When she turned around, he was bent over, examining his pants leg.

“What is it?”

“A cricket, I think.” The strange thing about it was it was stuck. He watched it wriggle on the khaki fabric. When with two fingers he gingerly plucked it off, a long streamer of gossamer followed, almost invisible, briefly recalling the luxurious strand swaying and glistening that morning in the courtyard, from awning to shrub.

“All good.” Though really, he was feeling feverish. His back was soaked where the pack pressed against it, the same spreading heat as before, in the clearing. The same spreading heat as when he woke drenched in sweat: hot, folded wings smothering a flushed patch of rash. At the same time, every inch of exposed skin—lips, face, and arms—felt oddly parched. His eyeballs were dried to their sockets, as when he'd underslept.

He lurched forward, catching up. "So...how is it you know so much about spiders?"

"Oh, I liked them a lot as a girl." She alternated between facing forward, and turning back to speak over her shoulder. "I saw a spider—in the top right pane of the living room window—eat a fly from its web once, just sink its mandibles into its head until it quit wriggling."

"That's macabre." Since the cricket, he'd grown sensitive to every graze and tickle. He found himself staring at the back of a finger where he had felt a gnat's tiptoe, incredulous there was nothing to be seen. And spiderwebs—you could never really be sure you'd gotten rid of them.

"I guess. I thought of them as...little spirits who protected against insects, guardians of house and home. Like hearths, big old pots, twig brooms, hanging satchels of spice."

The river gorge was sinuous, always hiding with a bend how far they had left to go. From time to time the trees parted to tease them with a glimpse of destination that seemed distant still. He kept his eyes lowered, on the trail. There were turns where a tree leaning sideways for light grappled with an outcrop. At such moments, he felt he was seeing the truth: the elemental thing, the obdurate structure they clambered. The rest was just dirt that the years would wash off along with whatever it anchored. As in their rented rooms where, thinly masked by their belongings, some abiding vacancy showed through, so one day, in the earth's old age, nothing would be left but bare rock jutting from the plain.

It occurred to him they had not seen a trail marker for some time. "How much further?"

"You're asking me?" She grinned.

Minutes later he stopped short, pointing through the branches at a spire of uneroded rock rising from the valley floor below. "I think that's Elephant Rock."

"I don't see it."

"Right there." His dry eyes twitched in the sunlight.

"No, I mean—the elephant."

"But it can't be, because...that means we're less than halfway. Unless we missed it earlier, and that's something else?"

"Don't worry," she said cheerfully. "There's still plenty of daylight."

"Is there?"

She showed him her phone. There was no signal, but the clock ticked on, unaffected. It felt later than it was.

"Hold still," she said, putting a hand on his shoulder. "You've got—"

Her finger touched his eyeball so briefly he barely had time to flinch. He stood there blinking madly, hoping for a tear. "Make a wish?"

She was peering closely at her fingertip, puzzled.

"I don't think so," she said at last. She held her finger out toward him. On the tip lay the leg of a fly.

Just then, he felt a touch of something on his neck, lighter than breath. He was jumping up and down, a frantic tantrum. "Get it off! Get it off, get it off, get it off!"

For a moment, she saw the spider abseiling into emptiness, lengths of silk behind like splintered light, and then, in midair, catch itself, check the force of his panicked fling. Now it rode the breeze, buffeted on updraft from his thrashing arms. How little it needed to stay aloft: a whisper, a stir of heated air!

"Did it bite me?" he was saying. It must have. He hadn't felt it, but that would explain everything. It must have crawled on him while he was fucking in the brush.

He was still slapping his neck and ears when she said, "Ssh, listen. Can you hear it?"

It was the river the trees hid. Invisible below, but they were closer.

"C'mon! We're almost there!" She darted off, reinvigorated. He hurried to follow.

They were descending now, sometimes steeply. The canyon walls began to narrow. They were too low by far, but what he wouldn't give for a vista, a glance back at where they'd begun. To see not how far, but simply how they'd come: to piece together from terrain a continuity, as if making sense of landscape might make sense of where they found themselves. But it was useless—looking back, he could see no further than the last rise or bend in the trail. And how to tell one clearing from another, this rock from that? There was no order to it, just sustained woodland sameness.

She heard him grunting and whuffling behind, exerting himself to keep up. It was odd—had her pace really changed that much? His footfalls were heavy, clomping, scraping.

"Where do you think this is going?" she heard him say.

"To a village where we can have beers on a terrace." She was thinking of the pleasantness, the plane trees, the long sweet evening slung like a silk hammock between the appointed hours of apéritif and sleep. "By a fountain, and watch the old men play pétanque."

"No," he said, "I mean us."

"Hey—isn't that my line?" How rare for her to be short, to dodge a subject.

"But...where are we headed?"

"Wherever this goes, as long as it's good for. Is that OK?"

Finally, he said, "I think so."

"I mean, isn't that what we agreed on?"

"Did we agree on something?" His voice came from far away, as if down a tunnel.

"Well, not in so many words. I just mean, I thought we both knew what this was." Her voice seemed not her own, but an echo. It was his style, and she felt she had usurped it.

"Let's just...enjoy what we have while we have it?"

From him, this protest would have sounded like a ploy. From her, it had the ring of...wisdom? In youth—he remembered it now—the days took ages, each hour a minor epoch. How vast time seemed to stretch, and he with no idea how to fill it. And at day's end awaited that special exhaustion, which made even squandered hours feel casually heroic. Moments still opened for her that special timelessness.

"I mean, it's beautiful here." Lifting her arms, she twirled to take in everything around them. To their right, the southern wall rose steeply, rimmed with brightness from the sun behind. It was hard, looking up, to believe they had come from such heights. The blue sky that the canyon had once yawned wide to gulp down was now but a strip.

She had stopped, waiting for him. His steps were slow, halting. She was suddenly afraid he might fall. When he drew abreast of her, she took his arm.

"Why do we have to worry about what happens next?" she asked.

Whatever happened next...she gave herself over to it gladly. It was fine with her, or not, but would happen anyway. Her trust, her confidence scandalized him. He wanted to run, arms open wide, shouting

No! as if after a child. But she was in no danger. What was it he feared?

"Because," he said. He was sweating freely. His mouth was dry. He felt a squeezing in his lungs. He could not think of a good reason. He could not think. His brow pounded. "Because..."

He wiped the corner of his mouth and the back of his hand came away with a long strand of spider silk.

"I'm really sorry," he said. He sat down heavily. His legs were trembling.

Her hand was on his shoulder. "Are you feeling all right?"

"I can't," he said. "I can't see from my left eye."

She bent to look. The eye was glazed and milky. At its outer corner, flush against his skin, was a web like a snowflake, starred by a single tear. Somewhere deep inside him, an itch built to a seizing of his chest before he coughed. As she watched, the fat glossy drop shuddered and rolled, scattering in smaller droplets like filtered dew. It did not occur to her to be terrified.

"I want to tell you something," he said. And before she could stop him, "I remember every woman who ever gave herself to me." He could not help seeing it as an act of generosity, even with those to whom it meant the least. "Like when I look at every photo I've ever taken, I remember what I was thinking right when I pressed the shutter, and why. Such trust."

As every lover believes he has invented love, so he now believed he had invented sadness.

"I've made so many mistakes," he said. "But someone had to be the one to worry."

In scant minutes, he was completely blind, his eyes sewn shut at the lashes. When she took his hand, her own was cool, and he allowed himself to be led.

The path ran by the river's edge, sometimes far, sometimes near, fringed with feathery grass and wildflowers. Through the trees they glimpsed the other side of the gorge, streaked tan or black with run-off, vegetation shelved in slate.

She was telling him about her grandmother's house, a steady stream of chatter to relieve and reassure. It was a humble cottage on an empty plain, at once cozy and drafty, the shingles like dead leaves peeling up in the wind. There were trapdoor spiders with their webs flat against the wood siding. In the final days of fall, crickets gathered on the screen door, dropping on the porch as the weather turned, while the spiders made their way inside, one to a room. As a child, she had watched them on the white walls, unmoving for days at a time and then, one morning, a foot to the left, three to the right. So long as they kept to their distant orbits there was a truce between her and them, an understanding. What strange, patient migration were they enacting, from one corner of the ceiling to another and back, toward the motionless fan? Their erratic progress hid a cryptic calendar, privy somehow to the true nature of time, its idleness, its fits and starts.

It was all happening so quickly now. The air was drying out the insides of his lungs, an ancient air, fine with grit. He felt the organs hollowed in his chest, preserved, like the liver of a camel he'd once handled in a museum, mapped with a brown mottle that had been the flush of health and blood's reverberations. His body was becoming a place of neglected things.

She could not touch him without drawing from him clinging strands of light that would have blinded but for their slenderness. She thought of the lavishing he called disrepair, webs strung with arachnid daring from eaves to peonies, across the side alley, and between the trash cans. Every night they put them up and every morning took them down; birds tore through the rest. She felt a rush of affection for the busy creatures. Webs were everywhere, holding the world together: every crack in glass, every cleft in wood, every filament of damage until the world was bound in rifts.

His lips hardly moved now when he spoke, and the barest breath passed through them.

"I've been there before," he was saying. Her hands on him were a balm: cool, soothing, water on a stone in the sun. His own hands were gauzy, the fingers almost mummified. "The village...I never told you."

It had been his first time abroad, a young man. Europe was a continent of buses. Every day was an endless exhilaration. He was curled into a seat with his massive pack beside him when he saw the village perched atop its hill, passing in the sunset. Shortly thereafter, he had fallen asleep, and when he woke in the dark, it was as if he had dreamed it. "I'm going back...but I've never really been."

At last, they came to the river. Sun had bleached the dusty pebble shores. Shale overhung teal pools rimmed by brown shallows. The water was milky with rock flour. Large slabs, frost-wedged from the walls, rose from its swirls, mighty except that they had already fallen.

She was carrying him now, cradling him as he had curled, like a child, though he was lighter than a child, a basket of reeds with no baby. Light, so light that if she bent him in any way he might crack. If she set him in the water, he would float away.

The spiders were a ballet in the air. How freely they swung from their invisible lines, at the whim of waft! How meticulously they flexed each spindly leg!

His skin where she could still see it was wizened. It had the lacquered feel of rattan, or palm fronds, stiff and burnished. His mouth was frozen, a small cavern where the wind whistled, and though he could no longer form words she knew from the way he implored her from his sightless sockets that he was asking her to sing.

She began, voice lilting and wavering like sunshine finding its way through leaves. The tune, slight as a breeze, grew tangled in the grasses by the shore. In the blue heights, the buzzards were no larger than the nearer dragonflies flushed from bushes by their passing.

She left him there, by the river, and moved on.

Arena

Daniel Mills

His shadow before me. Broad shoulders swallow dust and mud, the puddles and their reflected sky. His neck, bull-thick, merges with the helm he wears, which hides his face. The helm is bronze and flecked with blood, crowned by a lunging sea-serpent: Leviathan coiled at the bottom of the world. The crowd is deafening. They urge him forward, but his steps are slow and regular. His footfalls echo, overlap themselves.

The hiss of moving water. The fountain to which the centurion sent us.

My brother accompanied me, the clay jug carried between us. A holy man was there, a prophet dressed in the rags of a beggar, and he lifted his hands above his head, as though to compass the sun where it sat within the sky. The crowd swelled, thickened. The blind, the broken, the diseased: their wasted bodies pressed close, their dead hands lapping at us.

We were caught up. My brother, two years younger, clung to my arm as to drifting wreckage while the holy man blessed us with a voice like a slow-moving river: tranquil in aspect, inexorable in force. The square fell silent. Even the stones listened as he spoke of the passing of this age and of a kingdom still to come.

A judgment was coming, he said. The first would be last and the last would be first: the slave become master, the master made slave. He would break our chains. We would be free.

He said: "For I am not sent to bring peace, but a sword."

The words cut: I felt myself un-tethered, falling inside myself. Beside me, my brother wept, though for sorrow or joy, I could not tell. The kingdom was near, quickening inside of us, and from the realization we took flight, running. We reached the house and burst inside, panting—and only then did we recall the reason for our errand and the vessel we had left behind us, unfilled.

FIFTEEN PACES, TEN. He stops. Holds the sword level with his hip, the blade turned slightly so the fluid runs from it, mingling with his own blood on the ground.

He is wounded. His side is pierced and pulsing, half-concealed by the buckler he carries at his breast. Its once-ornate design has vanished, battered into obscurity by his previous opponents: two netmen, both dead.

The first lies on his back near the center of the arena, his trunk slashed open across the stomach. His innards show. The second man is nearby. He has also been gutted, the right arm hacked off at the shoulder. The sinews trail from it like water weeds.

All around us the crowd jeers and thumps their feet, a jagged rhythm. Women are chanting, but I cannot make out the words. My opponent raps his sword against his buckler. The blood flies loose in drops that catch the sun like red fires winking, going out.

He does not speak but bows his head. The great helm dips toward me, as if in recognition, and now he is in motion. His shadow sweeps toward me.

Moving with the sun. Circling the post to which I was chained, while my brother, kneeling, scrubbed my blood from the stones.

The centurion had made his judgment: we were to pay with our bodies for the jug we had lost. Its cost had been counted against our ration and the days had passed without food and with little water until I chanced to drop the master's helm and was whipped for it.

The day was hellish, hot. My brother went without tunic and the post-

shadow fell like the rod across his back. I tried to speak, but my throat was dry, and the brush moved rhythmically in his hand, back and forth over the stones, back and forth, a soothing sound.

The sun went out.

Sight returned, and pain.

Hours had passed. It was late afternoon, the sun high and riding. My brother lay before me, collapsed. His back was blistered, scored with dark lines: the master's whip, the sun's lash. Scraps of flesh had flaked away, sliding wetly off the bone, and he would not move for all I shouted, crying out to him, to anyone. I screamed my throat raw but none would come for us, not til evening, and later, in the night's agony, I watched the moonlight creep across the floor. A new kingdom, the holy man had promised, and in the thirst of my grief, I panted after it.

In dreams the heavens dimmed and turned black, the color of cooked flesh. The clouds caught fire and rained down plumes of flame like bolts of cloth unfurling. The seas boiled, over-heaving the ocean's banks, and the centurion, drowning, cried to heaven. But all were guilty, all consigned, and the sword that was promised felled all before it like fields of wheat at harvest.

HE CRASHES TOWARD me. His sword raised, the buckler swinging. I brace myself. I drop the net behind me and grasp the trident with both hands to thrust it out before me.

His strength is immense: his charge, the weight of it. His buckler strikes the trident to one side, wrenching the weapon from my hand and driving it point-first into the ground.

I stumble backward, unbalanced by the shock of the blow, and his sword is falling toward me, a closing arc like the moon in its waning. I lose my footing. The blade whistles past, cleaving light from sky and casting back the gleam: dazzling, white.

I catch myself, remain standing. My right hand is useless, numb from the shield-blow, but I gather the net from the ground with my left and throw it at my opponent's feet.

He retreats from it. I hurl myself forward, grabbing at the trident where it juts out of the dust. My left hand closes round it and I bring it up hard, turning with it to meet the next attack.

The trident catches his buckler. It caves in the iron round his fist and knocks him back. His sword goes wide, shearing open my shoulder and scraping the collarbone.

Heat runs down my chest, filling my navel, but there is no pain, not yet, and my opponent is winded, breathing hard. The air whistles in his helm. His wounded side pulses, spitting gouts of bright red fluid. He is losing blood, and quickly.

I press him. With the trident I strike to left and right only to meet the buckler again and again as we cross the arena, drawing near the dead men, their butchered bodies. Our shadows join and pass through one another, dancing, and the crowd thumps and cheers, keeping time.

His footsteps woke me. The other slaves were asleep but the old cook came and knelt before me, the damp standing in his eyes.

"You were at the fountain," he said. "You heard the teacher speak."

"Yes."

"You must not mourn," he said. "Your brother is dead, but the teacher has promised the just will be reborn. Even the teacher himself, it is said, will die to come again in glory. He has promised this much: his blood, though spilled, will serve to hasten the coming kingdom."

I asked: "Why do you tell me this?"

"Your grief," he said. "Your anger. You must leave it behind you as he told the fishermen to leave their nets."

I shook my head. "What is a fisherman without a net?"

And the cook told of how the teacher had sighted the fishermen from the shore and called to them to leave their nets and follow him. The teacher said: "I will make you fishers of men."

Fishers of men. *The phrase haunted me. I whispered it to myself when seeing to my work, and in the night, when sleep deserted me, I imagined the breaking of water, the sound, and saw the nets hauled up dripping with his naked shape inside.*

The centurion. He was stripped of robes and armor, white and twitching like a fish. His mouth worked soundlessly as I split him groin to throat, plunging my hands into the blood-hot viscera. The intestines in ropes. The bags of his lungs.

And always the eyes and mouth open, lips gibbering.

THE CLANGOR OF iron. Trident ringing off shield and helm as I beat my opponent back toward the far wall. His footing is careful, even as he withdraws, sidestepping the long washes of blood. His head remains upright. His eyes are hidden but locked on mine, probing me as to anticipate my every assault. The feeling returns to my right side, and I wield the trident with both hands now, driving him across the arena like an ox before the goad.

We reach the far wall.

He stands with his back against it, sword low, shield ready.

I jab at his neck, two rapid strokes that catch the buckler. He raises his shield to guard against a third attack and I lunge forward, this time aiming low.

He is too quick. His sword whips down across the trident, deflecting the blow. His buckler, upraised, swings out across his chest to smash into my temple.

Hearing deserts me, the sight in my right eye. My lips split open over my teeth, and the blood fills my mouth and throat. I gasp, reel back.

He surges forward to hack at my neck, but I dodge to the side, somehow, and now I am in retreat, stepping backward, guarding against his attacks with the trident.

The fluid moves in my deafened ear. In my skull, I hear the ocean.

Like the waves of their shouting. Men and women filled the streets, jeering as the condemned were led to the place of execution.

From an upper window, I saw the soldiers pass in two bristling ranks. The mob yielded, clearing the road, and I glimpsed the centurion alongside his men, cracking his whip at those who failed to let pass. His tall plumes swayed.

The shouts grew louder. The condemned appeared.

Their clothes were torn and stained, dripping where the lash-wounds had soaked through. Two of the men were plainly thieves, but behind them limped the one whom cook had called teacher, the holy man whom we had seen at the fountain.

His blood, though spilled. *I recalled the old cook's words and wondered at their prophecy while below me the whole of the city cheered the holy man's death.*

He struggled forward, saying nothing. His wounds left black trails in the dust behind him.

The centurion's whip cracked and snarled, biting.

HE IS RELENTLESS. The sword streaks toward me, alternating with the swing of his shield, and already, I am near to fainting. My ears ring, the blood in me a struck bell chiming ceaselessly, louder for the din of sword and trident.

His shield glances off my cheek, breaking teeth.

The sword blurs about my head.

I am nauseated, half-blind. I must act. I shift my footing to anchor the base of the trident against the ground. He takes aim at my head and I dodge to one side, catching the sword between the weapon's prongs. I twist with both hands, stomp down hard.

The sword snaps.

His buckler, cutting sideways, collides with my skull.

The air blows out of my lungs, and the broken sword, jabbing, strikes me through the side, plunging to the hilt. He pulls it free. He rips me open along its edge.

I do not fall. His helm gleams, sun-touched and glowering. The bronze serpent regards me, eyes round and black with dried blood.

The sun eclipsed. Leviathan, leaping, swallowed the light, and all was made dark, as in my dreams, if only for a time. The day returned and later the true night fell.

The old cook, returning to the house, told of how the teacher had expired. The end had come quickly, he said, a mercy. The women had anointed the dead man's wounds with oil and laid the body to rest in the tomb, and a great stone was rolled across the entrance to seal it off that none might violate it.

"It is finished," the cook said. He exhaled heavily. To me he appeared older than ever before. He said: "Your kingdom come."

They were hopeful words, but he would not meet my gaze, and afterward, he tottered off to the kitchen to sleep, to wait. I waited too but only until the hour before dawn when the whole of the house was sleeping and none awake to see me go.

The kingdom was imminent. I felt its coming in my blood and in the beating at my ears as I scaled the outer wall to the centurion's bedchamber. He was asleep. He snored and blubbered, drunk on wine or the day's cruelties. He did not stir and made no sound even as his own sword struck him through the chest. His eyes fluttered open, fell shut.

I wrenched out the blade, tearing wide the wound and spattering my face and hands. Beside him the sleeping woman woke, one of the lady's handmaids.

She saw me. She opened her mouth.

THE WOUNDS BELCH and spurt: his, mine. I thrust my left hand to my side and fumble at the ragged flaps of skin and muscle. I press down hard to dam the flow and stagger backward before his attacks. Five paces more and the net is at my feet.

My opponent advances, sword raised.

I release the pressure on my side. Warmth spills out, wetting my leg, and the arena starts to spin. I transfer the trident to my left hand and allow my right to drop behind me, fingers spread, straining at the fallen net.

He raps his fists together. Broken shield, broken blade.

Breaking stone. The noise of hammers underground. We were chained ankle to ankle, seeking for veins in the stone, for the glimmer of ore by the overseer's torch. A lifetime had passed since I fled the city of my birth but here the din of breaking sufficed to stretch time and swallow years until the day the heretic was sent to us.

The boy was too young to have known the teacher but even so he claimed discipleship, denying the facts of the holy man's death and of our subsequent abandonment. He spoke of the kingdom as though it were a place nearby, close enough to taste. In chains he pretended to freedom, and his eyes, luminous, caught the torch-light.

"The kingdom is here," he said. "It surrounds you and still you do not see."

Later, when the day's work was done, I heard him whispering to himself. He was praying for me or my deliverance. His hands were pressed together, raised to his mouth to catch the words, the softness of his voice. His eyes glimmered, pools of shining in the gloom.

The hammer, sweat-slick, slipped in my hands.

MY FINGERS IN the netting.

He is close, less than three paces away. He protects himself with the buckler and chops at my left arm where it holds the trident.

With my right hand, I sweep the net from the ground. The ends twine round his shoulders. His elbow, netted, strikes his side, and his hand opens to release the sword.

I must be quick. I jam the trident into the ground, then use both hands to pull fast on the net. My opponent stumbles forward and I sidestep to avoid his fall. He strikes the ground, stiff as a felled trunk with the net wound about him. I pull at the ropes with what strength is left to me, trapping his arms to his body, then reach with my left hand for the trident.

His breath is low and murmuring, his face upturned.

Eyes flash wetly in his helm.

Open doors. A light beyond all imagining the first time they prodded me out of the darkness and into the arena. Nothing was known of my past crimes save that I had murdered a man in the mines and now must face the judgment.

The heat dizzied me. The air itself was corrupt, tainted by the stink of torn bodies. Excrement. Organ-meat. They pushed me out toward the center of the arena while the surrounding crowd screeched for my death as they had for the teacher's long ago, and I, too, was naked, with only a net and spear to defend myself.

The arena's champion bore down on me, wielding a maul and clanking in his armor. He was taller than me, a giant of a man, but he died the same as the others while always the crowds roared their approval, cheering me on through the months and years in which I revenged myself on the hell of this creation, netting men like fish and piercing them, body and spirit.

I gutted the sun: I drank my fill of heaven.

BLOOD IN MY mouth. I swallow and choke on it, gasping after breath.

My opponent grasps at the cords that bind him. His hands are wet and cannot find purchase. I clench my fist and draw the ropes taut. I raise the trident, prepare to strike.

His fingers close. He has the net. He pulls hard, unbalancing me. My legs buckle and give and the trident impacts the ground. I fall across it, trapping it under my weight.

He stands and jerks upon the net, tearing it from my hands. He casts it over me.

I attempt to free myself, but he is too strong, the cords too tight about me. His foot connects with my ribs, a crunching sound. He rolls me onto my back then stands over me with one foot on the net, his outline looming across a blue sky without cloud.

The ropes hold. They bite through flesh like chains but I fight against them, rising. I cannot hear the crowd, only the breath in his helm. I am on my knees.

The tomb before me, the kingdom at hand. Soon their bodies will be found: the centurion, the handmaid. The soldiers will come for me and still I wait.

Dawn approaches. The tomb is sealed, as the cook has said, but I watch the boulder to see it rolled away. My shadow appears and lengthens to cover the ground at my feet. I hear birds, smell cooking fires from the city below. The night is spent.

Desperate, I scrabble at the side of the boulder. My hands are greased and slick, but I haul myself up by broken nails until I reach the gap between the stone and the hillside. I thrust my face to the earth and peer into the chamber beyond.

See nothing, nothingness. Darkness deeper than shadow in the place where no light penetrates. The teacher lies within, hidden beyond sight or rescue, his soul chained to bone and sinew as I too am shackled, even here, with the centurion's blood cracked and drying on my hands. Smoke rises from the city, visible now. My master's face fades with the daybreak to be replaced by another as the skies fire and lighten and morning blights the hillside.

HE REMOVES HIS helm. The eyes are familiar, the voice: the memory of rivers become river itself. I am drowning. My lungs fill. I pant after air that will not come even as the blood continues to pump from his wounded side, poured out without cease.

He says: "Did I not promise you I would return? That you would be free?"

The ropes strain, binding me.

His sword is raised: red hilt, red hand. And falling.

From the Fertile Dark

Rebecca J. Allred

As tendrils of spilled ink mingle with the pool of blood expanding around her knees, Charlotte paints the shadow child on a wall the shade of wilted daffodils. Upstairs, her husband packs his things, slipping quietly from her life even as the last of their children slips from her womb. There will be no call for the midwife who, with the blessings of the town elders, declared her pregnancy an abomination from the start. Neither will she seek the aid of the doctors from away. There is nothing either the ancient woman or the practitioners responsible for its inception can do to stay the flow of despair and failure seeping from Charlotte's sex, and she is already intimately familiar with the details of post-miscarriage self-care.

Hands trembling, she outlines the shape of a girl, four years old with soft curls that fall to her shoulders—an imitation of invented memory. With each stroke, Charlotte replaces the foul taste of Black Haw extract and Chaste tree berry with the flavors of vanilla ice cream and birthday cake; the acrid scent of antiseptic and bleached linens with the fragrance of baby powder and warm milk; and the repeated pricks of needles that promised a miracle at the price of her friends and family with the soft ticklish flutter of butterfly kisses. In her mind, the short, hurried footsteps traversing the hallway are not the clatter of a runaway spouse, but an echo of a toddler fleeing bath time. Charlotte chases the phantom memory into darkness.

Deceiver...

Instead of condolences and comfort, they bring casseroles and cake. Pariah or not, Charlotte is a grieving mother, and the neighbors have appearances to keep. Charlotte receives their charity with silent gratitude, stacking parcels one on top of the other like so many tiny coffins. With the exception of answering the door to accept tokens of feigned sympathy, she resides in the nursery.

Curtains closed, shelves lined with little socks and shoes, pacifiers, and containers of baby powder, the nursery is an altar for an absent god. Tucked in a corner, a handful of plush characters peek over the edge of a bassinet, glossy eyes connecting the dots of rust-colored stains that trace loss across the floorboards like chalk lines on pavement. Charlotte covers the walls with the residue of wishes, adding a jump rope, toys, and a swing for the shadow child's amusement.

Days stretch endlessly into weeks as time rushes past in a monochromic blur until the neighborly visits, much like the flow of blood that serves as a daily reminder of her failure, eventually slow and then stop altogether.

BEHIND THE HOUSE, near the edge of the surrounding woods, a pair of swings twists in an early winter breeze. Unable to contain her grief any longer, Charlotte's house invites the breeze to cleanse its stagnant halls, throwing open its doors and windows and spilling a kaleidoscope of sorrow into the night.

Charlotte gives chase, but for every lamentation recaptured and rebottled to nurture and protect, another escapes her lips, feeding the breeze until it becomes a gale. When it becomes clear her efforts are wasted, Charlotte takes to the swings. If she cannot stop her despair from taking flight, she will follow it into the sky. Charlotte swings up, up, up—toward the swollen moon as it drifts through the amnion of distant galaxies—and lets go. For a moment, she hangs suspended in the tempest. Then it retreats with all her cultivated misery in tow, and Charlotte plummets back to the earth to sow her garden of heartache anew.

"For what do you weep?" someone from within the wood whispers. The voice is low and dark, like distant thunder, and though it carries undertones of stealth and misdirection, it offers the first kind words Charlotte has heard in months.

"I weep for the death of my heart, that its ghost may forget how to love."

"Even those who walk between worlds are haunted by the memory of loss."

"I among them." Charlotte rises, brushing blades of winter grass from her dress and steps toward the edge of the wooded area. "Who are you? Why do you speak with me? Do you not know that I am forsaken?"

"I am a granter of wishes. I can give you that for which your heart breaks."

Temptation in the form of a flutter deep in the pit of Charlotte's stomach draws her nearer to the shadowed wood.

"Nothing of such value is given freely." Charlotte's voice trembles with an amalgam of hope and fear. "What payment is due such a service?"

"Love," the voice says. "Sacrifice."

A vine wide as her palm and armed with thorns like fangs twists from the foliage into the moonlight. It lashes out, slicing through the thin fabric of Charlotte's dress and leaving behind three sets of parallel wounds on her abdomen.

Charlotte cries out but does not flee. She touches the slits on her belly, smearing thick drops of blood against her shivering flesh. Fingers slick with red, Charlotte steps closer and attempts to wrap them around the vine, but it has no depth and passes through her grasp like vapor. She presses her fingers to her mouth.

"Love," she says, bending at the waist and brushing her bloodied lips against the shadow, returning its kiss. "Love is sacrifice."

The vine shudders. Its barbs scramble up the stem, coalescing into a razor sharp grin. "Flesh of your flesh."

Lapping at the fluid coursing down the concave hollow of Charlotte's stomach, the dark umbilicus sprouts arms and legs. They probe her wounds, diving between layers of muscle and disappearing into

Charlotte's body like smoke in reverse.

Her belly swells, the slits become gouges, and a sound like ruptured earth erupts from her throat. It is agony. It is rapture. It lasts forever and is over in the beat of a newborn's heart.

Charlotte kneels, clutching her abdomen. The slashes have disappeared; tiny fingers trace their absence from the inside.

Deceiver.

Whore…

Words like wasps hover round Charlotte's home, waiting for an opportunity to sting. Her much expanded midsection has captured the town's attention, and to the hive of buzzing tongues, each postulate regarding her condition is less palatable than the last.

THE PRESENCE OF another draws Charlotte from sleep. Fearing the worst, that the elders have come for her and the unborn child, she tumbles out of bed and heads for the door.

"It is only I," a calm, familiar voice reassures.

Charlotte ceases her escape and turns to confront her husband. He sits, hands clutching one another between his knees, on the edge of the bed they once shared.

"What are you doing here?"

"I came to make amends. To beg your forgiveness and be a father to our child."

Wrapping her arms protectively around her belly, Charlotte speaks the words she's practiced time and again inside her mind.

"This child belongs to me and me alone"

Her husband winces as if struck. "Not mine, then."

"No."

"I suspected as much. As do many of the others." It is clear from his face that while he accepts this explanation, her husband had hoped the earliest rumors were true. That the miscarriage had been no more than a deception and the child inside her was the sum of their shared efforts.

"And yet my errand remains the same." He rises and crosses to Charlotte, taking one of her hands in his own. "Forgive me, wife. I was a coward."

A sensation like falling into the sky forces Charlotte to her knees.

She looks into her husband's eyes and hopes the urgency reflected there is not her own.

"I forgive you, but you cannot stay. The elders will never allow it."

"It would not be the first time I rejected the will of the elders for the promise of a family."

"That was different."

"Was it? Tell me, wife. How came you to be with child this time?"

Charlotte pulls her hand away and returns it to its place upon her stomach which has begun to knot.

"Be it by medicine or by magic, it is the same in the eyes of the elders."

Instead of words, a wail of agony pours from Charlotte's throat and she curls round her tightening middle.

Her husband gathers her into his arms and rests her on the bed. "I'll fetch the midwife," he says when she's past the first contraction.

"No! They must never see!"

"See what?"

Charlotte cries out again as another wave of pressure threatens to split her open. "Help me," she pleads. "Help me, and you can stay."

Hours later, Charlotte's screams are replaced by the shrill cry of a newborn.

Deceiver.

Whore.

Murderer...

When they come to question her, Charlotte tells the elder's vassals that, despite his rumored claims to return home, she hasn't seen her husband in months—not since he left following her most recent miscarriage. About the infant sounds coming from the adjacent room, she tells them nothing, keeping the bundle of coos and gurgles tightly swaddled as they search the house and surrounding land time and again for evidence of a crime.

They find none, overlooking the dim, shifting outline of a man huddled in the bedroom corner. Charlotte too learns to overlook him, and in time, he disappears altogether.

AS THE GIRL blossoms from infant to toddler, Charlotte grows ever more pale, spending day and night watching her daughter play with toys inked upon the walls of their secluded existence. Her only regret is that, unlike the jacks and the swing, her daughter's dark touch is unable to animate the other shadow child and grant herself a playmate.

WALKING HOME THROUGH waves of winter ash, a bundle of groceries held close to her chest, Charlotte is confronted by a woman cloaked in familiar wounds.

"How's your daughter?" the woman asks, cheeks streaked with rage.

On both sides of the street, people have halted their journeys to bear witness. Charlotte's answer is tentative. "Well, thank you. I was sorry to hear of yours. I pray they find her soon and in good health."

The woman spits in Charlotte's face and hurries away, choked sobs trailing behind her. Sharp glares aimed at her heart pierce Charlotte's winter coat, but they fail to embed themselves in her fading flesh.

When she arrives at home, Charlotte is greeted by the sound of not one, but two children giggling. She rushes inside, terrified of what she knows she will find. Her daughter swings wide arcs across the nursery's yellow walls, dusky locks trailing behind her like smoke. A second, unfamiliar, shadow child pushes her as the original watches, silent and unmoving as a statue.

ONE BY ONE, the town's children vanish. One by one, their shadows appear in Charlotte's home, the ranks of her daughter's playground companions swelling into the dozens.

Deceiver.

Whore.

Murderer.

Witch...

Little more than a whisper, Charlotte watches as a mob gathers outside—larger, angrier versions of wasps equipped with more than mere stings. Near the back, draped in robes, the elders watch with a singular pious gaze.

"Give them back!"

"Come out, or we'll drag you out!"

Someone throws a stone; it crashes through the window, and a river of children's laughter leaks out.

"I hear them. They're inside."

"More lies. She must be destroyed!"

The children gather round Charlotte, pulling her away from the windows just as the first blazing torch sails into the living room. In the nursery, her daughter twists in the swing. Charlotte tries to gather the girl into her arms, but they no longer have any substance. The girl laughs and points to the original shadow child still inked upon the wall.

Exhausted, Charlotte sinks to the floor. This close to the shadow child, she can see flecks of dried blood admixed with the ink. Her blood.

The flames spread. They creep down the hall, a light made to devour shadow.

"Flesh of my flesh," Charlotte says. "Love is sacrifice." She presses her lips to the imprint and flows backward into herself. The children follow her into darkness.

CHARLOTTE WANDERS the boundless forest in a veil of midnight, surrounded by giggles and rustling leaves as tiny shadows dart from tree to tree through beams of moonlight. Ahead, she glimpses a break in the dense timber and, beyond that, a memory of her former self. Its slight frame shudders, exuding a fountain of grief.

Charlotte calls wordlessly to the shadows and draws one to her breast. Then she moves to the edge of the night and asks the woman a question to which she already knows the answer.

No Abiding Place on Earth

Matthew M. Bartlett

—MARY, DON'T FORGET *your cudgel.*

Mary mutters, how could she *possibly* forget, grabs the knotted, leaded blackthorn cudgel from the umbrella stand, knocking Daniel's cane to the floor. He shouldn't have said anything, he knew she was in a snit, and of course she knows to bring the cudgel, but…but a father's job is to err on the side of protecting his daughter if he can. And for his trouble, she snaps at him. Mary, little Mary-kins, not so long ago just a doll-faced girl, curious and giggly and adoring, now hardened, weary-eyed, humorless. She slams the door behind her as he pushes himself up from the chair, groaning like a man much older than his 54 years, bends slowly to pick up the cane, stabs it back into the stand. He pulls back the curtain, scans the barren treetops. Their stripped limbs wave in the wind, a skeletal convocation pleading for an offering from the frowning, furrowed sky. Tendrils of mist, the ghosts of snakes, curl around their trunks. The telephone wires bounce gently like recently deserted tight-ropes.

There don't seem to be any of *them* out there, not now.

From the other side of the hedges he hears the car door slam shut, the whinny and purr of the engine. She is okay. She will be okay. The cudgel will be enough.

November, that brown and brittle season, has swung in hard on the heel of Halloween, and most days linger in a dusky malaise from start to finish, suspended in a bluish-grey solution of dread and dead leaves. Last night the wind kicked up hard, barren limbs smacking at the house like dried husks of hands. The windows rattled and shook in their casements and the cat drew close to Daniel in his easy chair, her chin in the crook of Daniel's arm. When the wind yelped around the corners of the house, the cat whimpered, pressing closer. Daniel hoped fervently for the power to stay on.

Most of *them* keep their distance when the lights are on.

IT STARTED WITH the power outages. The first was in mid-September, resolved quickly, unremarkable. Another two days later, lasting nearly three hours. The next week brought four separate outages, over seven hours without electricity each go-round. Flashlights, candles, early to bed. Charge your devices while you can. When in doubt, throw it out.

Another call to MassGrid, a subsidiary of The Global Electricity Group PLC. The unhappy union of squirrel and transformer, said the voice somewhere back in the phone's speaker, distant, like a call from the outer reaches of the universe. *That's what you said every time I called last week. Are the squirrels committing mass suicide?* Silence for a beat, a rote apology. We're sorry sir. Crews are out and active, doing all they can.

Uh-huh.

The scratching at the windows starts up. The doorknob jiggles. The muttering, the guttural rumbling, the sighs at the windows, at the doorjamb.

After a time, the house awakens with a hum and the lights flicker bright, too bright, blinding, then back to their usual weak dimness. The things retreat to the trees, beyond the reach of the streetlights.

The outages still come, two or three a day, lasting hours.

IT WAS EARLY October when Daniel first saw them. He was out for a walk, and he chanced to look up high in the grey sky and one was descending, some kind of strange owl, plucked bare. Pallid, knobby breast; flimsy, webbed wings dangling from twig-like arms, it flew only with a great deal of exertion. When it was a few yards off it began to coast, spreading its wings wide, and lit in a copse of trees, its long-toed feet scrambling to grasp a gnarled branch. Twigs snapped and a flurry of leaves and…and the trees were full of the things. Daniel took a few tentative steps in their direction, then clasped his hand over his mouth. Their heads resembled those of elderly men, wispy white hair, wizened, slack mouths curtained with pink, blistered dewlaps. One turned its hooded, sagging eye in his direction. Then the others did the same. They coughed and wheezed and began flapping their sad wings as if to launch. It sounded like the smacking of slackened cheeks when someone rapidly shakes his head back and forth.

Then they did launch, all of them, at once. Daniel dropped to his knees, covered his head. They swarmed above him, flapping and wheezing and muttering. When they had passed, he turned and saw a boy—the Bernier kid, probably—running down Prospect Street, the horrid flock flying low above him, bellowing and belching and screeching. The front-most creature swooped down and grabbed the boy by the collar and left sleeve of his shirt. He cried out as he was lifted into the sky. The flock ascended into the clouds, the boy struggling to release himself, to punch at the horrid thing that carried him, small legs kicking uselessly at the sky. Daniel stared after them, helpless.

Since they came, everything deteriorates with alarming rapidity. The cat litter dampens and clumps into concrete. The milk curdles minutes out of the refrigerator. The bread, fresh from the machine, sprouts green bruises. Peaches erupt with black blisters and crumple, flies bursting from their rotten cores, buzzing madly. Tea cools before it reaches Daniel's lips. He cracks an egg and the yolk is black gelatin. The smell is rank, gag-inducing.

Even the bulbs in the lamps don't have the reach they once did.

The worst thing is that there's nothing about the creatures on the news. Daniel watches the two local channels, scans the daily paper, which the carrier, brave soul, still somehow manages to fling onto the doorstep every day but Sunday. There are three houses on the short dead-end street, three including the one he shares with Mary. The other two have shed their tenants and whatever belongings they could fit in their cars. Daniel wonders where they're going and whether they'll get there. He doesn't know how widespread the problem is. He wishes they'd talk about it on the news.

MARY'S BEEN GONE four hours, the longest stretch yet. The local markets are locked up tight or else busted open, trashed and looted, and she has to go further and further to find canned food and simple provisions.

Daniel is again left alone with his thoughts. They are not welcome companions. He considers his belly, now hanging over his belt-line. His belt digs into his flesh when he sits, carving painful welts into his waist. His own heartbeat nags him about his mortality. He is aware of it more and more as he ages, especially in the silences when Mary's gone out or sits sequestered in her room. It thumps out the years like a kitchen timer. Like anything else, it will stop, ring the harsh and jarring bell of finality. It could do so at any moment, as his father's had; the old man had simply crumpled to the kitchen floor while scrambling eggs, the spatula gripped in his white-knuckled hand.

Further, Mary has been complaining that she can hear his snoring from her room. He probably has sleep apnea. Stops breathing who knows how many times a night. And he speculates at what tiny cancers might even now be multiplying somewhere in the murky purple depths of his body. He turns over in his tired mind every fatal scenario he can conjure. Death flies among his thoughts, a black wraith tracing a zig-zag path among moon-drunk birds.

Daniel turns on the television to silence his thoughts. Channel 22 is interviewing a beloved coach about his retirement...and damned if one of the things isn't perched atop city hall in the background, blurry, but unmistakable; its spindly legs twitching; rheumy, hate-filled eyes surveying the town common. Daniel sits up in the chair, stares. His hands open and close. He wants to shout, to warn the people on the screen. The thing's talons scrape the brick, red clouds spill down onto the walk below. A couple walking below see the thing, flinch, scurry into traffic, protecting their faces with crossed forearms among the screaming of car brakes and the shouts of horns. Not a word from the reporter as the coach prattles on, oblivious. The thing launches awkwardly from its perch, lurches through the sky and off-screen.

He calls the station's You Report It Hotline. The phone rings and rings.

The door slams and the cat bolts from Daniel's lap and runs into the kitchen. Mary rushes in and the hood of her coat is torn, her forehead scraped, dots of blood clotting along a ragged line like points on a graph. Her strawberry blonde curls are matted, mud-caked. Daniel starts to rise and she flutters a dismissive hand in his direction.

—Fucking things. I'm fine. Where's the disinfectant...I've got it.

Off to the bathroom. The sink runs, water splashes. A door closes and music starts up and she's in her room ignoring everything. She has been stoic, sullen since before this thing began, since the disaster with Keith, about which she refused to give any information at all—an incident, Daniel supposed, or an unresolved argument—that saw her arrive at Daniel's unannounced with a suitcase full of clothes and unknown depths of unexpressed rage and disappointment. Now he is unwillingly cast in the role of the father who can't do or say anything right, and all he can do is wait for her to come around. It would feel better, he thinks, to have an ally. It would feel better for her too, he knows it. Until she comes around, the feline will more than suffice for uncomplicated companionship. As though summoned by the thought, the cat saunters back into the room, tail swimming lazily behind her. She jumps to Daniel's side and sinks into sleep.

THAT NIGHT, SOMETHING new, something bad. Daniel awakens to voices echoing outside, unintelligible, punctuated with dark chortling and sibilant whispers. He feels for the cat but she is no longer at his side. He rises, crosses the dark room to the window, parts the curtain. The moon is high and bright, the sky cloudless. Stars glint, smug and safe up in the firmament. The emptied houses' windows hang open, and the voices thrum within, in the dark, empty rooms. He can't make out individual words, can't even tell if they're speaking English. The voices overlap, converge and declaim in unison, then part into separate streams of droning monologues. They don't stop for breaths. Daniel turns on the fan to block out the sounds with white noise, but still he hears the percussive voices, now strident, now clandestine, now ecstatic. He falls into uneasy sleep as the cat, who has returned to his side, twitches and squeaks out complaints, her tiny teeth clicking.

In the morning Daniel dares step out onto the porch, then down to the lawn. It's warm for November. The sun glistens off the dewy branches that crowd the quiet street. He hears birdsong, a rare sound now. They sound cautious, staccato chirps and trills and titters. The windows of the other houses are still open, but all is still. He doesn't even see any of them. He usually sees two or three sleeping at dawn, tucked into the crook of a branch or on a housetop. They clench like wounded spiders, and they shiver and twitch. Their ribs stick out. Their sides heave. One will, on occasion, push out a loud, rattling fart. Daniel once saw one break wind, wake, and, grotesque arms pinwheeling, fall from its perch on a high telephone wire. He laughed—he could not help but laugh—but he stopped laughing when it hit the ground. He has to block his memory now of what happened when it hit the ground.

Beyond the hedge he spots Mary's shoe on the road and his heart starts to thrum in his chest. The air seems to buzz with menace. Dark droplets on the pavement lead to the shoe, or away from it. Are they blood drops? He backs up, keeping an eye on the space between the hedges. He closes the door and latches it, heads for Mary's room. The door is open, the bed unmade, the sheets and blankets piled at its foot.

He goes back outside, grabs his cane on the way out. A flimsy weapon, but a weapon nonetheless. The cat yowls as he passes. The shoe is still there, and now he hears something. A whimper. Holding the cane out in front of him in both hands, he advances toward the street. He braces himself, passes between the hedges. He looks at the shoe, kneels, touches a droplet and examines the tip of his finger. Brown liquid has settled into the whorls of his fingertips. He sniffs at it, wincing. Not blood. Motor oil.

Mary's car is still in its spot. He rises and turns to go back inside.

Three of them stand sentry in front of the front door. They are emaciated. Blue veins as thick as fingers pulse in their sagging wings. The layered, drooping folds under their eyes are black and bruised. One has a skin tag the size of an apple hanging on its cheek, dark red and bleeding at its root. Its weight pulls down the skin under its eye, creating a cradle of red below the pupil in which maggots cavort in a squirming orgy. The things open their mouths, revealing purple-soiled graveyards of disarranged grey teeth, and sing a high, mournful chorus, an alien, synchronized sigh. A barbershop quartet, Daniel thinks. But where is the fourth?

Hot, damp hands grasp the back of his neck and squeeze.

The thing whips him around, dropping him onto his back and pinning him, its wings flapping wildly. Daniel's cane flies from his hand, landing in the hedge. The thing's feet dig into his gut below the arch of his rib cage. Its eyes betray fierce anger rimmed around the edges with profound sorrow. It pulls Daniel's face to its own—Daniel deliberately unfocuses his eyes and lets his mouth go slack—and it kisses him gently on the lips, dry and feathery.

It loosens its grip and rolls off of Daniel onto the leaf-strewn walk. Its hands grapple uselessly at the air and it coughs, its body trembling with each concussive hack. Then the trembling quickens, its toes spread and stretch, and it dies, its eyes rolled rightward, staring through Daniel and into unknown abysses. It clenches and shoots a stream of miserable grey diarrhea onto the walk.

Daniel pushes himself into a sitting position, lurches forward, and stands. His legs are weak and shaking. The veins stand out in his arms as he puts his hand to the back of his neck to check for blood. It stings. It stings like a thousand jellyfish. The three things that had been blocking the door have flown up to the eaves, where they weep noisily, shining pendulums of yellow-green mucous swaying from their nostrils.

Daniel retrieves his cane, makes his way up the porch steps, caroms through the front doorway and into the dark living room, falls into his easy chair. He closes his eyes, listens to his own breathing as it calms. At some point the cat jumps onto the arm of the chair, then jumps back down and gallops out of the room hissing. His skin feels as though it's shrinking, tightening in increments like a blood pressure cuff. His arms feel weak and flabby. He tries to lift one and cannot. His eyes burn and he is unable to attend to them. *Am I dying?* he wonders. *Am I dead?*

The answer comes two hours later when the creak of the door awakens him. He lifts the lid of one eye and sees Mary silhouetted in the evening light. She smells of blood, of infected flesh. *Oh, Dad,* she says, and she comes and kneels next to him. She touches his face with one hand, lifts his wrist with the other. Her hands are as hot as fire.

Oh my god, Dad, she says.

Pause for Laughter

José Cruz

THE FACES IN the crowd look up to me and ask: *What good is a clown at the end of the world?* And if I'm not crying, I will turn to them and I will tell them. I will tell them that I am the last true residue of the human race.

They know it. Their children know it. They may shrink back from me, guard their eyes as I pass under the guttering bonfire sun of our dying city—as if afraid that my cursed hand should graze them, as if their souls should become heavy with the burden I pass onto them.

As if all of this is my fault.

Nighttime is another matter entirely.

At night the crowd comes to the theater to witness my magic. Only then can they see me for what I really am. I am not the monster. The monsters are the ones who lurk in the edges of our vision, shimmering in the periphery, spectral voyeurs at the harvest feast.

But at night when the ghost light gleams, it smiles upon me. The monsters watch the crowd; the crowd watches me; I watch them all. Everyone has a role to play in the great broken drama of the universe.

Every night the crowd comes to the theater and every night they ask themselves what I am. If they are patient they will see this in my act. If they are wise they will know it to be true.

I am their final hope.

EVERYTHING IS A modest affair during the apocalypse.

Before the world was reborn in Fire, I worked for companies of all creeds and colors: the Donovan Brothers' Travelling Electric Show; Le Cirque de la Bête; the Invisible Crime Festival. One outfit by the name of Uncle Diddly's Funny Farm was nothing more than a set of cages housing diseased lab animals overseen by a pack of unshaven men with angry jugular veins. The life of a clown is one of constant adaptability, and I am one of the greatest of my kind.

I am the greatest.

The gutted remains of an ice-packing factory serve as my Auditorium of Wonders now. There are no chairs, only piles of rubble I've stationed across the gashed concrete floor. The dozens of spectators that come at night take their seats atop the bathroom sinks and piecemeal bookcases and twisted traffic signs as if recalling from muscle memory, the association that this spot is "theirs," a thing for them to claim in a world bereft of any real ownership. My stage is a cluster of wooden pallets covered in rocky layers of dun-colored earth. Most of the building's corrugated tin roof has been clawed away, and in the evening the dim remembrance of stars can sometimes be seen by those who wish hard enough for them.

The Fever Men keep to the edges of the theater throughout the performance. The greasy flames from the trashcan fires reveal the jaundiced nest of epidermal tubing under their ragged shrouds that links their jaws and chests, the amber light swirling like drainwater in the infinite patience of their vacant, staring eyes. The crowd never acknowledges the Fever Men but they know that they're there all the same, just like they know when the Fever Men curl up next to them in the night to whisper loveliness in their ears and kiss their life away with the shriveled mouths of their claws.

Legends will breed in any time. It has been said that the Fever Men *were* men once, long ago, before their bodies were warped by flame and driven to infernal hunger from their trials. Others claim that they arrived during the Fire with all the others like them, doomsday riders without horses. If one were to journey to the ruins of the city's former ghetto, they would see this origin story splayed across the bared backs of fallen buildings in Neolithic shades of mud and bile, an unsavory pictorial record for the hoped-for generations of the future to read and understand from whence they came.

Not that a picture makes any of it true. The only thing that is certain is that there are less people in the crowd and more shadows along the walls every night.

As a boy I was bequeathed a fine *moplah* sword by a blind fakir who saw more than he told. It is never far from my reach during the nightly performances, its broad curve of steel always primed and freshly-whetted should the hooded shadows ever glide too close to the stage. Many people in the crowd have weapons of their own—crude newspaper shanks, nail-spangled baseball bats, gaping hand-saws with rusted teeth—but none wield them with any real precision or efficiency, only a kind of infantile mania. I have never been forced to bring the sword out during a performance, but the world is always becoming a different place these days. You can count on this and nothing else.

It is no secret that the crowd fears me more than the Fever Men. I can see it in their eyes, see it as their tear-gummed lids fight back against their own instinctual terror and open wide to take in the full breadth of my works. The crowd knows they will die at the hands of the Fever Men, but death has always been the great inevitable. I am the great unknowable. What I do on stage—how I do it—remains a mystery borne of their own flesh. To the crowd this is sacrilege; my magic is indefinable, intangible, a hand of uncertainty robbing them of their last remaining crumbs of security.

And yet: here they are. Chalk it up as another mystery of the universe. Or just an old joke.

Perhaps they understand my purpose here after all. Perhaps there is hope for us just yet.

A cloud of dust announces my entrance upon the stage, hangs in the cloying darkness like a lover's expectant breath. I clap, and the sound echoes across the frozen room.

The show begins.

Spreading my arms wide I grow my shadow for the crowd until it looms across the walls and reaches the tops of the smoke-crusted rafters. I flex my fingers like poisoned spiders, commanding the shadow to dance, a charcoal Cyclops twirling to the soundless music of the void. The crowd watches in a silence that would be reverent were it not for the bloodless clenching of their hands and lips.

Taking my cue, I step out of my Father's coat and leave my head resting on its frayed collar. I walk to the other end of the stage, clap twice, leap into the air as the empty arms of Father's coat tosses it into my hands. I twist the head back onto my neck and look out into the crowd's pinched, sooty faces, wondering if this will be the night that I finally see it: the blue spark of amusement, a flashing grin, the shaky birthing of a laugh…

But it isn't. It never is.

After I regale my public with further displays of Sights Never Before Seen and Other Comical Didos, I finish the performance by placing the water-stained cigar box labeled ZEPPO upon the stage and climb down into its fragrant brown gloom, waving my blue silk handkerchief in fond farewell as I descend. When I climb back out, I look upon an empty room. The crowd has left. Not even the shadows remain.

There are no roses left for me in tribute, no standing ovation to welcome my return. The only sound in the abandoned theater is the fanfare of dead leaves sighing down wayward aisles.

Hope is a dangerous thing to harbor in a world where nothing good can grow. And yet: here I am. Chalk it up as another mystery of the universe. Or just an old joke.

I wonder when the crowd will realize that destiny has brought me here to help them. That laughter is medicine. That it's all that we have left. That it's the only thing keeping us human.

The world is ending, but it isn't over yet. Yet I know that come the day I look out into the crowd and see a congregation of hungry, yellow faces staring back at me, it will be.

My first memory was the thundering of elephants.

I was born into the circus a small wormish thing, fish-belly white on a bed of hay laden with dung. Already I was the color of the clown, my destiny foretold in the shattered faces of the Tarot and heralded by the stamp of the gray mountains roaring wild-eyed in their chains.

The hermaphrodite who delivered me said I never cried once during the birth. After opening my eyes, all I did was laugh. My path was clear from the beginning.

Father was a fool and Mother was a joke. We lived in one of the listing, mold-devoured wagons that encircled the fairgrounds. Ours was said to be haunted by the spirit of the gypsy dwarf who last owned it, the victim of some foul marriage plot. Father feared these rumors because he came from a country where fairy tales were still real, so he'd drown his apprehensions in bitter blackberry wine until he was past the point of caring about ghosts or anything else that lived in the wagon.

And Mother. Mother was a joke.

One night during my fifteenth year Father beckoned me come over. He was still in the faded makeup and patched costume trousers of the weeping hobo. The stubble on his face was a livid blue scar. Mother stayed in her corner, moaning a lullaby and tapping at the spiders dancing across the window.

"So," Father said. "You want to be clown. Is that what clown looks like?"

He pointed to the leotard clinging to me like a second skin of dark matter, to the kohl-lined eyes popping out from under the mat of my rumpled hair.

"It's from a film," I told him.

I had spied the freaks watching it after-hours. Normally my eyes would cringe whenever I was forced to look upon their stumped, half-finished forms, but that night my attention was elsewhere. I watched from my hiding place as a flickering play was cast upon a wrinkled tent flap, the sharp licorice breath of absinthe cutting through the air like a green blade. In the film, a tall thin man held a knife over a sleeping woman. She awoke suddenly, screaming and writhing away before the man took her up in his arms and carried her across a maze of drunken roofs. The man never took the woman's clothes off, like in the other films. The line of Tarot that had been laid out at my birth was given its final player.

"Ay?" Father asked. "And who are you supposed to be?"

The film had told me what to do. It had given me the face of my destiny and then shouted my new name to me in silence from the glimmering prism of the makeshift screen, a name dank with the fungal taste of decaying books and forbidden fruit:

— I MUST BECOME CALIGARI —

"Shit name for clown," Father muttered. His rosy frown curled into a lopsided grin. "So show me what you do then."

Hurriedly, I grasped the dark puddle at my feet and proceeded to grow my shadow for him. In those days I could only make my shadow as tall as Father. Not like now. Father shifted uncomfortably in his chair, trying to look away.

Taking my cue, I snatched one of the mice nibbling on our dinner bread from the table and dropped it down my sleeve, opening my mouth wide-wide so Father could hear the frightened squeals that were echoing up from the pit of my stomach.

Father's throat quivered and he waved his hand impatiently, erasing me from his sight. "Dirty tricks," he said, and spat.

I cast my eyes to the floor and lifted my toeless shoe. The shivering mouse quickly fled back to the safety of its hole. I wrapped my arms around my chest and squeezed. I felt cold without it.

"Clown has only one true act," Father said. "Drum snare. Clown fall down. Everybody laugh." He scratched at his mouth and looked towards the mouse hole. "Everything else is just variation."

Mother giggled as she plucked one of the spiders off the window.

"You spend whole life try to make crowd smile," Father said. He held up his tremoring hand and contemplated his new, bloody fingers. "But where are your smiles?"

He snatched up the bottle of wine from the table. "It's like you keep them to yourself in big bottle, for rainy days. But the crowd comes and waves their cups at you, shouting—'Pour!' So you give, because you are good, and they drink. But then cups flash back. 'Pour!' they shout. Crowd is always thirsty, even on sunny days. So you keep pouring, and pouring. Finally crowd leaves, all happy, smacking lips. Toss empty cups at you like coins. Then you go fill your cup..."

He turned the bottle over. A single purple gem winked from its cracked lip and dotted the wormy board at his foot. He chuckled grimly. "Water, water, everywhere..."

The bottle slipped from Father's hand to the floor. The smoked glass spun on its edge and fell, tumbled over and over across the thrumming boards in the faint glow of the kerosene lamp, a steady beat rumbling in my chest like the approach of summer thunder.

One of the painted tears on Father's face came to life and cut a gray trail down his cheek. "That is what it is to be clown," he whispered.

Mother laughed and crushed the spider in her hand.

The bottle has never stopped moving. It is still rolling towards me, beating its snare, rising to its crescendo. Waiting for me to fall.

But Father was wrong. I know that now.

He has to be wrong.

His name is Boggs but he doesn't know it. "Boggs" is the name I have given him. We have never spoken. He appears to be around ten years old.

Boggs is the filthiest person I've encountered in the cratered streets of the old city. He wears his coat of grime proudly, like a family crest, and yet the child underneath it all is beautiful, a little prince dug up from years of enchanted slumber in the peat bogs of a land that still believes in fairy tales.

And so: Boggs.

It was the morning after a performance that I first noticed him following me. He had cleared away two round spots of caked dirt from his eyes and one from across his mouth to replicate a pale grin. The skin beneath shone white, clown color. The red handkerchief that covered his unwashed head would snap in the air anytime he raced to a hiding place when he thought that I might be looking, which was often. The game grew into ritual and after awhile I stopped reaching for the *moplah* hidden in the folds of my coat. There were always worse shadows to have.

I never see Boggs during the performances but I know he is there all the same, hanging from half-rotted beams like a limber alley cat, far away from the darkness whispering sweetness to him below, watching me watch for him.

During the day when the streets are free of Fever Men, I journey into the city to forage for food and stage crafts. Sometimes I can spot Boggs trying to grab his shadow and stretch it across a brick wall when he thinks that I'm not looking. Once I watched him from a hotel balcony as he danced and tumbled down a rancid alleyway so filled with polished bones that it resembled the gleaming horde of a cannibal emperor. Boggs laughed and laughed to himself the entire time.

His path is clear.

When I sleep, I dream, and when I dream, I remember how the end began.

It begins with the maestro dangling me high above the roaring earth from puppet strings sewn through my flesh. The quenching Fire breathes new red life into the world below even as it devours it. Monoliths tear their way into heaven with charred, broken fingers; floating tatters of skin crinkle and evaporate like a rain of shimmering confetti; steel streets quake with the death-rattles of a generation.

I watch as doctors and terrorists and newly-anointed mothers march through the ceremonial blaze hand-in-hand as if in mutual understanding, as if shackled to each other by their own guilt.

As if all of this is their fault. And perhaps it is.

Their screams are never as loud as the flames. They register only as a soft hum trilling through the veinwork of my strings: distant; faceless; always inside of me.

I look up to the maestro and ask: *Why this? Why me?*

He never answers, just glares down from on high with his flickering glass eyes, the golden tombstones of his mouth spread wide. All I can hear is the muttered creaking of the strings.

A scorching wind stirs and sweeps across the faces of the crooked things that are rising up from the settled dust. They clench their claws experimentally, tasting the electric air, shedding embers from their barren skulls like a crumbling afterbirth. Together they stand regarding the blasted remnants of our faith with ash-flaked eyes.

Boggs is in the center of their ring, waving his red handkerchief to me, his soft hair buffeted by the wind. I go to move but the strings hold me like a web, send violin shrieks of pain through my blood. I struggle wildly, blinded by grinding marrow and cartilage, broken prayers bleeding from my mouth.

Why him?

The maestro is silent. I reach down and shout my prince's name across the end of the world.

Boggs doesn't hear me, only stares up with the pale skin of his smile. The handkerchief is caught in a current of wind and spins up towards my outstretched hand. I make a grab for it but at the last second the cloth dances from my reach. The crooked things start to close around Boggs like the eye of a hangman's rope. As the circle tightens, the fiery priests turn their patient gaze upon me.

My strings hum with the sound of their laughter.

A furnace blast of night air blows through a vent in the theater's wall, snuffing out my dreams. I rise on cold, tingling legs, check the reinforced door of my shuttered annex at the back of the theater for signs of intrusion. The latches and padlocks are undisturbed, but sleep will be irretrievable now.

I gaze across the landscape of old circus posters that cover the walls, the paper as crinkled and browned as the leaves that fill my casket-bed, the child-wonders and Continental mystics and hardy daredevils all posing and preening with the fierce desperation of the dying and the forgotten.

Tonight will be a night for walking, a night for reminding. The *moplah* disappears within Father's coat and I am out in the city's veins once more.

Up above, pregnant thunderheads rumble with promise for the fresh bounty of acid rain they will deliver to the scarred dogs lapping at the overturned fire hydrant. Solid clouds of smoke boil from broken windows and canvas huts, the acrid stink of burning hair laced with the carnal musk of boiling fat. A sundried old man chained to a stoop recites poetry in a foreign tongue swollen with fever. He's being kept there either for safekeeping or as sacrifice. His sad, hoarse music offers no clues.

A tiny cry suddenly rings out, chills the stifling air. I glance towards the face of the moon, noxious through its haze of smog, and see the ragged outline of an airborne beast snapping its wings towards the sky. A small body hangs by its foot from one of the creature's barbed talons. Two stoop-shouldered tramps, man and woman, stand in the distance huddled together, watching the scene by the meager light of the smoldering pit at their feet. Chances say the stolen baby is theirs.

The man and woman observe the sight with the same helpless wonder as they would a shooting star. The figures in the sky are soon gone. The childless parents quickly stomp the faint embers into the ground and stumble away, perhaps back to their own nests to feast and rest from all the night's trials.

I walk on.

At the end of the street a car rocks steadily against a toppled lamp-post like a restless scarab, its fogged glass smudged with ominous runes. I pull on the rusted handle of the back door and the whole frame clatters into the gutter. A woman lies sprawled across slashed fabric, her skin already a pallid shade. The Fever Man has the fingers of his claws spread wide, their eager, gasping mouths breathing in the woman's misty essence as it pours out through the orifices of her skull.

The Fever Man snaps his face up, cutting off the life-flow streaming from his victim. He glowers from his perch, hissing quietly from the gas mask respirators of his jaws as I slowly remove the *moplah* from my coat. At the ringing glint of the blade, the Fever Man leaps forward from the car, claws eager for my skin.

His head makes it out of the door. I heave out the rest and toss it into the street.

I lean into the car. The woman is still alive. Her eyes flutter open and register me, widening in recognition, or fear. I smile and give her a soft, comforting laugh. A faint moan creeps out from her cracked lips. I shake my head and whisper to her.

"No. No, it's okay." I laugh again, to prove it. "It's all right. I'm here now."

The woman continues to moan. I can feel the sound inside of me, rising, rising. I crawl across the seat and nestle against her side. I hold my hands up.

"Look at me!" I tell her. "Nothing to be afraid of. See? Nothing to be afraid of!"

She writhes away from me but her flesh is beginning to ossify now, crumbling from all the life the Fever Man has drunk from her. She falls back in the seat, shaking as her ribcage caves in with an audible snap. I pull her up and look into her clouding eyes.

"Don't you see? I'm the *clown*." I choke on the second laugh as it hardens in my throat, dig my fingers deep to keep my hold on her. "You don't have to be afraid anymore. Not with me. Please. Don't be afraid. I can help you. I'm the clown. Please. Please. *Please*."

Several moments pass before I open my eyes again. When I do, the woman in my arms is gone. A cloud of cremated ash blows through the car's open portal, and I am alone once more.

Drying my eyes, I walk back out into the street, gaze up into a sky robbed of its wishes. I swallow and a compulsive shiver worms its way up my spine. The medicine has left a bitter taste in my mouth.

I turn to go and stop as a yellow face resolves itself from the shadows of the doorway to an old apartment block across the square. A thrill of violence grips my nerves, my rage coating my skin in a cold sweat. I raise the *moplah's* gory blade and consider going in to do my work, to set it all right again. I draw the weapon to my side and take a tentative step across the street. Like a candle sparked to life, a second pair of eyes light up in the doorway.

And another. Another.

Soon a mass of eyes stare back at me from the apartment block, glimmering their challenge. I stand in the street and regard the lone, decapitated body resting against the car. When I look back to the doorway, the Fever Men have already disappeared.

When I was a boy and Father was the clown, part of his act was to take a bouquet of giant roses and cut one of the buds off to stick into his lapel. Every time he did this two more rosebuds would grow in its place, so he'd cut them off and stick them into another spot on his coat, the coat I wear now. This game would keep going until the front of Father's coat was nothing but a curling wave of red. He would stagger comically from the weight and then fall onto his back, the bouquet sticking straight up from his chest in a mock-funeral pose, the sawdust of the midway exhaling and settling back over his still, still face. Father would be dead, and the roses would just keep growing. The crowd would scream with laughter.

It was a funny joke.

EVER SINCE THE Fire came the sun only burns. It bakes the fears inside our heads until we see only the fog of nightmares clouding our skulls.

I walk along the bank of a dried riverbed with only my heated thoughts to keep me company. The fog makes it easier to ignore the confusion of bleached limbs and drained torsos that broil from their towering mound in the dead river's throat. They are the bodies of the old and the lost, survivors who tired of surviving and came down here to die. Glassgreen blowflies drone merrily over the sun-withered scraps, happy to play their part in the broken drama.

I leave the fetid riverbank and re-enter the city through the shade of an overpass clogged with fossilized trucks. A sudden movement catches my eye and I turn just in time to see a shadow fleeing across one of the stone columns.

Impossible, I think. *The sun is still out.*

A piece of thick white construction paper flutters gently at the base of the column. I run over and snatch it up, unfold the intricate schoolyard design. A huge heart beams up at me from the page, scratches of red overlapping the magic marker outline. The fog in my skull begins to lift. I remember now how the top of the shadow's head appeared to wave as it ran to its hiding place once it had been spotted. I hadn't recognized it at first. It seems that Boggs can grow his shadow as tall as me now.

I refold the paper heart and put it in a pocket deep within Father's coat, a place where nobody but me will ever be able to find it again. Patting my chest, I drift calmly back to the theater, singing an old song I've forgotten the words to.

There can't be more than four people in the crowd tonight.

They watch me perform my wonders, but there's none of the old terror in them anymore. Their faces remain slack, neither laughing nor crying. Their eyes never once flinch, not even during the Figaro Earwig sequence. They sit hunched over on their thrones of garbage, hands upturned in lap, legs splayed in front of them. The absence of their fear brings me no comfort. They are exhausted, run to ground, too tired to notice shadows or anything else that might live in the theater.

I touch the paper heart in my pocket to remind myself, looking up to the beams dangling overhead. Not seeing, but still knowing.

I rise from the cigar box at the end of the performance and clamber back onto the stage, not even bothering to acknowledge the deserted room that awaits me.

A parched rustling resonates from the back of the theater.

Just the leaves. Then the sound comes again.

I look around, my eyes searching through the soughing light of the trashcans. The theater is empty. The crowd is gone. Nothing remains.

Nothing, except shadows.

There is a light pounding in the air now, like the first few tentative drops of rain upon metal, but the sound quickly doubles then doubles again until it is ringing from all four corners of the theater. The shapes of long-jointed fingers dance across the walls in tandem with the noise. I take an involuntary step back. From my place on the stage I stand and watch as the gathered Fever Men clap their hands together in a congratulatory rhythm of applause.

Slowly, I climb back into the box and don't come out until the thunder has finally passed.

EVERYTHING HAS CHANGED.

Nothing has changed.

We live in a world where two beliefs can call each other a lie and both be right. The crowd wonders how I can be a clown in a time like this. I wonder how they could choose to be anything else.

We conform reality to suit our survival. A person could lose their home, or the love of their life, or their right eye and continue to live by conditioning themselves into a state of acceptance. It's what allows the crowd to believe that creatures who gorge themselves on their essence are a conquerable obstacle, that a child's wagon in an old ice-house is actually a front row seat in a theater of magic and mystery.

But take away a person's shadow, and you've just stolen a part of their soul.

They may not notice it at first, their survivalist gene rationalizing it as some trick of the light, a deterioration of the eyes. Observe that person long enough though and you will see the realization drop over them like a great black curtain, watch them stumble through the blind alleys their life has become as they try to call their shadow back to them.

It's been two days since I've seen Boggs.

WHEN I SLEEP, I dream, and when I dream, it is only of him.

For the last two days I've scoured leveled plazas and raided diners and old whorehouses overgrown with cinders, chasing visions half-seen, answering echoes long-hushed. Whether it has been day or night I do not know. I see only darkness now.

I crawl out from the hard embrace of my casket-bed and trudge into the hollow expanse of the auditorium, my eyes swimming in a burning haze, gray leaves trailing behind me like breadcrumbs. The sun is setting on the shredded horizon, the overture to another lost night.

Two wretches stand outside the theater's warped doorway, shifting nervously on the stoop. They dip their heads in and give the stage a perfunctory look. They do not see me, or at least affect as much. The wretches start to hobble off and then quicken their limping pace as the first few manhole covers begin to lift up in the streets, the white eyes of the emerging Fever Men shining out.

I lean in the doorway and stare into my city's decrepit heart. Every muscle seems to be shouting at me for rest, but the sound of the strings is louder. I know that he is out there. There will be no respite, not until the great question is satisfied. The maestro rumbles overhead, twisting the strings in his soiled evening gloves as he tries to hold me to the course of my destiny. He tells me that my path is clear.

I turn and run the other way. The theater shrinks in the distance as I soar down the gnarled avenue, claws reaching out from below for my legs, the *moplah*'s curved steel burning through my clothes, searing my skin. The maestro bellows grim assurances from above in the voice of my Father but I do not hear him. I must not hear him.

The eye of the rope is closing.

My footsteps are a frantic staccato on the molten pavement, the shapes of tall thin men stretching and running across the maze of drunken roofs that curl over me in the bleak light of the moon, a host of demonic familiars. I crash through doors with a sound like cannonfire, shout into windows that throw my face back to me in funhouse contortions.

The paper heart beats its wings against my chest, so fast that I press my hand to it for fear of it breaking free and flying away. Flying away, never to return.

Boggs.

A scream rips across the air and catches in the web of my strings. I follow its magnetic vibrations until I round a corner and come to the yawning gums of an alley. A mortal stench drifts from its mouth. I unsheathe the *moplah* and hold it at my side, waiting for the source of the scream or its cause to make itself known.

A bloated shape flies through the air towards my face before the blade cuts it down. I pluck the limp thing from the sword's point and feel the warm trickle of its blood run over my wrist. Shaking, I hold it up to the waxen light to discern its form. Gripped between the pale knuckles of my fist is a red handkerchief.

The maestro cuts my strings.

Brick and concrete swirl around me, and I fall to the ground. The handkerchief comes to rest at my side. I make a weak grab for the fabric. Its wrinkled corner waves once and then is still.

I can hear the sounds coming from deep in the alley now, the whispers and small wet noises. Grabbing the handkerchief, I pull myself up with the sword and begin to tread slowly over the jewels of glass marking the entrance like scattered teeth. The ground slants hellward as I journey down the alley's sulfurous gullet. The chattering intensifies. A gathering of phantasmal shapes crouch in a pool of milksoft moonlight at the end of the alley. Three Fever Men all counted, making the most of a humble meal.

I stand still, listening to their harsh music. One of the Fever Men finally detects me from the shadows and emits a sharp *hiss* from his nest of tubes, his brothers huddling jealously over their prize. In the moon's glow, I can see my prince's face, his pale mouth still smiling up at the sky, sleeping forever in a depthless, dreamless bog. Within seconds it has crumbled and wasted away, never to return.

The life of a clown. An old joke, and nothing more.

My cursed hand passes the burden weighing down my soul and touches the rising blade of the *moplah* with a white, simmering fire. The bottle is rolling, the drum is beating, and the crowd is holding its breath as it waits for the funny-man to finish his act.

I am the greatest clown in the world, and my public shall want for nothing.

"Everybody laugh," I whisper.

My shadow swells with the taste of their fear and then descends, a great black curtain coming down.

From here, the city is just a memory.

Rolling dunes block most of its empty towers from my view. The sand blisters with radiation, sends its glistening breath into the air. The desert is not a traditional theater, but a clown's life is one of constant adaptability. The possibilities and the playing space are endless.

I can no longer remember how many fell at the end of my sword last night. It was a strange night, one of confusion and screams, a funhouse night. At some point the monsters began to disguise themselves, started to wear pleading human faces like masks of melting wax, thinking they could fool me. But you cannot fool a fool.

The *moplah* now stands atop the first hill of the desert that borders the city, its blade sunk deep, its haft bejeweled with fresh rubies and wreathed with two old handkerchiefs, one red and one blue, a sign-post for those horseless riders passing through to mark where that part of the ending stops and this one begins.

The little paper heart remains with me. I had intended to abandon it, to run it through with the sword and leave it pinned and weeping on the ground. But when I searched the pockets of Father's coat, I discovered that I couldn't find it. So it stays inside of me now, somewhere, fluttering gently.

Now there is only I, the sand, the arcane scavengers circling above, and the sun bowing its hooded head to the west. The maestro pulls me along no longer. My strings trail behind me now, phantom limbs dragging through the dust.

I crest a shining hill and look over the purple rim into the valley below. My eyes take a moment to adjust to the bite of the gritty wind before they recognize the shapes moving ahead.

A great circus tent, tall spires framed against fire, flaps with the scent of peanut oil and dirty rain. Gray sinewy mountains pull the tent across the desert by chains, marching solemnly towards the sunset. Their footprints are tremendous and instantly forgotten in the sand.

And there, just above the roaring of the earth, like the soft hum of a scream or a smile along a thin wire, is the dirge of an old organ playing the day down. Its jaunty, discordant tune makes promises to the desert of sights unseen, sounds unheard, of magic and mystery, of death and life. Those who are patient will hear this in its song. Those who are wise will know it to be true.

I look up to the sky and ask: *What good is the end of the world to a clown?*

Raw laughter bursts from my throat and echoes across the scarlet valley. The searing wind turns the tears on my cheeks to mercury and carries my laughter up, up into the wide, absolving sky, up where some greater mystery waits to hear it, dreaming of the end.

My path is clear now. I walk on.

ABOUT THE CONTRIBUTORS

MICHAEL GRIFFIN's collection *The Lure of Devouring Light* was published by Word Horde, and Dim Shores will soon publish his novella *An Ideal Retreat*. His work has appeared in magazines like *Apex*, *Black Static*, *Lovecraft eZine*, and *Strange Aeons*, and such anthologies as *Autumn Cthulhu*, the Shirley Jackson Award winner *The Grimscribe's Puppets*, the Laird Barron tribute *The Children of Old Leech*, and *Cthulhu Fhtagn!* Upcoming work will appear in *Eternal Frankenstein*, *The Madness of Dr. Caligari*, and the Ramsey Campbell tribute *Darker Companions*. He's an ambient musician and founder of Hypnos Recordings, an ambient record label he operates with his wife in Portland, Oregon. Michael blogs at griffinwords.com. On Twitter, he posts as @mgsoundvisions and writing-specific news appears as @griffinwords.

KRISTI DEMEESTER received her M.A. in Creative Writing from Kennesaw State University in 2011. Since then, her short fiction has appeared in publications such as *Black Static*, *Apex Magazine*, *The Dark*, *Year's Best Weird Fiction Volumes 1 and 3*, and several others. Her debut novel, *Beneath*, is forthcoming in spring 2017 from Word Horde. In her spare time, she alternates between telling people how to say her last name and how to spell her first. Find her online at www.kristidemeester.com.

CHRISTOPHER SLATSKY is the author of *Alectryomancer and Other Weird Tales* (Dunhams Manor Press, 2015). His work has also appeared in the *Lost Signals* anthology, *Strange Aeons Magazine*, and *Year's Best Weird Fiction vol. 3*. He currently resides in the Los Angeles area.

J.T. GLOVER's short fiction has appeared or is forthcoming in *The Children of Old Leech*, *The Lovecraft eZine*, *Goreyesque*, and *Pseudopod*, among other venues. His nonfiction has appeared in various markets, including *Thinking Horror* and *Postscripts to Darkness*. By day he is an academic research librarian specializing in the humanities, and he studies literary horror, writers' research practices, and related topics. He lives in Richmond, Virginia, and you can find him online at www.jtglover.com.

ERIC J. GUIGNARD's a writer and editor of dark and speculative fiction, operating from the shadowy outskirts of Los Angeles. His works have appeared in publications such as *Nightmare Magazine*, *Black Static*, *Shock Totem*, *Buzzy Magazine*, and *Dark Discoveries Magazine*. He's won the Bram Stoker Award, been a finalist for the International Thriller Writers Award, and a multi-nominee of the Pushcart Prize. Outside the glamorous and jet-setting world of indie fiction, Eric's a technical writer and college professor, and he stumbles home each day to a wife, children, cats, and a terrarium filled with mischievous beetles. Visit Eric at: www.ericjguignard.com, his blog: ericjguignard.blogspot.com, or Twitter: @ericjguignard.

MALCOLM DEVLIN's stories have appeared in *Interzone* and *Black Static* and the anthologies *Aickman's Heirs* and *Gods, Memes and Monsters*. His first collection, *You Will Grow Into Them*, will be published by Unsung Stories in June 2017.

GWENDOLYN KISTE is a speculative fiction writer based in Pennsylvania. Her stories have appeared in *Nightmare*, *Shimmer*, *LampLight*, and *Interzone* as well as Flame Tree Publishing's *Chilling Horror Short Stories* anthology. She currently resides on an abandoned horse farm with her husband, two cats, and not nearly enough ghosts. You can find her online at gwendolynkiste.com and on Twitter (@GwendolynKiste).

RALPH ROBERT MOORE's books include the short story collections *Remove the Eyes* and *I Smell Blood*, the novels *Father Figure*, *As Dead As Me*, and *Ghosters*, and the upcoming collection of ten novelettes, *You Can Never Spit It All Out*. He is a twice-nominated British Fantasy Society author whose work has appeared in a wide variety of literary and genre magazines and anthologies, including *Nightscript I*, *Black Static*, *Shadows & Tall Trees*, *Midnight Street*, and *Sein und Werden*. His website SENTENCE at www.ralphrobertmoore.com features a broad selection of his writings, videos, and photographs. Moore and his wife Mary live outside Dallas, Texas.

CHRISTOPHER ROPES lives in New Jersey with his family and their numerous pets. He is the author of the poetry collection *The Operating Theater* through Dynatox Ministries and the weird fiction chapbook *Complicity* from Dunhams Manor Press. He also writes occult nonfiction and lives in a perpetual "derangement of all the senses."

STEVE RASNIC TEM's last novel, *Blood Kin* (Solaris, 2014), won the Bram Stoker Award. His next novel, *UBO* (Solaris, January 2017), is a dark science fictional tale about violence and its origins, featuring such historical viewpoint characters as Jack the Ripper, Stalin, and Heinrich Himmler. He is also a past winner of the World Fantasy and British Fantasy Awards. A handbook on writing, *Yours To Tell: Dialogues on the Art & Practice of Fiction*, written with his late wife Melanie, will appear soon from Apex Books. Visit the Tem home on the web at: www.m-s-tem.com

JASON A. WYCKOFF is the author of two short story collections published by Tartarus Press, *Black Horse and Other Strange Stories* (2012) and *The Hidden Back Room* (2016). His work has appeared in anthologies from Tartarus Press and Siren's Call Publications, as well as the journals *Nightscript v.I*, *Weirdbook*, and *Turn To Ash*. He lives in Columbus, Ohio, USA, with his wife and their cats.

GORDON WHITE has lived in North Carolina, New York, and now the Pacific Northwest, collecting various terrors as he goes. His work has appeared in venues such as *Dark Fuse*, *Halloween Forevermore*, *Milkfist*, *Dark Moon Digest*, *Borderlands 6*, and others. In addition to writing, he also reads submissions for Kraken Press and Pantheon Magazine, and conducts interviews for various outlets. You can find him online at www.grizzlyspectacles.com.

NINA SHEPARDSON is a biologist who lives in the northeastern US with her husband. She's a staff reader at *Spark: A Creative Anthology*, and her writing appears or is forthcoming in over a dozen publications, including *Devilfish Review*, *The Colored Lens*, and *Electric Spec*. She also writes book reviews at ninashepardson.wordpress.com.

KURT FAWVER is a writer of horror, weird fiction, and dark fantasy. His short stories have previously appeared (or will appear) in venues such as *The Magazine of Fantasy & Science Fiction*, *Strange Aeons*, the *Lovecraft eZine*, and *Weird Tales*. He's also released one collection of short fiction, *Forever, in Pieces*. His non-fiction has been published in places such as *Thinking Horror* and the *Journal of the Fantastic in the Arts*. You can find Kurt online at www.facebook.com/kfawver or http://kurtfawver1.blogspot.com.

ROWLEY AMATO was born and raised in New York City, where he makes his living as a writer. "Aycayia" is his first published work. He's trying very hard to get a website together, but in the meantime, he tweets about movies and things at @rowleyamato.

CHARLES WILKINSON's publications include *The Pain Tree and Other Stories* (London Magazine Editions). His stories have appeared in *Best Short Stories 1990* (Heinemann), *Best English Short Stories 2* (W.W. Norton, USA), *Unthology* (Unthank Books), *Best British Short Stories 2015* (Salt), and in genre magazines/anthologies such as *Supernatural Tales, Horror Without Victims* (Megazanthus Press), *Theaker's Quarterly Fiction, The Dark Lane Anthology Phantom Drift* (USA), *Bourbon Penn* (USA), *Shadows & Tall Trees* (Canada), *Nightscript* (USA), and *Best Weird Fiction 2015* (Undertow Books, Canada). *Ag & Au*, a pamphlet of poems, appeared from Flarestack in 2013. His collection of strange tales and weird fiction, *A Twist in the Eye*, is now out from Egaeus Press. He lives in Powys, Wales.

H.V. CHAO's fiction has appeared in *Pseudopod, The Kenyon Review, West Branch, Epiphany, The Coachella Review*, and the anthology *Strange Tales IV* from Tartarus Press. It has also been translated in *Le Visage Vert* and *Brèves*. He is at work on a story collection called *Guises*. Home is wherever his wife and dog are.

DANIEL MILLS is the author of *Revenants: A Dream of New England* (Chomu Press, 2011), *The Lord Came at Twilight* (Dark Renaissance Books, 2014), and of the forthcoming *Moriah* (ChiZine Publications, 2017). He lives in Vermont. Find him online at http://www.danielmills.net.

REBECCA J. ALLRED lives in the Pacific Northwest, working by day as a doctor of pathology, but after hours, she transforms into a practitioner of dark fiction, penning malignant tales of suffering and woe. Her work has appeared in *A Lonely and Curious Country: Tales from the Land of Lovecraft, Gothic Fantasy: Chilling Horror Short Stories, Borderlands 6,* and others. When she isn't busy rendering diagnoses or writing, Rebecca enjoys reading, drawing, laughing at RiffTrax, and spending time with her husband and their cat. Keep up with Rebecca online at www.diagnosisdiabolique.com.

MATTHEW M. BARTLETT is the author of *Gateways to Abomination, The Witch-Cult in Western Massachusetts,* and *Creeping Waves.* His short stories have appeared in a variety of anthologies, including *Resonator: New Lovecraftian Tales From Beyond, High Strange Horror,* and *Lost Signals.* He lives and writes in a small brick house on a quiet, leafy street somewhere in Northampton, Massachusetts with his wife Katie Saulnier and their cats Phoebe, Peachpie, and Larry.

JOSÉ CRUZ is an author and freelance writer whose work has appeared or is forthcoming in print and online venues such as *Video Librarian, Turn to Ash, bare•bones e-zine, The Terror Trap, Classic-Horror,* and *Paracinema Magazine.* He lives in Southwest Florida with his wife and a very furry child. He can be found online at hauntedomnibus.-wordpress.com. "Pause for Laughter" is his first published story.

C.M. MULLER lives in St. Paul, Minnesota with his wife and two sons —and, of course, all those quaint and curious volumes of forgotten lore. He is related to the Norwegian writer Jonas Lie and draws much inspiration from that scrivener of old. His tales have appeared in *Shadows & Tall Trees, Supernatural Tales,* and *Weirdbook.* He hopes you have enjoyed the twenty-one tales collected herein.

For more information about NIGHTSCRIPT, please visit:

www.chthonicmatter.wordpress.com/nightscript

Made in the USA
Middletown, DE
28 September 2016